Emily Forbes is an award-winning author of Medical Romance for Mills & Boon. She has written over 25 books and has twice been a finalist in the Australian Romantic Book of the Year Award, which she won in 2013 for her novel *Sydney Harbour Hospital: Bella's Wishlist*. You can get in touch with Emily at emilyforbes@internode.on.net, or visit her website at emily-forbesauthor.com.

Amy Andrews is a multi-award-winning, *USA TODAY* bestselling Australian author who has written over fifty contemporary romances in both the traditional and digital markets. She loves good books, fab food, great wine and frequent travel—preferably all four together. To keep up with her latest releases, news, competitions and giveaways, sign up for her newsletter—amyandrews.com.au/newsletter.html.

REUNITED WITH HER BROODING SURGEON

EMILY FORBES

TEMPTED BY MR OFF-LIMITS

AMY ANDREWS

MILLS & BOON

First Published in Great Britain 2018
by Mills & Boon, an imprint of HarperCollins*Publishers*
1 London Bridge Street, London, SE1 9GF

Reunited with Her Brooding Surgeon © 2018 by Emily Forbes

Tempted by Mr Off-Limits © 2018 by Amy Andrews

ISBN: 978-0-263-93374-1

MIX
Paper from
responsible sources
FSC™ C007454

This book is produced from independently certified FSC™ paper
to ensure responsible forest management.
For more information visit www.harpercollins.co.uk/green.

Printed and bound in Spain
by CPI, Barcelona

REUNITED WITH HER BROODING SURGEON

EMILY FORBES

MILLS & BOON

To the fabulous Amy Andrews,

We've done it again!

Thank you—it's always fun to write with a friend.
Wishing you happy days as we send Grace, Marcus,
Lola and Hamish out into the world.

CHAPTER ONE

'DID YOU JUST say you have a spare kidney?'

Grace smiled. She knew her phone call would cause Connie Matera some disbelief but she also knew that would rapidly give way to relief and excitement once she explained the situation to her. 'Yes. I have a spare kidney and it's going to be yours,' she repeated.

'Did someone die?'

As the renal transplant co-ordinator at one of Sydney's biggest hospitals Grace knew that for transplant recipients their good fortune was often tinged with guilt that someone had died in order to give them what they needed. But that wasn't the case this time. 'No. It's from a living donor.'

'How—why?' Grace could hear Connie struggling to find the right words, to ask the right questions. 'How do you just get a spare kidney?'

'You've heard of the paired kidney exchange programme?' Grace asked.

'Yes. But I thought I needed to have someone, a family member or friend, who was prepared to give up a kidney in exchange for one for me? I thought that was how it worked.'

'Normally, yes, but you got lucky.' Grace knew that

Connie's family had offered to donate a kidney to her but, while her sister and mother had the same blood type, their tissue type hadn't been a match and therefore they hadn't been suitable donors. Which had left Connie having regular dialysis and waiting on the transplant list for a deceased donor. Until now. 'One of our patients on the exchange programme was a match with a deceased donor so now they don't need their living donation. That donor has offered to give their kidney anyway and you are the best match on the transplant list.'

'A stranger is voluntarily giving me their kidney?'

'Yes.'

'Has that ever happened before?'

'Not to my knowledge.' Was it fear or scepticism Grace could hear in Connie's voice? She didn't want her to refuse this offer. It was too generous and meant too much. 'This is good news, Connie. It's your lucky day.'

Grace heard Connie's deep intake of breath. 'Yes, yes. Of course it is. What do we do now?'

'I know you're scheduled for dialysis tomorrow but can you come in today at two for a pre-op appointment? We need to run some tests and I'm hoping to get your surgery scheduled for next week.'

'That soon?'

'Your donor was already scheduled for surgery next Wednesday as part of a paired kidney exchange exercise. The theatres and hospitals are all booked and your donor is happy to go ahead as planned, albeit with a different recipient. If I can get one more theatre here, and if all your pre-op tests are good, we'll add you to the list.'

'No more dialysis?'

'Hopefully this time next week, no more dialysis,' Grace confirmed. 'I'll see you at two.'

'Okay.'

'And, Connie,' Grace added with a smile in her voice, 'buy a lottery ticket on your way in here.'

She was still smiling as she said goodbye and hung up the phone. She loved this part of her job. As a member of the organ donation team it wasn't often she got to deliver good news without a side serving of sad news. But in the case of the paired kidney exchange programme, where living donors selflessly offered their organs, it was a rewarding part of the job and Grace was excited.

Some days were tough. Delivering bad news to people was never easy but today was a good day. Today she had a kidney to give away. And today she was going to be busy. The phone call to Connie had been the first piece in the final puzzle. All the other donors and recipients were checked and ready to go. Their surgeries were scheduled for next week but she needed to book one more theatre for Connie and pray that her tests results were what they needed to be. Then she needed to keep her fingers crossed that no one got sick between now and then. Or changed their minds.

She had twelve surgeries to schedule across five different hospitals in three different cities. It was going to be the biggest paired kidney exchange exercise that had ever occurred in Australia and she was part of it. She'd been working in the transplant unit for the past two years but had only recently been promoted to the co-ordinator position. She'd been involved in paired kidney exchange operations before but nothing of this magnitude.

She entered Connie's details into the nephrologist's appointment calendar and made sure all the relevant documents, recent test results, new test request forms and consent forms were attached before making a courtesy call to Connie's GP. Hopefully this time next week six people would each have a new, functioning kidney. She knew how much this meant to the families involved. She'd been one of those families herself.

Now she needed to organise a team meeting. Initially she'd had three of the twelve surgeries scheduled to take place here, at the Kirribilli General Hospital, but now she had a fourth, which meant she needed a fourth surgical team—two for the organ retrievals and two more to complete the organ transplants.

Finally, she made a call to the hospital's PR division. This would be a big story and some media coverage could be a huge benefit to the drive to encourage organ donation. If they pulled it off.

There was no if, she told herself. They *had* to do this. There was too much at stake for it not to work. It *had* to be a success.

Grace fought to subdue the swarm of butterflies that was taking flight in her belly as she stood out in front of the Kirribilli General and faced a barrage of television cameras and media crews. The countdown had begun.

The transplant surgeries were scheduled to begin tomorrow morning at eight, in just over seventeen hours' time, but first there was a media statement to be made. She wasn't alone, she was flanked by numerous members of the renal transplant unit and the hospital's public relations department. It was a glorious sunny afternoon and the media had turned out in force. Grace didn't know if it was because it was a slow news day or if they really were interested in the story. She hoped it was the latter. This was a fabulous opportunity for some good publicity and a chance to raise organ donor awareness.

She took a deep breath and tried to calm her nerves as the hospital's PR spokesperson introduced Professor Elliot Martin, the head of the renal transplant unit. Elliot would introduce the other nephrologists and then it would be Grace's turn to speak. Public speaking was *so* not her thing. She didn't mind talking to the doctors, liaising with other transplant co-ordinators, and even talking to the patients' families about death and organ donation. That she could handle, but ask her to stand up in front of a group of strangers, well that was a whole different ball game. And strangers with cameras and microphones were even worse. She'd been taking classes and learning a few tricks. She knew her topic so she didn't need to be nervous but knowing that and convincing her autonomic nervous system of that fact were two different things.

Peering over the shoulder of the person standing in front of her and scanning the crowd, her gaze landed on Lola—her friend, colleague and flatmate. Lola had given her some advice this morning and as she caught her eye, Lola mimed undoing the top button of her uniform and gave her a wink. Grace bit back a smile. Lola's advice had been to imagine the crowd naked—apparently that was supposed to make them less intimidating.

She flicked her gaze away from Lola before her friend revealed anything she shouldn't on national television and before Grace herself burst out laughing. She continued to scan the crowd but it consisted mostly of middle-aged men, doctors and hospital administration staff, all approximately twenty years older than her twenty-seven years, and not anyone she wanted to picture naked.

Whoa, hang on a minute. Her eyes had skimmed the crowd but something, or rather someone, had caught her attention, and she quickly reversed her gaze.

On the opposite side of the crowd, right at the front, stood a man she wouldn't mind seeing naked.

He was tall, easily over six feet, and his shoulders were broad and his chest solid, yet he seemed to balance lightly on his feet. Despite his size he looked calm and centred and relaxed and she wished she had a tenth of his composure.

His dark hair was closely cropped and a designer two-day growth accentuated his oval face. He had a strong jaw and full lips beneath a narrow nose. His forehead was smooth and there was a slight furrow of concentration between his eyebrows that belied his relaxed stance. His dark eyes looked brooding and serious but that didn't detract from his looks in the slightest. He was incredibly handsome but that wasn't the only thing that had captured her attention. It was the contrast between him and everyone else around him. It was more than his height and his perfectly shaped face and symmetrical features. All of this was enhanced by his coffee-coloured skin, making him different enough to stand out from the crowd.

He wore a steel-blue suit with a white shirt that highlighted his complexion. His suit fitted perfectly and was impeccably tailored and pressed. He looked like he took pride in his appearance, and when you looked that good, why wouldn't you? He was delicious.

There was something vaguely familiar about him but surely that was just her imagination? She'd remember if she'd met him before, he was not someone who would be easily forgotten. It must be one of those déjà vu things, she decided as a flutter of lust rolled in her belly, competing with the butterflies.

She ran her gaze down the length of his suit jacket, taking note of his lean hips and powerful thighs. He was *definitely* someone she wouldn't mind seeing naked. She pictured him shrugging out of his jacket and loosening the buttons on his shirt, her mind completely absorbed by the mental image she was painting until she realised she couldn't recall a word of her speech.

Focus, focus, she told herself, but it was impossible to picture him getting naked *and* remember her speech.

She averted her gaze and caught Lola grinning at her, eyebrows raised. She dropped her eyes before her friend could make her laugh and focused on her breathing, hoping no one else had caught her ogling this glorious stranger.

Marcus could scarcely believe his good fortune. He'd arrived at Kirribilli General Hospital on an exchange programme from Western Australia to spend twelve weeks as a visiting specialist with the transplant unit and found that he was just in time to take part in a multiple paired kidney exchange operation. This was *exactly* why he was here. He'd always avoided returning to the east coast but Kirribilli General was the leading hospital in renal transplants and had pioneered the paired kidney exchange programme.

He'd been in two minds about whether to accept this posting before finally deciding that it was something he needed to do. The opportunity had been too good to pass up, given that he was advocating for the Queen Victoria Hospital in Perth to become involved in the programme too. It stood to reason that he should spend some time in Sydney getting first-hand knowledge.

He looked around at the media throng that was gathered in front of the hospital. He realised that this was a big news story and he appreciated the fact that the hospital's PR division and the transplant team wanted to grab the opportunity for promotion but he could do without the circus. He itched to get going. He wanted to be in the operating theatre, with a scalpel in his hand. That was the one place where he always felt in control. Any surprises could be dealt with in a calm and clinical manner. He knew he had the skills to handle anything that could be thrown his way in Theatre. He'd spent years honing his skills. He liked to have control and being a surgeon afforded him that. Control and respect.

Elliot Martin, the head of the renal transplant unit, was speaking. Marcus knew he would be introducing the surgical teams soon and he returned his attention to his new boss, not wanting to miss his introduction.

He was excited. This was exactly the sort of opportunity he'd hoped to establish on his return to Perth and to get to be involved so early on was ideal.

He appreciated his good fortune and hoped that, rather than just observing the kidney exchanges, his surgical skills would be required due to the number of operations that were being scheduled. He breathed deeply as he thought of how it would feel to be offered the opportunity to conduct one of the surgeries himself. If it happened, it would most likely be one of the retrievals but he didn't mind. He just wanted to be involved. Just wanted a chance to showcase his ability. It was one of the few things he knew he excelled at. And a retrieval was still a surgical procedure. It was a little more routine than a transplant but the margins for error were small and it was still an important process.

Doing a retrieval meant he would be removing a healthy kidney from a healthy person, which really contradicted the medical charter of 'Do no harm' but, in this case, he believed in the cause, in the greater good such a procedure would mean. He believed in this case that the benefits outweighed the disadvantages. The improved quality of life the selfless donor was offering to an unknown recipient was an amazing gift, although he still found it incredible that people were willing to sacrifice one of their organs, to offer it to a stranger, in return for one of their own loved ones receiving the same gift.

He couldn't imagine loving someone that much.

He refocused, tuning back in to Elliot's speech just in time to hear his introduction.

'I would like to introduce you all to Dr Janet Hosking and Dr Marcus Washington from the Queen Victoria Hospital in Western Australia, who are joining the Kirribilli General renal unit for the next three months.'

He stepped forward as his name was announced and his gaze landed on a petite redhead who was standing to Elliot's left but had previously been hidden from view behind someone else's shoulder. She was staring at him with her mouth open. Her heart-shaped face was pale, her skin smooth and creamy but her lips were painted a bright red, almost the same colour as her fiery copper hair. He'd only seen hair that colour once before in his life.

That couldn't be right. There had to be millions of people with that colour hair in the world.

Maybe he was mistaken. It had been twenty years ago after all. His memory had to be misleading him. Surely this couldn't be the same girl? What were the chances of that?

But the coil of fear in his gut told him that the chances were high. It was just his luck.

CHAPTER TWO

THE GORGEOUS MAN with amazing bone structure stepped
forward and Grace's heart skipped a beat and her mouth
dropped open.

Marcus Washington.

She could not believe it.

It had to be him. Even though he no longer resembled
the twelve-year-old boy she'd once known, it *had* to be
him. There couldn't be two of him.

He was a doctor? A nephrologist?

She hadn't thought about him for years but if she had
she never would have imagined he would become a doctor. She knew that sounded harsh and judgemental but
what she remembered of Marcus did not fit with her
image of someone who had clearly ended up in a position of responsibility and service to others.

But what did she really know about him? She had
only been seven years old. What had she known about
anything?

Her father was a doctor and, at the age of seven, everything she'd known or thought had been influenced
by what and who she'd seen around her. Particularly by
her own family. And Marcus's family had been about
as different from hers as a seven-year-old could have

imagined. But she knew enough now to understand that it wasn't about where you came from or what opportunities you were handed in life, but about what you did with those opportunities, those chances. It was about the choices you made. The drive and the desire to be the best that you could be.

She would never have pictured Marcus as a doctor but now here he was, standing in front of her looking polished, professional and perfect. It had to be him.

Grace knew a lot could change in twenty years and by the look of him, a lot had.

She was still staring at him, trying to make sense of what was happening, when he looked in her direction and caught her eye. Grace blushed and, cursing her fair skin, the bane of a redhead, she looked away as his gaze continued on over her. She finally remembered to close her mouth and hoped her reaction hadn't been captured on camera.

Had he recognised her?

It didn't appear so but, then, why would he? She was nothing like the seven-year-old he had last seen.

She must have missed an earlier HR announcement about him coming to her hospital. She would have remembered if she'd seen his name. What had Elliot said? He would be here for three months? Attached to her department?

She swivelled her eyes and observed him through the curtain of her hair as he shook Elliot's hand. She took a second look. And a third. She had changed in the intervening years but so had he. There was nothing left of the skinny adolescent in him. Nothing at all.

Not that she was complaining. He looked just fine.

His dark hair was close cropped now, his wild curls

a distant memory. And where had those broad shoulders and powerful legs come from? Her last memory of him had been as a tall and thin pre-teen with skinny brown legs in shorts that had always looked as if he'd outgrown them. That boy was gone now. Replaced by a taller, more muscular, more confident and far better dressed adult version.

She didn't need to see him naked to imagine the toned, muscular body that was under the suit. She had always thought he was exotic in a slightly out-of-place way, but he appeared to have grown into his skin. She'd never known his mother but she'd heard she was Caribbean or something if she remembered correctly, and the mixture of her genes with Marcus's Caucasian father had combined to give Marcus the best of both worlds. And that had never been more obvious than today.

But the one thing that hadn't changed was that the adult Marcus was not paying her any attention. Just like the adolescent one. He had kept to himself as a child. It had seemed he'd never paid *anyone* any attention. Maybe he'd been trying not to draw attention to himself. He had been different from the other kids at school, different in looks and different in his background, and Grace knew that had made him a target for some of the other children. It didn't pay to be different when you were a kid. It didn't pay to stand out from the crowd.

But looking at him now it appeared that things had improved for him in the intervening twenty years. He still stood out from the crowd but now there was a sense of strength and confidence about him. All traces of the shy, quiet, reclusive child had been wiped out.

Grace was curious to know where he'd been, what had happened to him, but her questions would have to wait. It was almost her turn to speak and she needed to get her head back in the present. She was still new in this job and it was important to make a good impression. She couldn't afford to be distracted by the past. No matter how good it looked.

She picked Lola out in the crowd. That was a mistake too. Lola had obviously seen Grace's reaction to Marcus and was grinning wildly. At least she didn't know the full story. Grace glared at her and looked for someone else in the crowd to focus on as she tried to ignore Marcus, who had stepped back with the other nephrologists. He was no longer front and centre, but that didn't stop Grace from being totally aware of him. She imagined she could feel his presence even though she kept her eyes averted from him.

She took a deep breath and stepped up to the microphone as Elliot introduced her.

'As you know,' she addressed the crowd, 'we have four surgeries scheduled here tomorrow, which would not be possible without the generous gift of organs from family and friends of those in need.'

Her job today was to raise awareness about organ donation and, somehow, she managed to get through her spiel and ignore Marcus, even though she could feel his eyes on her. Most of the eyes in the crowd were on her but she could feel Marcus's piercing gaze more than most. There was an intensity about it and she knew she couldn't afford to look his way. She'd definitely lose her train of thought.

'The majority of Australians are willing donors,' she continued, 'so the problem we have is not a lack of interest but a lack of knowledge coupled with a lack of suitable organs. We need suitable organs and then we need permission to use those organs. If your family don't know your wishes or don't support your decision, we cannot use your organs. But, in some cases, living organ donations are a possibility and that is the case for the surgeries we have scheduled for tomorrow.

'All these surgeries are part of the paired kidney exchange, where living donors are giving up a kidney to a stranger in exchange for a better matched kidney for a loved one in need. There are twelve surgeries scheduled across the country, which makes it the largest paired exchange exercise ever conducted in Australia.

'Transplants using organs donated by the living have a higher success rate and you can imagine the freedom that this will afford someone—no more dialysis and fewer hospital visits. So thank you to those wonderful donors who are giving not just a kidney but the gift of a better life.

'If you are interested in finding out more there is further information on the organ donation website, but *please* also remember to talk about this issue to your families and let them know your wishes in this very important matter.'

Grace stepped gratefully back into her place after her speech and planned to bolt as soon as the media questions ended but Elliot called her name as she turned to flee. She stopped in her tracks and took a deep breath. She knew what he wanted. He wanted to introduce her to the two new doctors. Only they weren't both new to her.

She wondered if Marcus would remember her.

She pasted a smile on her face and turned around. Sure enough, Elliot was standing between Janet and Marcus. Grace tried to take control and introduced herself to Janet first, shaking her hand before looking up at Marcus.

He towered over her. Grace was tiny, only five feet two inches tall. Away from the hospital she liked to wear heels but they were impractical with all the running around she did and now, in her flat, sensible shoes, Marcus was easily a foot taller than her.

He stared down at her with a look that was far from friendly. She could only assume he remembered her. And not fondly.

She didn't think she'd ever given him a reason to dislike her yet his jaw was clenched and tense and his lips were firmly closed. No welcoming smile there!

She remembered other kids teasing him. But she never had, she'd been too young, and she doubted that her brothers would have either, they hadn't been raised that way, but Marcus certainly didn't look pleased to see her. He looked as if he was daring her to say something about his past and she wondered what he thought she might say after all this time.

She couldn't actually remember him leaving town. One minute he had been there, living in Toowoomba, going to school with her brother. The next minute he'd gone. Vanished. Just like his mother before him.

But now here he was. Fighting fit, successful and gorgeous.

So what was the story? She was desperate to know.

She put out her hand, waiting to see if he would say anything, wanting to know if he would divulge their shared past.

'Grace... Gibson, is it?'

You know damn well it is, she wanted to say, but the look in his eye stopped her short and made her hold her tongue. Which surprised her. Holding her tongue had never been her forte.

Her hand hovered in mid-air until Marcus's fingers curled around her palm. Perhaps he was just trying to make amends for his lack of manners but his touch flummoxed her. His tone was cool but his hand was warm. Warm enough to send fire through her fingertips. Her whole arm tingled and set her heart racing. Her breath caught in her throat and she barely remembered to nod her head in acknowledgement of his words.

What was he doing to her? How was he doing it? She was breathless, frozen to the spot, yet her body felt as if it was overheating. The colours around her intensified, making her feel dizzy, and sounds receded. She felt overloaded, as if her body couldn't cope with too many sensations at once. Marcus's touch was enough to cope with. More than enough.

What was wrong with her? She wondered if she was having a panic attack or if her system was shutting down. What had he done to her? She never lost her nerve.

She could feel another embarrassing rush of blood beginning to flood her body, only this time it wasn't in her face. This time it was starting somewhere south of that but she knew her face would soon be bright red also. She pulled her hand away, severing the contact.

Her hand was trembling. She was trembling.

She stuck her hand in her pocket to disguise her tremor and looked at her feet, unable to maintain eye contact.

If Marcus had been daring her to say something, he'd won the dare. She was completely tongue-tied.

Elliot was still talking, apparently oblivious to the feelings that were raging through Grace and completely unaware of the electric undercurrents flowing between her and his new colleague.

Perhaps it was all in her head, she thought, but she didn't really believe that.

'You've read the patient histories?' Elliot asked, and Janet and Marcus nodded. 'Janet, I thought you could perform the kidney removal on Rosa. I will assist and, Marcus, you are more experienced, you can observe that surgery and then you will perform the transplant later.'

Grace had decided not to be such a coward and had lifted her eyes again now that the attention was off her and she saw Marcus's small double take. He looked surprised by Elliot's words—had he not been expecting that?

Elliot continued speaking. 'Grace will have any other information you might need pre-op. If there's anything more you need, you can liaise with her. I will do the other transplant, with Janet assisting, and Andrew Murray will take care of the second organ retrieval. Your patients were admitted first thing this morning—'

'Already?' Marcus interrupted.

Grace knew it was unusual. Normally patients were admitted as late as possible, sometimes only on the day of surgery, mostly as a cost-saving exercise, but she'd advocated strongly that admission be brought forward.

Elliot nodded. 'Grace thought it would be prudent to get them admitted early to avoid the media circus that we're anticipating, and I agreed. We don't want to increase their stress levels by having reporters jostling for a comment as they arrive, and this also means we don't have to worry about traffic delays and other things that might be out of our control tomorrow.'

Marcus looked at Grace. She thought he might be about to say something and she wondered if it would have been complimentary but his expression remained guarded. Janet had no reservations. 'Great, I'll go and introduce myself to Rosa.'

Elliot moved away and Janet and Marcus followed him without a backward glance. Grace stood and watched them go. Had he forgotten about her already?

She watched as his long strides quickly put distance between them. Her legs were incapable of moving. Her knees were still shaky and she felt light-headed. She stood still and took a couple of deep breaths, getting the air back into her lungs, remembering to breathe as she sorted through her mental list of tasks ahead of her.

She had plenty to do before tomorrow. Final physical checks of their patients had to be co-ordinated, she had to confirm the courier arrangements and continue discussions with the other renal co-ordinators in Brisbane, Melbourne and North Sydney hospitals. She had a lot of balls in the air and she couldn't afford to drop any. She couldn't afford to worry about Marcus Washington and about what he was thinking or where he'd been for the last twenty years. There were far too many more important things waiting to occupy her time.

But that didn't stop her from immediately racing back to her office and checking her emails. There must have been one announcing the three-month appointment of Janet and Marcus. She couldn't believe she'd missed it. She typed Marcus's name into the search function and hit enter. An email from a month ago popped up. The heading gave no clue as to who the doctors were, and she was certain that if it had included his name that would have caught her eye. It was also in amongst dozens of emails relating to the paired kidney exchange, which would explain why she'd skimmed over it without even opening it.

She opened it now. She was eager to see what information it gave her.

She ignored Janet's CV and clicked on the file pertaining to Marcus. He had graduated from university in Western Australia. Had he moved there from Toowoomba? Why? Who had he gone to? Had his mother moved there? Was she alive? But if she was, why hadn't she taken him years before? Grace had more questions than answers.

She continued reading. He had spent some time in the US during his speciality years, returning to work in Perth. And now he was here. His career history was brief and, of course, there was no personal information included. Nothing to tell her if he was married, engaged, straight, gay—although she was pretty sure he was straight—or if he had a wife and kids back home in Perth.

She closed her email down. She didn't have time to do a wider search on him. She had all the final pieces of the transplant puzzle to put in place. She had dozens of phone calls to make, she needed to check in with the other hospitals to make sure that all their patients were still well enough to undergo surgery and that no one had changed their minds. One hiccup could ruin the whole exercise.

She was glad she'd made arrangements for her patients to be admitted early. As Elliot had outlined, her reasons were valid. There were enough other logistical arrangements to be made once the kidneys had been harvested, without adding to the complications with things going haywire prior to the surgeries. It would only take one problem to snowball and potentially disrupt all the surgeries, and she wanted everything to run smoothly.

By the time she ended her final call to one of the Melbourne hospitals it was dusk outside. She should have clocked off but there was still more to do. Her schedule didn't stick to regular nursing shifts any more, not since she'd become the renal co-ordinator. Her shifts supposedly ran from nine to five but it was not often that she stuck to those hours. Transplant patients could receive news day or night and she was often called back into the hospital to speak to the families of donors and to the transplant recipients. Plus, she had no reason to race out the door at the end of the day. She had nothing to race home for. No significant other, no children, no pets. If it wasn't for work, her life would be a bit empty.

She switched off her office lights but, still in no hurry to leave, she thought she'd check one last time on the four patients waiting for surgery.

She got two patients with her first visit.

'Gentlemen, how are you feeling?'

She greeted Rob and Paul, two brothers, one a donor, the other a recipient. Rob's donated kidney was going to Brisbane in exchange for a kidney for his brother, as unfortunately their tissue types didn't match. They were sitting together, chatting, when Grace entered Paul's room. They seemed quite relaxed but Paul had been through this before so it was nothing new for him. His first kidney transplant, from a deceased donor, had lasted twenty-five years but was failing now. It was wonderful to think that the paired exchange programme could hopefully give him another shot at a successful transplant.

As Grace chatted to the two men she quickly revised her opinion of how they were feeling. Paul seemed far more relaxed than Rob.

'Are you ready for tomorrow, Rob?' she asked gently when Paul went to the bathroom, leaving the two of them alone for a moment.

'I was told that the research shows that kidney disease most commonly affects both kidneys, is that right?'

'That does seem to be the case. You're worried about your remaining kidney?' Rob's nerves were not unusual in Grace's experience. The donor was often more on edge than the recipient. Grace didn't know if it was fear of the unknown or a lack of experience with hospitals or the fact that the donor wasn't actually sick but was giving up a perfectly healthy organ. Rob was going from being a healthy, intact individual to one who would be minus an organ. Granted, he could do without it but that was assuming his remaining kidney continued to function normally. Hence his question. She knew he'd heard these answers before but her role as co-ordinator was often as much about counselling as co-ordinating.

'We don't anticipate problems, Rob,' she reassured him when he nodded. 'We wouldn't let you do this if we thought it could create problems for you down the track.'

'There's no way I'm backing out,' he emphasised firmly, 'and my kidney only has to last long enough to see me out.'

'Okay. Get some rest and I'll see you in the morning.'

Grace made her way to Rosa's room across the hall next. Rosa's kidney would be going to Paul, not that either of them were privy to that piece of information, in exchange for a kidney for Rosa's son in Melbourne. Despite being across the corridor from each other, Paul and Rosa wouldn't meet.

Rosa was sitting beside her bed, knitting, the television on low volume. She was a widow with just the one son living interstate and Grace knew she was used to spending quiet nights alone. She'd told Grace she was fine as long as her hands were busy and she liked to knit.

She seemed calm and only had a couple of questions for Grace, both of which had to do with her son's prognosis. Rosa wasn't worried about herself at all.

'We have excellent results with kidney transplants,' Grace told her again, happy to answer her questions. 'Especially with living organ donors. Most kidneys will last ten years and some as long as twenty-five.' She wished she could tell Rosa that her kidney was going to Paul and that he was one of the people whose first transplanted kidney had lasted twenty-five years but she couldn't divulge that information, even though she knew it would make Rosa feel better. She said goodnight before popping into Connie's room, her last stop for the evening.

'Hey, Connie.'

Connie was the recipient of the spare kidney and even though in testing it had proved to be a good match there was a little bit of the unknown associated with this one, given the unexpectedness of the windfall, and Grace knew Connie was nervous.

Connie had moved to Sydney from the country eighteen months ago to have regular dialysis. She suffered from autosomal dominant polycystic kidney disease and Grace knew she was finding things difficult. She was only able to work part time and her support group of friends and family were not close by.

Because of her illness and medical appointments her social life was limited and Grace knew that this transplant would make a huge difference to her quality of life. Grace's sister-in-law had suffered from the same disease and had undergone a transplant five years ago, so Grace knew from personal experience how different Connie's life could potentially be. Connie was only twenty-seven, the same age as Grace, and because of that and her circumstances Grace felt a deeper affinity for her than for some of her other patients.

'Where is everyone?' Grace asked as she looked around. Although they weren't compatible donors, Connie's family were providing support to her in other ways, and when Grace stepped into the room she was surprised to find that Connie didn't have company. She knew her parents had come to the city to be with Connie for the surgery and the recovery.

'Mum and Dad will be back later, they've just gone to get some dinner.'

'How are you doing?' she asked as she flicked through Connie's chart, pleased to see everything looked stable and normal.

'I'm not worried about the operation. Just worried about what will happen if it doesn't work. I really want to be able to have kids. I need this to go well.'

Grace knew pregnancy was not out of the question for Connie if the transplant was successful but, as that was an unknown at this point, she couldn't make any promises. Who knew what would happen? The only thing you could do in life was to hope for the best. All they could do in this situation was hope the kidney was a viable, healthy and suitable match for Connie. And no one could control any of that. It wasn't her place to promise Connie things she might not be able to deliver.

'Have you spoken to Dr Washington about this?'

'OMG,' Connie gushed, 'thank you so much.'

Grace frowned. Connie's train of thought had clearly gone off at a complete tangent to the discussion Grace had thought they were having. 'What for?'

'Dr Washington. He is *hot*.'

Grace wasn't surprised that Connie had noticed Marcus, as he was difficult to miss, but she did *not* want to have this conversation. It felt inappropriate, even though she knew it was just chatter. She didn't want to talk about Marcus but she wasn't sure why. 'Seriously? You're about to have major surgery and you're thinking about your surgeon?'

Connie grinned. 'Thinking about him is proving to be a good distraction.'

'I guess I can see your point.' Grace could understand the fascination but she didn't have time to discuss Marcus's myriad attributes. She didn't know if she could be completely complimentary. 'But I really can't discuss him.'

'I just wish I didn't have to be asleep when he operates on me,' Connie sighed. 'He is totally gorgeous. Do you know if he's single?'

Grace had no idea. 'You know it's against the rules for doctors to get romantically involved with their patients, right?'

'I won't always be his patient.'

'He's only in Sydney for a few weeks. He's from Perth and once you get through tomorrow you will need to focus on your recovery, not chase after your surgeon.'

'But it would give me something to look forward to.'

This conversation was making Grace feel uncomfortable. She needed to end it. She turned her attention to a box of medical supplies that didn't need tidying but which gave her something to focus on. 'You shouldn't be getting excited, you need to keep your blood pressure stable,' she commented as she shuffled and sorted the small packets of wipes and dressings.

'What's this about your BP? It's not raised, is it?'

Grace had her back to the door and the sound of Marcus's voice made her jump. She didn't need to see him; his voice was already instantly recognisable. Deep, quiet and purposeful, it was a voice that commanded attention. When he spoke you wanted to listen. At least, she did. Grace turned and caught the tell-tale sign of a blush sweeping over Connie's cheeks as she greeted her surgeon.

'Nothing. It's all good,' Grace replied hastily.

Marcus swivelled his gaze to her but said nothing. He picked up Connie's chart and flicked through her records.

Grace bristled. Didn't he believe her? Not that she'd checked Connie's blood pressure herself but she *had* checked the chart. 'I am a registered nurse as well as the transplant co-ordinator,' she told him, deciding to give him the benefit of the doubt. Perhaps he wasn't aware of her qualifications. She'd only been the transplant co-ordinator for a few months but she was medically qualified and was gaining valuable experience all the time.

His gaze was cool and assessing when he looked at her again, his brown eyes imperturbable. He nodded once, but made no comment.

What was wrong with him? Did he have no warmth? Grace wondered, but then she recalled how her skin had burned when he'd held her hand. There was warmth in his touch but it was a pity it didn't appear to extend to his character.

He put Connie's chart away and perched on the edge of her bed and Grace watched as Connie's eyes nearly popped out of her head.

'Any last questions for me before I see you in the morning?' He smiled at his patient and Grace felt an unexpected stab of jealousy. His smile was incredible, transforming his features from striking and exotic to jaw-droppingly handsome, and she wished desperately that he would smile at her like that.

'Grace and I were just talking about what comes after the transplant. I really want to have children.'

Grace watched as Connie toyed with the ends of her hair and looked up at Marcus through her lashes. Was she flirting with him?

'If everything goes according to plan, pregnancy shouldn't be an issue after a transplant but it is recommended, and I certainly encourage my patients to follow this advice, to wait one year to ensure the transplant is functioning as we'd like and that your medications are stable.'

'That's okay. That will give me time to find a boyfriend.'

Yep, she was definitely flirting. She was all fluttering eyelashes and rosy cheeks. She certainly didn't look like a person who was critically ill and about to undergo major surgery. Not that Grace could blame her. Marcus was gorgeous, but if he noticed Connie's attempts to entice him, he didn't take the bait.

'You will need close monitoring during a pregnancy,' he replied, leaving Connie's comment well alone, 'but you would be closely monitored anyway and we can discuss any other issues post-surgery.'

'Great. If that's all, we'll leave you to get some rest now,' Grace said, keen to usher Marcus out of the room before Connie could actually proposition him.

As Marcus stood and started to leave, Grace shot Connie a warning glance behind his back, but Connie just grinned and then laughed it off, making Grace smile back. At least she was in good spirits.

Grace followed Marcus out of the room. His strides

were long and Grace found her gaze drawn to his hips. He'd removed his suit jacket, leaving the shape of his buttocks under his pants clearly defined as his legs ate up the length of the corridor. Grace forced herself to keep her eyes lifted. She didn't want to be caught ogling him or running into something because her attention was elsewhere.

She got the feeling he was trying to put as much distance between them as possible. But she had no idea why. Her curiosity got the better of her and she hurried after him. She wanted to know what his issue was. Why he was so abrupt with her. She didn't think she'd done anything to put him off, yet his aloofness was definitely directed at her. She had to admit he was an empathetic doctor with a good bedside manner and maybe she'd just have to be satisfied with that. But she still wanted some answers.

'Dr Washington!'

He stopped and turned towards her.

'Have I done something to upset you?' she asked as she caught up to him.

'No.'

Grace waited for him to elaborate but he didn't say another word. Man, he could totally be the poster boy for the strong, silent type.

Oh, well. Nothing ventured, nothing gained, she thought as she asked, 'Do you remember me?'

Marcus looked down at the petite redhead standing in front of him. She had her hands on her hips and looked as if she'd like to tear him to shreds. 'What do you mean? Of course I do,' he replied, attempting to use his most reasonable tone in an attempt to calm her down. 'We were just in Connie's room and I only met you a few hours ago.'

'I meant from before.'

He watched her with his steady gaze but said nothing. He wasn't going to admit to anything. Not until he knew what she wanted. She reminded him of a firecracker about to explode.

'You grew up in Toowoomba,' she said. It was apparent she wasn't going to be intimidated and she certainly wasn't asking him a question. She looked small and easy to handle but, just like a firecracker, he got the impression that once something set her off, you'd know all about it and there'd be nowhere to hide. 'I lived around the corner from you. You were at school with my brothers, Lachlan and Hamish Gibson.'

It was obvious she knew who he was. He'd suspected as much. He had recognised her too. Well, not her face as such, but her hair matched with her name was a dead giveaway. Her striking copper locks were so distinctive. He hadn't *wanted* to think she was the same person even though it was blatantly clear she was, just as it was clear she remembered him.

He cursed his luck. 'Was I?'

He knew he was being bullish but he couldn't help it. He'd spent twenty years trying to get away from his past. Twenty years spent reinventing himself and wiping away all traces of his childhood. He hadn't been back to Toowoomba in all that time and he'd even debated the wisdom of returning to the east coast for this three-month stint but the opportunity of this experience at the Kirribilli General Hospital had been too good to refuse. Guilt and opportunity had brought him back. And now it seemed it was about to make him pay.

He hadn't expected to run into anyone from his past and he certainly wouldn't have expected to be remem-

bered. He didn't want to remember who he had been and
the life he'd lived then. He didn't want to think about it
and he definitely didn't want to talk about it. So he stayed
silent, refusing to incriminate himself by admitting any
recollection. He couldn't admit to Grace that he had lied.
That he *had* recognised her.

'I guess I look a bit different,' Grace admitted when
he stayed mute. 'I must only have been about seven the
last time I would have seen you.'

Was there a question in there? Was she wondering why
he'd never come back? Had she even noticed?

He wasn't going to respond to vague insinuations but
she was right. She looked nothing like he remembered.
He remembered her brothers and he remembered their
little sister with skinned knees and missing teeth. The
only thing that remained of the seven-year-old she'd once
been was her hair. Her fiery copper locks hung in loose
waves over her shoulders, its rich colour bright and vibrant against the contrast of her navy uniform. He'd
hadn't seen a colour like it since leaving Toowoomba.

But everything else about her was different. She no
longer looked like anyone's kid sister. She had filled out
in all the right places. She was tiny, a good foot shorter
than his six feet two inches, but her proportions were
perfect. Her shirt was tucked into navy trousers, pants
which would have been unflattering on most figures, yet
his eye was drawn to her small waist, the swell of her
breasts and the curve of her hips. He felt an unexpected
surge of lust. Bloody hell, that was inappropriate. He
lifted his head and met her amber eyes. They blazed at
him. She appeared to have the fiery temper to match her
hair but what was getting her so riled up? Had she noticed his inappropriate once-over? He needed to douse

the flames of her temper and make sure he didn't set her off completely. Something told him there would be no stopping her if he did that.

Or maybe he should take up the challenge he could see in her eyes. She gave off an air of not being one to back down. Of having the courage of her convictions. That didn't appear to have changed. He remembered more about her than he cared to admit. She'd been loud and boisterous, full of energy; he'd always known when she was around and he suspected that hadn't changed in twenty years. He wondered what had.

The idea of putting a flame to her wick just to see what would happen was strangely exciting but he resisted the temptation. He didn't want to bring unnecessary attention to the two of them. He didn't want anyone asking awkward questions. Going under the radar was always best. He'd learnt that from experience.

But what did she want? What was she after? What did she remember of him? What secrets could she spill?

He hoped not many.

As a child he'd been quiet, shy and nervous. The complete antithesis to Grace. He'd been nervous around the kids at school and nervous around his father. His life had been unpredictable and devoid of routine but it hadn't been until he'd been at boarding school as a teenager that he'd realised that not everyone's lives were like that. He'd never experienced anything different. Most of the time he'd just tried to get from morning to evening without being noticed. It had seemed his presence had irritated people—his classmates and his father—and he had never been sure about what was going to happen, how people were going to react to him, although more often than not it had been unfavourably. He'd learnt to keep his head down, to try to be inconspicuous, but that had never been easy when he'd looked so different.

Thanks to his Caribbean mother he wasn't white but he wasn't indigenous either. He was part black but not the black that was common in Toowoomba. There wasn't another person in the town who had the same genetic mix as him and, if that wasn't enough to make him stand out, his family history and his unorthodox father had certainly made sure that everyone had singled him out.

His mother had disappeared when he'd been six, leaving him behind with a father who had chosen to develop a relationship with alcohol instead of with his son. His young life had been full of disappointments and he'd learnt early on not to ask for or expect much, and that the only person he could count on not to let him down was himself.

He'd been determined to escape a miserable childhood and to avoid all memories of his past. He'd worked hard over many years to forget who he was and where he came from. He didn't want to be remembered as that boy. That wasn't him any more.

And he didn't want anyone to remind him of it either.

Which made Grace the last person he wanted to see.

CHAPTER THREE

'I DON'T REMEMBER you from then,' he told her as he shook his head, but Grace knew he was lying.

She just didn't know why. Did he think he was above her now that he was a surgeon or was it for a more personal reason? He'd been perfectly pleasant to Connie. Not warm exactly but he was her surgeon and he certainly hadn't brushed her aside like he'd tried to do with *her*.

His dark brown eyes challenged her to say something more and for a moment she was tempted to but something stopped her. She couldn't have said what it was, and it was most unlike her to back down from an argument, but she had a sudden sense that she would regret the words that were itching to come out of her mouth so she bit down on her lip and kept quiet.

And Marcus turned and walked away.

Clearly the conversation was over and this time she didn't follow him. For some reason he seemed to have an issue with her. She didn't want it to be personal but, whatever it was, she wouldn't let it lie. But it would wait for another day. She returned to her office and collected her bag before heading to Billi's Bar.

As usual the bar was crowded with hospital staff. It was just across the road from the hospital and the staff kept it well patronised. She waved to Gary, who was serving customers, but made her way through the crowd, searching for Lola. She hadn't intended on calling into the bar tonight but she needed to vent her frustration. She wasn't sure why she was frustrated and that only made matters worse. Why did she care that Marcus was lying to her? Why did she care that he said he didn't remember her?

She found Lola towards the back of the room. She smiled in greeting but was looking over Grace's shoulder.

'Who are you looking for?' Grace asked.

'I thought you might bring the hot doc with you.'

Grace didn't need to ask who Lola was referring to but it had taken less time than she'd expected for the conversation to turn to Marcus. Was he all people could talk about? First Connie and now Lola.

'I'm the last person he would want to have a drink with.'

'Why? You haven't upset him already, have you?'

Lola's comment was not without merit. Grace knew she'd upset people before with her quick temper and tongue, but in Marcus's case she couldn't think of what she could have possibly done to make him behave so distantly towards her. She sighed and dumped her bag on the table then retrieved her phone. She needed to keep it handy as with so many surgeries scheduled for tomorrow she couldn't afford to miss a call. 'No,' she replied, 'but I don't think he likes me.'

Lola frowned. 'How can he not like you? He doesn't even know you.'

'So he says.'

'What does that mean?'

She pulled out a stool and sat down. She needed to debrief. 'He grew up in Toowoomba. He went to school with Lachlan and Hamish but he says he doesn't remember me.'

Lola laughed.

'What's so funny?' Grace's nerves were already frayed and having Lola laugh at her only irritated her more.

'You're upset because he doesn't remember you.'

'No, I'm upset because he's lying to me. He lived just around the corner from us. I used to walk past his house every day.'

'Was he there?'

Grace actually had no idea. She remembered walking past his house because it had always spooked her. The memory from years ago was still vivid in her mind but Lola was right. She couldn't actually remember if Marcus had been in there. She shrugged and admitted, 'I don't know.'

'Was he friends with your brothers?'

'Not really.' From what she could remember, he hadn't really been friends with anyone. She couldn't remember seeing him with friends. She thought he had played rugby but she could be imagining that.

'So maybe he really doesn't remember you. When did you see him last?'

'He left when I was about seven, so he would have been twelve. I haven't seen him since.'

'That's years ago! You can't blame him if he's forgotten you.'

But Grace didn't think she was wrong. She was certain he remembered her. There was something she couldn't put her finger on but she knew he wasn't telling her the truth.

'Where did he go when he left Toowoomba?' Lola asked.

'I have no idea. He just disappeared.'

'The whole family?'

Grace shook her head. 'No, just him. His father was still there.' Grace realised she hadn't thought about Mr Washington for years and she couldn't remember the last time she'd seen him either. Was he in a nursing home? Dead? She wouldn't have been surprised. Marcus's old house had been bulldozed after Grace had moved to Sydney and a new one was now in its place. With another family in it. But she had no idea what had happened to Marcus's father.

'So he left with his mother?'

'No. I never knew his mother. She disappeared years before.'

Lola leant forward, resting her elbows on the table. 'So his mother left suddenly, and then him? That sounds intriguing.'

'I really don't know much about it.'

There had been plenty of rumours about the family. Grace had grown up hearing them and then when Marcus had disappeared as well, the rumours had only intensified. The most popular theory amongst the kids at school had been that Marcus's father was responsible for the disappearances. They'd said he'd killed his wife and then he'd killed Marcus. As a seven-year-old that had frightened Grace immensely, and because of those stories it was unlikely she'd ever forget about Marcus Washington. The story of his disappearance had become an urban myth. The kids had been fascinated by it and Grace's imagination had led her to not only believe the stories but to embellish all sorts of gory details.

Her parents had told her and her brothers that Marcus had gone to live with his aunt but at the age of seven she'd put that story in the same category as the one about the

fate of their pet roosters. Her parents had told her that
the roosters were sent away to live on a farm because
they were happier there, but her brothers had gleefully
informed her that they really ended up in someone's pot
with their heads chopped off. Grace feared Marcus had
met the same fate and that her parents were lying to protect her because, surely, if he had gone to live with his
aunt he would still come back to visit his father. And he
never did. In Grace's seven-year-old brain this meant the
rumours must be true. Marcus was dead.

It wasn't hard for her to believe the rumours and to
imagine that Mr Washington had somehow played a hand
in the disappearance of his family. When they were never
seen again that story made sense. And, in Grace's young
opinion, Marcus's father was a strange man. Walking
past Marcus's house had always spooked her and after
his disappearance things had only got worse. The house
had been untidy and unloved. Paint had been peeling off
the woodwork, the iron roof rusty and the front garden
overgrown with weeds. If it hadn't been for the fact that
Mr Washington had often sat or slept on an old sofa on
the front veranda you would have thought the house had
been abandoned. He'd always looked dishevelled and, if
she saw him on his feet, unsteady.

She'd had to walk past the house on her way to and
from school and after Marcus's disappearance she had
always crossed to the opposite side of the road just in
case Mr Washington was out the front. Lachlan, who was
then twelve, had told her not to be ridiculous. He'd insisted that if Marcus's dad had killed him he'd be locked
up, not wandering the streets, but Grace had remained
wary for many years until she'd been old enough to un-

derstand Lachlan's logic and recognise the rumours for what they were.

Later she'd understood that Marcus's father had been an alcoholic but at the age of seven she hadn't got any of that. When she'd learned the truth she'd then wondered what had made him drink. Had it been losing his wife and son that had done that to him?

But Grace didn't share her thoughts with Lola. Normally she wouldn't hesitate to gossip with her but something about this felt wrong. Obviously Marcus hadn't been murdered and all her thoughts were based on rumour and supposition. She was sorry she'd brought up the topic now. She recalled the look in Marcus's eyes. The look that she'd thought had been daring her to say something. Maybe it hadn't been a challenge but fear? Was he afraid of what she might say about him?

What could she possibly say? What did he think she knew?

Did it matter? Even imagining she had tales to tell could be enough. She knew what that was like. After her boyfriend had taken his own life Grace had felt the eyes of a small town on her. Mostly the town had been supportive of her and her grief after Johnny's death but she'd still felt horribly exposed. That had been one reason why she'd wanted to leave Toowoomba. Too many people knew too much about her. She knew what it felt like when others made assumptions about you. How it felt when things you'd rather keep to yourself were discussed in public.

Was that what Marcus was worried about? That she would reveal his secrets?

But what did she know about him? What *could* she

know about him when she hadn't seen or heard anything about him for twenty years?

Nothing.

The truth of the matter was it wasn't her story to tell and she was sorry she and Lola had even been discussing him. She knew he wouldn't like it and for some reason that bothered her. She picked up her bag and tucked her phone inside it. 'I should go,' she said. 'I have a big day tomorrow.'

Grace was at the hospital bright and early the following morning. She had checked on her patients and found them in varying degrees of anxiety but otherwise okay. She'd contacted the renal transplant co-ordinators at the other hospitals, double-checking and making sure there were no last-minute problems, and now she was heading for the conference room to prepare her notes in anticipation of the doctors' meeting that was scheduled for half past seven to have a final run-through of the day's proceedings.

She scrolled through the messages on her phone, making sure again that she hadn't missed anything important as she waited for everyone to arrive. Elliot was first, followed by Janet and then Marcus. She wasn't watching the door but she knew the minute Marcus entered the room. She looked up to find him watching her. Was that what she could sense? The feeling of being watched? No, it was more than that. Her body recognised him. Her body responded to his proximity. But she suspected she was being fanciful. It was nothing more than an awareness of an extremely good-looking man. Who had absolutely no time for her.

He didn't hold her gaze. Didn't acknowledge her in

any way. He didn't smile. Or nod. He gave her nothing and she was disappointed. He greeted his colleagues as he found himself a seat but he did not make eye contact with her again. Was that deliberate or not? She wanted him to like her but she got an uneasy sense that something about her irritated him and that bothered her. She wanted him to like her but right now she didn't have time to think about why that might be. She lowered her eyes and looked over her notes. She refused to waste any more time wondering about Marcus. She was just as capable of ignoring him as he was of her.

She listened as Elliot ran everyone through the day's schedule. He was following the notes she had written on the whiteboard as soon as she'd confirmed every patient's status and he checked a couple of minor details with her. The surgeries were scheduled to commence at eight o'clock with concurrent harvesting of the kidneys. The donor patients were being prepped for surgery as he spoke and once Grace received confirmation that every patient was anaesthetised the surgeries would begin. The timing and, in a way, the success of the surgeries depended on her. She controlled the process and she needed to focus.

The actual transplant timeline varied and was dependent on when the donated kidneys arrived at their respective hospitals. There was still a lot to co-ordinate and it was going to be a long day for her. She would be on deck until the last patient went to Recovery. She was the link not only between the surgeons and the hospitals but also between the patients and their families. It was going to be hectic but while she would co-ordinate the surgeries the actual outcomes of them would be out of her hands. It was almost over. The final day was here and all that was left for her to do was to continue to liaise and to watch and to watch and to hope. And to wait. She crossed her fingers and hoped the day would be successful.

The medical staff split into their surgical teams at the conclusion of the meeting and Grace headed for the observation gallery that overlooked two of the theatres. She watched as the patients were wheeled in, Rosa in one theatre to her left, Rob in the other. She would be able to communicate with the operating teams via an intercom and she waited and watched as the anaesthetists began their job. The surgeons hovered, gloved and gowned.

She held her mobile phone in her hand, waiting for the sound of incoming text messages and constantly scanning the screen to check she hadn't missed anything. She saw Rosa's eyes close as the anaesthetic took hold and then, one by one, the messages started coming in. One, two, three and four. She waited for confirmation from the two theatres in front of her before sending her own reply.

'All donors confirmed asleep.'

Until everyone was under anaesthetic there was always a chance that one or more donors could change their minds. But no one could back out now. The six harvesting surgeries could begin.

Grace waited again, holding her breath until she got confirmation that all surgeries had begun. She breathed out and sank into a seat behind the viewing glass. Technically she could watch both Rosa's and Rob's operations but she concentrated on Rosa's. That was where Marcus was. She had vowed to ignore him but her eyes were repeatedly drawn to him regardless of her decision.

He stood slightly back from the operating table as he was in Theatre as an observer only, watching Elliot and

Janet operating, but Grace knew he was tall enough to see over the shoulders of the nurse who stood in front of him.

Janet and Elliot worked together. The surgery began as keyhole and Grace could watch proceedings on a monitor in the corner of the observation gallery. The kidneys were tucked up under the lower ribs and not always easy to access. The procedure was time consuming, requiring a steady hand and patience as the kidney needed to be carefully and precisely detached. All the important attachments needed to be preserved. Smaller blood vessels were cauterised but the ureter, renal artery and renal vein all needed to be harvested intact along with the kidney.

The surgery had begun as a laparoscopic procedure but once the kidney was detached Janet needed to remove it from Rosa's abdomen. She enlarged one of the incisions until it was the size of her fist and pulled the kidney free. It had taken a little over two hours before Janet was able to lift the left kidney out of Rosa's abdomen. It was major surgery and Rosa would need several days in hospital to recover.

In the second theatre, Rob's kidney was also being removed. It would be packed in ice and preservation fluid before being put in a medical tissue cool bag for collection by the courier company. They would take it to the airport and it would then head for Brisbane on the late morning flight.

Grace made a call to the courier company to confirm collection at the other end before checking the status of Rosa kidney. Elliot held her excised kidney in his gloved hands, checking Janet's handiwork. He looked up at Grace in the viewing gallery and, after returning Rosa's kidney to the iced water, he gave a thumbs-up signal to Grace, indicating that Rosa's kidney was looking good.

That kidney didn't have far to go. It was only going to a third theatre adjacent to the one they were in now to be transplanted into Paul. Despite their proximity, they still wouldn't meet even post-operatively. With private facilities there would be no need but if they wanted to communicate via letter Grace would assist them to do that. Often it was a useful exercise, for the donor in particular.

Even though living donors were usually donating a kidney to help out a loved one and therefore could see first-hand the difference a kidney transplant could make, they still often experienced feelings of loss. Hearing from the 'other half' in the exchange process, the person who received their gift of a kidney and the gift of a normal life could be immensely satisfying and help in their recovery process. They were often prepared for the financial losses incurred when they needed to take time off work, often weeks, to recover, but the emotional side of relinquishing a body part was often more stressful than they had anticipated.

Grace's role didn't end today. She would continue to liaise with and counsel all four of her patients. But having witnessed two successful harvesting procedures, she let herself relax just slightly as she slipped out of the viewing gallery to update Paul and arrange for him to be brought to Theatre.

He was in his room, ready and waiting in a hospital gown.

'How's it going? How's Rob?' he asked after his brother.

'He's doing well,' she told him. 'The surgeons are just closing him up now. All going to plan we'll have you in Recovery together in a few hours.'

'My kidney is already here?'

'It is and it's looking good.' Paul had never been told where his kidney was coming from and Grace knew it would be a relief to him to know that it was safely in the hospital. He didn't need to know it had literally come from across the hall. 'It's time to get you to Theatre,' she said.

All the other retrievals had gone to plan too. There had been no hiccups and apparently all the kidneys appeared viable. The courier process had begun and Grace's phone was never out of her hand as she kept tabs on all the transfers.

By midday Paul's surgery was under way, Rob's kidney was on its way to Brisbane, a third was on a flight from Brisbane down to Sydney, a fourth was being flown from Sydney to Melbourne and Rosa's son Steve was waiting in Melbourne for his kidney to be couriered across the city. It was enough to make her head spin but there was still one final piece in the puzzle. The one thing Grace was waiting for now was Connie's kidney, which was coming from Melbourne.

Her phone vibrated. Margie, the renal transplant coordinator in Melbourne, was on the line. 'Grace, the kidney is good. It's packed and on its way to the airport. I'll email you the courier tracking number.'

'Okay, thanks.' Grace checked the time on her phone as she disconnected the call. Five minutes past twelve. It was cutting it fine but she knew the airline was expecting the delivery.

She opened Margie's email and copied the tracking number into the courier's app and followed the progress of her delivery along Melbourne's freeways. She paced the hospital corridors as she constantly updated the app. Her stomach rumbled, making her realise how long ago breakfast had been. She pulled a protein bar from her pocket. She should probably go and get something more substantial for lunch but she didn't know if she could sit still long enough to eat anything. A bar on the run would have to suffice for now.

The tracking app showed the courier van had reached Tullamarine Airport at twelve forty-five. Her incoming mail notification flashed and a message popped up. The kidney had been delivered. Step two was complete. Now she needed to make sure it got put on the plane. She logged out of the courier company's app and opened the airline's web page to check the flight schedule. It showed the plane was still due to depart at one-fifteen and should land just after half past two. If everything went smoothly from here on, Connie should be in Theatre for a mid-afternoon surgery.

Grace updated Connie and the surgical team before checking on all the donor patients, who were now in various recovery suites around the country. So far, so good.

At one twenty the airline website marked the plane from Melbourne as 'Departed' but just as Grace was about to give another update to all concerned, the message changed and the plane was now listed as 'Delayed'. She frowned. How could it have taken off and now be 'delayed'?

She called the airline to check and was told the plane had left the terminal but hadn't taken off. It had a problem with its steering and had had to turn back. They were trying to fix it.

At two o'clock the website was still showing the flight as delayed and Grace was getting nervous. She placed another call and was given the same information—they were trying to fix the problem.

'Is there another flight you can put it on?' she asked.

'The next scheduled flight is at four, we're hoping to have the problem fixed by then.'

Grace hoped so too. She desperately wanted that kidney but it was completely out of her hands. Her heart was racing in her chest and she willed herself to stay calm. This was a big operation, her first major project as the renal transplant co-ordinator, and while she knew that, technically, it was out of her control she really didn't want anything to be screwed up. There was absolutely nothing she could do but she hated this feeling of powerlessness.

She should update everyone but she was reluctant to do that until she had more concrete information. At this stage everyone in Sydney would assume the kidney was on its way. She would update them when she had the facts to give them. She took a deep breath and sat down to wait.

Forty-five minutes later she knew she had to tell people something. They would be expecting to hear that the kidney had landed. She called the airline again and was told that the passengers and cargo were being unloaded and would be transferred to another flight when a plane became available.

'I need that kidney urgently,' Grace said, trying to quell the rising panic in her chest. 'Can you please get it on the next flight to Sydney, the one scheduled for four o'clock? It doesn't have to come with those passengers.'

'I will make sure of it,' the airline representative told her, but Grace's confidence was shaky.

She knew the kidney could stay on ice for hours but she was desperately worried that it would get misplaced or overlooked. She wanted it on a plane and then arriving safely in her hospital, but whatever happened she couldn't wait any longer to apprise people of the situation. She ended the call and headed for the PR department. They would be relatively easy to deal with. Then she'd tell Connie.

She took the news surprisingly well but Grace deliberately made it sound as though she had the situation under control. She left the surgical team until last. She'd start with Elliot. As head of the team she should speak to him first but she had to walk past Marcus's office to reach Elliot. Marcus was the lead surgeon on Connie's transplant so should she speak to him now?

She hesitated outside his door, but realised she was more nervous about telling him than Elliot. She didn't want to be the one bearing bad news to Marcus. She could only imagine the reception she would get as he was cool towards her at the best of times. Maybe she should stick with her plan and tell Elliot first. She knew he would understand. She'd tell him first and then *he* could tell Marcus.

That was a good solution.

But as she turned away from Marcus's door she saw him rounding the corner and heading her way.

'Are you looking for me?' he asked as he kept walking towards her.

She was caught, stranded between a rock and a hard place. There was no way she could pretend she hadn't seen him. She bit the bullet. 'I have an update on the kidney,' she said.

'Has it arrived?'

Grace shook her head. 'Not yet.'

'Is there a problem?'

He seemed to be standing very close to her. Maybe it was just that he was so much taller than her, so much bigger. She didn't feel intimidated but she did feel very aware of him, aware of the breadth of his chest, the warmth of his body and the smell of his aftershave. He smelt of the beach, of salt water and fresh air.

How he could smell like that after several hours in the hospital she didn't know but she knew that if she closed her eyes she would immediately think of the ocean. She resisted the urge to close her eyes and answered him instead. 'A minor one,' she admitted, and hoped that was all it was.

'You can tell me about it in here,' he said as he reached past her and opened the door to his office. His sleeve brushed her shoulder and she could feel the warmth of his breath and the heat of his skin. His proximity set her heart racing but his gaze remained steely and cold. He was such a contradiction of sensations and he stirred feelings in her that she didn't want to think about. And she wasn't sure that following him into his office was a good idea. She hadn't been alone with him out of the public eye yet and his inscrutable façade made her nervous. But she couldn't think of a good reason not to follow him in. At least, not one that she could verbalise.

'You told me it was on its way,' he said as she stepped into his office. She had assumed he would blame her and his tone suggested that she was in his firing line. She could feel her temper rising but she knew she couldn't afford to lose her cool. Now was not the time. 'What's happened?' he continued. 'Was there a problem with the kidney?'

'There's no problem with the kidney but there is a problem with the plane.'

She breathed a sigh of relief as Marcus walked to his desk and sat down, putting some space between them. If she was going to have this conversation in here, with him, she need to be able to think clearly and she knew that would be difficult if he stood too close. If she could smell him, feel his heat, she wasn't sure she'd be able to string enough words together to make a sensible sentence.

'What sort of problem?'

'The steering. It hasn't been able to take off. The kidney is still in Melbourne.' Her sentences were short and stilted. She was still struggling to think straight, her brain apparently too busy processing other thoughts.

'I assume it's already on another flight?' His tone matched the coolness of his gaze.

'Not yet.'

'What do you mean, "not yet"? It's Melbourne to Sydney, there must be a dozen other flights it can come on.'

He sounded irritated now and Grace could feel her face burning. Did he think she was completely incompetent? None of this was her fault. But, as the transplant coordinator, she supposed the buck really did stop with her. It was her job to get the kidneys where they needed to go.

'The next one doesn't leave until four p.m.,' she explained, fighting to keep a neutral tone. Losing her cool with him was not going to improve the situation. 'The airline has assured me it will be on that one unless they can get a replacement aircraft that can depart sooner. I've explained the situation to Connie. She's doing okay. She understands and I've explained that the delay shouldn't affect the outcome of the transplant. The team in Melbourne was pleased with the kidney.'

'It doesn't matter how good the kidney is if it's not here,' he snapped. 'I want that kidney.'

'And you will get it.'

'Can you arrange to bring it with another airline?'

It had been a long and stressful day and it wasn't over

yet, not by a long shot. Grace's nerves were stretched tight and her emotions were threatening to overwhelm her. She wanted things to go to plan and she hated the fact that there was a hiccup and she hated the fact that, because of the hiccup, Marcus thought her less than competent. She was close to tears but she wasn't about to let him see that his attitude was affecting her and she was teetering on the edge of a fight-or-flight response. Fight won. She had a redhead's temper, which she usually tried to keep under control, but something about Marcus pushed her buttons and she wasn't going to let him get the better of her. This wasn't about him and what he wanted, and she was getting annoyed.

She focused her energy on that emotion, which was more useful than feeling incapable, and, besides, she had considered all other possibilities and she didn't need him telling her how to do her job. She straightened her spine and tried to at least give the appearance that she was competent and in charge of the situation, even though they both knew that was far from the truth. 'The other airlines have a similar flight schedule,' she told him, 'and changing airlines means moving it from one side of the airport to the other. I don't want to risk it getting mislaid.'

'The longer Connie has to wait the more anxious she might become and you know that can affect surgery outcomes.'

He had a point but Grace would do her best to make sure Connie stayed calm. 'I'm not doing this on purpose.'

'I understand that but you have to agree this isn't ideal.'

It wasn't perfect but it also wasn't the worst thing that could happen under the circumstances. She wasn't sure why he was making such a big deal out of it. She was sure it would all be fine, why was he so pessimistic? 'Hasn't anything gone wrong for you before?' she asked.

Damn. The words had come out of her mouth before she could stop them. Stupid, thoughtless words. While she had no idea about the most recent twenty years of his life she knew his childhood had been far from perfect but it was too late now. She'd spoken without thinking and there was no taking back those words.

Should she apologise?

No. She knew that would only make matters worse. Apologising would reveal that she remembered more about him than he would want her to. She gathered he was a man who guarded his privacy zealously and she doubted he'd want to spend time reminiscing with her about his early years.

'Not lately,' he responded. His voice was deep and flat and his eyes were dark and intense. There was not a flicker of warmth in them. He looked at her like he was blaming her for everything that had gone wrong. Today and every day before it.

Grace felt her phone vibrate in her pocket. She broke eye contact to pull it out and check the screen.

'It's the airline,' she said without looking up as she took the incoming call and listened to the latest update.

'Your kidney is being put onto another plane,' the airline rep said.

'Have you double-checked that personally?' Grace asked. She didn't want to pass on false information. Not with the mood Marcus was in.

'I'm watching it being loaded now.'

Grace breathed a sigh of relief and was able to look Marcus in the eye again as she ended the call. 'They have a replacement plane. The kidney is being loaded now and is due to land in Sydney at five-fifteen p.m. I'll let you know as soon as it leaves the airport and is on its way here.'

'I'll be waiting,' he said, his tone dismissive. He nodded once, briefly, in acknowledgement, but offered no apology for his earlier brusqueness.

Grace took the hint and left his office. She had things to do now. Things that would keep her too busy to worry about Marcus and what he was thinking.

She called the courier company in Sydney to make sure they would be on hand to meet the plane and then went to let Connie know the state of play. She kept a close eye on the airline's website as well, not relaxing until she had seen the 'Departed' notation for her plane. Statistics showed that several hours on ice did not affect the success rate of a transplant but she wouldn't relax completely until the kidney was safely delivered to her.

This delay meant the journey was similar to transporting a kidney from Perth in Western Australia to the east coast. It wasn't ideal but it had happened before without problems. How long the kidney spent on ice was far less important than how good the kidney was and, by all reports, the team in Melbourne was very happy with it. Grace had to believe everything would be okay.

Marcus was ready. He took a calming breath, preparing himself for surgery, but he wasn't nervous or tense. He'd been preparing for this moment for days, years really if he considered all the study he'd done. He'd performed numerous transplants before but he'd never been involved in something on this scale. He was excited, filled with anticipation, and he couldn't wait to get started.

He looked around at his team. They were in for a

late night. It was after six already and Connie's surgery would take several hours but the sense of excitement and anticipation was palpable in the theatre. Everyone was happy to be involved.

Connie had been prepped and had moved herself onto the operating table but Marcus hadn't given the go-ahead for her to be anaesthetised yet. He wanted to see the kidney first. There was no point knocking Connie out if he decided the kidney wasn't viable.

'The moment of truth,' he said as he removed the lid of the container and lifted the kidney from its icy bed in his gloved hands. It was a good size without being too large for Connie and it looked healthy. He inspected it carefully and then smiled behind his mask. 'We are good to go, people. Let's do this.'

He put the kidney back in its bath. It would be warmed up later, ready to transplant, and returned to the operating table. His heart skipped a beat as he caught a glimpse of Grace standing on the opposite side of the room, a little behind the surgical team. Even though she was dressed in the same shapeless blue scrubs that everyone else was wearing, her face hidden behind a mask and her fiery hair disguised under a cap, there was no mistaking her.

He hadn't anticipated that she'd be in the theatre and her presence made him feel unexpectedly nervous. And not just because she would be watching and possibly judging his skills. She made him feel nervous in other ways as well. The way his body reacted to her presence was unsettling. He knew he was too aware of her and that made him uncertain. He hated feeling out of control and that was *exactly* how she made him feel. But he had no good reason to ask her to leave. He had to ignore her and get on with his job.

He looked down at Connie. The anaesthetist had sedated her and she was now asleep, draped in sterile cloths, her abdomen exposed and washed with an anti-septic solution, ready for surgery. Marcus held his hand out. 'Scalpel.'

The weight of the scalpel was reassuring, reminding him that this was what he did. This was what he was good at. He was a surgeon, competent, skilled, precise. He might not be any good at relationships, at social pleas-antries or thinking about the past, but he was an excel-lent surgeon.

He blocked out all thoughts of Grace and focused on his breathing, on slowing his heartbeat and steadying his hand ready to make the first incision. This was his chance to show her how far he'd come. To show her that he wasn't that adolescent from Toowoomba any more.

He placed the tip of the scalpel on Connie's skin and sliced through the soft flesh of her abdomen. The blade cut through the skin and subcutaneous fat just above her left pelvic bone. He breathed out steadily as he made the first cut. He was calm, focused and relaxed now that surgery had begun. This was where he was most com-fortable. Circumstances had made him determined to escape, excel and succeed, and his skills as a surgeon were the culmination of his drive and years of hard work and dedication. For him, being in the operating theatre represented the pinnacle of his achievements and it was something he was immensely proud of. He was good at his job and he was in control.

He continued to cut through layers of tissue. Cut, cau-terise and control until he was inside Connie's abdominal cavity. He made some space for the donor kidney. The donated organ was from the right-hand side of the donor but he would position it on Connie's left, below her existing kidneys, as that made it easier to connect the ureter to the bladder. Connie's old kidneys would remain in situ higher up in her abdomen, protected by her rib cage.

As he worked he imagined he could feel Grace watching him. What was she thinking? He knew he owed her an apology for his earlier behaviour. He'd been abrupt and discourteous and that didn't sit well with him. Nervousness had made him harsh. He hadn't been nervous about the surgery itself but about how he would appear to his team. It was important for him to be in control and for others to see him that way. Losing that donated kidney or losing control was something he couldn't risk. He would complete this surgery and then he would figure out how to apologise to Grace.

The donor kidney was ready, warmed and waiting. It was gently placed into position and Marcus could then begin the delicate task of connecting it to Connie. The renal artery and vein had been carefully preserved and with tiny, precise sutures he attached these vessels to the external iliac artery and vein, ready to bring the kidney back to life. Once he was satisfied, the vessels were unclamped and he watched the blood flow closely, checking for any signs of leakage at the suture lines.

All good. Step two was complete. Now he needed to move on to step three, to connect the ureter. This was a straightforward process. Access and visibility was good and his hand was steady. His confidence was high as he completed the surgery. Once the ureter was connected he inserted a catheter into Connie's bladder and gave a silent prayer of thanks when he saw fresh urine flow into the bag. Immediate urine output sometimes occurred when kidneys from living donors were transplanted and it was always a good sign. The kidney was healthy and functioning.

He did a final inspection of his handiwork before closing Connie's wound with small stitches. He could have used staples but he preferred stitches as they would leave a less obvious scar, which he felt was important in a female of Connie's age. He might not understand much about women but he knew the importance of appearance. Once he was confident that everything was working, he instructed the anaesthetist to reverse the anaesthetic and thanked and congratulated his team.

'Great work, everyone.'

Surgery had gone smoothly and he breathed out a sigh of relief. Once Connie was out of the anaesthetic and stable in Recovery he could go home. He could escape.

But it seemed Grace had other ideas.

'I think this calls for beer and pizzas at Billi's,' she said. 'You've all missed tea break and I'm sure you'd like a chance to wind down. Who's up for that? The hospital is paying.'

'Hell, yeah,' was the first response. Free food and beer was rarely declined, and this offer was swiftly followed by a chorus of positive answers with only a few declining the invitation. Marcus stayed silent.

'Dr Washington?' Grace queried.

He looked around the room before replying. It seemed the majority of the team was heading to the pub, barring a couple who had families, which left him no choice. He had no one to go home to, no family, no excuses. He nodded. 'Sure. That sounds good.'

In the time it had taken him to shower and dress and check on Connie's recovery, Marcus had changed his mind about stopping in at Billi's Bar at least a dozen times. Even as he walked into the bar he was still in two minds about whether or not this was a good idea. He didn't drink and he didn't socialise. These situations made him feel awkward and he did his best to avoid them. He was never one hundred per cent comfortable in a group setting. The trace of the uncertain boy remained, always making him wonder how people perceived him, what people thought of him and whether he was saying the right thing.

In a hospital and particularly in an operating theatre he knew how to behave. He'd taught himself those skills but he always felt like he failed dismally with any social interactions. He'd never had a foundation for that. The psychological scars of his childhood ran deep and not even his surgeon's confidence could hide them completely.

Even in Theatre tonight he'd taken a moment or two to reply to Grace's invitation because it had taken him a few seconds to work out what he was expected to do. He'd waited to take his cues from the others and when it had seemed the majority of the surgical team was going to the bar he'd found himself accepting the invitation. Because it had seemed to be expected. It was pushing him out of his comfort zone but declining the invitation would have drawn more attention to him so it had been safer to accept. He didn't want to examine whether he'd been more enticed to accept because Grace had organised it, because she would be there, but that was beside the point now. He was here. So he would use this opportunity to apologise to her and then he would leave.

She was the first person he looked for when he stepped through the door and the first person he saw. Even in the dark recesses of the bar her bright hair shone like a beacon.

He'd been totally aware of her in Theatre today and not solely because he remembered her from his childhood. Recollections of her were still vague and triggered mainly by the unusual colour of her hair, but he couldn't deny he felt some sort of connection to her. Somehow he'd managed to keep his focus on his work and he'd kept up the required amount of conversation with the theatre staff, but even though Grace had stayed silently in the background, he'd been totally aware of her presence. He'd wanted to do his best work, not only because he was the new kid on the block but because he'd wanted to impress her.

An unfamiliar twinge of desire unwound in his belly as he watched her profile now as she chatted animatedly with her workmates. She looked completely comfortable and vibrant and he found it difficult to keep his eyes off her. He didn't want to admit it but the connection he felt was attraction.

And that put him on the back foot. He was completely out of his depth emotionally and he knew that usually made him defensive so he'd have to watch himself. He'd come here to apologise, not to make matters worse.

He wanted Grace to like him, he'd decided it would be safer that way, and he knew he'd been unpleasant earlier in the day. He knew he'd made a less than favourable first impression on her, but he hoped it wasn't too late to remedy the situation.

He made his way to the bar while he tried to sort through his new-found dilemma. An apology to her was necessary but he wasn't going to do it in front of a crowd of colleagues. And he had to work out how to deal with the fact he was attracted to her. That hadn't been a page in his playbook for Sydney.

He leant on the bar, half turned away from the group he was supposed to be joining as he ordered a soft drink. He didn't know if he could force himself to approach his colleagues. Didn't know how long he would last, but his position at the bar enabled him to keep half an eye on Grace. He couldn't resist. She looked up and met his gaze. She gave him a half-smile, picked up a pizza box and started moving. Was she coming to him?

Marcus couldn't take his eyes off her as she crossed the room.

He wondered whether she had someone to go home to or whether she was single like him. Would she have organised pizzas for everyone if she had someone waiting at home for her? Probably. She seemed like that type of person—one who was good at looking after others.

He very much doubted she was single. Girls like her never were. She was vivacious, determined, opinionated and fiery. If she was single it was because she wanted to be, he thought as she stopped in front of him.

'Hungry?' she asked as she flipped the lid open to reveal a pepperoni pizza.

He was starving and the pizza smelt fantastic but he didn't think he could eat a thing. He felt like the adolescent schoolboy of years ago. A bundle of nerves and insecurities. Why did she make him feel so nervous? Was it because she was linked to his past? A past he'd rather forget? Or was it because of the feelings of desire she evoked in him and that he was finding difficult to ignore? If he could work out why, and how, she made him feel this way he'd be able to fix it. He'd be back in control, but for now he felt like making a run for it.

But he had come here with the intention of apologising and she looked like she was about to present him with the perfect opportunity. They were away from their colleagues so he would apologise and then he'd leave. He shook his head and she closed the box, trapping the smell of pepperoni, but now he could smell her. She smelt fresh and clean and he wondered what perfume she wore. She looked pure, young, innocent and honest, but he didn't know if she was any of those things so before he could get distracted by how she looked or smelt he launched into his apology.

'I wanted to ask you to forgive my earlier behaviour,' he said. She was looking at him with a slightly mischievous glint in her amber eyes and he could see the corners of her mouth twitching. Was she trying not to laugh? Was she going to laugh at him? Could he not even apologise properly?

He repeated his sentence in his head. God, he'd sounded so pompous and pretentious. That wasn't what he'd intended. He tried again, accompanying his second effort with what he hoped was a self-deprecating smile. 'I'm sorry about earlier, I was being an arse.'

Grace's face broke into a wide smile and suddenly his day, which in all honesty had gone pretty well, improved even further. Her smile was amazing. Warm, wide and white, it showcased perfect teeth and lit up her already beautiful face. He couldn't help but smile in return.

'Apology accepted,' she said as she put the pizza box down on the bar and climbed onto the stool beside him.

Her knee brushed against his thigh as she swivelled on her seat and turned to face him. His heart missed another beat and desire swelled in his belly and settled in his groin. Hell, he was in trouble. He needed to get a grip.

She was just a girl. No one special. Just a girl with creamy skin, wide amber eyes and glorious hair, but there was no need to behave as if he'd been locked in a monastery for a decade even if he couldn't remember the last time someone had made him feel like this. He recognised the feeling. He felt happy. Open to possibilities. Filled with hope and promise.

He was being ridiculous, he chided himself. Women didn't make him feel like this. He was responsible for his own happiness. Being in Theatre, catching a wave or riding his horse made him happy. Not sitting next to a pretty slip of a woman. Operating, surfing and riding, those were his safe environments, the places where he felt he could relax and be himself without fear of ridicule or judgement.

In a hospital, wearing his white coat or his operating scrubs as a shield, was the only time he felt confident in company. When people deferred to his knowledge but didn't expect idle conversation. Other people, women especially, usually only made him feel uncomfortable and emphasised his awkwardness. He got a kick out of being at work or being outdoors on his own. But women he tried to steer clear of.

It wasn't always easy to do as there always seemed to be a new one on his periphery. He knew he was considered a catch. He knew that people assumed he was wealthy because he was a surgeon and he also knew, without being vain or narcissistic, that he had grown into his physical features and was now described as good looking. He knew it was often his unusual genetic mix that intrigued women, but that usually made him cautious.

Were they genuinely interested in him or was he an

experiment? He usually assumed the latter, which gave him licence to indulge in casual relationships, giving the women a taste of what they wanted in exchange for sating a thirst in himself before letting them go on their way. No harm, no foul, no commitment.

A night or two of physical company. Nothing serious. Never anything serious. He didn't need a serious relationship. He didn't need the angst or the complication. Didn't need the heartache. His affairs were brief. They were about fulfilling a need for sexual release without any emotional commitment.

He didn't romance the women. There were no candlelit dinners, no bouquets of flowers, no gifts of jewellery, nothing that could give the women the impression that their relationship was anything more than sexual. They might share a casual meal, a glass or two of wine but there was no sharing of dreams. He was a master at separating physical intimacy from emotional.

In short, he didn't date. His spare time was spent on his surfboard or out in the paddocks on his horse and there was no room for a woman in either of those scenarios. It had been a long time since someone had even caught his eye. And it wasn't just because of her fiery copper hair.

Not that it mattered. Grace wouldn't be interested in him. She knew where he'd come from. She'd known him before he was Dr Marcus Washington. She'd known him when he'd just been Marcus. The quiet, lonely, sad little boy.

'I am sorry,' he repeated, keen to make amends and still worried that she would think him an arrogant surgeon, a trait so often associated with his profession. He could be called a lot of things but he didn't want to think arrogant might be one of them. You didn't come from a childhood like his and grow up arrogant. 'I don't normally speak to people like that. I wanted to make a good impression here and if I didn't get that kidney I wouldn't get the chance. But that was my issue, not yours, and I apologise.'

'Who were you trying to impress?'

You. 'Everyone.'

But mostly you.

He kept that thought to himself, feeling he'd embarrassed himself enough for one day. 'Having an opportunity to be involved in this paired kidney exchange wasn't something I wanted to miss out on. I'm afraid I got a little bit caught up in it all. Congratulations, by the way, you did a fabulous job with co-ordinating everything.'

'You weren't too bad yourself,' she said, with another easy smile. She was poised and comfortable and he wished he had some of her confidence. 'We've come a long way from Toowoomba, haven't we?' she added, and his heart stopped in his chest.

He still hadn't admitted to her that he remembered those days but it looked like his tactic of ignoring the obvious wasn't going to work.

'Do you think I could ask you a favour?' he asked, still choosing not to comment on her statement per se, neither confirming nor denying her observation. 'I'd appreciate it if you don't mention that I'm from Toowoomba,' he went on when she nodded.

'Why not? What's wrong with Toowoomba?'

The defensive note in her voice grated on his conscience. 'Nothing,' he responded. Not from most people's perspective anyway, but he knew his view was definitely tainted. 'But my years in Toowoomba aren't relevant to my work.' They might be relevant to other aspects of his life but he wasn't prepared to discuss that with her. He didn't even want to think about it. 'That's another thing I should apologise for,' he said. 'I told you I didn't remember you but I do.'

'Why did you lie?' Her eyes were wide. Was he imagining the hurt he could see in their amber depths?

'You took me by surprise,' he said honestly. 'I wasn't expecting to see anyone I knew. Or who knew me. And I'd prefer not to be reminded of my life there. I thought that if I admitted that was where I came from you'd want to talk about it and I do my best to ignore those years.' He was happy to talk about work, anything in his professional life was up for discussion, but that didn't apply to his private life. That topic of conversation was off limits.

'I understand.'

'Do you?'

Grace nodded her head and his eye was drawn to the glossy shine of her copper hair as the light bounced off it. 'In a fashion, and don't worry, I'll respect your request.'

He wondered what she meant by 'in a fashion' but he was reluctant to prolong any discussion about the town where they had both grown up. He had no idea if he could trust her to keep her word but as there was precious little he could do about that he had to take her at face value. 'Thank you.'

'Don't mention it.'

Marcus stood up. It was time to leave. He'd managed to tie up all the loose ends. His apology had been given and accepted. His explanations made and accepted. He could move on. There was nothing more to gain by staying. Nothing good would come of spending more time with Grace. It would only serve to confuse his already addled brain even further.

'Are you going?'

He nodded. 'This isn't really my thing.'

'After-work drinks?' she asked. She swung her head and looked around the bar and Marcus was enveloped in her scent. It wasn't a perfume, he realised, it was her shampoo.

'Yes.' Or talking about his past to an attractive woman. To anyone really. It was time to go.

She was a danger to him and his equilibrium. She'd been in his peripheral vision all day. Her red hair a fiery distraction. He'd blocked her out during the surgery and kept his head bent over his patient but the minute he'd lifted his head as he'd wrapped up the surgery his eyes had been drawn to her again.

What was it about her?

There was a fascination there but he sensed it was dangerous.

He was attracted to her but he knew it was risky.

He was in danger of exposing himself, his past, all his secrets. People saw him now as someone successful, intelligent, powerful. They weren't to know that it had taken him years to achieve that. But Grace had known him before. She was the very last person he should be drawn to. She was high risk.

She was gorgeous and good at her job and people, both staff and patients, seemed to like her, but seeing her brought reminders of the shy, unloved, unwanted boy he had been when he'd lived in Toowoomba.

Only he couldn't help himself. His attraction to her presented him with a host of complications that he didn't want or need. His nerves were stretched tight whenever she was near. She was testing his resolve. She was dangerous.

And he needed to stay away from her.

CHAPTER FOUR

GRACE HAD BARELY set foot inside her flat on Thursday evening when she received a call summoning her back to work.

'I'll be there as quickly as possible,' she said as she pressed 'end' and immediately called for a cab. On her way to the hospital she phoned Marcus.

'Marcus Washington.'

He was the on-call specialist for the night and, despite the fact she knew he would answer, the sound of his voice rushed through her and set her nerves jingling.

'It's Grace.' Her voice sounded breathless to her ears but she didn't think he would notice.

'Is there a problem?'

He was obviously expecting a work call and assumed there would be a problem. She wondered what he'd say if she told him she was phoning to invite him to dinner.

But she knew what he'd say. Despite their truce they weren't in that place yet. Their relationship over the past ten days since the kidney exchange surgery and the night in Billi's Bar had improved but it had remained purely professional. He was less cool towards her, but still reserved.

'Is everything all right with Connie?'

Connie was recovering well after her surgery and Grace knew Marcus had plans to discharge her in the morning. She would have frequent check-ups, as would Rob, but both transplant patients, and the donor patients, had experienced smooth recovery phases to date.

'Connie is fine,' she told him, 'but one of our other patients on the transplant register has been brought into Emergency. Her husband is asking for me but I know they are about to call you next for a consult. Can you meet me in the ED? I'm in a cab, heading to the hospital now,' she explained, wanting him to know that she couldn't divulge any more details over the phone where the cab driver could hear.

Grace was first to the hospital and had got limited information about their patient by the time Marcus arrived. The smell of Chinese food accompanied him into the ED, disguising his familiar fresh ocean scent, and she saw a carrier bag holding takeaway containers hanging from his fingertips. The bags drew her eye to his thighs, encased in well-worn jeans and topped with a white polo shirt that drew her eye higher. The white fabric skimmed his chest and highlighted his skin tone. He was casually dressed but looked just as good as when he was wearing a suit or surgical scrubs.

'Did I catch you in the middle of dinner?' she asked, wondering if he'd asked for a doggy bag for his leftovers. It looked like a large amount of food.

'No. I was just collecting my order when you called and I didn't want it to go to waste. I figured the staff would be just as hungry,' he said as he deposited the bags on the triage desk and told the nurses, 'Go your hardest.'

Grace knew they wouldn't need to be asked twice and Marcus had just won himself a few more fans. He turned back to her after being thanked. 'Now, I'm all yours. What can you tell me?'

Grace looked away quickly, flustered at being told he was all hers, afraid her face would colour with its tell-tale flush. She turned and led Marcus into a side room but not before he'd lifted two of the containers and some chopsticks from a bag. He put the containers on the stainless-steel bench and removed the lids to reveal six steaming dumplings and a dipping sauce.

'Want one?' he asked as he picked up a dumpling with his chopsticks and dipped it in the sauce. Her eyes were drawn to his long, slender fingers, his prowess with the chopsticks rivalling his skill with the scalpel.

'What flavour are they?'

'Prawn.' He handed her a pair of chopsticks.

The dumplings did smell good and Marcus *looked* really good. It might not be a dinner invitation in the sense she hoped for but in the interests of maintaining their truce she thought it would only be polite to accept his offer.

'Thanks.' Her fingers brushed his as she took the offered chopsticks and her skin tingled and sighed as it came into contact with his.

Not that Marcus seemed to notice. 'Okay, tell me about this patient.'

Grace dipped her dumpling as she gathered her composure. 'Louise Edwards. Age thirty-eight. She has end-stage renal disease and type one diabetes. She has her dialysis here so I touch base with her once a week since she's on the transplant register, but she presented today with hypertension, vomiting and dehydration. It appears the dialysis isn't clearing enough of the toxins from her system. The registrar is with her now and she called for a renal consult.'

'She's only thirty-eight?'

Grace nodded. She bit into the dumpling but had difficulty swallowing it, not because it wasn't melt-in-the-mouth delicious but because her appetite waned as she thought about Louise.

'What else?' Marcus asked.

Grace looked up at him.

'Something is bothering you. What is it?' he said as he took another dumpling.

'I know I need to wait for you to review her but it's not looking great. She has a young family. Three kids. She needs a transplant soon, before it's too late.'

Marcus finished the dumpling and threw his chopsticks into the bin. 'Right, where is she?'

Grace took Marcus to the exam cubicle and introduced him to the ED registrar, Louise and her husband, Daniel. Grace left him to his assessment and waited outside. The cubicle was already crowded and there was no need for her to be there. She had no idea what Marcus would be able to do but she prayed for a miracle, just in case.

He was out within ten minutes.

'How is she?' Grace asked, but she really only needed to look at his expression to know the answer. *Not good.* Her heart fell.

'You were right. She needs a transplant urgently. I've got her on meds for hypertension and nausea. We're running a drip but she needs monitoring. I'll increase her priority on the transplant list and then all we can do is hope and pray and wait that we get a kidney in time,' he said as he headed for the triage desk. 'Give me a minute to increase her priority and to make sure we have a bed for her and then I'm going back to the Chinese restaurant to get some more food—everything here's pretty much gone. Would you like to join me?'

His invitation took her by surprise. 'I don't know if I could eat anything.' She felt sick with worry over Louise.

'There's nothing you can do for Louise tonight,' he said, reading her mind.

The reality was there was nothing she could do for Louise at all and that didn't sit well with her. Her natural instinct was to help people. To make things better. But Marcus was right. She was powerless. She really didn't feel hungry but she didn't want to go home to an empty flat either, as Lola was also working. Keeping Marcus company would at least keep her mind occupied. 'You're right,' she replied with a nod. 'I will come with you.'

Grace entered the restaurant, which was tucked down a side lane behind Billi's Bar. As Marcus held the door she had to remind herself this was not a date. The restaurant was small but brightly lit and noisy. It wasn't intimate or romantic.

'If you could grab a table,' he said, 'I'll get us some food. Any preferences?'

Grace shook her head. She slid into a seat at the only vacant table in the back corner of the restaurant and watched as Marcus's order was taken quickly. She wondered how often he'd eaten here in the short time he'd been in Sydney. The staff obviously knew who he was.

'Daniel said living kidney donation wasn't an option in this case,' Marcus said as he put a bottle of water and two glasses on the table and sat down. 'Do you know why not?'

The table was tiny and his knees knocked Grace's as

he sat in his chair. Her heart stuttered, missing a beat. She took a steadying breath. They were two colleagues sharing a quick meal, she told herself. Nothing more.

She nodded and gathered her thoughts. 'Daniel wasn't a match and Louise has no siblings. Her father died a few years back and her mother isn't well. Unless a friend is willing to give up a kidney, and is a match, we'll just have to wait and hope. Do you want me to speak to Daniel again tomorrow and ask about any friends or cousins he may not have already thought of?'

'I'm not sure that we even have the time to go down that path,' he said as their food was brought to their table. 'Let's see what tomorrow brings.'

The food smelled incredible. 'I think my appetite just returned,' Grace said as she helped herself to the chicken hotpot, pleased to have something to focus on other than Marcus's face, which was way too close across the small table, and his knees, which continued to bump against hers. 'I had no idea this place even existed.'

'How long have you lived here?' He glanced around at the crowded space and sounded surprised that she hadn't found this restaurant before.

'Five years.'

'You're staying here?' he asked. 'No plans to go back to Toowoomba?'

'Not at the moment. I like Sydney. And not everyone goes back, as you well know.' She smiled, hoping that would soften her words.

He gave a quirky half-smile that lifted one corner of his mouth but didn't reach his eyes. 'But I assume you still have family there.'

'Yes. Don't you?'

'No,' he replied as he spooned more food into his bowl.

Was he avoiding eye contact? She wasn't sure. He didn't seem edgy. He looked relaxed. In Theatre he looked in control, in Billi's Bar he had looked uncomfortable but here he looked calm. They were packed shoulder to shoulder with the other patrons but, despite the crowd, it was the most comfortable she had seen him. She wondered if it was because no one knew him. Most of the other diners were speaking Chinese. No one was interested in Marcus.

Except for her.

She wondered again where his father was but she was afraid she'd ruin the mood if she pried.

'What brought you to Sydney?' he asked, ending the silence that had stretched between them.

'My career.' She still loved saying that. She was proud of her achievements and her career was everything to her at the moment. Despite the fact that it wasn't the whole story, it was enough to divulge for now. 'My sister-in-law had a kidney transplant down here and I found the whole process fascinating so I applied for a job in the renal unit and I got it.'

'Your sister-in-law had a transplant?'

His dark eyes watched her intently and Grace lost her concentration for a moment before she eventually nodded. 'She had polycystic kidney disease. She's the reason I'm here.'

'How's she doing?'

'She's doing well. She's married to Lachlan and they're happy, planning on having a family.' She paused, curious to know if Marcus would ask after Lachlan or Hamish, but when he stayed silent she continued. 'Her transplant was five years ago, just before I moved here, and since then I've worked my way into the renal co-ordinator position. It's new, I've only had the role for six months but I love it. And I can't do this in Toowoomba so...' she shrugged '...here I am. I get home when I can.'

'Which is how often?'

'I don't know. A few times a year.' Other than her family there wasn't a lot for her in Toowoomba any more. Her new life was in Sydney. Her career. Her friends. 'I go back for birthdays, Christmas, weddings, that sort of thing.'

'Do you go to lots of weddings?'

'Not any more,' she admitted. 'My friends who stayed in Toowoomba tended to get married early and they're all having their second or third babies now. Or getting divorced.' It was hard to believe now that had almost been her life too. Sometimes she didn't recognise that part of herself any more. The girl who had thought she was happy to settle down at a young age was long gone. The world was so much bigger than Toowoomba.

'And you escaped?'

'Sort of.'

'Sort of?'

She'd been looking for an escape. She'd wanted to get away from a place where she had experienced so much distress. Merridy's transplant had opened her eyes to a whole world of other possibilities. After she had lost Johnny she'd been desperate to escape and start again, and she had jumped at the chance to move to the city. She had some understanding of Marcus's reluctance about small towns and their long memories. She still carried the memories of her loss but the passing of time had eased the pain and the guilt. Johnny was gone but it had been his choice to go. Her choice had been to move forward and, with time, the wounds had healed and now she was able to visit Toowoomba without being haunted by the tragedy she'd experienced. But tonight was not the night for that story.

'I was looking for a challenge,' she said. Something to take her mind off things. She'd needed a new start and fresh surroundings and she knew that moving to Sydney had been the right decision. She'd embraced city life, its challenges, the excitement, and she'd needed to be somewhere that helped push the memories aside, somewhere where people weren't constantly reminding her of what had happened. Naturally she still wanted to find true love but she knew now that Johnny hadn't been the right one for her. She was prepared to wait. She enjoyed her life in Sydney and her job. The rest would happen in time. She was sure of it.

'And have you found challenges?' Marcus asked, bringing her back to the present.

'I've found plenty,' she replied. One was sitting opposite her. She suspected her quest to find out more about him might be the biggest challenge she would face in the near future. And it was one she was prepared to take on.

But rather than pick up on her comment he was looking at his watch.

'Are you going back to the hospital?' she asked.

He nodded. 'I want to make a few more calls.'

Grace stood, taking her cue from him. 'Thank you for dinner, I'll remember this place.'

Marcus walked her to the taxi rank in front of Billi's Bar and waited until she was safely in a cab. Grace sat in the back with a smile on her face. He might take some work but she thought Marcus Washington could provide her with both a challenge and some excitement. She looked forward to it.

* * *

Grace liked it when she had time to watch the operations. It was a reward for all the time and effort she put into getting the process happening. She spent hours counselling, organising and liaising, and she enjoyed watching it all come together. She loved this part of her job—a successful, happy outcome for everyone. Except for the donor family, although she knew from experience that the knowledge that their loved one's death was helping others often helped in the healing process.

And she particularly enjoyed watching Marcus. He was a completely different person when he had a scalpel in his hand. He came alive and she found it fascinating to watch. He was an excellent surgeon and there was no hesitation when he was operating. He made good, quick, well-judged decisions, whereas in other circumstances he was far more deliberate; Marcus hesitated before answering and appeared cautious.

She'd noticed that he held himself back in social situations but in Theatre he joked and laughed with his team and Grace hadn't seen that side of him before. It was like a mask had been removed. He obviously felt comfortable in Theatre. He was confident, almost chatty, although he still didn't share anything personal. While everyone else was talking about their plans for the weekend Grace still didn't have any idea what Marcus was up to but he joined in with the general conversation.

The discussion turned to music people liked listening to—he liked country music—and their favourite food. Grace already knew he had a preference for Chinese and knowing she was privy to that information before anyone else gave her a little burst of satisfaction. When the topic changed to where they were all going on their next holidays she learned his favourite place was anywhere he could ride a horse or a wave but, in particular, Margaret River, three hours south of Perth in Western Australia.

By the end of the surgery she'd learnt far more about him than she'd known at the start but it really only served to reinforce that they had nothing in common. She liked pop rock, the Blue Mountains and Italian food was her go-to. She couldn't surf, although she did like the beach but needed to be careful in the sun. They had nothing in common other than spending their early years in Toowoomba and they were now both working in renal medicine. But both things were circumstantial. Their common ground certainly didn't bind them together.

It was late when Grace got out of Theatre but she went back to her office hoping that by some miracle a kidney had been found for Louise.

But today was apparently not the day for miracles.

She went to visit Louise anyway, to see how she was, and found her room bursting at the seams with Daniel and their children. The children often accompanied Louise to the hospital for her dialysis during school holidays and Grace had met them several times. The eldest girl was quite solemn and Grace suspected she'd had to shoulder some of the responsibilities at home and, even now, she had her little brother on her lap as they read his school reader. Grace wondered how she'd managed to get him to sit still. He was only six years old and usually full of energy.

The second daughter was usually far more verbose but today even she seemed quiet. It was highly likely that they were picking up on the tension and stress and worry that surrounded Louise but Grace wasn't able to ease their concerns.

As she left Louise and her family she saw Marcus at the nurses' station. He was still in his surgical scrubs and had his back to her but she knew the set of his shoulders, the shape of his head, the length of his legs. She didn't realise she'd spent so much time studying him that his physique was imprinted in her brain but, then again, it was a very impressive physique.

She went to him. 'Are you going to see Louise?'

He nodded. 'I take it we don't have a kidney yet?'

'No.'

He picked up Louise's file but before he could walk away Grace spoke again. 'You didn't mention in Theatre whether you have plans for the weekend.' She went on hurriedly, not wanting to give him an opportunity to interrupt before she'd finished. She half expected she knew what he would say but she wanted to extend the invitation anyway. 'Lachlan and his wife are in town and I'm having lunch with them tomorrow. If you're not busy you're welcome to join us.'

'Why?' Marcus still wasn't exactly cheerful and approachable but she felt he was less wary of her. His eyes held a little more warmth but his tone remained guarded, almost suspicious.

She shrugged. 'I thought you might like it and I owe you a meal.'

'No, you don't. Thank you, but I'm busy tomorrow.'

She wondered what he was busy doing. He hadn't mentioned anything in Theatre when everyone else had discussed their plans for the weekend. For a moment she wondered if he wasn't busy at all but was just brushing her off. Had she misread the situation? Mistaken his openness in Theatre for a willingness to socialise? His eyes had gone blank again.

She cut her losses. She was grateful that their working relationship had improved but she knew when her company wasn't welcome. 'No problem. Another time, perhaps.'

Grace liked people to be happy and she knew she had a tendency to try to make that happen, even when she suspected it was an uphill battle. She'd failed before but she didn't let that stop her. She would continue to try to bring some positivity and happiness into people's lives and that would include Marcus. She felt that he, in particular, could use some happiness but he didn't seem to think it would come from her and she'd have to deal with that.

Marcus sat out the back on his surfboard, waiting for his turn to catch a wave. He'd got home late last night and he'd slept badly but he'd needed to burn off energy this morning and surfing was his only outlet while he was in Sydney. Surfing was relaxing and he needed that today. Surfing gave him the opportunity to be part of something without having to be involved. He could nod a greeting or comment on someone's ride but there was no expectation that he would have a conversation or have to reveal anything about himself. It was a solitary pursuit, which suited him just fine. The only problem was that it left him with too much time to think.

He'd spent last night the same way he'd already spent several other nights, tossing and turning. There were too many thoughts racing through his head and he blamed his return to the east coast. He was battling thoughts about his past. About his mother and father. About Grace. He wasn't sure what to do about most of it. Doing nothing about Grace would be the sensible option but it wasn't the one he was tempted to take. Thursday night was a prime example of not taking the sensible option. He hadn't needed to invite her to dinner and it was completely out of character for him to invite a woman he didn't plan on sleeping with out at all, but he'd done it anyway and he'd enjoyed it. More than he wanted to admit. And he didn't want to think about what that meant.

As he waited for a wave he caught a glimpse of a red-headed girl walking along the beach. From this distance it was impossible to see who it was but before he could really process his actions, he had dropped in on another bloke's wave. He knew he'd annoyed the other surfer but he didn't care. He had an intense, overwhelming desire to know if the girl on the beach was Grace.

He grabbed his board and carried it out of the water, heading in the girl's direction, hoping he looked like he was walking with a purpose and not behaving like a stalker

Not that it mattered.

She wasn't Grace.

Disappointment flooded through him but now he couldn't get the thought of her out of his head. Not that he'd been having much luck with that before either.

He remembered the look in her amber eyes when he'd asked her to eat with him. She'd been hesitant, unsure. Of him or his motives? He wasn't certain but he could hardly blame her. He wasn't even sure of his motives. He seemed to lose all sense of perspective when he was around her. He was still awkward but something about her made him feel safe.

He should feel anything *but* safe around her. She knew where he came from, she knew far too much about him, yet he trusted her when she said she would keep her own counsel, and the time they'd spent eating and talking had been the most enjoyable social interaction he'd had since moving to Sydney.

He loved being in Theatre but that was work and he usually avoided all social activities, or as many as he could, but something about Grace drew him to her. She was easy company. Relaxed and happy, not to mention vivacious and chatty. What was the saying? *Opposites attract.* Whoever had coined that phrase must have had them in mind. There was nothing to say that she was attracted to him but that didn't stop him from wanting to find out. Only the idea that it could potentially be a complete disaster was stopping him. She was too close. Much too close. Yet he knew he was going to have trouble staying away.

And he still hadn't worked out why she had invited him to lunch. He had no desire to see Lachlan. He didn't want anything to do with his past and he couldn't see the point of having a meal with someone he hadn't seen for twenty years and probably would never see again. But the idea of lunch with Grace was surprisingly attractive and he knew that if the offer had been to have lunch just with her he might have been tempted to take her up on it. So much for keeping his distance. So instead he'd made an excuse that he was busy. He did have somewhere else to be but it wasn't nearly as enticing as spending time with Grace.

He knew it was one way to get his mind off her. It wasn't a pleasant way, but it was guaranteed to work.

He stripped off his wetsuit, strapped his surfboard to the roof of his hired four-wheel drive and jumped into the driver's seat.

* * *

'How is he today?' Marcus asked the RN on duty in the nursing home as he walked down the corridor.

Karlie raised her eyebrows. 'Not his best day. He had one of the carers in tears this morning. He was having trouble with his buttons but he won't wear a T-shirt and he refused to let the carer help him get dressed. He's been a bit agitated.'

Marcus steeled himself. He had visited every day for the past fortnight. Ever since he'd arrived in Sydney. He could handle this visit. He *would* handle it.

He took a deep breath as he turned the door handle and stepped into the room.

'What do you want?'

His father was sitting in a chair by a window. The garden outside was well cared for with neat lawns, clipped hedges and the occasional garden seat and bird bath strategically placed. Not that his father would notice or care.

Marcus remembered his father as a big man. He'd certainly been both physically and emotionally intimidating. Marcus's facial features resembled his mother's side of the family but he had inherited his dad's muscular physique. But his father had shrunk. Wasted away from a lack of nutrition and exercise. He wasn't old, only in his mid-sixties, but he looked at least a decade older. His skin was grey, his hair was grey and his clothes were grey. It was sad and depressing but Marcus didn't want to feel any empathy. He didn't think his father had done anything to deserve it but it was difficult to reconcile the old man in the chair with his memory of his father. A father he had avoided for twenty years.

He hadn't expected to feel so guilty. He knew he had nothing to feel guilty about, he and his father didn't have anything even resembling a functional relationship, yet he still felt guilty. If he hadn't promised his aunt he'd visit he knew he would find plenty of reasons to stay away. Starting with the fact that his own father didn't recognise or even remember him. What was the point?

He knew the point was that he still had the hope of a twelve-year-old boy that his father would pay him some attention. Would choose to love him. But he'd soon realised his hopes were going to be cut down. He doubted his father had ever loved him.

'I thought you might like a visitor.'

'Why? Who are you?' His father was looking at him suspiciously. They'd had the identical conversation every day for two weeks and Marcus prepared himself for more of the same. He was an adult now, he could handle a few weeks of this while he was in Sydney. Twelve weeks of repeated conversations with no connection in exchange for the one thousand weeks that he'd stayed away.

It should make it easier that his father didn't recognise him. It should make it easier to keep his visit brief and then to walk away but it didn't stop the guilt.

'I'm your son.'

'I don't have a son. You look like a Yank. Are you a Yank?'

His father had fought in the final years of the Vietnam War and his mind had regressed back to that period of his life. He didn't seem to recall having a wife, a son, a life after his early twenties.

Marcus shook his head and repeated. 'I'm Marcus. I'm your son.'

Marcus knew he looked nothing like his father would expect his own son to look like. Not if he didn't remember his wife, Marcus's mother, and the fact that she was from

Barbados. His father was so anti-American, anti-Asian, anti most things that Marcus was finding it increasingly hard to believe that he ever would have fallen in love with someone who wasn't a white Australian.

Marcus wiped his hand across his eyes. He didn't remember much about his mother but he'd remembered her smile. He was so sure she'd loved him yet she'd left when he was only six. And hadn't taken him with her. She'd left him behind with a father who may have loved him but who had loved his vices even more. Marcus's memories of his mother were fleeting and he often wasn't sure which ones were real and which he'd created himself. By contrast he had plenty of memories of his father but none of them were pleasant. They were all tainted by the detritus of his childhood.

What a total disaster his life had been.

Which begged the question: what the hell was he doing here?

He knew why. He wanted some answers. That was why he was here.

He knew he needed some closure. His career was going from strength to strength but personally he was struggling. He wasn't happy and he knew he needed some information about the past in order to be able to make sense of who he was and where he had come from. He was terrified that if he didn't get some closure he could find himself following his father into addiction just to forget about it all. Just to block out the stories that had multiplied in his head. He had no idea how many of his memories were based on fact or how many had simply grown out of his imagination over the years. Why had his mother left? Why hadn't she taken him with her and why had his father chosen to drink himself into oblivion?

'I'm not a Yank,' he replied as he sat in the only other chair in the room and unzipped his backpack. He pulled out a bottle of beer and noticed how that immediately caught his father's attention. He went quiet and still as he waited to see what Marcus would do next.

Bringing in alcohol wasn't exactly against the rules but it wasn't actively encouraged and yet Marcus had learnt that one small bottle seemed to calm his father down. He guessed that was how the slippery slide into alcoholism started. Just one to take your troubles away, and that became two and then three. Until you ended up here. In a nursing home, battling alcoholic dementia and advanced liver disease.

It was a horrible combination. But from the perspective that distance and a medical degree gave him he knew his father didn't have long left and Marcus couldn't really see the point of depriving him of the one thing he still got enjoyment from.

He cracked open the bottle and his father sat up a little straighter in the chair at the sound of the unmistakable pop. He handed the bottle to his father, who took a long drink.

He pulled out another bottle for himself. A non-alcoholic version. Somehow it didn't seem so bad if it looked like his father was sharing a drink with his son rather than drinking alone while a stranger sat by his side.

It didn't look like he would get any useful answers today. He'd share a beer and then be on his way, he decided as one of the catering staff brought in a tray holding his father's lunch. Marcus wondered where Grace was having lunch with her brother. He imagined it was somewhere a lot more pleasant than here. He imagined them sitting in the sunshine by the beach while he sat in a room watching a stranger eat a sandwich and rice pudding.

But regardless of his circumstances, or because of them, he knew he'd made the right decision in turning down her invitation. What could he possibly have in common with someone he hadn't seen since he was twelve and, to be honest, someone he hadn't had much in common with even then?

Grace's father was a doctor, her mother was a nurse. His father was an alcoholic and his mother had abandoned him. The childhood he imagined Grace and her brothers had had couldn't have been more different from his own reality. Visiting his father was enough of a trip down memory lane without adding lunch with virtual strangers into his day. He had no desire to reminisce about old times. He'd spent far too long trying to forget them.

But that didn't stop him from wishing he was anywhere but here.

CHAPTER FIVE

MARCUS WAS BACK at the beach early the next morning. He'd learnt years ago that surfing was an excellent stress reliever and while he was enjoying his work in Sydney he was finding many other aspects of this visit less than relaxing.

His father's condition was stressing him out more than anything. If he was going to manage to continue with daily visits, albeit short ones, he had to make time to hit the surf as well. While he was at work he was able to block out all extraneous thoughts and focus on his job but away from the hospital he was finding it difficult to escape the memories and guilt without the release of surfing.

But when he arrived at Manly the surf was flat. He hadn't thought to check the surf report. After another almost sleepless night he'd tossed his things in his car and headed for the beach, hoping for the best.

The only upside of the lack of surf was that the beach was almost deserted. He untied his board and dropped it into one of the local cafés where he'd discovered they were happy to mind surfers' personal possessions provided the surfers made a purchase. He might not be able to surf but a swim might clear his head and ease the tension.

He swam for thirty minutes, parallel to the coast, up and back, until his muscles were fatigued but his mind was clear. As he started to tire he bodysurfed on a small wave into the beach. He rose out of the water and scanned the shore as he shook his hands dry.

A redheaded woman was walking towards him. She wore a visor that shaded her face and she was too far away to see her clearly but the visor left her hair exposed and it was definitely red. Once again, like yesterday, he imagined the woman was Grace. Was it the same woman he'd seen yesterday?

She was wearing a pair of short denim shorts with a long-sleeved top. Her legs were amazing. Toned and slim. It wasn't the same woman. He would definitely have remembered her legs.

He stepped out of the water onto the hard sand and continued to watch. A red kelpie streaked across the beach towards her, a ball in its mouth. It was definitely a different woman. There had been no dog yesterday. He intended to wait until she drew nearer but his feet were already moving towards her.

She was still fifty metres from him but the closer she got the more vibrant her hair looked. The closer she got the more her hair began to resemble the fiery copper colour of Grace's.

She threw the ball for the dog and it bounced high, headed for Marcus. The dog raced along the beach in his direction.

He stretched out his hand and caught the ball just before the dog reached him. The dog ran in circles around his ankles, waiting for him to throw it again. He reached down and handed the ball to the dog but the animal dropped it at his feet, not wanting to give up his game. He threw the ball back towards the woman and kept walking, meeting her halfway. The dog beat him to her. It *was* her. The dog stood looking up at Grace eagerly, waiting for attention, and he felt a surprising affinity with the dog.

He dragged his eyes up from Grace's toes, away from her amazing legs and up to her face. She was tiny, barefoot and barely dressed. Her copper hair glowed in the sun and her eyes glittered. She was looking up at him and smiling. She looked gorgeous and happy to see him. He couldn't remember the last time someone had really looked that pleased to see him.

'Hello.'

'You have a dog,' he said. He loved dogs. He'd never had a pet. Not in Toowoomba and not in boarding school. He'd had working dogs, farm dogs, but not a pet.

'Reg isn't mine. He belongs to Lachlan and his wife. I'm just taking him for a walk to let them have a sleep in.'

'Would you like some company?'

'I'm just on my way home, actually.'

Disappointment surged through him. He'd been so sure she'd say yes.

'Can I buy you a coffee first?' he asked, hoping he'd be able to encourage her to stay.

He threw the ball for Reg, needing to avoid eye contact. He didn't want to appear desperate but he wasn't ready for more of his own company yet. He'd spent a lot of time on his own over the past two weeks and while he was normally content in his solitary ways he suddenly found the idea of sharing a coffee and some more conversation with Grace quite appealing. He tried, and failed, to tell himself it was because his conversations outside work had been mostly one-sided discussions between him and his father, which had been far from satisfactory, but he knew the appeal lay in Grace's company. Nothing else. He was drawn to her. She calmed his mind but stirred his body. Made him feel excited but relaxed at the same time. She was the human equivalent to surfing—the antidote to his stress. He'd never met anyone who had that effect on him before and it was captivating. Reg returned the ball and he threw it for him again as he waited for her answer.

Grace hesitated, gathering her thoughts. His sudden appearance had taken her by surprise and she had a dozen questions swirling through her mind. What was he doing here? Why was he inviting her for coffee? And how good did he look?

She was trying not to stare but it was difficult when his bare chest was at her eye level. His body was brown, smooth and muscular. Droplets of water glistened on his skin, making him shine in the early morning light. His arms were strong and he had swimmer's shoulders, broad and straight. His stomach was flat, save for the ridges of his abdominal muscles, and she wasn't quite sure where to look.

He picked up the ball, which Reg had dropped at their feet, and threw it. The muscles in his shoulder rippled and Grace forgot to answer. She was mesmerised.

'My shout,' he added, when she didn't reply.

'Your shout?' Her gaze travelled below his hips. He was wearing a pair of short, red swimming trunks and she was pretty sure he didn't have anywhere to hide his wallet. He didn't have room to hide much in those shorts, she thought, feeling herself start to blush.

'I've got some cash with my car keys,' he said as he started walking up the beach. Had he seen her checking him out and followed her train of thought? She assumed he had—she'd been less than surreptitious—but at least he'd only followed one train of thought.

'And where are they?'

'Are you always this suspicious?' he replied. 'I promise I have money and I also have honourable intentions.'

That was a pity, she thought as she followed him. She hadn't said yes yet but she was intrigued enough by the invitation that she knew she'd accept.

'The café up there...' he pointed towards a small café that faced the beach '...has lockers for hire and they're also minding my surfboard for me with the expectation that I'll at least buy a coffee before I leave. They'll be happy to sell me two.'

He keyed in the code for the locker as they reached the café and pulled out a shirt. He threw it on, hiding his chest and disappointing her again. He placed their order and led her to a seat at one of the outdoor tables with a view of the beach.

Grace was aware of the sideways glances of several other café patrons as she followed behind him. All women. All taking a second look at Marcus. He looked fit, toned, healthy and very, very masculine.

'How did your lunch go yesterday?' he asked as they sat.

Grace wondered if he was being polite or if he was really interested. 'You really want to know?'

'I would. I'd like to hear about someone else's day.'

He sounded as though he had the weight of the world on his shoulders. 'You sound like you've had a bad day already.'

'Today's been good so far. Yesterday afternoon was nothing fabulous.'

'What happened?'

'I'd rather talk about your afternoon.'

'Are we going to have a proper conversation,' she asked, 'or are you just going to sit and listen to me talk?' She could see the sorrow in his dark eyes and her heart ached as she imagined all the things that could have put that unhappiness there. Grace hated seeing other people hurting and her instinct was always to try and make things better. That's what she did. But with Marcus she had no idea where to start.

'I thought a woman would love that opportunity.'

He smiled at her as he spoke. It was the first time he'd smiled at her and it was as incredible as she'd imagined. She quite literally felt her heart skip a beat. She'd always thought that was a silly expression. Until now.

'Possibly,' she replied. She wanted to make him feel better and he'd asked her to talk. Maybe he just needed a distraction. Something to take his mind off whatever it was that was bothering him. She could manage that.

'Lunch was interesting,' she said, as the waitress brought their coffees and the toasted banana bread Marcus had ordered. 'My sister-in-law, Lachlan's wife, had a really intriguing idea. You might like it but you'll need to hear the background first. Let me know if I'm boring you. I think I told you that Merridy had a kidney transplant four years ago. She had PCKD and Lachlan donated one of his kidneys. That's what got me interested in the paired exchange programme and the renal unit, but I'm getting off track.'

She paused and sipped her coffee before continuing. 'Merridy has become a big advocate for organ donation. She is often interviewed by the local media and regularly visits schools and gives talks but she has a bigger plan.

She and Lachlan are on the land, they work with cattle and run a feed lot in Toowoomba, and Merridy's latest idea to raise awareness about organ donation and also to raise funds is to organise a cattle drive. Her idea is to get people to sponsor cattle in the muster or pay to ride along and the funds raised will go towards putting dialysis machines into country hospitals and training nurses.'

'Does she think country people will pay to do something they probably already do for free?' Marcus asked.

'It's not country people she's aiming for. She wants to run it for city people.'

'She thinks enough people would go out to the country to take part?'

'She doesn't want to do it in the country. She wants to bring it to the city.'

'To the city?'

Grace nodded and broke off a piece of banana bread and popped it in her mouth. 'You know how popular television shows set in rural Australia are. Merridy thinks there are plenty of people who would love the chance to be involved in something like this. She thinks it has an element of romance to it and that city folk would get behind it. There are heaps of young girls in pony clubs who would love it and people could walk with the cattle if they can't ride. She thinks it's the sort of event that would get massive exposure in the media and I think she might be right.'

'Where does she want to hold it?'

'This is the really good part,' she said before pausing for effect. 'She wants to drive the cattle over the Harbour Bridge.'

'The Sydney Harbour Bridge? Seriously?' Marcus's eyes were wide now but Grace was pleased to see that the traces of sadness had been replaced by amazement. If the idea was enough to distract him she could only imagine how incredible it would be if they could bring Merridy's idea to fruition. She could only imagine how the muster could inspire and engage other people.

She nodded. 'Yep. Wouldn't that be fantastic?'

'Is it possible?'

'We have no idea. I said I'd look into it. What do you think?'

'I honestly don't know. It's certainly an interesting idea.'

'Now I just have to convince the hospital, the transplant foundation and the council to get on board.'

'You're going to do all that?'

'Yes. Merridy will engage with sponsors. She'll do all the social media and sort out the registration process but we have to get approval first and I'm hoping I've got enough contacts in Sydney to organise that side of things. Are you going to eat that?' Grace asked, eyeing the last piece of banana bread. Marcus shook his head and pushed the plate closer to her. 'You said you ride—would you support something like this?' she asked.

He didn't answer immediately and Grace steeled herself for a refusal before remembering that he was a man who seemed to consider his answers and organise his thoughts before verbalising them. He was measured and calm, quite the opposite of her. Her tendency was to speak first and think later.

'Yes,' he finally declared.

'Where did you learn to ride?'

'In Western Australia.'

'Is that where you went when you disappeared?'

His brow furrowed. 'I didn't disappear.'

Another prime example of her shooting her mouth off and then thinking afterwards, she realised. She shrugged. 'One minute you were living around the corner and the next you weren't. People wondered what had happened to you.'

Marcus hadn't thought anyone would have given him, or his circumstances, a minute's consideration after he'd left Toowoomba.

'Why would anyone wonder where I'd gone?'

Grace looked uncomfortable. She picked up her coffee and drank from the cup, even though he was sure she'd already finished it, avoiding direct eye contact.

'I don't know. You became a bit of a local legend.'

'What does that mean?'

'People wondered what had happened to you and when no one knew, I guess they came to their own conclusions.'

'What sort of conclusions?'

'They were just stories…' she said quickly.

'What sort of stories?'

'We were only kids. You know what they're like.'

Marcus knew all too well what kids were like. It was one reason why he'd been happy to leave Toowoomba and never return. 'What stories?' he repeated.

She hesitated before answering. Considering her reply, he assumed, but her reply when it came took him by surprise. 'The one that freaked me out the most was when they said you'd been murdered.'

'Murdered! By whom?'

'I don't know,' Grace said, but he knew she was being evasive. He wasn't going to force her to tell him, though.

'Nothing happened to me. I just went to boarding school.'

'In Western Australia?'

He nodded.

'Was your mother there?' she asked.

'No. Why would you think that?'

'You never came back. Who did you stay with? You can't have been at school all year.'

'I spent holidays with my aunt and uncle and cousins on their farm down near Margaret River.' He'd never wanted to return to Toowoomba, not then and not now. He'd left that behind a long time ago.

'What happened to your mother?'

'I have no idea. My aunt said she just packed up and left one day.'

'You've never heard from her since then?' Grace asked softly.

'No.'

'Have you tried to find her?'

He had but he'd been unable to find any trace of her. Eventually he'd figured she'd changed her name and simply didn't want to be found.

Grace was sitting, watching and waiting for an answer, her creamy skin, amber eyes, innocent expression and amazing hair casting a spell over him, tempting him to let his guard down. But he couldn't do that. Didn't do that. Ever. Things went awry whenever he was tempted to.

'I looked for her. Unsuccessfully,' he said, deciding that was enough information to reveal, reminding himself that Grace was the last person he should reveal anything to. She already knew too much about him.

But he couldn't deny she was easy company. He wouldn't go as far as to say he enjoyed it, he wasn't one to enjoy the company of others, he was a solitary man, but Grace was so open and engaging. It was an unfamiliar experience to share a meal with no expectations.

Normally his conversations with women were work-related or very limited. In a social setting it was only a means to an end and conversation was almost always instigated by the woman. Conversation usually consisted of an introduction, maybe they'd share a drink and talk about what they did for work and then they'd share a bed. A single night usually. There was no talk of anything private or personal. He made sure of that. And his relationships didn't last long enough to include walking a dog and sharing breakfast. He made sure of that too.

'I'm sorry,' Grace said as she reached out and put her hand over his. Her hand was cool and soft and small and her pale skin was a sharp contrast to the darker hue of his. He couldn't remember the last time someone had held his hand. Had they ever? He also couldn't remember the last time he'd been physically intimate with anyone. He didn't do intimate. Sex didn't count. Sex for him was a physical exchange, something primal and necessary, but it wasn't intimate.

He thought about withdrawing his hand but it felt good under hers. He thought about turning his hand over and threading his fingers through hers but wondered what she'd make of that.

He looked at Grace, wondering if he could read her thoughts in her amber eyes, wondering if she would give him any clues as to what he should do, but as their eyes met the waitress arrived to clear the table and his opportunity was gone. As if realising what she'd done, Grace looked at her hand, lifted it and removed it from his. Then she removed herself. She stood up and picked up Reg's lead. 'Thank you for the coffee. I'd better get Reg home before he starts a ruckus. He's not good at doing nothing.'

And before he could say anything she was gone. Leaving him alone again.

Alone had never felt quite so lonely before.

'We have a kidney!'

Grace felt like she'd uttered those words days ago. It had, in fact, been only hours since she'd received the phone call advising that a deceased donor had tested to be a match for Louise and Grace had set the wheels in motion. Marcus was operating now and Grace was sitting with Daniel, keeping him company. She longed to be in Theatre, watching Marcus work a miracle, but she knew Daniel needed her support. Waiting for news was almost as difficult as waiting for a kidney.

'Does it normally take this long?'

Daniel was edgy. Grace could understand that and he'd been asking a variation of the same question for the past hour, but now she was starting to wonder too. She should have had some news by now. The surgery had started well over two hours ago.

'Would you like me to go and get an update?' she asked.

'Can you?'

'Yes. Give me a minute.'

Grace headed to the theatres but instead of wasting precious time scrubbing in she went upstairs to the viewing gallery. It was late in the evening and the gallery was empty save for two interns. They were standing at the window and appeared tense.

She shivered as a chill of foreboding ran down her spine. 'What's going on?' she asked.

'Cardiac arrest.'

'What?'

The viewing gallery overlooked two theatres, maybe the interns were watching a different surgery, she thought as she hurried to the window. Her stomach fell as she saw that the second theatre was in darkness. They were talking about Louise.

Grace squeezed her eyes shut before opening them slowly, as if she might find that she was in the middle of a dream and that the nightmare would disappear if she blinked. But nothing had changed.

'What happened?'

'I'm not sure, but they've been working on her for over half an hour since the arrest.'

'Oh, no.' That was not good news.

She stood with her forehead resting on the glass. She held her breath as she watched but within minutes she saw Marcus strip off his gloves and glance at the clock and she knew he was calling time on Louise's life.

Poor Daniel.

Poor Marcus.

Those poor children.

The interns left the room as Grace stood still with tears rolling silently down her cheeks.

She pressed her hand to the window. Wanting Marcus to know she was there. Wondering if she should go to him.

This wasn't supposed to happen. No surgery was without its risks but no one would have anticipated this. Louise was supposed to get a new kidney and live a long and healthy life.

Grace sank onto a chair as she watched Marcus leave the theatre. She knew he would be going to speak to Daniel. She probably should go too but she couldn't make her legs work.

But she knew her dilemma was nothing compared to Marcus's. He had the unenviable task of telling Daniel that his wife was dead.

Her heart ached for all of them, Daniel, the children, Louise's widowed and now childless mother and Marcus.

She sat in the viewing gallery until her tears had stopped and she thought she might be able to stand. She went down the stairs on shaky legs, clinging to the handrail.

Walking out of the theatres, she saw Daniel in the Reflections Suite, talking to the chaplain. She didn't interrupt. She would get in touch with him later. He would be in shock and there was nothing she could say, or do, that would bring Louise back.

She went in search of Marcus instead, unable to leave without seeing him. She had to know he was okay.

Grace was told he was in the theatre change rooms. She waited outside.

And waited.

No one came out or went in.

If he was still in there he would be alone. She knew this would have been a tough night for him. The toughest. He shouldn't be alone.

She pushed open the door and went in.

Marcus had no idea how long he'd been sitting in the change rooms. He was still in his scrubs, everyone else having long since left the hospital. He was cold and his spine was stiff. He needed a shower but his muscles felt as though they'd seized up and he knew it was going to be an effort to stand and make it to the showers. He didn't know if he could be bothered. He'd just sit for a little while longer.

Talking to Louise's husband had been a horrendous experience. How did you tell someone that their wife wasn't coming home? That your children wouldn't feel their mother's arms around them again, that she wouldn't be there to wipe their tears or kiss them goodnight or hold their babies one day?

Marcus knew all too well what it was like to grow up without a mother. He'd been exactly the same age as Louise's son was now when his mother had left him. The only difference was that Louise hadn't chosen to leave her little boy. He hoped the father held it together better than his had done.

He couldn't remember what he'd said but he'd never forget the blank look in Daniel's eyes as he'd processed the news and the sound of his anguish as the truth had hit home.

Marcus had no idea what sort of man Daniel was. How he would cope with his loss.

He sighed and dropped his head into his hands. He heard the door of the change rooms open but he didn't lift his head. He didn't want to see anyone, didn't want to make eye contact, didn't want to have a conversation.

'Are you okay?'

He knew the question was directed at him. The change rooms were empty save for him but even if there had been other people in there he knew the person was addressing him because the person was Grace.

But even Grace, with all her optimism and joie de vivre, wasn't going to be able to lift his spirits today.

He lifted his head from his hands. She was standing in front of him, a worried crease between her brows, her amber eyes unusually sombre.

'Not really,' he admitted.

How could he explain what he was feeling? The guilt, the grief. He knew it wasn't all about Louise. He had enough insight into his own mind to know he was dealing with a lot more than what had happened today but how could he tell Grace that? How narcissistic would that make him seem? How out of touch with reality? His thoughts were best kept to himself.

She sat down next to him. Right next to him. He could smell her shampoo. Light and floral. She smelt fresh.

Her leg pressed against his and he felt her warmth. She placed her hand on his thigh and he could feel the weight of her palm.

'Is there anything I can do?'

He looked at her pale hand where it rested on his leg. He almost believed he could feel the blood pumping through her body, keeping her alive. Warming him. He needed some of her warmth. He was still so cold. He turned his head to look at her. She was only inches away.

Her fiery copper tresses added to her vibrancy. Her hair was mesmerising. Looking at her was like looking into the flames of a fire. He wanted to reach out and wind his fingers through her hair. He wanted to reach out and touch her. He wanted to bask in her warmth. He wanted her to bring him back to life but he knew he'd only get burnt in the attempt.

He should tell her to leave him alone. Tell her to leave him to wallow in his guilt and misery and despair.

His normal routine in times of crisis would involve going surfing or taking his horse out for a ride but it was ten o'clock at night and his horse was thousands of miles away in Western Australia.

And Grace was right here.

He stared at her face. Her amber eyes had softened,

her pupils wide and dark. She had a few bronze freckles scattered across the bridge of her nose and her lips were plump and pink. He could kiss her now and forget about everything for a few moments.

Was that the answer?

He knew it would take his mind off things. He was sure that kissing her would be a hell of a distraction but would it be the right one?

He didn't know and he didn't care. Now that the idea had crossed his mind it was all he could think about and he didn't think he could resist her even though he knew he couldn't trust women. But one night of comfort couldn't hurt. What harm could there be in that?

He leant towards her. Her eyes widened and he could feel her breath on his cheek. Her lips were slightly parted and he could see the tip of her tongue, small and red behind her teeth. He heard her tiny intake of breath as he reached for her. He cupped his hand at the back of her neck, sliding his fingers through her glorious hair, and pulled her to him.

CHAPTER SIX

HE BENT HIS head and covered her lips with his. Her lips were soft and moist and she sighed as his mouth claimed hers. He'd thought she might push him away but instead he felt her lean into him. He could feel the curve of her breast, plump and ripe against his chest, and he felt the answering swell of excitement in his groin as his blood finally began flowing through his body again as Grace breathed life back into him.

He closed his eyes and increased his pressure. He felt her lips part further under his. Her mouth opened to his and his tongue explored her. She tasted of peppermint.

He wanted her closer. Needed her closer. He wanted to possess her. For her to possess him.

He lifted her easily off the bench and sat her astride his hips, her knees on either side of his thighs. He pulled her shirt from the waistband of her uniform trousers and slid his hand under the hem, resting against the warm, soft skin of her waist. He moved his hand around her back and undid her bra with a practised snap of his fingers. Her breasts sprang free and he held one in the palm of his hand as he ran his thumb over her nipple. A throaty moan escaped from her lips as she tipped her head back and broke their kiss.

She held onto his shoulders and arched her back as she thrust her hips towards him, closing the minuscule gap that had existed between their groins. His erection was thick and long between her thighs.

The fabric of his scrubs was thin but there was still too much between them. He wanted to feel her skin against his. He wanted her naked legs wrapped around him. He wanted to bury himself inside her. To lose himself in her warmth.

His hand stilled, his thumb resting over her peaked nipple. He could make love to her now but, while it might be the time, he didn't think it was the place. The hospital was quiet but the change rooms could be used by other staff at any moment. He needed to take this somewhere else but he knew he wouldn't be able to make it much further without tearing her clothes off or losing control. He needed to prove to himself he could stop. That he still had control. Even if it was only fleeting.

'I need a shower. Are you going to join me?'

Grace didn't stop to think. She was incapable of thinking. She was far too busy feeling. Her body was a quivering mass of nerve endings, her senses heightened, touch, taste and smell being flooded with information courtesy of Marcus's lips and fingers.

She nodded and this time she kissed him as she offered herself to him.

He stood and lifted her up effortlessly and carried her across the room. She wondered if he was afraid to put her down, afraid she might change her mind. There was no chance of that.

He stepped into the shower cubicle and spun around, holding her against him with one arm as he closed and locked the door. He pressed her back to the door, trapping her between his hips and thighs. She lifted her arms and he pulled her shirt over her head, disposing of her bra with the same movement.

Marcus ducked his head and took one breast in his mouth as Grace clung to him. His tongue flicked over her nipple, sending needles of desire shooting down to the junction between her thighs. It felt amazing but she wanted more. She was desperate for more.

'I don't think I can wait,' she said. She was barely able to find the breath to speak.

He set her down on the floor and she kicked off her shoes as her fingers tugged at the drawstring of his pants. She hooked her thumbs into the waist of his scrubs and pulled them off his hips, the palms of her hands skimming over his buttocks. They were tight and firm and warm under her fingers. She pulled him towards her, pressing her stomach against his erection. He stepped out of his shoes and scrub trousers in one go and reached his hand over his head and grabbed a fistful of his top, ripping it off over his head as she slid her pants off.

He was naked but, more importantly, so was she.

She pressed against him, her soft, pale skin against his warm brown muscles. She reached down and wrapped her hand around his shaft. It throbbed under her touch, springing to life, infused with blood. She could feel every beat of his heart repeated under her fingers.

His fingers slid inside her, rubbing the sensitive bud that nestled between her thighs. Her knees were shaking. 'I can't stand,' she panted. 'You'll have to hold me.'

Her eyelashes fluttered and her eyes closed as he lifted her up in one easy motion and she spread her thighs wider, eager to welcome him. She felt the tip of his erection nudge between her legs and held her breath as she waited for what came next but she felt him hesitate.

Her eyes sprang open as he said, 'I haven't got any protection.'

She had no idea if she could stop now. And she didn't want to. She blinked and said. 'I'm on the Pill. Are you clean?'

He nodded.

She took him at his word.

He took her at hers.

There would be time enough later to think about their level of trust and where it had come from.

'I want you inside me.'

She didn't need to ask him twice.

She wrapped her thighs around his waist as she spread her legs. She heard him sigh as he plunged into her. She enveloped him as he thrust into her warmth.

God, that felt good.

She moaned as he pushed deeper.

'I'm not hurting you?'

'No.' The word was a sigh, one syllable on a breath of air.

She closed her eyes as she rode him, bucking her hips against his, her back arched, and she was completely oblivious to everything except the feel of him inside her as she offered herself to him. His face was buried in her neck and she tipped her head back as he thrust into her, rapidly bringing them to their peak.

'Oh, God, Grace, that feels incredible.'

Hearing her name on his lips was her undoing. Her name had never sounded so sweet and she had never felt so desired. She gave herself up to him and as he exploded into her she joined him, quivering in his arms as she climaxed.

He kissed her forehead and her lips and held her close until she stopped shaking.

She had let him seek comfort in her body, had offered herself willingly to him, but, having experienced him once, she knew that once would never, *could* never, be enough.

'You look like you've had a good time.'

Grace hadn't expected Lola to still be up when she got home and she was surprised to find her in the kitchen when she bounced in with a broad smile on her face.

'I just had sex with Marcus,' she announced.

'You did *what*?'

Lola's reaction was just the one Grace had expected and she'd never imagined *not* telling her. It was a force of habit. They had shared a flat for the best part of two years and their friendship had grown to the point where they told each other everything and this news was way too exciting *not* to share. She started to fill her friend in on the details of the last part of her evening, all traces of tears almost wiped from her memory by the past hour, but she didn't get far before Lola interrupted her.

'You had sex in the doctor's change rooms? What if someone came in?'

'We didn't think it through,' Grace admitted.

'And how was it? Pretty good, by the look on your face.'

'It was amazing,' she said with a grin. 'He certainly knows what he's doing.'

Lola laughed. 'I suspect a man who looks like he does

has had plenty of practice. What did he say to get you to sleep with him?'

'What did he *say*?'

Lola nodded. 'You always fall for the boy with the story. Someone who you think needs you in some way to help them fix their troubles. How did he talk you out of your clothes?'

She had a point. Grace's first serious boyfriend had died in tragic circumstances for which Grace still felt she was somewhat to blame. She hadn't been able to save Johnny and it had taken her a long time to recover from his death. And ever since she had been drawn to men who'd had some sort of crisis. Men who, she thought, needed her. Whether it was survivor's guilt or part of the healing process she wasn't sure. Sometimes the crises had been real, sometimes they had just been spinning her a story and she'd been caught up in the lies.

Most recently it had been Anthony, a radiologist who had told her a story about his wife leaving him and taking the kids. His heart had been broken and he needed Grace to help him recover. Only it had all been a lie. He'd still *had* a wife and kids. Grace knew she was far too honest and she expected the same of others, which meant she often didn't recognise the stories she was hearing were just stories. Not until it was too late.

But she was positive Marcus was different. There was something damaged about him, a deep hurt, and she'd known he'd genuinely needed her comfort. But had it been about her or had she just been convenient?

No, she didn't want to believe that.

'He didn't have a story,' she said. Not tonight. It hadn't been his story that had made her abandon her clothes, it had been the look in his eyes. He'd looked at her and she'd been able to see that he'd needed her to take his mind off his troubles. And she'd wanted to help. She hadn't been able to refuse him. He'd needed comfort and she had been prepared to offer it, had *wanted* to offer it. What was wrong with that?

But she wasn't about to admit that to Lola. Some secrets were meant to be kept. 'He didn't say anything. He just kissed me and that was it.'

'What do you mean, that was it?'

'I couldn't stop, I didn't *want* to stop.' There had been no subterfuge, no lies, no half-truths. She knew him. And she knew he'd needed her. But what she didn't know was what would happen next.

'What happens now?' Lola wanted to know, as if reading her mind.

'I have no idea.'

'This is serious. You don't do casual sex. It's always dinner and conversation, something that could be considered a date. Have you ever even had a one-night stand?'

'Who said anything about a one-night stand?'

'Did he make plans to see you again?'

'No.'

Lola raised an eyebrow.

'All right, I admit I got carried away,' she said, without sharing any further details. Lola would hear soon enough about the outcome of Louise's surgery and she didn't need to know how distraught Marcus had been. That was between him and herself. 'But I'm not sorry. You do this all the time, so why do you get a different set of rules?' She couldn't deny she really liked the idea of finding 'the one' but there was no reason she couldn't have some fun along the way. Lola seemed to manage

that all right. She insisted she was happy being footloose
and fancy-free. Maybe Grace should try it.

'That's not what I'm saying and I don't make the rules
but you must admit this is out of character for you. What
if that's it, one night, thank you very much, and he moves
on to the next girl? I don't want you to get hurt. I'm not
sure you're tough enough to handle it.'

Grace knew she wouldn't be okay if Marcus did do
that to her, but it was too late to worry about that now.
They hadn't made plans or promises. It had just been
great sex and she'd have to handle it if he didn't want to
see her again.

'It's fine, Lola. It was just sex.'

'That's not how you do things, Grace.' Lola's voice
held a hint of warning and Grace knew she was worried
as well as right. Grace had never had a casual fling before. She'd never jumped into bed with a guy on the first
date, let alone *without* a first date. But while she heard
her friend's concern she chose to ignore it.

'It's fine,' she repeated.

Grace lay in Marcus's bed, satisfied and also a little bit
smug. Despite Lola's warnings she *had* seen Marcus
again and this was the third time in a week they'd spent
the evening together. He'd taken her to dinner at the Chinese restaurant again; it wasn't fancy but Grace didn't
care, in her mind it was now 'their' restaurant and she
was more than happy to eat there. With him.

And tonight, instead of putting her in a taxi and sending her home, he'd taken her to his apartment and now she
lay in his bed with her knee nestled between his thighs,
her head on his shoulder as she listened to him breathe.

He had his fingers in her hair, playing with the ends, and she could tell his thoughts were drifting.

She longed to know what he thought about. They spent a lot of time talking about her. They spoke about work and her family, the muster and her friends. He'd shared a few stories about his life in Perth but he was reluctant to share more than that and every time she tried to change the topic he quickly changed it back, which made it difficult to get a sense of who he was. She did know he'd gone to a boys' boarding school from the age of twelve and had spent holidays on a farm with his three male cousins so it wasn't surprising he wasn't a good communicator. But she could teach him. It wasn't healthy to keep every emotion bottled up. She hoped he'd eventually learn to share his thoughts and feelings with her. Maybe he would learn by example.

She'd ignored Lola's warnings about getting involved with someone who wasn't planning to stay in Sydney and who was also emotionally distant. Was she setting herself up for heartache, as Lola predicted?

She'd decided she didn't care. Lying in his arms, she thought it was a risk worth taking. An opportunity she found she couldn't resist. It might end in tears but she couldn't walk away. He was sexy and smart and knew what he was doing in the bedroom—it was no sacrifice on her part. Besides, she felt he needed a connection to someone and, at the moment, she didn't mind that for a few nights or weeks it might be her. A few weeks wasn't long enough to risk everything. It wasn't long enough for him to break her heart.

'Are you going to Louise's funeral tomorrow?' he asked.

That was where his thoughts had gone. The coroner's

inquest had absolved him of any blame but she knew he still felt a sense of responsibility for Louise's death.

'Are you?' she asked. She'd be surprised if he attended.

'No. I don't think it would be appropriate.' His chest rose and fell with his words.

Grace hated funerals but she felt a duty to attend. She sighed. 'I have to go.'

'You don't have to.'

'I've known Louise and her family for three years. I've seen her at least once a week every week during that time, so I think I should be there to pay my respects to Daniel and their children,' she explained. Louise's death was affecting everyone in the renal unit and Grace knew she wouldn't be there alone. There would be a lot of support for Louise's family, friends and the hospital staff who had worked so closely with her.

'I wish I didn't have to go. I hate funerals, they are so sad, so final. People talk about funerals being a chance to celebrate life but what is there to celebrate when a life has been cut so short? Louise should have been able to celebrate being alive. All those dreams shattered.' Louise had had everything to live for but now she was gone. Grace hated to think about all the things Louise was going to miss out on and all the things her children would miss too.

'Life isn't always like that,' he said. 'You don't always get to live happily ever after.' Grace wondered if this was an opportunity for her to talk to Marcus about his childhood, he certainly hadn't had a happy start to his life, but before she could formulate a question that didn't sound too intrusive he had already shifted the focus onto her. 'This is about more than just Louise, isn't it?'

'Why do you say that?'

'In the work we do we lose people and we work out ways to deal with it. I know there are some patients we form stronger bonds with than others but Louise's death seems more personal to you than I would have expected. I'm not saying you shouldn't be upset by it but are you sure there's not more going on in your head? Who are you thinking about? Who did you lose too young?'

For someone who kept his emotions close to his chest he was quite intuitive when it came to other people. Grace thought about brushing his question aside—after all, that was what he would do to her—but she was too honest. And maybe, if she shared something important with him, he might learn to do the same with her. 'I lost a friend. A good friend,' she said, 'when we were twenty-two. It was too young and, even now, I still feel like there was more I could have done, *should* have done, to help him.'

'Do you want to tell me what happened?'

In the hours they had spent together Grace had learned that Marcus was a good listener. It was probably because he preferred to listen rather than talk, but she was prepared to talk about Johnny. She'd found it was better to express her emotions. That was something losing Johnny had taught her.

'Johnny was my first serious boyfriend. He was from Toowoomba. We met when we were still at school. He suffered from depression and it got worse as he got older. He was on medication but he hated the way it made him feel. Said the tablets dulled him, made him feel like he was existing but not living. It was an ongoing battle to get him to keep taking them. One day he stopped and I didn't notice. I was studying and working, I was too busy. Johnny had grown up in the country on a property where everyone had a gun. He took one out one day and shot himself. He left a note saying it was all too difficult, that living with the disease was too hard. He killed himself and I couldn't save him. I've hated funerals ever since I went to his.'

Grace had grown accustomed to Johnny's absence but talking about him still made her feel sad. Fat tears were rolling down her cheeks. Marcus wiped them away with his thumb. 'Do you still miss him?'

'I miss the friendship we had,' she admitted. 'We'd been friends for ever, before we started dating, and that's the part I miss. I'm not sure that I miss the future we would have had, and part of me is relieved that I got a chance to do something different from what we'd planned, but then I feel guilty about thinking like that.'

'Relieved?'

'Everyone assumed we'd get married, settle down to a life in Toowoomba, but I honestly don't know if that life would have been enough for me. I think I would have had a lot of regrets. After Johnny died I felt trapped by the emotion. There were too many people feeling sorry for me without knowing how I was really feeling. It was a mixture of grief and relief and that made me feel like a bad person. I had to get out of there, away from all the expectations and the sorrow. When Merridy came to Sydney for her surgery I saw my chance for a new beginning. I could start fresh, somewhere no one knew me. Or Johnny.'

'And yet…' she still lay with her head on his chest but she could hear a trace of a smile in his voice '…on my first day at Kirribilli General you were defending the small-town lifestyle.'

'Lifestyle maybe, but I never said the people were

easy. Moving here was a good decision for me. I can go back now with a bit of perspective. I'm not the same person I was, I'm stronger and I've learnt a lot about myself. If I'd settled down five years ago I would have regretted all the things I never got to do. I know I need more challenges than I would have got in Toowoomba. I'm happy here. I'm happy, full stop.'

She still dreamed of settling down. She still wanted a husband and kids one day but she could wait. She wasn't prepared to settle for second best. She needed excitement and challenges and she suspected Marcus might give some of that to her.

'So that's the full story of how I ended up here,' she said as she ran her hand down Marcus's bare chest, 'and now I think that's enough time spent talking about my past. I, for one, have better things to do tonight.'

'Tania?' Grace approached the nurse at the nurses' station and introduced herself after reading her name badge. 'I'm Grace Gibson, the renal transplant co-ordinator. Someone called asking me to review a file for a patient who might need a transplant?'

'That was me. We have a patient who was admitted yesterday with end-stage liver disease and the specialist is advocating for him to be placed on the transplant register but our liver transplant co-ordinator is on leave and I need to know what the process is.'

'I don't have control over who goes on the register,' Grace explained.

'I know but the patient has a complicated medical history and I doubt he's suitable for a transplant. Would you mind taking a look at his file and just giving me your thoughts? It might help us clarify what to do next.' Tania retrieved the patient's case notes when Grace nodded and handed them to her as she elaborated further. 'He has dementia and is also an alcoholic. Not a reformed alcoholic either.'

The name on the front of the file caught Grace's eye: *William Washington.*

Was that a coincidence? She was certain that was Marcus's father's name but surely he would have said something if his father had been admitted to hospital?

She took the file to a vacant workstation and flicked to the personal details.

Age—67
Next of kin—Marcus Washington, son.

She continued to turn the pages, trying to get a picture of the man who was Marcus's father.

His address was listed as a veterans' affairs nursing home in the northern suburbs of Sydney. Grace did the maths—he must have served in the Vietnam War. Was that relevant at all?

She continued to flick through the notes. He was underweight for his height and blood-test results were less than ideal, with several relevant increased markers consistent with cirrhosis. Iron levels and platelets were also low.

From his notes it was apparent that due to social factors, lifestyle choices and his medical history he wasn't a suitable transplant candidate but Grace couldn't forget that Marcus hadn't said anything. She returned to the nurses' station.

'Tania, it says here his son is his next of kin. Do you know if he has been in to see him?'

Tania nodded. 'He was here last night when Bill was admitted.'

So Marcus did know and had chosen not to share that information with her.

Grace's job was to look at his file but she couldn't resist going to his room. She got to his room at the same time as the catering staff were delivering lunch trays. Grace offered to take his in with her. She pushed the door open and found Marcus's father lying in the bed, his eyes closed. He looked a lot older than the sixty-seven years she knew him to be. He was a tall man who was much too thin. His skin was grey and he looked shrunken.

'Mr Washington?' Grace said as she balanced the tray against her waist and knocked on the door she'd just opened and stepped further into the room. 'I have your lunch.'

He opened his eyes and stared vacantly at her.

'Do you know where you are?' she asked as he continued to stare vaguely. 'You're in hospital. You were brought in last night. Are you hungry?' She put the tray on the overway table and pushed it over his bed. He lifted the insulating cover with shaky hands and Grace wondered when his last drink had been.

She stayed with him for a few minutes, making sure he could feed himself and trying vainly to make conversation. He either wasn't interested in talking to her or wasn't able to maintain a conversation so she eventually gave up and left the room. She had another member of his family she urgently needed to talk to.

She found Marcus in his office. She knocked on his

door and entered when he looked up. 'I need to talk to you about a patient,' she said.

'Sure. Who is it?'

'William Washington.'

She waited to see how he would respond but he gave her nothing.

'Why didn't you tell me he had been admitted here last night?' she asked.

Marcus frowned. 'Why would I? It's not relevant to anything. How did you know he was here?'

'I was asked to see him.'

'What for?'

'His specialist wants to put him on the national register for a liver transplant. I was asked to review his file because the liver transplant co-ordinator is on annual leave and the nursing staff wanted an opinion from someone on the transplant team.'

'He's not a candidate for a liver transplant.'

'I know,' she agreed. 'I need you to talk to his specialist. Explain the situation.'

'I know as much as you do.'

'Marcus, I haven't seen your father in close to ten years. How could I possibly know as much as you about his condition?'

'Until I arrived in Sydney four weeks ago I hadn't seen him for *twenty* years. You're probably more qualified than I am to have the necessary conversations.'

'Twenty years? You haven't seen him at all?'

'No.'

She desperately wanted to know what had happened but getting any information from Marcus was like getting blood out of a stone. He gave her tiny snippets of information but the rest she had to go hunting for. 'Is that why you came to Sydney?'

'No. I came to Sydney for this career opportunity but I figured I could use this trip to see Bill before it was too late.'

'Too late for what?' she asked.

'For answers.' He sighed. 'Bill sent me to boarding school in Perth and my aunt became my guardian. Until this past month the last time I saw him was when I was twelve years old. He sent me off to the other side of the country with no explanation. We were never close and I can't deny I was happy to go, but as I've got older I've started wondering about the circumstances that led me to Perth. What was the catalyst?'

For once Grace felt like she could actually understand what Marcus *wasn't* telling her and it gave her far more insight into his character than she imagined he realised. He'd been hurt. Not by a lover—but by his parents. Grace noticed that he didn't even refer to his father by that title but called him 'Bill'.

'You've been by yourself since you were twelve?'

'I spent school holidays with my aunt and my cousins but I learnt to become self-sufficient.'

He wasn't going to trust easily. She would have to build that trust. 'How are things going now with your father?'

'It's a complete waste of time. He has no idea who I am.'

'He doesn't recognise you at all?' That didn't surprise her. If the two of them had had no contact for twenty years it wasn't all that surprising given Bill's dementia.

'It's more than that,' Marcus said. 'He doesn't even seem to remember that he has a son at all.'

'Maybe given some time he will remember you,' she said.

'We both know he doesn't have that long,' he said. He clicked the mouse and woke his computer monitor as he dismissed her by adding, 'If that's all you wanted to discuss, I have work to do.'

Grace was ready to go. She found the whole situation terribly sad, loss of any kind affected her deeply, and she wanted to get out of there before she burst into tears. She knew he'd hate to see her crying for him, knew he would hate her pity, but she couldn't imagine how it must feel to have a parent who didn't remember you. But what was almost worse was the realisation that Marcus had been on his own for twenty years. No mother. No father. No siblings. He'd had no one to kiss him goodnight, no one to listen to his dreams, to tell him he could do anything. No one to love him. He had no one. It wasn't surprising then that he found it hard to share his feelings.

She headed to the ICU in search of Lola, as she badly needed to debrief, but by the time she found her she was in floods of tears.

'What's wrong?'

'Marcus—'

'I *knew* he would break your heart,' Lola interrupted as she wrapped Grace in a hug. 'What's happened?'

'No.' Grace shook her head as she sobbed into Lola's shoulder. 'My heart is breaking but not because of anything Marcus has done. It's breaking *for* him.'

Lola stepped back, releasing Grace from her embrace but not letting go of her completely. 'What does that mean?'

'He's all alone. His mother left him when he was very young and his father has dementia and doesn't remember him. Marcus has no one, he's been by himself for twenty years.'

'He's probably quite used to being alone, then,' Lola said matter-of-factly. 'Has he said he's unhappy? He seems fine.'

'On the surface maybe, but how could he be happy to be so alone?' Grace relied heavily on her family for support. She knew she would never have recovered from Johnny's death without their help, and even though they hadn't necessarily agreed with her move to Sydney they had supported her in that too. They had always been there for her and she couldn't understand how Marcus, or anyone else, could be perfectly happy alone. No one should be alone. She believed in love and family but listening to Marcus talk about his family she knew he didn't believe in either of those things.

'Grace…' Lola's voice held a hint of warning '…don't assume he needs help or that things need fixing. You can't solve all the world's problems.'

She knew that and she didn't want to fix everyone's problems. Just Marcus's.

CHAPTER SEVEN

MARCUS HESITATED AT his father's door. The visits weren't getting any easier but he had an obligation and so he continued to come, even though he wasn't getting any further in his quest for answers.

He knew Grace thought he should be more direct with Bill—she'd told him as much, told him he should ask specific questions if he wanted specific answers. He knew that waiting for Bill to volunteer information was never going to work so why couldn't he ask a straight question? Was he afraid of the answers? Afraid of the truth? Or afraid he wouldn't *get* the truth?

He knew Grace disapproved of his methods and he didn't want the stress of her disapproval on top of everything else. He didn't want to deal with any additional guilt. It was clear she would never understand the issues he and his father faced and she obviously still expected their differences to be resolved. But reconciling their differences had never been his goal and he had made his peace with that. Striving for that outcome was only ever going to end in disappointment but he'd hoped to get some closure, or at least some answers, but, because of Bill's condition, that wasn't likely to happen either.

He took a deep breath at Bill's door as he mentally

prepared himself to enter and hoped Grace was there to act as a buffer. Her presence was the only thing that made the visits manageable. Her presence in his father's hospital room over the last week had eased the tension between the two men.

Grace had formed a connection with his father and Bill seemed to enjoy her company. With Grace there was no pressure, no expectation that he would remember her or anything they talked about. Quite literally, she just gave him company.

Marcus, however, remembered everything he talked about with her. He also remembered every minute they had spent together. Every curve of her body, every freckle on her shoulders, the feel of her skin under his hand, the smell of her shampoo and the way her dark eyelashes rested on her pale cheeks when she closed her eyes as he kissed her. He'd learnt a lot about her in the time they had spent together. That didn't concern him as he enjoyed her company, in bed and out, but he was worried that she was learning more about him than he wanted to reveal. He knew she wanted him to open up to her, but he found that difficult. He'd taken her to dinner, which, while not completely out of character, he always did before he had sex with a woman, not afterwards. *Never* afterwards. And he had never let a woman stay overnight, he'd never even invited one to his house before. He'd done things with Grace that he'd never done with anyone. He hoped he wasn't making a mistake.

She fascinated him and he wanted to know everything about her. He wouldn't normally bother to learn about the women he took to bed—did that make him selfish? He didn't think so as those women didn't care about him either. But he was beginning to care about Grace. She was kind and gentle and honest and he enjoyed her company very much.

He refused to be concerned about that. He wasn't here for long so he could enjoy her company for a few more weeks and then return to Perth, heart and soul intact. Secrets safe.

He was fully aware that he was avoiding the major issues in his life—his feelings about his father and his feelings about Grace—but he'd never let himself examine his feelings before and he had no idea where to start or even if he *wanted* to start. He was terrified of how exposed he would be.

The irony of the fact that he could cope with just about anything professionally and then become a mass of indecision and uncertainty around his father, who didn't even know who he was, hadn't escaped him. He just didn't know what to do about it.

He opened the door and stepped inside.

Grace was there and she greeted him with a smile. He knew she was trying to make things easier for him. She was trying to help him mend the bridges and he appreciated it but she didn't realise that the bridges had been damaged so badly a long time ago and there wasn't going to be the time or opportunity to mend them. He wasn't even sure if he wanted to, he really only wanted answers, but he knew Grace wouldn't understand that. She believed in happily ever after.

He didn't want to disappoint her but she wasn't going to get what she wanted as far as he and his father were concerned. He had the potential to forgive Bill, and it was obvious that Grace would like him to, but he didn't think he had it in him. His hurt was still raw after all these years. Grace would be disappointed in him but he felt incapable of doing anything else.

'Hi.' She was still smiling as she greeted him. 'I was just telling Bill about the muster.'

He'd noticed she always carefully avoided saying 'your dad' in front of him and Bill. The phrase agitated Bill and irritated Marcus. He appreciated her candour even though he couldn't be the son Grace wanted him to be, just like Bill couldn't be the father she wanted for *him*.

It was what it was.

He tried not to feel jealous that Grace had developed a good rapport with his father. She never seemed to run out of conversation. Perhaps it was because she was happy to chat about anything that captured Bill's interest. It was easy to hold a conversation when you weren't emotionally invested. It didn't matter to Grace what the topic was, her only agenda was to keep Bill company.

Marcus wished he could say the same for himself but he was too aware that time was running out. He didn't have months at his disposal to get the answers he was seeking. He didn't even have weeks. His father was getting frailer and it was clear he wouldn't be leaving the hospital to return to the nursing home. The hospital was his last stop. There could be worse things than having Grace's company for his last days.

'Have you had some success?' He picked up Grace's lead and continued the conversation. His father had been a stockman when Marcus had been young. He'd had to give that up when Marcus's mother had abandoned them but perhaps he remembered those days and, who knew, maybe he and his father would finally find some common ground with Grace's help. Stranger things had happened. Grace had managed, in principle, to get support for the muster from the hospital and the transplant foundation but the local council was proving more difficult to persuade. 'Have you had the route approved yet?'

Grace shook her head. 'No. The council is being really stubborn. Even though we've offered to do the muster early on a Sunday they say they can't close the bridge to traffic. But they close the bridge for several hours for the New Year's Eve fireworks *and* for the running festival. They even had cows on it a few years ago for a fundraising breakfast but now they've decided it's too disruptive.'

'You've done your homework.'

'Of course I have.'

'Is it a financial issue? Road closures for major events are costly, and I imagine it's an even more expensive exercise to close the bridge.'

'You're not suggesting I bribe them?' She smiled and his mood lifted instantly.

'No, but you could offer to compensate them for their costs and time and effort. Call it a little sweetener.'

'But not a bribe?'

'No.'

She laughed. 'You probably have a good point but the muster is for a charity. I want to maximise the profits and it would annoy me to have to hand over good money after we'd worked so hard to raise it. Merridy has organised lots of sponsors, companies have been very generous, but I'm sure they would want their money going to the cause, not the council. They are the only sticking point.'

Marcus figured it was highly likely that the companies wouldn't care where their money went as long as they got some positive exposure and the tax benefits but that thought probably wasn't helpful at all. 'Have you considered alternative routes?'

Grace sighed. 'Merridy has her heart set on the bridge. It would bring massive publicity.'

'I don't disagree, but it might just not be possible.'

'Which stock route are you using?' Bill asked.

Grace and Marcus both looked at him in surprise. It was unusual for him to keep track of a conversation like this, particularly when it was occurring between two other people, but it seemed he had followed the topic after all.

'It's not technically a stock route,' Grace told him. 'We want to truck the cattle in to Sydney's north shore and walk them across the Harbour Bridge but the council is giving me grief. They say it can't be done.'

'Well, they're wrong.'

'What do you mean?'

'You're talking about the Sydney Harbour Bridge?'

'Yes.'

'It's a designated stock route,' Bill said.

'A what? How do you know that?'

'I am a drover. Stock routes are my bread and butter. Cattle need water, which means I need to know the stock routes and the watering holes. Not that I've ever needed to use the Harbour Bridge but I'm telling you, it's a stock route.'

Grace looked at Marcus. He shrugged. There was no way he'd take his father's word for it. But he could see Grace was getting excited.

'Are you saying I can request to walk the cattle over the bridge and the council will have to let me?' she asked Bill.

Bill frowned and shook his head and Marcus could feel Grace's disappointment. 'How many cattle are you talking about?'

Marcus wasn't sure if Bill was losing his train of thought but Grace went with him. 'I'm not sure. A few hundred hopefully. It depends on how many people want to be involved.'

'That might work. The stock route is not the whole bridge. It's only the pedestrian walkway so it will depend on the size of your herd.'

'That's better than nothing. In fact, that's the best news I've had all day. Thank you.' She stood up and gave Bill a big hug. He looked surprised but didn't resist. He was probably too taken aback to protest. Marcus couldn't remember ever hugging his father. Or his father ever hugging him. 'I'm going to go and do some digging right away,' Grace said.

Marcus followed her out of the room. She stopped outside the door and turned to him. Her face was alight, her amber eyes shining. 'Isn't that brilliant news?' she said. 'I just need to get that information confirmed and then the council will *have* to approve my request.'

'I don't want to rain on your parade, so to speak, and maybe it *was* a stock route once, but who knows if it still is?'

'Well, I intend to find out.'

'Don't you think that if what Bill is saying is true, the council would have told you?'

'They probably don't know. It must be years since anyone has tried to do what we're doing. I didn't mention stock routes.' She paused and gave him a considered look. 'You don't seem very enthusiastic.'

'I don't want you to get your hopes up. Do you think it's sensible to base your expectations on the ramblings of an alcoholic with dementia?'

'He seemed pretty certain.'

'You think he can remember a stock route from his droving days, which were thirty years ago, when he can't remember what he had for lunch?'

'You know that's how dementia works. Short-term memory is affected far more than long-term.'

'You think he can remember a stock route that he said he *never* used but he can't remember his own son? I was also there thirty years ago.'

Grace returned to her office. She had to investigate Bill's claim. She understood that Bill's unreliable memory was upsetting for Marcus. She knew how badly he wanted his father to remember him, to be able to give him the answers he was seeking, but she couldn't do anything about that. What she could do was follow Bill's lead.

She trawled the internet but her searches returned no results. She phoned the council but the person who it was recommended she speak to was away for the day. She left a message and decided she'd go back to see Bill at the first opportunity to see if he could tell her anything more. She didn't get a chance to get back to his room again that day and she was held up the following day too. It was after lunch before she got a moment to make the dash to his ward.

She almost collided with the empty meal trolley being wheeled along the corridor and she knew Bill's lunch would have already been delivered. She pushed open his door and was greeted by an empty room. Her heart plummeted. The bed had been stripped but there was no accompanying pile of clean linen indicating that someone was halfway through a task. Bill didn't have many personal effects dotted around the room but Grace had seen enough hospital rooms to know when someone was just out of bed or the room had been vacated. It could only mean one thing.

She backtracked to the nurses' station and glanced at the wall. The box next to room sixteen was empty. His name had been wiped from the board.

He was gone.

She was aware what that meant but she would check anyway. Maybe he had just been moved.

She was pleased to see that Tania was on duty. Grace wasn't Bill's family, she didn't need to be informed of what was going on, but, as a staff member, it was possible she'd be kept in the loop.

'Bill Washington?' She asked the question.

Tania shook her head. Nothing more needed to be said. He was gone.

'When?'

'About two o'clock this morning.'

'Was anyone with him?'

'Marcus was here.'

Marcus knew. And, once again, he hadn't said anything to her. What was the matter with him? Why did he insist on keeping everyone out? She had bared her soul to him, he knew everything about her, everything about her fears and her losses. Why couldn't he share anything with her?

She marched back to the renal ward and found him in his office, going through some papers. His door was open and she didn't bother knocking. If he thought she was just going to let this go he was very much mistaken. She closed the door behind her, making a poor attempt not to slam it. He looked up in surprise.

'Were you going to tell me?' She knew she should

start with condolences but they were already way past that point.

'Tell you what?'

'About your father? Did you not think I'd want to know?' She made sure to keep her tone neutral, even though she was furious with him and his refusal to share any personal thoughts or emotions with her.

'I knew you'd hear.'

'Well, maybe I wanted to hear about it from you.'

'Why?'

'Because he was your *father* and I thought you might be upset. I thought you might want some company. I would have come in to the hospital if you'd asked me to.' She tried to stay calm but her fiery temper was threatening to get the better of her.

'Grace, I'm fine. It's all okay.'

'How can you say that?'

'Bill hasn't been part of my life for a very long time and the man who was here wasn't even him.' He shrugged. 'Nothing has changed now he's gone.'

'But you wanted answers.'

'And I didn't get them and there's nothing I can do about that. So, can we move on?'

He returned his attention to the papers in front of him and it was obvious from his body language that he thought the discussion was over. Grace begged to differ.

His words had really hurt her. She knew this shouldn't be about her but how could he be so blasé? Was Bill's death really so insignificant to him? She worried that he was bottling things up and that frightened her. She had seen what happened when people buried their emotions and refused to acknowledge their issues—they became ticking time-bombs until one day they exploded.

Was he really so self-contained and self-sufficient?

She knew a little about his childhood and it really wasn't surprising he didn't confide in others or rely on their support but she wasn't just a colleague, neither was she just a friend. Surely she was more than that, wasn't she? Why wouldn't he talk to her? Did she mean nothing to him?

She needed to work out a way to make him talk to her. He had to be hurting and she wasn't going to ignore a friend in need. She'd made that mistake once before and she wouldn't do it again. She would make a dignified exit and deal with this later but as she walked towards the door Marcus's exasperated tone stopped her in her tracks.

'You're kidding me!'

Unsure if he was addressing her, she hesitated and turned back to him but he wasn't looking at her, he was still reading the papers.

'What is it?' The question was out of her mouth before she realised he probably wasn't about to share anything with her but to her amazement he looked up.

'The nursing home sent some of his papers over.' He held up the page he was reading. 'This is his funeral instructions. Apparently he wants to be cremated and have his ashes scattered on a plot of land he owns in Toowoomba.'

'Is that a problem?'

'I didn't know he had land there.'

Grace frowned. 'Does it make a difference?'

Marcus either chose to ignore her question or didn't know the answer. 'I guess I shouldn't be surprised. Even when he's dead, he's still keeping secrets.'

He might say that nothing had changed but Grace could see traces in him of the little boy he'd been, a boy looking for answers and looking for love. But she knew he'd never admit that.

She could love him if he'd let her.

'I'm sure you can arrange for someone else to do it for you if you prefer,' she said, her voice softening.

'His lawyer is also in Toowoomba. I'll have to have a meeting with him.'

Grace suspected that if Marcus really wanted to avoid Toowoomba he could arrange to meet the lawyer in Sydney if he offered to pay expenses. She didn't think money was an issue but she thought it would do him good to go back to Toowoomba. It might be a cleansing experience, it might give him some closure. She suspected his memories of Toowoomba were far more onerous than the reality. Maybe he should face his demons. Maybe then he would finally get some perspective.

Memories could be powerful but experience had taught her that at some point difficult memories needed to be confronted, otherwise they kept all the power, and she doubted that the memories of a twelve-year-old boy were terribly accurate. She didn't doubt they were powerful—they had shaped the last twenty years of his life, after all—but maybe it was time to take back control. He needed to address his issues rather than ignoring them, or they would only fester and grow.

Something had to be done to help him move on. He thought he was coping but Grace could see the weaknesses in his argument. If he was coping that well with everything that had happened in the past, then going back to Toowoomba wouldn't be the stumbling block it appeared to be.

She would help him.

'I'm going home to Toowoomba in a couple of weeks,'

she told him. 'Why don't you come with me? We could do this together.' He looked at her and she knew he was going to make an excuse, to reject her suggestion, but she was certain it was a good one and she wasn't going to let him refuse to consider it. 'Think about it,' she added. 'You can let me know over the next day or so.'

CHAPTER EIGHT

SINCE BILL'S DEATH Marcus had thrown himself into work and retreated further into his shell. He couldn't admit that Bill's death had rattled him but it had spelt the end of his chances to get the answers he'd so desperately wanted. He'd avoided Grace, keeping their contact to a minimum, mainly so that he didn't have to talk about his feelings. She'd only be disappointed to find that they were of anger, frustration and disbelief rather than the more appropriate ones of sadness, loss and grief.

Grace had insisted on going to the funeral. He'd tried to talk her out of it—after all, she'd told him she hated funerals—but she hadn't been dissuaded. He'd settled on a private funeral that he'd let the war veterans' nursing home organise and in the end he gave in to Grace. Partly because her presence would distract from the fact that he couldn't be the grieving son everyone expected to see but mainly because, quite simply, he wanted her there.

The funeral had been bittersweet. Grace recounted stories Bill had told her from his droving days, painting a picture of a man Marcus had never known. Marcus himself had no stories to tell. No happy memories to share. He wondered if Grace had put on a brave face for him but he didn't reiterate that there was no need, he wasn't mourning, he'd lost his father a long time ago.

He didn't need his father and he didn't need Grace. He'd let her get much too close and it had been a mistake all along.

Though he didn't know how he was going to resolve the problem. He didn't know if he wanted to. And after two weeks of shutting her out, sitting next to her on the plane as they approached Toowoomba was doing his head in.

The irony of his situation wasn't lost on him. If he didn't need her, why had he accepted her suggestion that they fly back to Toowoomba together? He knew having her company would make it easier and she certainly was a distraction. He could smell her familiar floral shampoo and it made his head reel in longing. As she leant across him to pass her meal tray to the hostess her breast brushed against his arm and he just wanted to take her in his arms, hold her tight and forget about the rest of the world and his dysfunctional past.

The way she made him feel frightened him.

She made him feel as if he was worth something.

He had even found himself imagining having a future with her. Could he stay in Sydney? Could it work?

She made him believe he could be happy. That his past didn't matter. But he knew it did.

He wasn't good enough for her.

He should let her go before he disappointed her, he thought that was inevitable, but he couldn't let her go. Not yet. And so here he was, travelling to Toowoomba with Grace beside him.

Toowoomba. The last place on earth he ever thought he'd return to.

He grew increasingly nervous as they approached their destination. The funeral had been just one thing on the list of responsibilities. He had been going through the motions, ticking off the formalities and now, finally, he was able to embark on the final step of his duty. He jiggled his legs up and down and Grace reached across and held his hand. Her gesture was comforting but he was dismayed that he'd let her see his nervousness.

'It'll be okay,' she said. 'Are you sure you don't want some company at the lawyer's?'

'No. I don't want to think about it.' He had a meeting scheduled with Bill's lawyer to find out the details of the land Bill owned and to get other instructions. 'Tell me about your plans for the weekend.'

'It's my sister-in-law's birthday. That's why I'm coming home. There's a party at my brother's place tomorrow.'

'Is it a special birthday?'

'No. But this is Merridy, my sister-in-law who is organising the muster. After her transplant she said she's going to celebrate every birthday in style so I always make an effort to get back if I can. They run a feed lot so it's hard for them to get away. I always have to come to the party. It's a good chance to catch up with everyone and I get to see my goddaughter as well.'

'You have a goddaughter?' Despite knowing that they'd spent far more time talking about her than him over the past few weeks, he still continued to discover new things about her. She was far more extroverted and social than he was and her family and friends were an important part of her life. He couldn't imagine anyone asking him to be a godparent for their child.

'Merridy's sister is my best friend from high school. Her daughter, Chloe, is my goddaughter.'

Her reply reminded him of one of the reasons he hated small towns and Toowoomba in particular. Everyone knew everyone and everything. There was no way people would have forgotten him. Grace hadn't. What the hell was he doing, going back?

The plane touched down and he stood and lifted the box containing Bill's ashes from the locker above his head. This was it. A weekend of memories and loneliness stretched before him.

Grace stood up. 'You're welcome to join us for the party tomorrow,' she said, and for a moment the idea appealed as an alternative to a lonely, empty day before he registered that there would be way too many people from his past all together in one place. He was happy to see Grace but that happiness didn't extend to meeting her family again. He was already too involved. It was going to be difficult enough to walk away from Grace before he disappointed her without having to handle her family's criticism too.

He shook his head. 'Thank you, but I'm good.'

'You know I'm here for you if you need me.' Grace said as they prepared to part ways.

He could see her inherent traits of trust and honesty reflected in her amber eyes. Her world was black and white. So different from his. His was all shades of grey. The only bright light in his personal life was standing in front of him, offering to help.

He didn't deserve her. She was too good for him. 'I'll be fine.'

He'd let her brother Hamish collect her and he would pick up his hire car, see the lawyer and check into his hotel. He'd have dinner and read through some journal articles he hadn't had time to look at yet. He shook his head. His weekend was looking more depressing by the minute. He was tempted to change his mind. To race after Grace and ask her to go with him.

He could handle this, he told himself as he settled into the car. He plugged the lawyer's address into the navigation system and pulled into the light traffic as he tried to ignore the empty seat beside him.

Marcus had some time to kill before his appointment, so he switched off the navigation and drove through town, looking for the ghosts of his childhood. He drove past his old house but it had been demolished and a mansion had been built in its place. Most of the houses in the area had been renovated. There were lots of gracious Queenslanders, neat and well kept with their wraparound verandas and large blocks of land.

His old house was only a couple of streets from the primary school and close to the centre of town and, judging by the houses, he guessed the land values had gone up in the past twenty years. He turned the corner and drove past Grace's family home. He remembered it but hoped that no one would notice him drive by. He continued up the hill to Picnic Point. It was mid-morning on a Friday. There were a few mothers with young children in the park and a few older people who looked as though they'd just finished an exercise class, sitting having coffee.

He parked the car and walked to the lookout that took in the view over the ranges. Picnic Point was where teenagers came to hang out late on a Friday and Saturday night—it was a rite of passage once they got their driver's licences—but he had been long gone by then. Maybe he should have brought Grace with him. They could have parked the car and fooled around. It would certainly have kept his mind off the impending lawyer's appointment. He smiled, feeling a little bit brighter, and returned to the car.

He found a space in the main street right outside the lawyer's office. Some things may have changed, buildings had been demolished and new ones built in their place, but parking in a country town was still easy.

Marcus introduced himself to the receptionist, still in some measure of disbelief that he was actually back in Toowoomba.

He was ushered into the office. Charles McDonald stood up behind his desk. He was in his late fifties, Marcus guessed, and extended his hand in greeting as he said, 'My condolences about Bill.'

Marcus assumed he knew about his estrangement from his father but the lawyer had the courtesy not to mention it and allowed Marcus to get down to business without engaging in small talk.

Marcus's first order of the meeting was to get the details regarding the block of land. He was anxious to scatter Bill's ashes. In his mind it would take him one step closer to the end and he was in a hurry to get there.

'It's a bit more than a block,' Charles informed him, 'and there's the will to be read. You are the sole beneficiary.'

'Of what?'

'Bill's estate.'

Marcus hadn't expected Bill to have anything to leave behind. He knew his father had had a pension and enough money to live on. He had topped up Bill's account via a monthly direct debit. It had been his way of assuaging guilt for not visiting him. Ever.

'It's not extensive, just the land and some money in the bank,' Charles said as he handed a piece of paper to Marcus. He looked at the figures in surprise. It was clear from the balance that Bill had never touched a cent of Marcus's money. All of his money would be coming back to him. With interest.

That made Marcus smile. Maybe he and his father had had something in common after all. Both could be stubborn bastards. So certain that they knew best.

'I don't want it,' he said. He wanted nothing from his father. Nothing except answers and it was too late for those.

'It's yours but what you choose to do with it is also up to you,' Charles explained. 'You can donate the money, set up a trust for future generations and sell the land. The neighbours might be willing to buy it. They made an offer once before but Bill wasn't able to give instructions so I had to turn it down. It was a fair offer. You could see if they are still interested.'

'Do you have their details?'

'I do. This is the address of your land and these are the neighbour's details.' He slid two more pieces of paper across the desk to Marcus. 'Lachlan and Merridy Gibson.'

Marcus tried to hide his surprise. Nothing about this whole process should surprise him any more but Bill just kept on delivering curve balls.

'There's also a file with some letters and personal effects that Bill left with me,' Charles said as he handed Marcus a slim box file. 'Have a look through it all and if you have any questions give me a call.'

Marcus took the file and pulled out the title of the land along with the map. With no other commitments for the day he decided he would drive out to see the block. It would give him time to think.

The wide tree-lined streets of town gave way to the familiar small hills and valleys filled with eucalypts and tea trees. He had his window down and the air temperature dropped as he drove north-west. He could smell rain and saw clouds gathering in the distance. The change looked far enough away and he hoped it would hold off until he'd seen the property. He drove past a wide dirt driveway bisected by a cattle grid and noticed a sign nailed to the wooden fence post—'L&M Gibson'. His neighbours. Grace's brother. He kept driving.

His driveway was another five kilometres along the road, the entry marked with a sign that simply listed the lot number. The fences appeared in reasonable condition and a metal gate restricted entry. He unlocked the chain around the gate with the key Charles had given him, pushed it open and drove onto the property. His property.

He drove around, following rutted tyre tracks, getting a feel for the land. From what he could see, it appeared he'd inherited several hectares of prime land. He shook his head. His father might not have known how to raise a son but he knew about cattle and what they needed to thrive. None of this made sense.

He completed a circuit of the property before he eventually parked beside a creek bed. Taking Bill's ashes, he scattered them under one of the willow trees, honouring him in death as he'd been asked to. The air was still and heavy as he let go of his final link to his family. It was a fitting end to his father's life, he felt. Bill had lived a solitary existence, so it seemed right that it should end this way. Just one person there to mark the occasion. As the last of the ashes drifted to the ground he wondered who would be at his own funeral one day. Who would he leave behind? Was he more like his father than he wanted to admit?

Marcus shook his head. There was no way of knowing what the future would bring.

He returned to the car and put the empty box in the boot beside the box of papers that Charles had given him. He took out the file and sat in the car, flicking through the documents and growing increasingly disturbed by the information before him.

When he finished he returned the papers to the file. He'd been given yet more questions and fewer answers but at least this time he had an idea of where to begin looking for them. He started the car and returned to town.

The rain had come and gone as he visited the local council offices and searched the internet. Finally, he had unearthed some answers to his questions and now he was more determined than ever to make sure he had no reason to return to Toowoomba. He was done with this town.

He would tidy up the loose ends and make sure he never had to set foot here again, he thought as he knocked on the door of Grace's brother's house.

The door opened and a streak of red fur dashed out through the gap and darted around Marcus's legs. Reg nudged his wet nose into Marcus's palm, seeking attention. Marcus recognised the cattle dog and patted him automatically as the door opened wider.

'Marcus! How did you know I was here?'

He looked up from the dog into Grace's amber eyes and his heart lifted immediately at the sight of her. She was a sight for sore eyes or, more aptly, for a sore heart and he longed to take her in his arms and let her distract him from his troubles, but she wasn't the person he'd expected to see. 'I didn't. I came to speak to your brother. Isn't this his house?'

Grace nodded. 'Yes, but I don't know where he is. What did you want to see him for?'

'The block of land my father owns shares a boundary with this property. The lawyer said that Lachlan and Merridy had made Bill an offer but he hadn't accepted it. I wanted to know if they were still interested.'

'The land is yours now? He left it to you?'

'Yes.'

'And you're going to sell it?' She frowned as she spoke.

'Of course. What else would I do with it? I don't need a block of land in Toowoomba.' Despite the fact that Toowoomba had changed, it still didn't hold happy memories for him. Despite what he'd discovered today, he still wanted nothing to do with his father or what he'd left for him. 'I never want to come back here again. I want nothing to do with the place.'

Grace stepped back and opened the door wider. 'You'd better come in. Lachlan's not here but I'll introduce you to Merridy.'

Merridy was in the large, farmhouse-style kitchen, which had been extended to open out into a large living space that overlooked the paddocks.

'Merridy, this is Marcus Washington. He's a nephrologist doing a temporary stint at Kirribilli General but his dad was Bill Washington.'

Merridy had an apron tied around her waist and wiped her hands before shaking his. 'Was?'

'He died a couple of weeks ago,' Marcus told her.

'I'm sorry to hear that.'

'Marcus has inherited Bill's land.'

'The land next to us?' She directed her question at Marcus.

'Yes. Bill's lawyer told me you and Lachlan had made an offer to purchase it once before. I wondered if you were still interested.'

'You want to sell?'

'I do.'

'Lachlan will be back shortly, in time for dinner. You're welcome to stay and eat with us,' she said. 'We can discuss it then.'

'Thank you but no. Perhaps the two of you could talk it over and see if you're still interested. I'll leave you my number.'

'We're definitely interested. It's a great piece of land.'

Marcus pulled out a business card and wrote his mobile number on it before handing it to Merridy.

'Are you okay?' Grace asked as she walked with him back to his car, Reg at their heels. 'What else happened at the lawyer's? What else did he tell you?'

'What makes you think he told me anything else?'

'You're edgy. Unsettled. Something has upset you.'

He was all of those things. Usually that would make him retreat until he had sorted through his problems. On his own. He would have gone for a surf or ridden his horse until his mind cleared but he had neither of those options here. All he had was Grace. But she was enough. She listened well and without judgement. She had proven herself to be a good, impartial listener and he really didn't fancy more of his own company.

'Do you want to go for a drive with me?' he asked.

'Sure.' She didn't hesitate. Unlike him, she never seemed to overanalyse things. She took things at face value. Trusting. Easy. 'Just let me put Reg inside and tell Merridy so she doesn't think you've abducted me.'

She was gone only a few minutes but returned with a picnic basket and a blanket.

'What's that for?' he asked as he reached out and took the basket from her.

'Merridy said you looked like you needed to eat. It's a beautiful evening, it seems a shame to waste it. Do you feel like a picnic?'

'Why not?' he replied, realising he'd go just about anywhere with her. His spirits had lifted in the last ten minutes alone.

'Where do you want to go?'

'I have no idea.'

'Would you take me to see your land? There has to be a spot for a picnic there.'

For a lack of any better ideas he took her suggestion. For the second time today he parked beside the creek, near the willows. The sun was dipping below the hills and the sky, clear now after the rain, was turning pink but the air was still warm.

'This is beautiful,' Grace said as she spread the picnic blanket under a willow. She looked around and took in the scenery. She breathed in deeply and sank down onto the rug. 'Did you scatter Bill's ashes?'

'Yes. Why do you ask?'

'I thought this looked like a good place if you hadn't done it already.'

He smiled, wondering why it was he only seemed to smile when Grace was around. He hadn't thought he would smile at all today but, once again, she was making everything better. 'This is the spot I chose,' he told her. 'I scattered them under that willow just over there.'

'It's perfect.' She reached out a hand and pulled him down beside her on the blanket. He set the picnic basket down and Grace opened it and assembled a platter of cheese, pâté, bread and cold meats.

He opened a bottle of wine and poured Grace a glass when she nodded in response to his gesture. He took a bottle of water for himself and said, 'Merridy got all this organised in the few minutes that you were inside?'

Grace smiled. 'It's the country way. She always seems to have food ready to go. She's a good organiser. The muster is in excellent hands.'

'How are things going with that?' he asked, but Grace shook her head as she cut a piece of cheese.

'We're not going to talk about that today. It can wait. Have something to eat and tell me what the lawyer said that's bothering you.'

'He didn't say anything. But he had a box of papers that Bill had left with him for safekeeping. To be passed onto me.'

'What was in there?'

'It was partly what *wasn't* in there. All the things you would expect were there—Bill's legal documents, his birth certificate, his passport, property titles, his will, but there was no marriage certificate.' Marcus felt like he was never going to get to the end of his search for answers. Every time he discovered one thing it led to two more questions, meaning he still had more questions than answers. 'Apparently, they were never married.'

'Does it matter?' She had a puzzled expression in her amber eyes but he could see the exact moment when one thought led to another. She was easy to read, her expressions open and honest, just like she was. There was nothing guarded about her, so totally different from him. 'You said you looked for her. Do you think that's why you never found her? Were you looking for her as a Washington?'

He nodded. 'It would have been helpful to have had this information years ago. I never knew her maiden name either. I don't know why Bill never gave these papers to me before. I don't know why he kept the information from me and now I'll never know.'

'Are you going to look for her again?'

'I have,' he admitted. 'And I've found her.'

'Already!' Grace's amber eyes glowed in the soft light of the evening and her fiery red hair shone, reflecting the rays of the setting sun. She looked beautiful and her expression was full of expectation. Marcus knew she was thinking he had good news to share but it was far from that.

'I could have found her a lot sooner if I'd been given these pieces of the puzzle before today.'

'Where is she? What are you going to do?'

'Nothing.'

'What do you mean, "nothing"?'

'She's dead.'

'What? No! What happened?'

'There was also a letter in with Bill's things.'

'I'm not following you. What letter? A letter to you?'

'No. A letter from my mother to Bill. A letter she wrote to him after she left.'

'What did it say?'

'She'd had an affair. She told Bill she had fallen in love with someone else and she was leaving to be with him. Knowing they were never legally married meant she could just walk out. But she didn't take me with her.'

'Did she say why?'

'She said her boyfriend didn't want to take on another man's child. She said she would work something out and come back for me. But she never did.'

'Maybe she died before she could come back.'

'No. That wasn't it. She married that man and changed her name. In the letter she gave her new name and address. My father never shared that information with me. For years I'd been looking for a person who didn't actually exist. But today I did a search for her online. She died when I was eleven. Five years after she left me. Five years after she said she'd come back for me. She had time to do it if she'd really wanted me.'

The details in the letter confirmed that his mother had abandoned him, rejected him. She'd never come for him even though she'd had the opportunity to do so. The contents of the letter had shocked and upset him. He hadn't thought anyone could upset him more than his father had but today he'd discovered that his mother had been the cause of all his angst. He'd blamed his father all this time, assumed Bill must have done something that had pushed his mother away. He hadn't been able to forgive his father when he'd been alive and had blamed him for his awful childhood, but now he'd found out Bill hadn't been the only one to blame.

'I don't know whether Bill loved her or loathed her. Was that why he drank? We never spoke about her. Was I a reminder of her? Did he send me away because he couldn't stand the sight of me?'

Grace put her wine glass down and knelt between his legs. She took his hands in hers and held onto them. He let her hold him. It comforted him. 'Maybe he couldn't cope on his own but whatever their reasons your parents made their own choices. Whatever they did was their decision. Their responsibility. You are not responsible for their actions. You were a child. You are the victim in this.'

Maybe she was right. It was his history but maybe it wasn't his fault. And as his history maybe it was time he put it behind him. He kept trying to tell himself he wasn't that boy any more. That boy who had grown up unloved and unwanted. Maybe it really was time to let him go.

He sighed. 'They're both dead. This is it. The end of the line. Both of them are gone now. I know as much as I'll ever know.'

'Is it enough?'

It wasn't nearly enough but it was all he would have. 'It will have to be. So now I have to put it all behind me.' Like he'd done before. He knew he would mentally box the information up and quite possibly refuse to think about it any further. 'What's done is done.'

'Is there anything I can do?' she asked.

She was curled between his legs. Her shirt was untucked and he could see a sliver of bare skin beneath the hem. He slid his fingers under her shirt and rested his hand on the warm skin of her stomach.

Dusk was settling over the land, a warm breeze stirred the branches of their willow tree and frogs called out to each other, their sound replacing the chatter of birds. He felt as though they were miles from civilisation. His fingers slid higher on Grace's belly until he reached the swell of her breast. He slipped his hand inside the cup of her bra and felt her nipple peak as he ran his finger across it.

Grace sighed and shifted between his thighs. Her eyes closed and her lips parted and he decided he'd spent enough time for one day sifting through the past and trying to find answers that were probably not there. Here, under the willows, on the banks of the creek they were a million miles away from other people and that was just how he liked it. He could forget about everything that had happened today and focus on Grace. She made him feel calm and content. She made him feel happy. He knew it wouldn't last, nothing good ever lasted in his personal life, but he decided he'd enjoy it while he could.

He bent his head and kissed her. He would lose himself in her and everything would seem better. At least, for a while.

CHAPTER NINE

'MERRIDY SAID TO tell you that things are just about ready inside.' Grace spoke to her brother as she stepped outside to the barbeque.

'No worries,' Lachlan said as he turned the chicken skewers. 'Can I ask you something? Do you think Marcus is really serious about selling his land to us?'

She and Lachlan had discussed Marcus's offer over coffee the night before. Merridy and their parents had been there for the conversation too and Grace had filled them in on some of the details of Marcus's past twenty years but had kept the details about her personal involvement with him negligible. She figured all her family needed to know was that they worked together. She'd seen her mother and Merridy exchanging glances and wondered if they could see something in her face or hear it in her voice but if they suspected she was editing the story they didn't press her for further information.

'He's serious,' she replied. Lachlan should be having this conversation with Marcus, not her. It wasn't her business and she really didn't know much. But while she'd invited Marcus to the party a second time he'd, unsurprisingly, not accepted. She knew he wasn't overly comfortable in social situations and she knew he was even

more unsettled by being back in Toowoomba. He had a
lot of stuff to sort through, and she understood that, but
that didn't stop her wishing he'd accepted her invitation.
It might have done him good to be surrounded by a bit
of normality or, at least, what passed as normality in the
Gibson family.

'He doesn't want anything to do with Toowoomba,'
she added, 'and considering he lives in Perth, what would
he do with the land?'

If she had, even briefly, entertained the notion that
things could become serious between them she knew the
way Marcus felt about Toowoomba would be problem-
atic. While she didn't plan on living here, she did visit
regularly. She was inextricably tied to the town. Her family was here. In a way it was still home for her but Marcus felt very differently about it and she didn't think he
was likely to change his mind. He'd gone just about as
far away from here as was possible without leaving the
country. He'd said he was finished with Toowoomba and
she believed him.

Time hadn't healed his wounds as it had done for her.
Maybe now that he had closure over his mother's disappearance he would find peace, if not forgiveness. She
hoped so.

'We made an offer to Bill a few years ago,' Lachlan
said, 'but his lawyer turned it down. I don't want to start
the process again if it's just a hypothetical.'

Grace might wish she could help Marcus but she knew
he needed to release his emotions, willingly, before he'd
be able to move on. In the meantime, perhaps she could
help by assisting him to divest himself of his land. It
seemed to be what he wanted. 'Marcus told me that the
sale didn't go ahead because Bill wasn't in a sound frame

of mind and his will stipulated that Marcus would inherit the land so the lawyer had to reject your offer. The lawyer had power of attorney. If Marcus had had it, he would have sold it to you then. But he's meeting a property valuer there today. He means business.'

Knowing Marcus was literally next door made her wish even more that he'd accepted her invitation. But she hadn't wanted to push it. She hadn't wanted to pressure him into doing something he might not enjoy.

'Good to know. Can you let Merridy and Mum know I'll be done in ten minutes?' Lachlan asked as he put the steaks on the grill.

Lillian was in the kitchen when Grace went back inside.

'Lachlan will be done in ten,' Grace told her mother. 'Where's Merridy?'

'Gone to get some paracetamol, she said she had a bit of a headache.' Lillian glanced at the microwave clock. 'She's been gone a while—do you want to check on her? I'd hate for her to miss her own party.'

Merridy and Lachlan's bedroom door was ajar. Grace knocked and pushed it open. Her sister-in-law was lying on the bed.

'Are you okay?' Grace asked.

Merridy opened her eyes. 'I think I might be coming down with something. I've had a bit of a headache all day,' she said as she sat up. 'Oh.' She put a hand to her temple.

'What is it?'

'My headache's worse.'

'Do you want me to get you something stronger than a paracetamol?'

'No. I can't take anything stronger.' Merridy looked

at Grace. 'We were going to tell everyone at lunch but I'll tell you now. I'm pregnant.'

'That is so exciting! Congratulations.' Grace hugged her gently, taking care not to jostle her too much. She knew that Lachlan and Merridy had been hoping for this and that they'd had to put their baby plans on hold while Merridy recovered from her kidney transplant. 'Do you think this is morning sickness?'

'No. I'm twelve weeks, it's almost passed. This feels like a virus.'

'Have you got a temperature?' She put her hand on Merridy's forehead but that felt normal. 'Do you want to see a doctor?'

'No. I'm sure it'll pass. Just give me ten more minutes to see if the painkillers work.'

'I think it would be a good idea to get someone else's opinion. Why don't I get Dad or Hamish?' Grace's gut was telling her there was more going on here than just a virus. Merridy's colour wasn't quite right and she seemed a little vague. Her father was a doctor, and Hamish was a paramedic. Merridy's transplant meant she was prone to infections and now that she was pregnant Grace was uncomfortable ignoring her symptoms. A second opinion couldn't hurt.

She ducked out of the room to look for the others. She found Hamish first.

'Hame, can you find Dad, and ask him if he's got his medical bag in the car? I want him to check Merridy's BP.' Grace knew that, being a country GP, her father rarely went anywhere without his bag, which contained all the essentials for home visits and emergencies. He'd have his sphygmomanometer in there.

Grace went back to Merridy. She was lying down

again and Grace made her stay supine until Hamish and her father appeared. Grace quickly recounted Merridy's symptoms and the fact she was expecting, but there wasn't time to celebrate the news before she sent Hamish off again to fetch Lachlan while George wrapped the cuff around Merridy's arm and listened for her heartbeat.

'One fifty-five over one hundred and four. You need to go to hospital,' George announced as Grace's brothers entered the room.

'Do you want me to call a crew?' Hamish asked.

'We can drive her,' George replied. 'We'll be just as fast as the ambulance if we go now.'

Lachlan's face was drained of colour and Grace knew he was desperately worried. Merridy was almost oblivious to what was going on around her now. Happy just to let other, more qualified people make the decisions for her. 'We've got this,' Grace told Lachlan. 'You've got a doctor, a nurse and a paramedic here and I'll call Marcus too. She'll be okay.'

Grace sent Lachlan with Hamish, their father and Merridy. The rest of the family followed and Grace called Marcus as the convoy departed.

'Marcus. I need a favour,' she said when he answered. 'It's Merridy, my sister-in-law, the one who had the kidney transplant. She's not well. Her BP is dangerously high—one fifty-five over one hundred and four—and we've just found out she's twelve weeks pregnant. We're taking her to the hospital. Can you meet us there?'

Marcus made good time and pulled into the hospital car park, where he found Grace waiting for him by the emergency entrance.

'They've just taken Merridy inside,' she said as she greeted him with a hug.

Marcus was surprised by her greeting. They hadn't been publicly affectionate, and he never was, but he could see by Grace's expression that she was upset and realised the hug was for her own sake. He hugged her back, hoping that in some small way he could make her feel better.

'Thank you for coming,' she said as she released him, 'I know Dad will make sure she gets the proper attention but it can't hurt to have your opinion too. You're the expert.'

'Who is her nephrologist?' he asked, switching quickly into his professional persona. He was far more comfortable in that role.

'Elliot.'

Good. Knowing Merridy's specialist personally would make things easier, he thought as fell into step beside Grace. He would assess Merridy and then place a call to Elliot if necessary.

Grace stopped next to the triage desk and introduced him to her father. 'Dad, this is Marcus. Marcus, my dad, George.'

'We've got you on Merridy's paperwork as the consulting specialist,' George said as he shook Marcus's hand. There was no time and no need for Marcus to be nervous, they were just two doctors with Merridy as their focus. 'And I've sorted your visitation rights.'

Marcus nodded but didn't bother asking if everyone was happy to have him treat Merridy. Grace was right. He was the expert when it came to nephrology. This episode of hypertension might be completely unrelated to Merridy's transplant but his opinion was still worthwhile. Her transplant could not be ignored and treatment needed to be administered accordingly but also needed to take into account the fact that she was in the early stages of a pregnancy. 'Where is Merridy?'

'They've just taken her into a bay.'

Marcus cleared the cubicle of people, with the exception of Lachlan and the nurse who was hooking Merridy up to the monitors. He got Merridy's medical history from Lachlan as he waited for the monitors to start giving him the information he needed. No temperature, oxygen sats normal but BP dangerously high. According to Lachlan, when they'd seen Merridy's obstetrician a week ago her BP had been fine.

He ordered blood tests, looking in particular for infection of the kidneys or urinary tract, started medication for hypertension and got the nurse to hook up a saline drip. He put a call in to Elliot and also to Merridy's obstetrician, who confirmed Lachlan's recall, before going out to speak to Merridy's family. Lachlan didn't look as though he was capable of remembering the information so it was easier for Marcus to inform the family himself.

The waiting room was bursting at the seams and he was surprised and a little overwhelmed to find that most of the people there were Merridy and Lachlan's family. The entire party seemed to have relocated to the hospital.

'Other than high blood pressure, everything else looks normal so far,' he said reassuringly. 'She doesn't have a temperature, which is a good sign, but I'm running some tests for infection and started her on methyldopa to bring her BP down. You may remember, high blood pressure is a common side-effect of anti-rejection medication so this isn't unusual to see, but her pregnancy is a complicating factor.'

Merridy would need careful monitoring even once her

BP normalised as women who developed hypertension in their first trimester were twice as likely to develop pre-eclampsia than other women, but Marcus would let Merridy's obstetrician deal with that. His job was just to get things under control for now. 'The medication may take a few days to work so I'll get her admitted overnight. The hospital staff have my number and will let me know when the test results come back. Her GP should be able to manage things from here on but I will check on her in the morning before we go back to Sydney.'

Grace was shaking her head. 'I'm going to change my flight,' she said. 'I'll take a couple of days' leave and stay here. I can't go back now.'

He waited while everyone thanked him for his help, even though he was anxious to escape.

He headed for the car park but, aware he was being followed, he stopped walking and turned around. Grace's mother was behind him. She hadn't called to him, hadn't said anything, but he knew she wanted to speak to him. Why else would she be there?

She was an older version of Grace. The same petite build, her hair a slightly faded shade of red, the same amber eyes and with a few more lines. He experienced a flash of familiarity. Did he remember her or was he just seeing what Grace would look like in another thirty years?

'Thanks for your help,' she said as he stopped walking. 'I know my family would have managed but it's hard when the patient is a relative. We appreciate your expertise.'

'Don't mention it.' Marcus felt uncomfortable. Out of the confines of the hospital he was awkward and uneasy. He was eager to get away but it was obvious she had more to say.

'I also wanted to pass on our condolences about your father.' She hesitated and then continued, 'It seems wrong just to let it go unsaid, despite the circumstances.'

Marcus nodded. 'Thank you. It may have been a blessing in disguise, I'm not sure how much living he was doing.'

'Grace said his dementia was very bad. We hadn't seen him for several years. I didn't know he had deteriorated that badly.'

'You knew Bill?' Marcus couldn't reconcile the man he knew having had much to do with anyone in Toowoomba.

Lillian nodded. 'He was a patient of George's and I was the practice nurse. We knew your father.'

'And me?'

'Of course. But it's been a long time. I feel responsible for that.'

Marcus frowned. 'For what?'

'For sending you to Perth.'

'What are you talking about?'

'I was the one who rang your aunt. I was the reason she took you to Perth.'

'You?' It took Marcus a moment to process what he was hearing. What exactly was Grace's mother saying? 'I don't understand.'

'I phoned your aunt. Your father's…health was deteriorating rapidly.' Marcus could hear Lillian choosing her words carefully. 'The school had notified authorities and there were concerns for your welfare. We did what we could, bringing meals over and doing washing, but your father was…difficult. I was worried that you would be put into foster care and I didn't think that was a good solution, not even in a small town, and I knew you had other family. Your aunt was listed as your father's next of kin and so I called her. But I never imagined that my actions would mean it would be twenty years before you would see your father again.'

Marcus had wanted answers but this revelation was completely unexpected.

He needed to think.

'Thank you for telling me.' Lillian's admission reminded him that everyone in town knew everyone else's business. Reminded him of why he wanted to stay as far away from Toowoomba as possible. Although things had changed in twenty years, they hadn't changed enough for him. 'If you'll excuse me, I need to go.'

Lillian wasn't responsible for the fact that he hadn't seen his father for twenty years, he alone had made that choice. But it had always been based on the idea that his father had sent him away and apparently that hadn't been the case. Although there could be no denying that his father hadn't taken care of him while he had still been living with him. His father had chosen alcohol over his son and Marcus couldn't blame Lillian for trying to help him. She might have instigated getting him out of Toowoomba but this hadn't been the place for him anyway. It hadn't been at twelve and it wasn't now.

He didn't belong here. Not in Toowoomba and not with Grace's extended family. All these people were here for Merridy and the same people would be here for Grace if she needed them. But he had no one. He needed to leave. He didn't fit in with her world. And he would never belong.

* * *

'Grace, you need to come back to Sydney. Marcus is leaving.'

Grace had mentally replayed the conversation she'd had with Lola for the entire flight home from Toowoomba. Marcus had given notice and was leaving a few weeks before his time was up. If Grace didn't get home on the next available flight, she risked missing him altogether.

She couldn't understand what was going on. She'd called and left messages. He'd texted back but his messages had been impersonal—'Pleased to hear Merridy's doing better', 'Connie says hello'—and there was no sign of the intimacy she'd thought they'd so recently shared. No exchanges of confidences and never a hint that he was planning on leaving early. Part of her hoped Lola was wrong. Perhaps the hospital grapevine had made a mistake, but the chances were good that Lola knew something so Grace was returning to Sydney as quickly as she could.

Lola collected her from the airport and dropped her at Marcus's apartment block. She managed to get into the building as someone else left and she caught the lift to his floor. As she pressed the doorbell for his apartment she shifted her weight nervously from foot to foot. What if she'd missed him?

She couldn't believe he hadn't told her or that he'd been going to leave without saying goodbye. She had been so confident that they were building something worthwhile, had felt as if she was slowly peeling back his layers, that he was starting to share some of his feelings and emotions with her. Grace knew about the issues he'd had with his father and that he felt abandoned by his mother. She wasn't sure if she'd ever get him to reveal his whole self, she knew he had a lot to deal with and was still hurting, but she'd thought she was helping. She'd thought he trusted her.

Grace blamed herself. Her family. Her mother had told her of the conversation she'd had with Marcus. Was that why he was leaving Sydney early? Was it narcissistic to think it was all because of her?

He answered the door and Grace's heart gave a little flip. She hadn't thought it would be possible but in the week since she'd seen him she'd forgotten just how handsome he was and he almost took her breath away. He was clean-shaven and dressed in light cotton pants and a red T-shirt. He looked gorgeous.

'Grace. I wasn't expecting you.' His tone was flat and her heart plummeted. This hadn't been the greeting she'd been hoping for.

'Can I come in?' He hesitated and she was tempted to put her foot in the door in case he tried to close it. She wasn't going to let him leave without some sort of explanation. 'Lola told me you're going back to Perth early.'

He didn't deny that her information was correct. He stepped back and made room for her to pass.

'Is it because of me?' she asked bluntly. She didn't want to make it all about her but what other reason could there be for his abrupt departure? Honesty was important to him. Was that what this was about? Did he think she'd lied to him? Kept secrets from him that she should have shared?

'I had no idea my mother had had any role to play in removing you from your father. You can't think I wouldn't have told you that if I knew,' she said. 'My mother feels terrible. She feels responsible for you not going back to see your father.'

'It's not because of you. One of the nephrologists at the Queen Victoria Hospital in Perth has been diagnosed with pancreatic cancer. He's resigned from his position to spend time with his family. I'm going back to Perth to take over his caseload.'

'This has nothing to do with what happened last week, then? With my mother?'

He shook his head. 'This has nothing to do with what happened last week or twenty years ago and even that wasn't your mother's fault. I've spoken to my aunt. I would have been removed from Bill's care with or without your mother's involvement.

'According to my aunt, I never asked why I was in Perth. I just assumed Bill sent me away and I barely spoke about him after that. I never asked to see him and my aunt never made me visit. I doubt our relationship would have been any better if I'd stayed in Toowoomba. Losing his son wasn't enough to get Bill to sort out his life and that has nothing to do with your mother. There's no denying my life would have been different if I'd stayed in Toowoomba but your mother's actions meant I went to family and got opportunities I would never have got otherwise. I have a lot to be grateful for. This isn't her fault.'

Grace wanted to believe him but she sensed there was more to this than he was telling her. She wanted to know what that was but as she was trying to work out if she dared press him for more information she saw a suitcase in his bedroom, a laptop bag leaning against it. He was halfway out the door.

'You're leaving today?'

He nodded.

'That's it?' she said. 'You're not coming back?'

'No.'

He didn't apologise. He didn't say he'd miss her or invite her to go with him. He'd said his reason for going wasn't anything to do with her but she wondered if there was something more she could do, some way of making him stay. She almost asked him to take her too.

She realised that for their relationship to work he needed to be shown commitment, trust, love and respect but he had to offer those things in return. She wanted him to consider her. To want her. To need her.

But perhaps he didn't share the same feelings for her that she did for him.

Who was she kidding? It was perfectly apparent that he didn't.

She should tell him how she felt but she couldn't bring herself to. She couldn't bring herself to give him all of her as it was quite likely she would get nothing in return.

She had to set him free. Set them both free. If he didn't realise on his own that they were meant to be together, she couldn't force it on him. She'd tried to give him happiness but it seemed it was out of her control. He had to find it on his own.

She was prepared to stick with him through thick and thin but he had to be prepared to do the same. He deserved to be loved and she could do that. She loved him with all her heart but she needed his love in return.

And that was the crux of the problem. She'd done the one thing she hadn't planned on doing. The one thing she'd known would end in heartbreak. She'd fallen in love with him. And he was walking away from her without even a backward glance.

She swallowed her pride, her tears and her heartache.

She hugged him and wished him happiness in the future, and then she left. She couldn't let him see her tears. This time they were all for herself.

Marcus sat on the front veranda of his house near Margaret River. It was one of the few shacks that was still in almost original condition but its lack of modern amenities was superbly compensated for by its position. He could see the ocean from where he sat and could check out the surf conditions from his front door. He'd gone for a surf at first light and had not long returned.

This was usually his favourite time of the day, it was calm and peaceful, but today he felt lonely. He had never felt lonely until he'd met Grace. Until he'd started *missing* Grace. And he'd never felt lonely here before. Margaret River and this house was his sanctuary. Three hours south of the city, it was his escape and he loved it here. He had never shared this space with a woman but today he wished that Grace was here with him. Today he was missing her more than ever.

Leaving her was the hardest thing he'd ever done but at the time he'd thought it had been the right thing to do. He'd told her his reasons for leaving had had nothing to do with her family and he'd meant it, up to a point. It had had nothing to do with the past but everything to do with the future. Her family was at the centre of her world and he didn't belong there with them. He didn't know how to be a part of that life.

He would not be the kind of man her parents wanted for their only daughter. He wasn't enough for her. He couldn't be what she needed and he knew he would only disappoint her. She was better off without him. He wanted to be the person for Grace just as he knew she was the person for him, but he was terrified of letting her down. What did he know about love and commitment?

Marcus stared out at the ocean. The sea had always calmed him, given him a chance to think clearly and get perspective on his life, but he didn't like where his thoughts were heading today. Since leaving Sydney, he was being forced to face some harsh realities about himself. He'd always thought he had strength of character but now he was having doubts. Perseverance and persistence he had in spades when it came to his career, but he couldn't say the same about his relationships. He'd never had a serious relationship but whether that was due to a lack of desire for one or a lack of example to follow he didn't know. He'd certainly never wanted to try. Was that because he had an overwhelming fear of failure?

He didn't like to think like that of himself but he was worried it might be true. He'd told Grace he'd wanted answers from Bill and yet he'd been relieved to an extent when Bill's illness had made it impossible to have the difficult discussion. Had he deliberately left his visit too late? Knowing he would be able to blame a lack of communication for being unable to repair their relationship rather than blame himself?

He didn't want to leave things too late with Grace. He'd been getting too close to her and, afraid of failure, had left at the first opportunity. He had been afraid she wouldn't choose him.

This had nothing and everything to do with Grace.

She didn't need him, no one ever had, but he realised now that he desperately needed her. He'd been happy with her. And he hadn't been happy in a very long time. Maybe ever. In surgery he was content, satisfied with knowing he was good at his job. On his horse or his surfboard he was relaxed but neither of those pastimes could compare to how he felt when he was with Grace.

She'd told him to follow his heart. To be happy.

But he wasn't happy. He was lonely. And miserable.

Maybe he deserved it. Maybe it was genetic. His father had loved and lost. His father had been damaged and lonely. But he didn't want to end up like that.

Sitting on his veranda, contemplating his solitary existence, he knew he'd made a mistake. The reason to return to Perth had come at the perfect time, it had given him an opportunity to leave and he'd taken it, thinking it was the right thing to do, but then hindsight could be a terrible thing.

He'd definitely made a mistake. A huge one. It was his problem to deal with and he needed to fix it.

He missed her. He needed her. He wanted her.

He loved her.

CHAPTER TEN

THE SKY WAS beginning to lighten in the east, a soft pale blue tinging the horizon, and Grace knew it wouldn't be long before the harbour would be bathed in the golden glow of a new dawn. It was going to be a beautiful crisp, clear, winter's day, perfect for the 'Herd across the Harbour' muster.

The crowds were already gathering and she could hear the soft snuffling of the cattle that Lachlan and his stockmen had corralled in the park. She loved the sound of the cattle. They were surprisingly quiet considering their size and they seemed calm and relaxed. She knew Lachlan had chosen beasts that were used to being around people and horses, had specifically selected them for their temperament, and they were all used to being haltered. They couldn't afford to have any animals go rogue on them.

She smiled. She almost still couldn't believe that she'd been able to pull this off and that Bill Washington had been right. The Sydney Harbour Bridge remained a dedicated stock route. After Bill had dropped his bombshell she'd discovered that, provided you paid a toll, stock could be taken across the bridge between midnight and six in the morning. She had wangled permission to start the muster at six on a Sunday but, given that it was expected to take about two hours to get all the animals and the people to the south side, the walkway would be cleared and open for regular foot traffic before nine. The official stock route was the eastern pedestrian walkway so, in theory, the bridge was open to traffic but the council had agreed to reduce the speed limit and close some lanes to separate the traffic from the muster and avoid spooking the animals. And now they were almost ready to start.

The muster had been a lifesaver for Grace over the past four weeks. The project had kept her busy outside work. Too busy to think about Marcus.

Almost too busy.

She and Lola had spent hours talking about Marcus— she was kidding herself if she thought he was going to be easy to forget.

She loved him. But obviously that wasn't enough.

She missed him and she hoped he was okay but he had made his decision and she had to get on with her life now.

She checked the time. Five thirty a.m.

News helicopters buzzed overhead and there were several news vans parked on the side of the road. One of the national morning television shows was doing their weather broadcast from the bridge and several reporters had signed on for the walk. The crowd of people numbered in the hundreds now and all participants should have checked in for registration. Some were walking and some had paid extra to ride. So far they had raised close to two hundred thousand dollars and the television morning show hosts would advertise the 'Herd across the Harbour' website so that viewers could also donate to the cause if they wished. Grace was committed to a short interview on camera prior to the start but she had time to do one more thing.

Each participant was able to write an individual message on a 'Herd across the Harbour' ribbon that would hang around their animal's neck, either their cow or their horse, and they could take that home with them, along with their commemorative T-shirt, at the conclusion of the event. Prior to the walk they were able to have their photographs taken with their beasts before professional stockmen led the animals across the bridge.

Grace knew that Marcus had sponsored an animal, donating a huge sum of money to the cause in Bill's name and almost doubling their previous fundraising efforts with his gift, and she wondered if he had sent instructions for a message to be written. She went in search of Lola, who was in charge of handing out the ribbons. If Marcus hadn't left instructions, maybe she would write a message in memory of Bill. After all, this event wouldn't have been possible, not in the way she and Merridy had imagined, without him.

She bumped into Connie and her parents and sister on her way to the official registration area. Connie was recovering well post-transplant and she was thrilled to be taking part in the muster. Grace hugged her and wished her well before continuing on to the registration desks. Merridy, whose blood pressure was once more back under control, was seated at one of the desks alongside Grace's mum. Her father and Hamish were also at the event, co-ordinating the first-aid volunteers. It was a real Gibson family affair but Grace wouldn't have it any other way.

She found Lola standing nearby, chatting to Hamish, with the remaining few ribbons draped over her arm.

Considering it was five thirty in the morning, Lola looked amazing. Her skin glowed, she had curves in all the right places and her golden curls had that just-got-out-of-bed look that most men, as far as Grace could tell, couldn't resist, and that seemed to include her brother. Lola was touching Hamish's arm and he was hanging on her every word. He hadn't even noticed Grace's arrival.

Hamish's chiselled good looks would appeal to Lola too. Any good-looking man was on her radar and even though he was her brother Grace knew women found Hamish attractive. She wondered who had introduced them or had Lola recognised him from all the family photos Grace had displayed in their flat?

She wanted to warn Hamish that Lola was a serial flirt but she knew they would both laugh at her, and although Lola had had more lovers than Grace could count, she thought there was no way Lola would actually sleep with Hamish. Sleeping with your best friend's brother would be weird. So what harm could come of a little casual flirting?

She cleared her throat as she casually stepped between them. She didn't want to lecture them but that didn't mean she had to encourage them. 'Haven't you got something better to do than flirt with my best friend?' Grace teased her brother.

'Dad has everything under control,' was his response, although Grace noticed he barely took his eyes off Lola as he replied.

Grace didn't doubt that their father would be running a tight ship and it seemed Hamish had no intention of budging. She rolled her eyes and turned to Lola instead.

'I'm just wondering if Marcus sent any instructions for the wording on his ribbon?' she asked her.

'No. Would you like to write something?'

Grace hesitated. She knew what she wanted to write but would Marcus think it was appropriate?

'I don't think he'd mind,' Lola said with a smile as she handed Grace a ribbon and a marking pen.

Grace leant on the table and printed on the ribbon.

In memory of Bill Washington
1951-2018

Then, with a quick backward glance to find that Hamish and Lola were still chatting animatedly, she went to find a spare cow to claim for Marcus. She had too many things to do this morning to worry about Hamish and Lola. Besides, Hamish was only here overnight and Lola was working later. How much trouble could they get into in the next few hours?

She paused for a moment, thinking of both Bill and Marcus as she hung the ribbon around the cow's neck. She had a sense of being watched but as she looked around the crowd she realised everyone was too busy with their own experience to be interested in her. She gave one last thought to Marcus. It was three in the morning in Perth so he would be in his bed, not thinking about her, but her jealous streak hoped that he would at least be alone.

She spoke to the stockman who was responsible for a handful of cows, including this one, and asked him to meet her at the front of the herd before she went to check in with Lachlan. He was busy assembling the herd ready to be led off with the stockmen. The herd would be followed by the riders on horseback who would be followed, in turn, by the pedestrian sponsors. They were almost ready.

Grace found the television crew and took them to meet the stockman and Marcus's cow beside the starting line. She would use the cow as a prop for the interview. She waited while a battery pack and microphone were clipped to her clothing and for the lighting and sound technicians to get into position. The muster wouldn't begin until after her interview but she was eager to get it over and done with.

The reporter gave a summary of the event before introducing her. 'I have Grace Gibson with me. She is the renal transplant co-ordinator at the Kirribilli General Hospital and one of the event organisers. Grace, can you tell me how much money you are hoping to raise and where it will be going?'

'Good morning, Grant. We are aiming to raise two hundred thousand dollars and we are already close to that target.' Fundraising had exceeded their expectations, thanks to Marcus's generous gift in Bill's name, and Grace was confident viewers would continue to donate online throughout the course of the muster.

'Money raised will be used to purchase dialysis machines for rural and remote hospitals and to train nursing staff to use them. Each machine costs thousands of dollars but, given that dialysis is required three times a week and takes several hours each time, you can imagine the disruptive impact it has on people's lives. Country people also have to factor in travel time to the hospital if dialysis can't be done locally, or have the expense, stress and upheaval of moving to the city.

'Supplying dialysis machines to country hospitals will save time and money and reduce stress, but a kidney transplant is even better than dialysis for the majority of people. It's a cheaper option but, even more important, the long-term outcomes are better. Thank you to everyone who has already donated, but if you haven't yet donated to this cause and would like to, our website is up on the screen and you will also find more information about organ donation, living or deceased, there too. And now let's get this mob on the bridge.'

Grace stepped back and unclipped her microphone, waiting as an assistant unhooked the power pack. She made her way to the back of the herd where she had planned to follow behind with the walkers. She watched as the cattle started moving sedately onto the access ramp ready to traverse the bridge. She couldn't help the grin that spread across her face. It was really happening.

The cattle passed by and the horses began to follow. The noise level increased slightly as riders chatted as they guided their horses onto the ramp. Grace stepped further to one side, making room as she listened to the snippets of conversations in passing.

'Grace?'

A horse stopped beside her right shoulder and she looked up as she heard her name. Marcus was looking down at her.

She blinked, not sure she could trust her eyes. Was she imagining him?

'Marcus?'

He smiled at her, his teeth white in contrast to the designer stubble that darkened his jaw. He wore a padded vest to combat the crisp morning air. Under the vest, with its familiar embroidered longhorn logo, he wore a checked shirt, along with jeans that moulded to his thighs and stockman's riding boots. He looked good on horseback. He looked good in general. Actually, he looked better than good.

'What are you doing here?'

'I told you I'd ride.'

Her heart was racing. 'But that was before you left.'

'I came back. Will you ride with me?'

The horse nuzzled Grace and she lifted her hand and rubbed its face and looked at it for the first time as she wondered where Marcus had got a horse from. It looked familiar and seemed to recognise her. She frowned. 'Is this one of Lachlan's horses?'

He nodded. 'It's Percival.'

'I don't understand.'

'Hop up here with me and I'll tell you everything.'

He leant over in the saddle and held out his hand. The horse was an Arab and could easily manage to carry them both the relatively short distance over the bridge. Grace reached out and put her hand in his. His fingers closed around hers, warm and safe. Her palm tingled and her heart beat increased its pace a little further. He lifted her off her feet in one smooth movement and swung her into position behind him. She tucked herself tightly against him and wrapped her arms around his waist. She rested her head on his back, feeling the warmth of his body seep into her bones. She could smell the tang of the ocean, the fresh saltiness in the air as Marcus's familiar scent mingled with the smell of the sea.

She closed her eyes and breathed him in. She'd missed him. She gave herself a few moments to enjoy having him back in her arms, to enjoy the feel of him. This was where she belonged. With him. She knew it. She recognised it. She just wished he did too.

Marcus sat easily in the saddle. He held the reins

loosely and threaded his fingers through Grace's as he guided Percival forward with slight pressure from his knees.

'I don't understand how you're here, and how you've got Percival too,' Grace said.

'I will explain it all once we cross the bridge but for now I want you to have a look around and take all this in. You and Merridy have done an amazing job to bring this to fruition and I want you to savour the moment. You should be really proud of what you've achieved here.'

His advice was good and Grace listened to it. He was here and his words suggested they would have time to talk later. While the muster would take a couple of hours, Grace knew it would seem to pass in the blink of an eye. She wouldn't get this opportunity again. She needed to embrace it.

The view from horseback was incredible. Lines of cattle stretched in front of them and the walkers stretched out behind them. The walkway had become a functioning stock route once more. The sky was clear and bright as the sun began to warm the air. Helicopters circled the bridge and boats zipped across the harbour beneath them. It was a beautiful day. And Marcus was back. It was a perfect day.

By the time they reached the south side of the bridge the crowd was buzzing. On an adrenalin high from the experience, people milled around, reliving the muster and checking out the social media posts.

'Do you want to dismount and join in?' Marcus asked her.

Grace looked at the crowd. She had no desire to change her position. She was happy right where she was, with her arms wrapped around Marcus. Lachlan and Hamish would supervise loading the cattle and horses back onto the trucks that had followed them across the bridge and she suspected it was going to take longer than they'd anticipated as people did not seem eager to disperse. She had no urgent tasks to attend to. No one needed her right this minute. 'No,' she said with a shake of her head.

She didn't know what she'd expected Marcus to do next but she definitely hadn't expected him to keep on riding. 'Where are you going?' she asked as he turned the horse west and headed away from the bridge. 'We need to load Percival onto a truck.'

'Your family have everything under control, we've got some time. You're free to come with me, if you wish.'

She didn't need to think about her answer. 'I wish,' she said.

Marcus directed Percival up Observatory Hill, where he dismounted beside the old bandstand. He looped the horse's reins around the wooden balustrade and lifted Grace down before taking her hand and leading her up the steps into the rotunda, where they had a view back across the harbour past the bridge to Luna Park.

Grace wasn't interested in the view any more. Marcus was watching her intently and she couldn't think about anything other than the fact that he was back and looking at her like he never wanted to let her go.

He lifted his hand and ran his fingers over her cheek and Grace's breath caught in her throat. 'I missed you,' he said.

She wanted to reach up and hold his hand against her face. She wanted to keep him close for ever. 'I missed you too,' she replied, 'but I'm still confused as to what you're doing here.'

He wrapped his arms around her and held her close.

'I've been in Toowoomba. I flew over to see Lachlan and Merridy about the sale of Bill's—my—land. I told them I intended to come down to Sydney for the Herd across the Harbour and one thing led to another and Lachlan offered to lend me a horse. I wanted to see you, although I hadn't expected such a huge crowd. I was really worried I wouldn't find you.'

'I'm glad you did.'

'Are you?'

'I think so,' she said with some nervousness. Last time they'd had a face-to-face conversation it hadn't unfolded as she'd anticipated and she needed to know what had really brought him back. 'But I guess it depends on why you're here.'

'I'm here for you.' He lifted a strand of her hair and tucked it behind one ear. Grace's heart stuttered as his fingers brushed over her skin. 'I'm sorry I left you to go back to Perth. I should have asked you to come with me.'

'Why didn't you?'

'Because I wanted to save myself the pain of rejection. I've been trying to get away from my past and although you've shown me that my past can't hurt me any more, I was still afraid that no one could love me. That *you* couldn't love me. My parents both chose to prioritise other things over me. My mother ran away to start a different life with a new man, my father sought oblivion in the bottle. They didn't choose me.

'How could you love me if my own parents didn't? Your family is here, your work is here, your life is here. What could I offer you? I was afraid you wouldn't choose me and I was too scared to find out, but the pain of not having you, of knowing that I'd lost you and wondering if that was inevitable or if it was my own fault, was even worse. I thought you were better off without me. I didn't think I was enough for you. I didn't know if I could make you happy.'

Grace regretted the fact that she hadn't made her feelings clear to Marcus before he'd gone back to Perth. It was uncharacteristic of her to hold her tongue but she knew why she'd kept quiet. She'd been afraid of getting her heart broken, just as Lola had warned her. This was her second chance at happiness. He was here, he'd come back for her and she knew he needed to hear how she felt. 'You excite me, delight me, content me.' She smiled. 'And sometimes frustrate me, but all that is so much more than just making me happy. You make me feel alive. You let me breathe. I have been holding my breath for so long, waiting for something, but it wasn't something in the end, it was someone. It was you.'

'Me? You want me?'

'I want you.'

'Even with all my demons?'

'Demons?'

'Who knows what I've inherited from my parents? My mother's abandonment tendencies, my father's addictions? What if I break your heart?'

'Marcus.' Grace took his hands in hers, stilling him, making him listen. 'Look at everything you have achieved in the past twenty years. How far you've come. The choices you've made have been good ones. I don't think you have abandonment tendencies—you've stuck with your studies, you've come back for me, you've chosen wisely. You are a good man and you deserve good things in your life. You should have asked me if I wanted to be with you,' she told him. 'I would have chosen you.'

'Am I enough for you?'

'You are enough for me. You are *everything* for me.' He needed to know he had her love and commitment. He needed to know she wouldn't leave him, that he could trust her to stay. That he could trust her to give him her word and to keep it. 'Since the first moment I saw you again on the day of the press conference I was drawn to you. You captured my heart and you have it still.

'I need you to believe in me,' she said. 'I need you to believe in us. You have to believe me when I tell you that I will not leave you, that I will not choose someone or something else over you because if you are always waiting or expecting me to leave you, this won't work. I can't build a relationship without trust. Or love. I have always been open and honest with you. You just need to ask for my opinion or my thoughts and I will give them to you. Willingly. I will give you everything willingly. I will be here for you always. I love you and I choose you. Together we can be happy, so why don't you ask me again to come to Perth with you?'

'No.'

'No?' she asked, flinching.

'I've been offered a job back here. At Kirribilli General. Andrew Murray is retiring. So I thought, if you would have me back, I'll take the job and move to Sydney.'

She couldn't stop the smile that spread across her face. He was really coming back. To her. 'Are you sure this is what you want?'

His smile matched hers. 'I have never been more sure of anything in my life. You are everything I need. You have put me back together and you make me feel that nothing is impossible. Not even love. I'm in love with you, Grace—'

'You love me?' she gasped.

'I love you so much. I want a life with you, a family with you. I want to grow old with you but I am really here to ask you one thing.' He dropped to one knee and Grace's smile grew even wider. 'I came back to ask you if you would be my wife. I love you and I don't ever want to let you go. If you will have me, I promise to spend the rest of my life making you happy, making you proud and making you so crazy about me that you will wonder how you lived without me.'

'I'm already crazy about you.' She knelt down with him and cupped his face in her hands, pulling him towards her until their lips were millimetres apart. 'I love you too and, yes, I will marry you,' she said, seconds before he kissed her.

And with that kiss they sealed their future, their promises and their love.

* * * * *

TEMPTED BY
MR OFF-LIMITS

AMY ANDREWS

MILLS & BOON

I dedicate this book to my brother-in-law
Ron MacMaster, a great husband and father
who was taken too young.
You are greatly missed.

CHAPTER ONE

LOLA FRASER NEEDED a drink in the worse way. Thank God for Billi's, the bar across the road from the Kirribilli General Hospital. The ice-blue neon of the welcome sign filled her with relief—she didn't think she could wait until she got home to Manly and it was less than a thirty-minute drive at nine-thirty on a Sunday night.

The place was jumping. There was some music playing on the old-fashioned jukebox but it wasn't too loud. Most of the noise was coming from a large group of people Lola recognised as belonging to the Herd Across the Harbour event. It had taken place earlier today and they were all clearly celebrating the success of the fundraising venture.

Grace, Lola's bestie and flatmate, was the renal transplant co-ordinator for the hospital and had been one of the organisers. In fact, her entire family had been heavily involved. Lola had also been roped in to help out this morning before her afternoon shift, and although she'd gratefully escaped horses, cows and, well…anything country a long time ago, there had been something magnificent about all those cattle walking over the Sydney Harbour Bridge.

Talk about a contrast—one of the world's most iconic

architectural landmarks overrun by large, hooved beasts. It had certainly made a splash on news services all around the world. Not to mention the pile of money it had raised for dialysis machines for rural and remote hospitals. And then there was the exposure it had given to the Australian Organ Donor Register and the importance of talking with family about your wishes.

A conversation Lola wished her patient tonight had taken the time to have with his family. Maybe, out of his tragic death, some other families could have started living again.

And she was back to needing a drink.

She moved down the bar, away from the happy crowd. Their noise was good—celebratory and distracting—but she couldn't really relate to that right now.

Gary, a big bear of a man, took one look at her and said, 'You okay?'

Lola shook her head, a sudden rush of emotion thickening her throat. Gary had been running the bar over the road for a lot of years now and knew all the Kirribilli staff who frequented his establishment. He also knew, in that freaky bartender way, if a shift hadn't gone so well.

'Whaddya need?'

'Big, *big* glass of wine.'

He didn't bat an eyelid at her request. 'Your car in the multi-storey?'

Lola nodded. 'I'll get a cab home.' She had another afternoon shift tomorrow so she'd get a cab to work and drive her car home tomorrow night.

Within thirty seconds, Gary placed a chilled glass of white wine in front of her. It was over the standard drink line clearly marked on the glass. *Well* over.

'Let me know when you want a refill.'

Lola gave him a grateful smile. She loved it that Gary already knew this was a more-than-one-glass-of-wine night. 'Thanks.'

Raising the glass to her lips, Lola took three huge swallows and shut her eyes, trying to clear her mind of the last few hours. Working in Intensive Care was the most rewarding work she'd done in the thirty years of her life. People came to them *desperately* ill and mostly they got better and went home. And that was such an *incredible* process to be a part of.

But not everyone was so lucky.

For the most part, Lola coped with the flip side. She'd learned how to compartmentalise the tragedies and knew the importance of debriefing with colleagues. She also knew that sometimes you weren't ready to talk about it. And for that there was booze, really loud music and streaming movies.

Sometimes sex.

And she had no problems with using any of them for their temporary amnesiac qualities.

Lola took another gulp of her wine but limited it to just the one this time.

'Now, what's a gorgeous woman like you doing sitting at a bar all by yourself?'

Lola smiled at the low voice behind her, and the fine blonde hairs at her nape that had escaped the loose low plait stood to attention. 'Hamish.'

Hamish Gibson laughed softly and easily as he plonked himself down on the chair beside her. Her heart fluttered a little as it has this morning when she'd first met him on the Harbour Bridge. He was tall and broad and good looking. And he knew it.

Patently up for some recreational sex.

But he was also Grace's brother and staying at their apartment for the night. So it would be wrong to jump his bones.

Right?

She *could* have a drink with him, though, and he wasn't exactly hard on the eyes. 'Let me buy you a drink,' she said.

He grinned that lovely easy grin she'd been so taken with this morning. She'd bet he *killed* the ladies back home with that grin. *That mouth.*

'Isn't that supposed to be my line?'

'You're in the big smoke now,' she teased. 'We Sydney women tend to be kinda forthright. Got a problem with that?'

'Absolutely none. I love forthright women.' He gestured to Gary and ordered a beer. 'And for you?'

Lola lifted her still quite full glass. 'I'm good.' She took another big swig.

Hamish's keen blue eyes narrowed a little. 'Bad shift?'

'I've had better.'

He nodded. Hamish was a paramedic so Lola was certain she didn't have to explain her current state of mind. 'You wanna talk about it?'

'Nope.' Another gulp of her wine.

'You wanna get drunk?'

'Nope. Just a little distracted.'

He grinned again and things a little lower than Lola's heart fluttered this time. 'I give good distraction.'

Lola laughed. 'You *are* good distraction.'

'And you are good for my ego, Lola Fraser.'

'Yeah. I can tell your ego is badly in need of resuscitation.'

He threw back his head and laughed and Lola followed the very masculine line of his throat etched with five o'clock shadow to a jaw so square he could have been a cartoon superhero. Was it wrong she wanted to lick him there?

Gary placed Hamish's beer on the bar in front of him and he picked it up. 'What shall we drink to?'

Lola smiled. 'Crappy shifts?'

'Here's to crappy shifts.' He tapped his glass against the rim of hers. 'And distractions.'

They were home by eleven. Lola had drunk another—standard—glass of wine and Hamish had sat on his beer. They'd chatted about the Herd Across the Harbour event and cattle and he'd made her laugh about his hometown of Toowoomba and some of the incidents he'd gone to as a paramedic. He *was* a great distraction in every sense of the word but when she'd started to yawn he'd insisted on driving them home and she'd directed.

But now they were here, Lola wasn't feeling tired. In fact, she dreaded going to bed. She wasn't drunk enough to switch off her brain—only pleasantly buzzed—and sex with Hamish was out of the question.

Completely off-limits.

'You fancy another drink?' She headed through to the kitchen and made a beeline for the fridge. She ignored the three postcards attached with magnets to the door. They were from her Aunty May's most recent travels—India, Vietnam and South Korea. Normally they made her smile but tonight they made her feel restless.

She was off to Zimbabwe for a month next April. It couldn't come soon enough.

'Ah…sure. Okay.'

He didn't sound very sure. 'Past your bedtime?' she

teased as she pulled a bottle of wine and a beer out of the fridge.

He smiled as he took the beer. His thick, wavy, nutmeg hair flopped down over his forehead and made her want to furrow her fingers in it. There were red-gold highlights in it that shone in the downlights and reminded Lola of Grace's gorgeous red hair.

'I'd have thought Grace would still be up.'

Lola snorted. 'I'm sure she is. Just not here. Did you forget she got engaged to Marcus today?'

'No.' He grinned. 'I didn't forget.'

'Yes well…' Lola poured her wine. 'I'm pretty sure they're probably *celebrating*. If you get my drift.'

The way his gaze strayed to her mouth left Lola in no doubt he did.

'He's a good guy, yeah?'

'Oh, yeah.' Lola nodded. 'They're both hopelessly in love.'

Lola was surprised at the little pang that hit her square in the chest. She'd never yearned for a happily ever after—she liked being footloose and fancy-free. Why on earth would she suddenly feel like she was missing something?

She shook it away. It was just *this* night. This awful, awful night. 'Let's go out to the balcony.'

She didn't wait for him to follow her or even check to see if he was—she could *feel* the weight of his gaze on her back. On her ass, actually, and she wished she was in something more glamorous than her navy work trousers and the pale blue pinstriped blouse with the hospital logo on the left pocket.

Lola leaned against the railing when she reached her destination, looking out over the parkland opposite, the night breeze cool as befitting August in Sydney. She could just detect the faint trace of the ocean—salt and sand—despite being miles from Manly Beach.

She loved that smell and inhaled it deeply, pulling it into her lungs, savouring it, grateful for nights like this. Grateful to be alive. And suddenly the view was blurring before her eyes and the faint echo of a thirteen-year-old girl's cries wrapped fingers around Lola's heart and squeezed.

Her patient tonight would never feel the sea breeze on his face again. His wife and two kids would probably never appreciate something as simple ever again.

'Hey.'

She hadn't heard Hamish approach and she quickly shut her eyes to stop the moisture becoming tears. But he lifted her chin with his finger and she opened them. She was conscious of the dampness on her lashes as she was drawn into his compelling blue gaze. 'Are you sure you don't want to talk about it?'

His voice was low and Lola couldn't stop staring at him. He was wearing one of those checked flannel shirts that was open at the throat and blue jeans, soft and faded from years of wear and tear. They fitted him in all the right places. He radiated warmth and smelled like beer and the salt and vinegar chips they'd eaten at the bar, and she *wanted* to talk about it.

Who knew, maybe it would help? Maybe talking with a guy who'd probably seen his fair share of his own crappy shifts would be a relief. Lola turned back to the view across the darkened park. His hand fell away, but she was conscious of his nearness, of the way his arm brushed hers.

'My patient... He was pronounced brain dead tonight.

We switched him off. He had teenage kids and…' She shrugged, shivering as the echo of grief played through her mind again. 'It was…hard to watch.'

Her voice had turned husky and tears pricked again at the backs of her eyes. She blinked them away once more as he turned to his side, his hip against the railing, watching her.

'Sorry…' She dashed away a tear that had refused to be quelled. 'I'm being melodramatic.'

He shrugged. 'Some get to you more than others.'

The sentiment was simple but the level of understanding was anything but and something gave a little inside Lola at his response. There were no meaningless platitudes about *tomorrow being another day* or empty compliments about what an *angel* she must be. Hamish understood that sometimes a patient sneaked past the armour.

'True but… Just ignore me.' She shot him a watery smile.

'I'm being stupid.'

He shook his head. 'No, you're not.'

Lola gave a half laugh, half snort. 'Yes. I am. My tears aren't important.' This wasn't about her. It was about a family who'd just lost everything. 'This man's death shouldn't be about my grief. I don't know what's wrong with me tonight.'

'I think it's called being human.'

He smiled at her with such gentleness and insight she really, really wanted to cry. But she didn't, she turned blind eyes back to the view, her arm brushing his. Neither said anything for long moments as they sipped at their drinks.

'Was it trauma?' Hamish asked.

'Car accident.' Lola was glad to be switching from the *emotion* of the death to the more practical facts of it.

'Did he donate his organs?'

Hamish and Grace's sister-in-law, Merridy, had undergone a kidney transplant four years ago, so Lola knew the issue meant a lot to the Gibson family.

She shook her head. 'No.'

'Was he not a candidate?'

Lola could hear the frown in Hamish's voice as she shook her head, a lump thickening her throat. What the hell was *wrong* with her tonight? She was usually excellent at shaking this stuff off.

'He wasn't on the register?'

The lump blossomed and pressed against Lola's vocal cords. She cleared her throat. 'He was but...'

Her sentence trailed off and she could see Hamish nod in her peripheral vision as realisation dawned. It was a relief not to have to say it. That Hamish knew the cold hard facts and she didn't have to go into them or try and explain something that made no sense to most people.

'I hate when that happens.' Hamish's knuckles turned white as he gripped the railing.

'Me too.'

'It's wrong that family can override the patient in situations like that.'

She couldn't agree more but the fact of the matter was that family always had the final say in these matters, regardless of the patient's wishes.

'Why can't doctors just say, too bad, this was clearly your loved one's intention when they put their name down on the donation register?'

Lola gave a half-smile, understanding the frustration but knowing it was never as simple as that. 'Because we don't believe in further traumatising people who are already in the middle of their worst nightmare.'

It was difficult to explain how her role as a nurse changed in situations of impending death. How her duty of care shifted—mentally anyway—from her patient to the family. In a weird way they became her responsibility too and trying to help ease them through such a terrible time in their lives—even just a little—became paramount.

They were going to have to live on, after all, and how the hospital process was managed had a significant bearing on how they coped with their grief.

'Loved ones don't say no out of spite or grief or even personal belief, Hamish. They say no because they've *never* had a conversation with that person about it. And if they've never *specifically* heard that person say they want their organs donated in the event of their death. They...' Lola shrugged '...err on the side of caution.'

It was such a terrible time to have to make that kind of decision when people were grappling with so much already.

'I know, I know.' He sighed and he sounded as heavy-hearted as she'd felt when her patient's wife had tearfully declined to give consent for organ donation.

'Which is why things like Herd Across the Harbour are so important.' Lola made an effort to drag them back from the dark abyss she'd been trying to step back from all night, turning slightly to face him, the railing almost at her waist. 'Raising awareness about people having those kinds of conversations is vital. So they know and support the wishes of their nearest and dearest if it ever comes to an end-of-life situation.'

She raised her glass towards him and Hamish smiled and tapped his beer bottle against it. 'Amen.'

They didn't drink, though, they just stared at each other, the blue of his eyes as mesmerising in the night as the perfect symmetry of his jaw and cheekbones and the fullness of his mouth. They were close, their thighs almost brushing, their hands a whisper apart on the railing.

Lola was conscious of his heat and his solidness and the urge to put her head on his chest and just be held was surprisingly strong.

When was the last time she'd wanted to be just held by a man?

The need echoed in the sudden thickness of her blood and the stirring deep inside her belly, although neither of them felt particularly platonic. Confused by her feelings, she pushed up onto her tippy-toes and kissed him, trapping their drinks between them.

She shouldn't have. *She really shouldn't have.*

But, oh…it was lovely. The feel of his arms coming around her, the heat of his mouth, the swipe of his tongue. The quick rush of warmth to her breasts and belly and thighs. The funny bump of her heart in her chest.

The way he groaned her name against her mouth.

But she had to stop. 'I'm sorry.' She broke away and took a reluctant step back. 'I shouldn't have done that.'

His fingers on the railing covered hers. 'Yeah,' he whispered. 'You absolutely should have.'

Lola gave him a half-smile, touched by his certainty but knowing it couldn't go anywhere. She slipped her hand out from under his, smiled again then turned away, heading straight to her room and shutting out temptation.

CHAPTER TWO

BUT LOLA COULDN'T SLEEP. Not after finishing her glass of wine in bed or taking a bath or one of those all-natural sleeping tablets that usually did the trick. She lay awake staring at the ceiling, the events of the shift playing over and over in her head.

Her patient's wife saying, *'But there's not a scratch on him...'* and his daughter crying, *'No, Daddy!'* and his teenage son being all stoic and brave and looking so damn *stricken* it still clawed at her gut. The faces and the words turned around and around, a noisy wrenching jumble inside her head, while the oppressive weight of silence in the house practically deafened her.

She felt...alone...she realised. Damn it, she *never* felt alone. She was often here by herself overnight if Grace was at work or at Marcus's and it had never bothered her before. She'd *never* felt alone in a city. But tonight she did.

It was because Hamish was out there. She knew that. Human company—*male company*—was lying on the couch and she was in here, staring at the shadows on the ceiling. And because it wouldn't be the first time she'd turned to a man to forget a bad shift, her body was restless with confusion.

Was it healthy to *sex* away her worries? No. But it wasn't a regular habit and it sure as hell helped from time to time.

Lola had no doubt Hamish would be up for it. He'd been flirting with her from the beginning and he'd certainly been all in when she'd kissed him on the balcony. The message in his eyes when she'd pulled away had been loud and clear.

If you want to take this to the bedroom, I'm your guy.

And if he hadn't been Grace's brother, she would have followed through. And not just because she needed the distraction but because there was something about Hamish Gibson that tugged at her. She'd felt it on the bridge this morning *and* at the bar.

It was no doubt to do with his empathy, with his innate understanding of what she'd witnessed tonight. She didn't usually go for men who came from her world, particularly in these situations. Someone outside it—who didn't know or care what she'd been through—was usually a much better distraction.

Someone who only cared about getting her naked.

Who knew familiarity and empathy could be so damn sexy? Who knew they could stroke right between your legs as well as clutch at your heart?

Lola rolled on her side and stuffed her hands between her thighs to quell the heat and annoying buzz of desire. *Wasn't going to happen.* Hamish was Grace's brother. And she *couldn't* go there. No matter how much she needed the distraction. No matter how well he kissed. No matter the fire licking through her veins and roaring at the juncture of her legs.

Lola shut her eyes—tight.

Go to sleep, damn it.

* * *

At two o'clock in the morning, Lola gave up trying to fight it. Grace wasn't here—she'd texted an hour ago to say she was staying at Marcus's—and Hamish would be gone in the morning.

What could it hurt? As long as he knew it was a one-off?

Decision made, she kicked off the sheet and stood. She paused as she contemplated her attire, her underwear and a tank top. Should she dress in something else? Slip on one of her satiny scraps of lingerie that covered more but left absolutely nothing to the imagination? She'd been surprised to learn over the years that some guys preferred subtlety.

Or should she go out there buck naked?

What kind of guy was Hamish—satin and lace or bare flesh?

Oh, bloody hell. What was wrong with her? *Had she lost her freaking mind?* Hamish was probably just going to be grateful for her giving it up for him at two in the morning and smart enough to take it any way it was offered. She was going to be naked soon enough anyway.

Just get out there, Lola!

Quickly snatching a condom out of the box in her bedside drawer, she headed for her door, opened it and tiptoed down the darkened hallway. Ambient light from a variety of electrical appliances cast a faint glow into the living room and she could make out a large form on the couch. She came closer, stepping around the coffee table to avoid a collision with her shins, and the form became more defined.

He'd kicked off the sheet, which meant Lola could see a lot of bare skin—abs, legs, chest—and she looked her fill. A pair of black boxer briefs stopped her from seeing *everything* and his face was hidden by one bare arm thrown up over it. The roundness of his biceps as it pushed against his jaw was distracting as all giddy up.

As was the long stretch of his neck.

It was tempting to do something really crazy like run her fingers along that exposed, whiskery skin. Possibly her tongue.

But she needed to wake him first. She couldn't just jump on him, no matter how temptingly he was lying there.

Lola clenched her fists, the sharp foil edges of the condom cutting into her palm as she took a step towards him. Her foot landed on the only squeaky floorboard in the entire room and he was awake in an instant. She froze as his abs tensed and his body furled upwards, his legs swinging over the edge of the couch. His feet had found the floor before she had a chance to take another breath.

He blinked up at her, running his palms absently up and down the length of his bare thighs. 'Lola?'

Lola let out a shaky breath as she took a step back. 'I guess it's true what they say about country guys, then.'

'Hung like horses?' He shot her a sleepy smile. His voice was low and rumbly but alert.

She laughed and it was loud in the night. 'Light sleepers.'

'Oh, that.' He rubbed his palm along his jawline and the scratchy noise went straight to her belly button. 'Are you okay?'

Lola shook her head, her heart suddenly racing as she contemplated the width of his shoulders and the proposition she was about to lay on him. 'I…can't sleep.'

'So you came out for…a cup of warm milk?'

The smile on his face matched the one in his voice, all playful and teasing, and Lola blushed. Her cheeks actually heated! What the hell?

Since when did she start blushing?

Most nurses she knew, including herself, were generally immune to embarrassment. She'd seen far too much stuff in her job to be embarrassed by *anything*.

'No.' She held up the condom, her fingers trembling slightly, grateful for the cover of night. 'I was thinking of something more…physical.'

His gaze slid to the condom and Lola's belly clenched as he contemplated the foil packet like it was the best damn thing he'd seen all night. 'I have read,' he said after a beat or two, refocusing on her face, 'that *physical activity* is very good for promoting sleep.'

Lola's nipples puckered at the slight emphasis on 'physical activity' and she swallowed against a mouth suddenly dry as the couch fabric. 'Yeah.' She smiled. 'I read that too.'

He held out his hand. 'Come here.'

Lola's heart leapt in her chest but she ground her feet into the floor. They had to establish some ground rules. 'This can only be a one-time thing.'

'I know.'

His assurance grazed Lola's body like a physical force, rubbing against all the *good* spots, but she needed to make certain he was absolutely on the same page. 'You're leaving tomorrow,' she continued. 'We'll probably never see each other again.' This was the first time she'd met Hamish after all, despite having lived with Grace for almost all the last two years. 'And I'm good with that.'

'Me too.'

'I don't do relationships. Especially not long-distance relationships.'

He nodded again. 'I understand. We're one and done. I *am* good with it, Lola.'

'Also… I don't think we should tell Grace about this.'

He sat back a little, clearly startled at the suggestion, looking slightly askance. 'Do I look like I took a stupid pill to you?'

Lola laughed. He looked like he'd taken an up-for-it pill and heat wound through her abdomen. Hamish leaned forward at the hips and crooked his finger, a small smile playing on his wicked mouth.

'Come here, *Lola*.'

The way he said her name when he was mostly naked was like fingers stroking down her belly. Lola took a small step forward, her entire body trembling with anticipation. She took another and then she was standing in front of him, the outsides of her thighs just skimming the insides of his knees.

He held his hand out and she placed the condom in his palm. He promptly shoved it under a cushion before sliding his hands onto the sides of her thighs. Lola's breath hitched as they slid all the way up and the muscles in her stomach jumped as they slid under the hem of her T-shirt, pushing it up a little.

Leaning closer, he brushed his mouth against the bare skin, his lips touching down just under her belly button. Lola's mouth parted on a soft gasp and her hands found his shoulders as their gazes locked. One hand kept travelling, pushing into the thick wavy locks of his hair, holding him there as they stared at each other, their breathing low and rough.

Then he fell back against the couch, pulling her with

him, urging her legs apart so she was straddling him, the heat and pulse at her heart settling over the heat and hardness of him.

His hands slid into her hair, pulling her head down, his mouth seeking hers.

Her pulse thundered through her ears and throbbed between her legs and she moaned as their lips met. She couldn't have stopped it even had she wanted to.

And she didn't.

He swallowed it up, his mouth opening over hers, a faint trace of his toothpaste a cool undercurrent to all the heat. He kissed her slow but deep, wet and thorough, and Lola's entire body tingled and yearned as she clutched at his shoulders from her dominant position, moaning and gasping against his mouth.

He was all she could think about. His mouth and his heat and the hardness between his legs. No work, no death, no stricken children, no disbelieving wives. Just Hamish, good and hard and hot and *hers*, filling her senses and her palms and the space between her thighs.

Lola barely registered falling or the softness of landing as his hands guided her backwards. But she did register the long naked stretch of him against her. The way his hips settled into the cradle of her pelvis, the way his erection notched along the seam of her sex, the way his body pressed her hard and good into the cushions.

He was dominating her now and she loved it. Wanted more. *Needed* more. His skin sliding over hers. His body sliding *into* hers. It was as if he could read her mind. His hands pushing her shirt up, gliding over her stomach and ribs and breasts, pulling it off over her head before returning to her breasts, squeezing and kneading, pinching her nipples, his mouth coming back hard and hot on hers, kissing and kissing and kissing until she was dizzy with the magic of his mouth, clawing at his back and gasping her pleasure.

He kissed down her neck and traced the lines of her collar bones with the tip of his tongue before lapping it over her sternum and circling her nipples, sucking each one into his mouth making her cry out, making her mutter, *'Yes, yes, yes,'* in some kind of incoherent jumble. And he kept doing it, licking and sucking as his hands pushed at her underwear and hers pushed at his until they were both free of barriers.

He broke away, tearing the foil open and rolling the condom on, then he was back and she almost lost her breath at the thickness of his erection sliding between her legs. He was big and hard, gliding through her slickness, finding her entrance and settling briefly.

'You feel so good,' he muttered, before easing inside her, slowly at first then pushing home on a groan that stirred the cells in her marrow and lit the wick on her arousal.

She flared like a torch in the night, insane with wanting him, wanting him more than she'd ever wanted anybody before, panting her need straight into his ear, *'God yes*, like that,' revelling in the thickness of him, the way he stretched her, the way he filled her. 'Just like that...'

And he gave it to her like *that* and more, rocking and pounding, kissing her again, swallowing her moans and her cries and her pants, smothering them with his own as he thrust in and pulled out, a slow steady stroke, the rhythm of his hips setting the rhythm in her blood and the sizzle in her cells. Electricity buzzed from the base of her spine to the arch of her neck.

Her mind was blank of everything but the heat and

the thrust and the feel of him. The prison of his strong, rounded biceps either side of her and the broad, naked cage of his chest pinning her to the couch and the piston of his hard, narrow hips nailing her into the cushions. And the smell of him, hot and male and aroused, filling up her head, making her nostrils flare with the wild mix of toothpaste and testosterone.

Lola gasped, tearing her mouth from his as her orgasm burst around her, starting in her toes, curling them tight before rolling north, undulating through her calves and her knees and her thighs, exploding between her legs and imploding inside her belly, breaking over her in waves of ever-increasing intensity until all she could do was hold on and cry out *'Hamish!'* as it took her.

'I know.' He panted into her neck, his breathing hot and heavy, his body trembling like hers. 'I know.' He reared above her, thrusting hard one last time, his back bowed, his fists ground into the cushions either side of her head. *'Lola-a-a-a...'*

He came hard, his release bellowing out of him as his hips took over again and he rocked and rocked and rocked her, pushing her orgasm higher and higher and higher, taking her with him all the way to top until they were both spent, panting and clinging and falling back to earth in a messy heap of limbs and satisfaction.

Lola hadn't even realised she'd drifted off to sleep when Hamish moved away and she muttered something in protest. He hushed her as she drifted again. Somewhere in the drunken quagmire of her brain she thought she should get up and leave, but it was nice here in the afterglow.

Too nice to move.

Hell, a normal woman would have dragged him back

to her bed. It was bigger with a lot more potential for further nocturnal activity of the carnal kind. But then he was back and he was shuffling in behind her, his heavy arm dragging her close as he spooned her and she could barely open her eyes let alone co-ordinate her brain and limbs to make a move.

She was finally in a place where there was *nothing* on her mind and she liked it there.

She liked it very, very much.

CHAPTER THREE

Three months later...

HAMISH WASN'T SURE how he was going to be greeted by
Lola as he stood in front of her door. Sure, they'd *spoken* in the last few weeks since Grace had arranged for
him to live with Lola for the next two months while he
did his urban intensive care rotation, but they hadn't *seen*
each other since that night.

And he still wasn't sure this was the wisest idea.

He'd assured Lola that he could find somewhere else.
Had stressed that she shouldn't let Grace steamroller her
into sharing her home with him because his sister felt
guilty about her snap decision to finally move in with
Marcus. It was true, someone paying the rent for the next
eight weeks would give Lola time and breathing space to
find the *right* roomie rather than just *a* roomie, but Grace
wasn't aware of their history.

Unless Lola had told Grace. But he didn't think his
sister would be so keen on this proposed temporary arrangement if that had been the case. Neither did he think
for a single second that he wouldn't have heard from her
about it if she did know.

Lola had assured him she hadn't felt backed into a

corner and it made perfect sense for him to live with her temporarily. It would help her out and their apartment was conveniently located for him.

Perfect sense.

Except for their chemistry. And for the number of times he'd thought about her these past three months. He'd told her it had been unforgettable and that had proved to be frustratingly true. How often had he thought about ringing her? Or sending her flirty texts? Not to mention how often he'd dreamed about her.

About what they'd done. And the things he still wanted to do.

Things that woke him in the middle of the night with her scent in his nostrils and a raging erection that never seemed satisfied with his hand. He shut his eyes against the movie reel of images.

Just roomies.

That's what she'd insisted on when they'd spoken about the possibility of this. Insisted that what had happened between them was in the past and they weren't going to speak of it again. They definitely weren't going to *act* on it again

Just roomies. That was the deal-breaker, she'd said.

And he'd agreed. After all, it hadn't seemed *too* difficult over a thousand kilometres away. But standing in front of her door like this, the *reality* of her looming, was an entirely different prospect. He felt like a nervous teenager, which was utterly idiotic.

Where was the country guy who could rope a cow, ride a horse, mend a fence and fix just about any engine? Where was the paramedic who could do CPR for an hour, stabilise a trauma victim in the middle of nowhere in the pouring rain, smash a window or rip off a door and insert

an IV practically hanging upside down like a bat in the
shell of car crashed halfway down a mountain?

That's who he was. So he *could* share a home, in a
purely platonic way, with a woman he was hot for.

Because he was a grown man, damn it!

Hamish knocked quickly before he stood any longer
staring at the door like he'd lost his mind. His hand shook
and his pulse spiked as the sound of her footsteps drew
nearer.

The door opened abruptly and Lola stood there in her
uniform. He wondered absently if she was going *to* or
coming *from* work as his body registered more basic details. Like her gorgeous green eyes and the blonde curls
pulled back into a loose plait at her nape, just as it had
been that night at Billi's.

Suddenly he was back there again, remembering how
much she'd *touched* him that night. *Emotionally.* How
much he'd wanted to comfort her. To ease the burden so
clearly weighing heavily on her shoulders.

To make her smile.

She smiled at him now and he blinked and came back
to the present. It was the kind of smile she'd given him
when she'd first met him on the harbour bridge that
morning—friendly and open. The kind of smile reserved
for a best friend's brother or a new roomie. Like they
were buddies. *Mates.*

Like he'd never been inside her body.

She'd obviously put what had happened between them
behind her. Way, *way* behind her.

'Hey, you.' She leaned forward, rising on tiptoe to kiss
him on the cheek.

Like a sister.

It was such an exaggeratedly platonic kiss but his body

tensed in recognition anyway. She was soft and warm and smelled exactly like he remembered, and he fought the urge to turn his head and kiss her properly.

She pulled back and smiled another friendly smile and he forced himself to relax. Forced himself to lounge lazily in the doorway and pretend he didn't want to be inside her again. *Right now.* Because he really, really did.

This is what you agreed to, *dumbass.*

'That all you got?' She tipped her chin at his battered-looking duffel bag.

Hamish glanced down, pleased to have some other direction to look. 'Should I have more?' She didn't seem impressed by his ninja packing skills.

She tutted and shook her head. 'After two months in the city you'll need that for your skin products alone.'

Laughter danced in her eyes and Hamish was impressed with her ability to act like nothing had happened between them while he felt stripped bare. Lola Fraser was as cool as a cucumber.

'I'll have you all metrosexual before you know it.'

Hamish laughed. Was that what she liked in a man? A guy who spent more time in front of the mirror than she did? Who used skin care products and waxed places that he wouldn't let hot wax anywhere near? 'Thanks. I'm happy with the way I am.'

And so were you. He suppressed the urge to give voice to the thought. He wasn't naive enough to think he'd been anything other than a port in a storm for Lola. A convenient distraction. He'd known full well what he'd been agreeing to that night.

Hell, he'd been *more* than happy to be used.

'Ah I see. You can take the boy out of the country—'

'But not the country out of the boy.' He laughed again as he finished the saying.

She grinned and said, 'We'll see,' then stood aside. 'Come on in.'

Hamish picked up his duffel bag and followed her inside. Lola gave him a quick tour even though he was familiar with the layout from that night three months ago and nothing appeared to have changed.

The couch was *definitely* the same. He had no idea how he was going to sit on it with her without some seriously sexy flashbacks.

'And this is Grace's room.' Lola walked past a shut door on the opposite side of the short hallway, which Hamish assumed was Lola's room. 'She moved out a couple of days ago.'

Hamish hadn't been in his sister's bedroom when he'd last been here. He hadn't been in Lola's either. Not that that had stopped them…

'Make yourself at home.' She swept her arm around to indicate the space. 'It's a good size with big built-in cupboards and several power points if you want a TV or something in here.'

Hamish looked around. Grace had left her bed for him and the bedside tables. Everything was ruthlessly clean as per his sister's ways. They could have taken an appendix out on the stripped mattress. Although now they were both in the room together with a massive bed dominating the space, other things they could do on the mattress came to mind.

Lola was staring at it too as if she was just realising the level of temptation it represented. 'There are sheets, pillows, blankets, etcetera in the linen cupboard in the hallway.'

'Thanks.' Hamish threw his bag on the bed to fill up the acres of space staring back at them. And to stop himself from throwing her on it instead.

The action seemed to snap Lola out of her fixation. 'And that's it.' She turned. 'Tour over.'

Once again Hamish followed her down the hallway and into the kitchen, where she grabbed her bag and keys off the counter top. 'I'm sorry, I have to run now or I'll be late for work. I couldn't swap the shift.'

She didn't sound that sorry. In fact, she was jingling the keys like she couldn't wait to get out of there.

'It's fine.'

A part of him had assumed she'd be home this weekend to help him get settled. *Which was ridiculous*. He was a thirty-year-old man living in one of the world's most exciting cities—he didn't need to have his hand held.

And Lola was a shift worker, just like him. With bills to pay and a twenty-four-hour roster she helped to fill, including Saturdays. She had her own life that didn't involve pandering to her friend's brother.

'I'm sure I can occupy myself. What time do you finish?'

She fished in her bag and pulled out her sunglasses, opening the arms and perching them on the top of her head. 'I'm on till nine-thirty tonight. I should be home by ten, providing everything is calm at work.'

'Cool.'

'Help yourself to whatever's in the fridge. There's a supermarket three blocks away, if you're looking for something in particular. Grace and I usually shopped together and split the bill but we can discuss those details tomorrow.'

Hamish nodded. 'I'm having dinner with Grace and

Marcus tonight actually. At their new apartment. So we'll probably be getting in around the same time.'

'Oh…right.' She glanced away and Hamish wondered if she was remembering the last time they'd been here together at night. She had some colour in her cheeks when her gaze met his again. 'Don't feel like you have to be home for me. If you want to have a few drinks and end up crashing at theirs, that's fine. I'm often here by myself, it doesn't bother me.'

Hamish didn't think anything much bothered Lola. There was a streak of independence about her that grabbed him by his country-boy balls. But *he* knew that under all that Independent Woman of the World crust was someone who could break like a little girl and he really hoped she didn't feel the need to pretend to be tough all the time to compensate for how vulnerable she'd been the last time they'd met.

That would be an exhausting eight weeks for her.

And he just wanted Lola to be Lola. He could handle whatever she threw at him.

'And miss my first night in my new home?' He smiled at her to keep it light. 'No way.'

'Okay, well…' She nodded. 'I'll…see you later.'

She turned and walked away, choosing the longer route rather than brush past him—*interesting*—and within seconds he was listening to the quiet click of the front door as it shut.

Well…that was an anti-climax. He'd been building this meeting up in his head for weeks. None of the scenarios had involved Lola bolting within twenty minutes of his arrival. Still, it *had* been good, seeing her again. And she had *definitely* avoided any chance that they might come into contact as she'd left.

That had to mean something, right?

Hamish rolled his eyes as he realised where his brain was heading. *Get a grip,* idiot. *Not going to happen.*

And he went to unpack and make up his bed.

It was a relief to get to work. A relief to stop thinking about Hamish. It was crazy but Lola hadn't expected to feel what she'd felt when she'd opened the door to him. She'd actually been looking forward to seeing Hamish again. Quite aside from the sex, he was a nice guy and a fun to be around. Even a few months later she still caught herself smiling at the memory of the note she'd found the morning after they'd had sex on the couch.

You looked so beautiful sleeping I didn't want to disturb you.
I'm heading home now.
Thank you for an unforgettable night.
Hamish

He'd drawn a smiley face beside his name and Lola had laughed and hugged it to her chest, secretly thrilled to be *unforgettable*.

Sure, she'd known their first meeting after that night would be awkward to begin with but had expected it to dissipate quickly.

She'd been dead wrong about that.

His presence on her doorstep—big and solid, more jaw than any man had a right to—had been like a shockwave breaking over her. She'd felt like she was having some kind of out-of-body experience, where she was above herself, looking down, the universe whispering *He's the one* in her ear.

She'd panicked. Hell, she was *still* panicking.

Firstly, she didn't believe in *the one*. Sure, she knew people stayed together for ever. Her parents had been married for thirty-two years. But to her it was absurd to think there was only *one* person out there for everyone. It was more statistically believable, given the entire population of the world, that there were many *ones* out there.

People just didn't know it because they were too busy with their current *one*.

Secondly, she honestly believed finding *the one* didn't apply to every person on the planet. Lola believed some people were destined to never settle down, that they were too content with the company of many and being children of the world to ground themselves.

And that was the category into which Lola fell. Into which Great-Aunt May fell. A spinster at seventy-five, May hadn't needed *the one* to be fulfilled. Lola had never known a person more accomplished, more well travelled or more Zen with her life.

And, thirdly, if Lola fell and smacked her head and had a complete personality change and suddenly *did* believe in such nonsense, her *one* would never be a guy from a small town.

Never.

She'd run from a small town for a reason. She hadn't wanted to be with a guy who was content to stay put, whose whole life was his patch of dirt or his business, or the place he'd grown up. Which was why her reaction to Hamish was so disconcerting.

Hamish Gibson *couldn't* be the one for her.

No. She was just really…sexually attracted to him. Hell, she'd thought about him so much these past three months it was only natural to have had a reaction to him when she'd opened the door and seen him standing right in front of her.

But she wasn't going there again.

Which was why work was such a blessing. Something else to occupy her brain. And, *yowsers*, did she need it today to deal with her critical patient.

Emma Green was twenty-three years old and in acute cardiac failure. She'd been born with a complex cardiac disorder and had endured several operations and bucketloads of medication already in her young life. But a mild illness had pushed her system to the limit and her enlarged heart muscle into the danger zone.

She'd gone into cardiac arrest at the start of the shift down in the emergency department and had been brought to ICU in a critical condition. Which meant it was a whirlwind of a shift. There were a lot of drugs to give, bloods to take, tests to run. Medication and ventilation settings were constantly tweaked and adjusted as the intensive care team responded to Emma's condition minute by minute.

As well as that, there was a veritable royal flush of specialists and their entourages constantly in and out, needing extra things, sucking up time she didn't have, all wanting their orders prioritised. There were cardiac and respiratory teams as well as radiologists and pharmacists, physiotherapists and social workers.

And there was Emma's family to deal with. Her parents, who had already been through so much with Emma over the years. Her mother teary, her father stoic—both old hands at the jargon and the solemn medical faces. And Emma's boyfriend, Barry, who was not. He was an emotional wreck, swinging from sad to angry, from positive to despondent.

Not that she could blame him. Emma looked awful. There was barely a spare inch of skin that wasn't criss-crossed by some kind of tubing or wires. She had a huge tube in her nose where the life support was connected and securing it obscured half of her face, which was puffy—as was the rest of her body—from days of retained fluid due to her worsening cardiac condition.

Lola was used to this environment, to how terrible critical patients could look. She was immune to it. But she understood full well how hard it was for people to see someone they loved in this condition. She'd witnessed the shocked gasps too many times, the audible sobs as the sucker-punch landed.

The gravity of the situation always landed with a blow. The sudden knowledge that their loved one was really, *really* sick, that they could die, was a terrible whammy. So Emma's boyfriend's reactions were perfectly normal, as far as Lola was concerned.

And all just part of her job.

'It really is okay to talk to her,' Lola assured Barry as he sat rigidly in a chair by the window, repeatedly finger-combing his hair. It was the first time he'd been alone with Emma since she'd been admitted. Her mother and father were taking it in turns to sit with Barry at the bedside but they'd both ducked out for a much-needed cup of coffee and a bite to eat.

Barry glanced at Emma and shook his head. 'I don't want to get in the way or bump anything.'

Lola smiled. 'It's okay, I'll be right here keeping an eye on you.' She kept it light because she could tell that Barry was petrified of the high-tech environment, which was quite common. 'And I promise I'll push you out the way if I need to, okay?'

He gave a worried laugh, still obviously doubtful, and Lola nodded encouragingly and smiled again. 'I'm sure she'd love to hear your voice.'

His eyes flew to Lola's in alarm. 'I thought she was sedated.'

'She is,' Lola replied calmly. 'But even unconscious patients can still hear things. There have been plenty of people who've woken from comas or sedation and been able to recite bedside conversations word for word.'

Barry chewed on his bottom lip. 'I...don't know what to say to her.'

The despair in his voice hit Lola in every way. Barry was clearly overwhelmed by everything. She gestured him over to the seat Emma's mother had vacated not that long ago. He came reluctantly.

'Just tell her you're here,' Lola said, as he sat. 'Tell her you love her. Tell her she's in safe hands.'

'Okay.' Barry's voice trembled a little.

Lola turned to her patient. 'Emma,' she said quietly, placing a gentle hand on Emma's forearm, 'Barry's here. He's going to sit with you for a while.'

There wasn't any response from Emma—Lola didn't expect there would be—just the steady rise and fall of her chest and the rapid blipping of her monitor. Lola smiled at Barry as she withdrew her hand. 'Just put your hand where I had mine, okay? There's nothing you can bump there.' Barry tentatively slid his hand into place and Lola nodded. 'That's good. Now just talk to her.'

Lola moved away but not very far, hovering until Barry became more confident. He didn't say anything for a moment or two and when he started his voice was shaky but he *started*. 'Hey, Emsy.' His voice cracked and he cleared it. 'I'm here and… I'm not going anywhere. You're in good hands and everything's going to be okay.'

Lola wasn't entirely sure that was true. She knew how fragile Emma's condition was and part of her was truly worried her patient wasn't going to make it through the shift. But humans needed hope to go on, to *endure*, and she'd certainly been proved wrong before by patients.

Barry was doing the right thing. For him *and* for Emma.

CHAPTER FOUR

'SO? WHEN *ARE* you going to settle down?'

Hamish sighed at his sister, who was slightly tipsy after a few glasses of champagne. They were sitting on the balcony of their new apartment, which was also in Manly but at the more exclusive end, with harbour views. Marcus had moved out of his apartment near Kirribilli General when he and Grace had decided to move in together because they'd wanted an apartment that was *theirs*.

'God, you're like a reformed smoker. You're in love so you want everyone else to be as well.'

Grace smiled at Marcus, who smiled back as he slid his hand onto her nape. Hamish rolled his eyes at them but it was obvious his sister was in love and he was happy for her. She'd had a tough time in her first serious relationship so it was good to see her like this.

'You're thirty, Hamish. You're not getting any younger. Surely there has to be some girl in Toowoomba who takes your fancy.'

'There's no point getting into a relationship when I'm hoping to spend a few years doing rural service after the course is done.'

Hamish had recently been passed over for a transfer

to a station in the far west of the state because he didn't have an official intensive care paramedic qualification, even though he had the skills. It had spurred him to apply for a position on the course.

'It's hardly fair to get involved with someone knowing I could be off to the back of beyond at a moment's notice,' he added.

Grace sighed in exasperation. 'Maybe she'd want to go with you.'

Unbidden, an image of Lola slipped into his mind. He couldn't begin to imagine her in a small country town. She'd cornered the market in exotic city girl. She was like a hothouse flower—temperamental, high maintenance—and the outback was no place for hothouse flowers.

Women had to be more like forage sorghum. Durable and tough. And although Lola *was* tough and independent in many ways, there was something indefinably *urban* about her.

'I don't know whether you know this or not, but you're a bit of catch, Hamish Gibson. Good looking even, though it pains me to admit it. Don't you think so, Marcus?'

Grace smiled at her fiancé, a teasing light in her eyes. 'Absolutely,' he agreed, his expression totally deadpan. 'I was just saying that very thing to Lola the other day.'

Lola.

It seemed the universe was doing its best to keep her on his mind. 'And did she agree?' Hamish was pretty sure Marcus was just making it up to indulge his sister but, hell, if they'd had a conversation about him, then Hamish wanted to know!

'Of course she'd agree,' Grace said immediately. 'Lola can pick good looking out of a Sydney New Year's Eve crowd blindfolded.'

Hamish grinned at his sister. 'I'll have to remember that this New Year.'

Something in Hamish's voice must have pinged on his sister's radar. Apparently she wasn't tipsy *enough* to dull that sucker. Her eyes narrowed as her gaze zeroed in on him. '*No*, Hamish.'

'What?' Hamish spread his hands in an innocent gesture.

'You and Lola would *not* be good for each other.'

Hamish grabbed his chest as if she'd wounded him. 'Why not?'

'Because you're too alike. You're both flirts. You like the conquest but suck at any follow-through. You have to *live together* for two months, Hamish. That's a lot of awkward breakfasts. And I don't want to be caught in the middle between you two or have my friendship with Lola jeopardised because you couldn't keep it in your pants.'

Hamish didn't think Lola would be the one who'd get burned in a relationship between the two of them. He at least was open to the idea of relationships—she, on the other hand, was not. He glanced at his soon-to-be brother-in-law. 'Help me out here, man.'

Marcus laughed and shook his head. 'You're on your own, buddy.'

'C'mon, dude. Solidarity.'

Grace shook her head at her brother. 'In an hour I'm going to take my fiancé to bed and do bad things to him. You think he's going to side with you?'

Hamish glanced at a clearly besotted Marcus, who was smiling at Grace like the sun rose and set with her, and a wave of hot green jealousy swamped his chest. He wanted that. What his sister had found with Marcus.

Contrary to *apparent* popular opinion, he'd never been

opposed to settling down. He just hadn't found the right woman. For ever was, after all, a *long* time! But watching these two together...

They were the perfect advertisement for happily ever after.

Once upon a time the idea of eternal monogamy would have sent him running for the hills but these two sure knew how to sell it.

'Okay. Well, that was TMI.' He gave the lovebirds an exaggerated grimace. 'And is definitely my cue to go.'

He stood, but his sister wasn't done with him yet. 'I mean it, Hamish. I wouldn't have suggested you move in with Lola if I thought you'd make a move on her.'

'I'm not going to,' he protested.

Clearly, Grace didn't believe him. 'She's off-limits, okay?'

He was much too much of a gentleman to suggest Grace have this conversation with her bestie who had all but jumped him three months ago. But it did annoy him that somehow he was the bad guy here. 'I think Lola can take care of herself.'

Grace shook her head at his statement, thankfully a little too tipsy to read anything into his terseness. 'She comes across that way, I know. Brash and tough and in control. But she feels things as deeply as the next woman.'

A memory of Lola's glistening eyelashes flashed on his retinas, the weight of her sadness about her patient as tangible now as it had been that night. Hamish sighed. Yeah. He knew how deeply Lola felt.

'Lola and I are roomies *only*.' He moved around to his sister and kissed her on the top of her head. 'Thank you for dinner.' She went to stand but he placed a hand on her shoulder. 'You guys stay there. I can let myself out.'

Grace squeezed the hand on her shoulder. 'Good luck on Monday. Ring me and let me know how your first shift went.'

'I will.' Hamish shook Marcus's hand. 'Goodnight.'

He left them to it, happy that his sister had found love but pleased to be away from their enviable public displays of affection.

Lola enjoyed about five seconds of contentment when she woke on Sunday morning before she remembered who was sleeping in the room across the hallway.

The feeling evaporated immediately.

She rolled her head to the side. Nine thirty. Normally she'd stretch and sigh happily and contemplate a lazy Sunday morning. No work to get to. No place to be. Her time her own.

Normally she'd walk down to one of the cafés that lined the Manly esplanade to eat smashed avocado and feta on rye bread while she watched people amble past. Maybe even stay in bed, read a good book. Or sloth around in front of the television, watching rom coms and eating Vegemite toast.

But she wasn't going to be able to sloth around for the next two months. Because Hamish was here.

Lola stared at the ceiling fan turning lazy circles above her. It was dark and cool in her room as it was on the western side of the apartment but the prediction was for a warm day. She strained her ears to hear any movement from outside.

Was he up?

Lola shut her eyes as that led to completely inappropriate thoughts and a strange dropping sensation in the pit of her stomach.

Do not think about Hamish being *up,* Lola.

Was he out of bed? That was more appropriate. She couldn't hear any noises but she'd bet her last cent he was. He was a country boy after all. And she'd known enough of them in her life to know they liked their sunrises.

Ugh. Give her a sunset any day.

Gathering her courage, she sat up and swung her legs out of bed. She had to face him some time. She couldn't spend the next two months avoiding him like she had yesterday, running out on him about twenty minutes after he'd arrived and nodding a quick hello to him last night before heading to her room with the excuse of being tired.

So just get out there, already, and face him!

Dressing quickly in a simple floral sundress with shoestring straps, Lola pulled the band on her plait and fluffed out her hair a little. She'd left it in overnight to help with knot control and to tame the curls to a crinkly wave instead of a springy mess.

But that was it—she refused to make herself pretty for Hamish. Normally when meeting a guy she'd put on some make-up, spray on her favourite perfume and wear her best lingerie. Today she was wearing no make-up, she smelled only of the washing powder she used on her clothes and she deliberately chose mismatched, *comfortable* underwear.

Not that he was in the kitchen or the living room when she made an appearance and, for a second, a ribbon of hope wound through her belly before she flicked her gaze to the balcony to find him sitting at the table. Resigned, Lola poured two glasses of juice, slamming most of hers down before topping it up and wondering if it was too early for a slug of vodka.

Pulling in a steadying breath, she picked up the glasses and went out to make polite conversation. He turned as she slid the screen door open. Her heart was practically in her mouth as she prepared herself for her body to go crazy again but the incredibly visceral reaction from yesterday didn't reappear and Lola smiled in relief.

It had clearly been an anomaly.

He smiled back and her belly swooped but it was still an improvement on yesterday. Plus, he *was* sitting there shirtless. A damp pair of running shorts clinging to his thighs was the only thing keeping him decent and that was up for debate.

'You've been for a run?' Lola gave herself full marks for how normal she sounded as she slid his glass across the tabletop. She was going to need to channel a lot of that if he was planning on walking around here shirtless very often.

'Yep.' He lifted the glass as if he was toasting her and swallowed the whole thing in several long gulps. Gulps that drew her gaze to the stretch of his neck and those gingery whiskers. 'Thanks.' He put the glass on the table. 'I needed that.'

She noticed he had an empty water bottle by his elbow.

'I can get you some more.' Lola stood. She needed a moment after that display of manliness. Escaping to the fridge seemed the perfect excuse.

He waved her back down. 'Nah. I'm good.'

'So you…run every morning.'

'Not every morning. But regularly enough. I figured it was a good way to get to know the neighbourhood.'

'Did you make it to the beach?'

'Yep. Ran along the esplanade. It's very different to the scenery I'm used to.'

It was about five kilometres to the beach so he'd already run ten kilometres this morning. *While she was sleeping.* She'd have felt like a sloth if she was capable of feeling anything other than lust.

'A lot more beach, I'd imagine.' Toowoomba was a regional inland city, well over a hundred kilometres to the nearest beach.

'Yes.' He laughed. 'Are you a runner?'

It was Lola's turn to laugh. 'I'm more of a hit-and-miss yoga in the park kinda gal.' If she was going to get hot, sweaty and breathless, she could think of much more satisfying ways to do it. Preferably naked.

'I saw a group doing that.'

'Yeah, there's a regular morning and afternoon class not far from the beach.'

Lola hadn't been in a while. Who knew, maybe living with Mr Exercise would guilt her into being more energetic herself and she was clearly going to need to put her sexual energy somewhere. Just sitting opposite him was hell on her libido.

'What are your plans for the day?' Time to move the conversation to safer territory.

He shrugged those big bare shoulders and Lola resisted the urge to stare. 'Thought I'd do a bit of sightseeing. It's pretty full on for the next couple of weeks. Might take me a while to get out again.'

'That's a great idea. It's not your first time to Sydney, though?'

'No. I've been a few times but until recently not for almost ten years.'

Lola only just stopped herself from gaping at Hamish.

Ten years? Had he been *anywhere* in a decade? 'So you'll be doing the usual, then? You saw the bridge a few months ago, probably more intimately than anyone in the city, actually. You should definitely climb it while you're here.'

Lola had climbed the Sydney Harbour Bridge several times. She loved the rush of adrenaline that heights gave her. That any kind of precarious situation gave her—from white-water rafting to bungee jumping to zip lining.

The thrill. The buzz. It was better than sex.

It was also why she was such a good ICU nurse. She knew how to ride the adrenaline in critical situations. She appreciated how it honed her reactions and sharpened her focus. She thrived on how well she anticipated orders, knowing what was going to be asked for even before it was, putting her hand to something a second before the doctor wanted it.

'I'd love to climb it. It's on my to-do list. Today I was just going to get a ferry across to Circular Quay and check out the Opera House and Darling Harbour.' Lola glanced at the layers of blue sky crowning the ancient trees in the park opposite, pleased for the distraction from his body. 'It's a good day for it. And an easy walk into the city from there.'

Especially for someone who'd just run ten kilometres. And had those legs. And those abs. And that chest.

Bloody hell.

'Grace's favourite haunt is the Rocks area; you'll find a lot of old convict-era stuff there. You can walk it or jump on one of those hop-on, hop-off buses.'

'And what's *your* favourite haunt?'

Lola's breath caught at the tease in his tone and the

flirt in his smile. 'Sydney's such a beautiful city, it's hard to choose.'

'Oh, come on.' He rolled his eyes at her. 'You must have a place you love more than any other.'

She did. But… 'My favourite place is not a tourist spot.'

'Ah. It's a secret? Even better.'

Lola smiled at him—she couldn't not. He was hard to resist when he was teasing, so endearingly boyish. He must have broken some hearts in high school.

'Not a secret. It's just a street I really love.'

'Does this street have a name? Spill, woman.'

Lola laughed. This was better. If she could hide behind some friendly teasing and banter the next couple of months might not be so awkward. 'I find these things are more meaningful if you stumble across them yourself.'

He snorted. 'I'm here for two months. How long did it take you to find it?'

She smiled. 'About two years.'

'Well, then.' He stood and Lola's pulse fluttered. 'I insist you take me there. Today. And I solemnly swear…' he slapped a clenched fist against his sternum, which was dizzily distracting '…to keep it a secret, on pain of death.'

Lola hadn't shown anyone her spot. Well, she'd told Grace and May about it but neither of them had seen it yet and she'd never really wanted to share it with a guy. She couldn't have borne it if he'd been dismissive of something that was essentially girly.

But, surprisingly, she *wanted* to show Hamish. Maybe she was being influenced by the whole country-boy thing but she had a feeling he appreciated nature and that he'd understand why she loved it so much.

And she hadn't checked it out this season yet so what

better way to visit than playing tour guide? Plus it would occupy the day and give them a chance to establish a rapport that wasn't sexual. After today they'd probably pass like ships in the night—the hazards of shift work— so starting as she meant them to go on was a good idea.

'Okay.' She nodded. 'But only because this is actually the most perfect time of year to see it.'

'Well, that sounds even more intriguing. I'll just have a quick shower. Give me fifteen minutes.'

Lola's gaze followed him into the apartment. Broad shoulders swept down to a pair of fascinating dimples just above the waistband of his shorts. Two tight ass cheeks filling out said shorts in a way that almost made Lola believe in miracles.

And possibilities.

She tried really hard not to imagine him stripping off and stepping into the shower, water clinging to his body, running *everywhere*, wet and soapy and slippery.

She failed dramatically.

CHAPTER FIVE

WITHIN HALF AN hour Hamish was following Lola onto one of the harbour's iconic yellow and green ferries, enjoying the way her sundress fluttered around mid-thigh and the way she kept scooping up her right shoulder strap as it slipped off repeatedly.

He was pleased but surprised she'd agreed to this outing. He'd been expecting to be rebuffed, for her to keep putting him firmly at a distance. But then she'd invited him to her secret spot as if she'd made some kind of decision to accept him and their situation and wild horses couldn't have dragged him away.

He liked Lola and, who knew, maybe they could even become friends? He doubted they were the only two people in the world who'd fallen into bed and wound up as friends.

'So, we're taking the ferry?' Hamish said as Lola led him to the bow and lowered herself into one of the open-air seats. She looked very city chic in her big sunglasses, short and cute and curvy, her hair blowing around her shoulders, her cutesy dress riding up high on her thighs.

Hamish felt very *country* next to her.

'Yep. Have you been on the harbour before?'

He nodded. 'When I was in high school. Mum and Dad took us on the ferry to Taronga Zoo.'

The engines rumbled out of idle and the boat pulled away from the wharf. She breathed in deeply and sighed. 'I love taking the ferry. We're so lucky here, the harbour is gorgeous. The best in the world.'

Hamish laughed. 'Biased much?' It *was* a beautiful day, though. The sky was a stark blue dome unblemished by clouds, the sun a glorious shining bauble, refracting its golden-white light across the surface of the water like a glitter ball.

'Nope.' She shook her head and her curls, already fluttering in the breeze, swung some more. 'Trust me, I've been to a lot of harbours but Sydney wins the prize.'

'Well travelled, huh?'

Hamish realised he didn't know much about Lola at all. And the only person he could ask was his sister, who would have been highly suspicious of his interest.

'I've done quite a bit of travelling, yes.'

'What's quite a bit?'

She crossed one leg over the other and Hamish tried not to look at the dress hem riding up a little more. 'I lived in the UK for several years after I finished my degree. I did a lot of agency nursing to support my travel obsession. I've been back here for four years but go travelling again at least once a year. I've backpacked extensively through Asia, Europe and America and seen a little of Africa.'

Hamish whistled. 'Intrepid. I like it. Got any favourites?'

She didn't hesitate. 'India. It's such a land of contrasts. And Iceland. So majestic.' She glanced at him and he could just make out her eyes behind those dark brown lenses. 'It's my goal to go to every country in the world before I die.'

'A worthy goal.'

'I'm off to Zimbabwe next April.'

'On a safari thing?'

She smiled. 'For some of it. What about you? Ever had a hankering to see the world or are you one of those people who think living in the country is the be all and end all?'

Hamish blinked at the fine seam of bitterness entrenched in her words. 'Hey,' he protested, keeping it light. 'What have you got against living in the country? Don't knock it till you've tried it.'

She snorted and even that was cute. 'No, thanks. I spent seventeen years in the middle of bloody nowhere. I've paid my dues.'

Hamish stared at her. Lola Fraser had come from the sticks? He'd never met a female more *urban* in his life. 'Whereabouts?'

'You won't have heard of it.'

Hamish folded his arms. 'Try me.'

He was pretty sure she was rolling her eyes at him behind those shades.

'Doongabi.'

Yeah...she was right. He hadn't heard of it. 'Nope.'

'Imagine my surprise.' He could *hear* the eye-roll now. 'It's a rural community way past west of Dubbo, population two thousand.'

'And you couldn't wait to get out?'

'You can say that again.'

'Was it that bad?' Hamish was intrigued now.

She sighed. 'No.' Her strap slipped down giving him a peek at the slope of her breast before she pulled it back into place. 'It's a nice enough town, if that's your thing, I suppose. But it's hard to be put in a small-town strait-jacket when you were born a free spirit.'

'So you're a gypsy, huh?'

Physically she was far from the traditional gypsy type—she was blonde and busty rather than exotic and reedy—but he supposed *gypsy* was a state of mind.

'Yes. I am.' The ferry horn tooted almost directly above their heads. 'Always have been. I'm a living-in-the-moment kinda woman, although I suspect...' A smile touched her mouth. 'You probably already know that.'

Hamish acknowledged her reference with a slight smile of his own and she continued, 'I've always craved adventure. I wanted to bungee jump and climb mountains and parasail and deep sea dive and jump out of planes.'

He nodded. 'And you can't do any of that in Doongabi.'

She laughed and Hamish felt it all the way down to his toes before the breeze snatched it away. 'No.'

'Have you ever gone back?'

'I've been back a few times. For Christmas.'

'Are your parents still alive? Don't you miss them?'

'Yes. They're both still on the farm.'

The farm? Try as he might, Hamish couldn't believe Lola had come from a farming background. She was as at home in Sydney as the sails of the Opera House.

'And, yes, I do miss them in the way you miss people you love when you haven't seen them for a long time. But they don't really *get* me and I think it's honestly as much a relief for them as it is for me when I head back to Sydney.'

'Why don't they *get* you?' Hamish felt sorry for Lola. Sure, his family had their disagreements and their differences but he'd always felt like he belonged. Like his parents *got* him.

She glanced away, the back of her head resting on the wall behind. 'Doongabi's the kind of place that people tie themselves to. Generations of families, including my father's and my mother's, have come from the district. And that's fine.' She rolled her head to look at him, the frown crinkling her forehead speaking of her turmoil. 'It's their lives and it's their choice. But…how can it be a choice?'

Her eyebrows raised in question but Hamish was sure the question was rhetorical.

'They don't *know* anything else. Women…tie themselves there to Doongabi men and have Doongabi babies, without ever venturing out into the world to see what else is on offer. They're so stuck in their ways. Unwilling to change a century of this-is-the-way-we-do-it-here.'

She sighed heavily and, once again, Hamish felt for Lola. She obviously grappled with her mixed feelings.

'And I…wanted to fly. So…' She shrugged. 'My mother blames her aunt.'

'Her aunt?'

'My Great-Aunt May.'

'Oh…the postcards on the fridge.' She smiled at him then and it was so big and genuine it almost stole Hamish's breath.

'Yes. She's the family black sheep. Hitchhiked out of Doongabi when she was eighteen. Never married, never settled in one place. She's lived all over the world, seen all kinds of things and can swear in a dozen different languages. I have a postcard from every place she's ever been. I was five when I received my first one.'

Hamish nodded. 'And you knew you wanted to be just like her.'

'No.' Lola shook her head, her curls bounced. 'I knew I *was* just like her.' She gave a half-laugh. 'Poor Mum. I don't think she's ever forgiven May.'

'She sounds fabulous.'

'She is.' Lola's gaze fixed on the foam spraying over the bow and Hamish studied her profile, as gorgeous as the rest of her. 'I can see the bridge.' She pointed at the arch just coming into view and sighed. 'I never get tired of that sight.'

Hamish dragged his gaze off her face, following the line of her finger. But he didn't want to. He could look at Lola Fraser all damn day and never get tired of *that* sight either.

They alighted from the ferry at the North Sydney Wharf about fifteen minutes later. 'It's a few minutes' walk from here.'

Hamish fell in beside her as they sauntered down what looked very much like a suburban street. 'What suburb is this?'

'It's Kirribilli.'

'So the hospital's not far, then?'

'Um, yes. Up that way…somewhere.' She waved her hand vaguely in the general direction they were heading. 'At the dodgy end.'

Hamish laughed as they passed beautifully restored terraced houses, big gnarly trees that looked as if they'd been in the ground for a century and cars with expensive price tags. It was hard to believe this harbourside suburb—*any* harbourside suburb—had a dodgy end.

She turned right at an intersection. 'So, are you going to tell me what's so special about this street?'

'Nope.' Lola shook her head. 'You'll see soon enough.'

'Mystery woman, huh?'

She just shrugged and kept walking but there was a bounce to her step. Like she couldn't wait to get there. Like *maybe* she couldn't wait to show him? It was intriguing that a woman who'd just confessed to having itchy feet and being a bit of a daredevil would choose a place so quiet and unassuming to take him.

They passed a park and Hamish could see down to the harbour again, glittering like a jewel and the massive motor boats moored at what looked like a marina. A personal trainer was putting a group of people through a session and a large gathering of people were picnicking under the shade of a tree.

'This,' she said as she turned left at another street, 'is my favourite place to visit in Sydney.'

Hamish turned the corner to discover an avenue of massive Jacaranda trees alive with colour. The dry, gnarly branches knotted and tangled together overhead to form a lilac canopy down the entire length of the street. A carpet of dropped, purple-blue flowers covered the road.

It was stunning. Toowoomba had plenty of Jacarandas as well but this avenue was something else, the trees all lined up together to create an accidental work of art. A sight so *purple* it was almost blinding.

The kind of purple usually only found on coral reefs or in magic forests.

He glanced at Lola. She'd taken her sunglasses off and was staring down the street with rapt attention, like she'd discovered it all over again. Like she was seeing it for the first time.

She switched her attention to him and caught Hamish staring at her, but she didn't seem to mind. 'Isn't it the most beautiful thing you've ever seen?'

It was. *She* was. Looking down the street like a kid staring at an avenue of Christmas trees just lit up for the season, giddy with the magic shimmering in the air.

And she'd shared it with him. This beautiful place she loved so much.

'Yes. It's stunning.' *Just like you.*

She smiled at him and for a crazy second he wanted to pull her close and kiss her. Kiss her in this place she'd taken nobody else, so every time she came here she'd remember that she'd taken *him*.

But he didn't. He just said, 'Shall we walk up and down a few times?'

She gave a half-laugh, a girly edge of excitement to it as he offered her his arm and she looped hers through it. 'I thought you'd never ask.'

They didn't speak for a while, just strolled along, admiring the scenery as lilac flowers floated down all around them, quiet as snowfall. It was like walking in a purple wonderland. He turned to tell her that as two almost luminescent blue-purple flowers drifting in the gentle harbour breeze landed in Lola's hair.

It couldn't have been more perfect. 'You have flowers in your hair.'

'So do you.' She stood on tippytoes and plucked out the trumpet-shaped blooms. Their eyes locked for a moment and Hamish's pulse spiked before she dragged her gaze to the flowers in her palm. 'Only in nature could you get this colour.'

She blew them both off her hand, her gaze tracking them as they fluttered to the ground. 'Where are mine?' she asked, fixing him with a gaze that was all business now.

Hamish lifted his hand to remove them then decided

against it. 'Wait.' He pulled his phone out of his pocket. 'I think this needs a picture first.'

She rolled her eyes but acquiesced. 'I get to veto it if it's terrible.'

He took the pic, zooming in tight on her face but conscious of snapping the background blaze of purple too, of framing this woman just right. He took several in quick succession then handed over his phone for Lola to approve what he'd taken.

'They're all pretty good,' she said, her thumb swiping back and forth between them. 'Hard to screw up with that background, I guess.'

Hard to screw up with the *foreground* too.

'This one.' She handed the phone over. 'Can you send it to me?'

Hamish glanced at it. She'd chosen one he'd zoomed out on a little but she was smiling a big, crazy smile that went all the way to her eyes and squished her full cheeks into chipmunk cuteness. The flowers in her hair drew attention to its blonde bounciness and the way it brushed her shoulders drew attention to her fallen-down strap.

'Sure.' His fingers got busy as they walked on again.

'So, Grace's big brother…' She smiled at him. 'Have *you* travelled?'

'Sure. I'm afraid it's kinda tame compared to you.'

She rolled her eyes. 'It's not a competition.'

Hamish thought back to that first trip, a smile spreading across his face. 'I did a tour of the Greek Islands with some mates when I was nineteen. Got a snowglobe from every place we stopped.'

Lola blinked. 'A snowglobe?' *In Greece?*

'Yeah. You know, those terrible, tacky things they sell in tourist traps everywhere.'

Lola laughed. 'I know.'

'Had to get something to remember the best damn trip of my life.'

'The Greek islands are beautiful, aren't they? And the people are wonderful. So generous.'

His smile became a grin. 'You have no idea.'

'Oh, *really*?' She cocked an eyebrow at him. 'I take it you were a recipient of some generosity? Of the female kind maybe?'

He laughed. 'I lost my virginity in Mykonos.'

'Ah. Was she a local or one of the women on the tour?'

Hamish shook his head. 'She was Greek. The daughter of the innkeeper. She couldn't speak much English and all I could say was please, thank you, good morning and can I have some ouzo.'

She laughed. 'What else do you need?'

'Nothing, as it turned out.' Hamish laughed too. 'A little ouzo and good manners go a long way.'

'That's a great life motto,' she said as they crossed to the other side of the street, trampling a sea of fallen purple flowers. 'I don't suppose there was an *I lost my virginity in Mykonos* snowglobe?'

'No, sadly… I would have bought the hell out of that.'

Lola shook her head as they headed back the other way. 'Where else?'

'I did a tour of Europe the following year. Fifteen countries in twenty-five days.'

'Oh, God,' Lola groaned. 'This isn't where you tell me that you could only ever get laid on a tour so that's all you've ever done?'

'No.' He grinned. 'But it is surprising how…accommodating being on holiday makes a woman.'

'I would say that is most definitely true.'

Hamish didn't really want to think about how much travelling Lola had done and how much adrenaline she must have had to burn off after all her death-defying adventures. But he was jealous as hell of whoever had been in the right place at the right time to be the recipient of all that excess energy.

He knew how mind-blowing she was in grief. He could only begin to imagine how amazing she'd be pumped with devil-may-care.

'Since then I've been to LA and New York for brief visits. And to New Zealand for a ski trip last year.'

'Let me guess, you have snowglobes from all of them?'

'Absolutely. It's worth, like, fifty bucks, that collection.'

She laughed. 'And where's your favourite place out of everywhere you've been?'

'Well, Mykonos, obviously.'

He smiled and she rolled her eyes. '*Obviously*. What about your second favourite place?'

'London. I was only there for three days and I need to go back because I loved it. What about you? What's your number one pick of all the places you've been?'

She sucked in air through her teeth. 'That's a hard call.'

'I bet. But there must be something that just grabbed you by the gut?'

'Last year I went on a tandem hangglider flight over an Austrian lake. It was…magical. We hovered for so long, riding the air currents I actually felt like I was flying and the Alps in the distance were all snow-capped. It was almost…spiritual, you know?'

'It does sound spiritual but I'd rather get my thrills with both feet planted firmly on the ground.'

'Afraid of heights?'

Hamish's breath caught at the amusement in her voice. She was something else when she teased him. She wasn't flirting exactly but it felt good to have her green eyes dancing at him.

'Afraid of plunging to my death attached to some dude I don't know is more like it.'

She shrugged. 'Life's too short to worry about the what-ifs.'

'Maybe. But I tend to see all the disastrous things that go wrong for people indulging in high-risk ventures. I think it skews my view somewhat.'

'Hey, there are plenty of ICU patients who were doing risky things that didn't work out. But you could trip over your feet tomorrow, smack your head on the ground and die. Just getting out of bed each day is a risk.'

'Exactly.' Hamish grinned. 'Which is why I plan on dying in my bed at the grand old age of ninety-six after having sex with a beautiful woman.'

A smile played on her mouth as she stopped and looked up at him. 'Sex, huh? Wow, you do like to push the envelope.'

'Hey, sex at ninety-six *is* pushing the envelope.'

She laughed. 'Come on. Let's walk down again and keep going. There's a great little café that overlooks the harbour. We might not be able to get a seat but you don't know if you don't try, right?'

Hamish cocked an eyebrow. 'You even like to take risks with tables.'

'You really need to take a walk on the wild side, Hamish Gibson.'

Hamish grinned. He'd grown up around horses and cattle and farm machinery. He'd done his fair share of wild *and* stupid. He didn't feel like he had anything to prove. But Lola could probably persuade him to do anything. 'I'm starting to see the attraction.'

CHAPTER SIX

LOLA TRIED NOT to make too much noise the next morning as she crept down the hall of the silent apartment, tightening the knot on her short gown. Hamish was on a couple of days of orientation so he didn't start till nine but she didn't want to disturb him at five thirty in the morning with her fridge opening and toast popping and teaspoon clinking.

Grace had always been a light sleeper and Lola figured it probably ran in the Gibson family. Her parents were the same so she knew it was a *country* thing. She needn't have worried, though. Her toast had just popped when she heard the front door open and a sweaty Hamish appeared a few moments later, his damp shorts and shirt clinging to him.

'Is that coffee?'

Lola nodded, lost for words both at his appearance and the fact he was not only out of bed but had already been for a *run*.

Who was he?

'Is there enough for two?'

Lola nodded again, still finding it difficult to locate adequate speech. His pheromones wafted to her on a wave of healthy sweat and she leaned against the kitchen bench as her legs weakened in an exceedingly unhelpful way. She ground her feet into the floor to stop herself launching at him.

'Can you pour me one? I'll just have a quick shower.'

And then she was looking at empty space, the tang of salt in the air a tangible reminder he *had* been here, an image in her head of Hamish in the shower a reminder of where he *was* right now.

Lola hoped like hell these shower fantasies weren't going to be a regular thing.

Determined to think of something else, her mind drifted to Hamish's confession about his virginity. The fact he still enjoyed the memory in a sexily smug way over ten years later was either testament to the greatness of the event or the depth of his gratitude. Both were endearing as all giddy-up.

Was it crazy to feel a tiny bit jealous of the woman on Mykonos?

She'd lost her virginity travelling too. She'd been eighteen and in Phuket where she'd met a backpacker called Jeremy. He'd been exotically handsome—Eurasian with a sexy Brit accent—and had known it. But she hadn't cared. She'd wanted to show her parents and everyone in Doongabi she was sophisticated and worldly. Plus there'd been cheap beer and a little too much sun earlier in the day.

Lola didn't remember a lot of it. Unlike Hamish, who appeared to remember his first time in great detail. She wondered if Jeremy still thought about that night with the same mix of pleasure and reminiscence that Hamish obviously did. How awesome would it be, knowing there was a guy out there in the world who got a secret, goofy grin every time he thought about his first time with you?

Knowing that you'd rocked his world?

She thought about that note again, the one Hamish had left for her the morning after, with its goofy smiley face. Did he smile like that whenever he thought about what *they'd* done together?

Had she been as *unforgettable* as he'd claimed?

Hamish reappeared fifteen minutes later as she sat in front of the TV, listening to the morning news, And, hell, he looked seriously hot in his uniform. Like a freaking action man in his multi-pocketed lightweight overalls with a utility belt crammed with all the bits and bobs a paramedic needed on the road.

He looked strong and capable. Wide shoulders, wavy cinnamon hair with a sprinkle of ginger, powerful thighs. He looked like he could fix anything—*anyone*—and Lola's heart fluttered just looking at him. When he plonked himself down next to her on the couch—the same couch where they'd done *it*—any hope of following the news reports was dashed.

Lola took a sip of her coffee. 'Are you nervous? About your first day?'

He seemed to consider the question for a beat or two. 'Not of the work. I know Toowoomba may seem like a country backwater compared to the size and population of Sydney, but it's a decent-sized regional city and I've seen a lot on the job. I *am* nervous about the people I'm going to be working with. I don't know anyone so I'm not sure who knows what and who to be wary of.'

Lola nodded. Finding out colleagues' levels of experience and their limitations always took a little time. Sometimes that could be detrimental, especially in emergency situations.

'Well, if it helps, I know quite a few of the paramedics stationed at Kirribilli. They all seem professional and they all get along, work as a team. A lot of them go to Billi's after their shift. Make sure you go along. It's a great place to de-stress.'

It was also a great place to pick up women—as he would know. The sudden thought was like a hot knife sliding between her ribs as she thought about him hooking up at Billi's, bringing her back here. Which was crazy. He could sleep with every woman in Sydney if he wanted to—it wasn't any of her business or her concern.

'Right. Well...' She stood. 'I'd better get ready.'

She didn't wait for his reply, scooping her plate off the coffee table and heading to the kitchen. She was going to be late if she didn't hustle.

Lola had another busy morning with Emma. The condition of her heart was worsening. Her body was becoming more oedematous which was putting pressure on other organs. Even the conjunctivas of her eyes bulged with oedema, requiring frequent ointment to prevent them drying.

The specialists were now at the stage where they were talking about a transplant. The question, though, was whether they could stabilise Emma enough to survive the rigors of such a massive operation and if they could, how long could they keep her heart going in its current state while they waited for another to become available?

Sadly, they didn't grow on trees. Even an emergency listing could still sometimes take weeks. And nobody was confident Emma's heart could last that long.

Her family were beside themselves with worry and Lola spent a lot of the morning trying to meet their growing need for comfort, assurance and answers. Lola could give the first and she did, she just wished she could give the other two as well.

At least Barry was more comfortable about being near Emma now. He'd grown more confident and had taken to reading out all the supportive messages that family and friends had left for Emma on social media. There were hundreds every day and Lola knew the outpouring was not only good for Emma to hear but for Barry and her parents as well.

'I think she *can* hear me,' Barry said.

Lola smiled and nodded. 'I do too.' She'd noticed how Emma's heart rate settled a little every time Barry or her parents touched and talked to her. 'Keep it up.'

By the time Lola was heading to lunch she felt like she'd been working for a week. Seeing Grace in the kitchen alcove of the deserted staffroom was a fabulous rejuvenator.

'Hey, you here with the team?' Lola asked as she threw a tea bag into her mug and filled it with hot water from the boiler attached to the wall. Although she was the renal transplant co-ordinator, Grace often stepped in when a co-ordinator from a different department was on annual leave.

Grace nodded, following Lola's lead and also filling her mug. 'Just finished the Emma Green meeting. You're looking after her?'

Lola settled her butt against the edge of the kitchen counter. 'Yep.'

Grace settled hers beside Lola's. 'She's not doing very well, is she?'

Lola shook her head as she blew on her hot tea. 'No. She's going backwards at the moment, which is a worry.' Emma's chances of survival decreased every minute they couldn't stabilise her condition. 'She's just about reached maximum drug support.'

'Do you think she'll stabilise?'

It wasn't an unusual question to ask. Experienced nurses often had gut feelings about patients. 'Well, her body's been pummelled over the years so… But she's got this far. She's obviously a fighter. I just…don't know.' Lola took a sip of her tea. 'Are they going to list her?'

Lola knew they didn't list people just on the gut feeling of the nurses. But she also knew that if Emma pulled through, if she stabilised, she was going to need a transplant because she couldn't stay on life support for ever and she couldn't survive without it. Unless she had a new heart.

Grace sipped her tea. 'The team is discussing it now.'

'Good.' Relief flowed through Lola's core and she smiled. 'Fingers crossed.'

They sipped at their tea for a moment or two. 'Hamish tells me you took him to see the jacarandas yesterday.'

Lola was instantly on guard, not fooled by Grace's casual slouch against the bench. 'Yes.'

One elegantly arched eyebrow lifted. 'I thought that was a state secret?'

'I told you about it,' Lola protested, dropping her gaze to the surface of her tea.

Grace regarded her over the rim of her cup, speculation coming off her in waves, even though Lola was finding the depths of her tea utterly fascinating.

'He's going back to Toowoomba, Lola.'

'I know.'

'And then he's moving to a rural post.'

'I know.'

'And you're not interested in settling down, remember?'

'I know.'

She wasn't. There were still places to go and people she hadn't met yet. And she couldn't do that being with Hamish in some rural outpost somewhere.

'Lola?'

Lola almost cringed at *that* note in her friend's voice—that mix of suspicion and dawning knowledge were a deadly accurate cocktail. She girded her loins to look directly at Grace as if she and Hamish hadn't got naked and done the wild thing already and this conversation wasn't too late.

'I said I know, Grace. Take a chill pill.' Lola plastered a smile on her face. 'He wanted to know my favourite spot in Sydney and I figured a country boy would probably appreciate some nature.'

Grace studied her closely. 'But *you* went with him.'

Lola shifted uncomfortably under her friend's all-seeing gaze. 'I haven't seen it yet this year. Plus, he's your brother. I thought it might be…polite to play tour guide.'

The expression on Grace's face finally cleared and she nodded slowly, as if she'd reached her conclusion. She glanced around to make sure no one had slipped into the room unnoticed while they'd been deep in conversation. 'You two have *slept* together.'

It wasn't a question and it took all Lola's willpower not to glance away, to hold her friend's gaze and brazen it out. 'Don't be ridiculous. He's been here two nights during which we have *not* slept together.'

Which was the truth.

'No.' Grace slowly shook her head. 'Not this time. Last time.'

Oh, hell. Grace had missed her calling as a PI. 'As

if I would sleep with Hamish.' Lola lowered her voice. 'He's your *brother*.'

Grace waved a hand. 'I don't care about that.'

Lola blinked at Grace's easy dismissal. She'd thought her friend would care but it ultimately didn't matter— *Lola* cared.

That was what mattered.

'I care about the fact that while you two are exactly alike in a lot of ways, you want completely different things, which means that you're both going to get hurt and that I'm going to be in the middle of it all.'

Lola had to admire how well Grace could summarise things. 'There's nothing going on, Grace.'

Another *almost* truth. There *was* an undercurrent between them but they weren't acting on it. And that was the most important thing.

'Lola?'

For a brief second, the sudden appearance of one of the shift runners was a welcome relief until concern spiked Lola's pulse. 'Emma?'

'No, sorry, she's okay. Just thought you'd like to know Dr Wright is heading in to talk to the family now.'

'Is he?' She plonked the mostly untouched mug on the bench. 'Sorry,' she said to Grace. 'I've gotta go.'

'Isn't this your lunch break?'

Lola nodded. 'But I have to sit in on it.'

She hated it when the doctors had a family conference without the nurse present. Invariably a patient's loved ones only heard some of the conversation or misheard it or didn't understand it but nodded along anyway because they were too overwhelmed by everything. When they had questions later—and they always had questions later—Lola could answer them, could reiterate what the doctor had said exactly, could interpret *and* correct any misperceptions.

But only *if* she was privy to what had been discussed.

Grace nodded. 'That's fine. Go. I'll pop around later this afternoon after I have some ducks in a row and introduce myself to the family.'

'Okay. Thanks.' Lola scuttled off to the conference room.

Lola was on her second glass of wine on the balcony when she heard the front door open. Her pulse spiked followed by a quick stab of annoyance. She had to stop this stupid behaviour around him, for crying out loud.

Why couldn't she just look at him and think, *Oh, a guy I once slept with*, and act normal. Instead of, *Holy cow, a guy I once slept with. Danger! Danger! Danger!* Why was having to deal with him again after they'd got naked and done the wild thing *such* a problem?

She usually handled the ex-lover stuff really well.

It was probably just the newness of the situation. It'd only been a few days since Hamish had come to stay after all. She probably just needed time to get used to their living arrangements.

Of course, Grace's speculation about them hadn't helped. Lola hadn't had much of a chance to think about the implications of that during the remainder of her shift but she'd been thinking about it plenty since. She should have known Grace would guess something was going on. They may not have been besties since kindergarten, but they had known each other for several years and had lived together for the last two.

Of course Grace could read her like a book.

Which meant she was going to have to give Hamish a

heads-up, because Lola had no doubt Grace would soon be seeking an explanation from her brother.

And she needed to get ahead of that.

Despite the inner uproar at the thought and Hamish's tread getting closer and closer, Lola forced herself to stay right where she was, her feet casually up on the railing of the balcony. They at least weren't throbbing any more after her long, busy day with Emma. A good soak in a bath had helped.

So had the wine.

'Hey.'

'Hey.' Lola plastered a smile on her face as she half turned in her seat.

He stepped onto the balcony, returning her smile, his gaze shifting to her legs before quickly shifting back again.

'How was orientation?'

He gave a half-laugh as he undid his utility belt and discarded it on the table with a dull thud. 'Let's just say I can't wait to get out on the road.'

Lola nodded. Orientation days were generally tedious. They were a necessary evil and HR boffins loved them, but staring at a bunch of policy and procedure manuals all day was not fun for most people.

He pulled up the chair beside her, turned it around and plonked himself in it, raising his feet to the railing also, his legs outstretched. Fabric pulled taut across powerful thighs as he crossed his feet at the ankles. Lola fixed her gaze on the darkening outline of the Norfolk pine in the park opposite.

'Met my partner, though. A woman called Jenny Bell. She seems good. Know her?'

Lola nodded. 'Yeah. She's an excellent intensive care paramedic. One of the best.'

'Good.' He dropped his head from side to side to stretch out his traps. 'How was your shift?'

'Long.' She took a sip of her wine, resolutely pushing worry for Emma out of her mind. 'One of those shifts where you're on your toes every second.'

'Well, I've been sitting on my ass all day, so I can cook us something to eat if you like.'

Lola blinked at the unexpected offer. 'You can cook?'

'Well…' He smiled. 'Nothing too gourmet but I manage.'

'Good to know. But—' Lola grabbed a menu off the table she'd been studying earlier. 'Let's just order something gourmet and get it delivered for tonight.'

He took the menu and opened it. 'Delivered, huh?'

Lola laughed. 'Yeah, *Country*, it's a city thing. Choose something from the extensive menu then I order it through an app and a nice person delivers it right to the door.'

'I like the sound of that.'

They chose some pasta and garlic bread and Lola ordered it online. 'Should be here in thirty.'

'Good.' He stood and reached for his utility belt. 'I'll take a shower.'

Lola shut her eyes against a sudden welling of images in her head. *Enough with the shower already.*

At least she knew something that could combat the seduction of those images this time. 'Before you go…'

He paused, belt in hand, his gaze meeting hers. 'What?'

Lola sighed. Damn Grace's observation skills for putting her in this position. 'Look, I know I said we weren't to speak of this again but…'

'But?' Two cinnamon eyebrows rose in query.

She let out a breath. *Just say it!* 'Your sister knows we slept together.'

His face went blank for a second before his eyebrows lifted in surprise this time. 'You told Grace we slept together?'

'No.' Lola shook her head. 'Not exactly. She kinda guessed.'

'Ah. Yeah…she's like a bulldog when she scents blood.'

'I denied it. Told her there wasn't anything going on but… I'm sure you'll be hearing from her so I thought you might like some prior notice.'

'I have a missed call from her actually. I was going to ring her soon.'

'Well…that's probably why.'

He gave a soft snort. 'She always was one of those pain-in-the-ass, know-it-all little sisters.'

Lola laughed. 'Well, like I said, I did deny it. I just don't think she believed me so…sorry if you cop some flak from her.'

'Don't worry.' He grinned. 'I know how to handle Gracie.'

In Lola's experience men tended to underestimate a woman's tenacity when her mind was made up but that was between him and his sister and, to be honest, it was good to be able to pass that hot potato on to someone else.

'All right. I'll hit the shower.'

She didn't watch him go. She stared straight ahead at the trees silhouetted against a velvety purple sky. Did he *have* to constantly announce his intention to take a shower? Couldn't he just go and do it without informing her all the time?

Planting images in her head. Naked images. Wet images.

It was going to be a very long two months.

CHAPTER SEVEN

A FEW WEEKS later Hamish was sitting in the work vehicle, eating lunch under a shady tree. It was exceptionally hot today and they were between jobs. He was flicking through images on his phone to show Jenny some pictures of the feed lot his family ran back in Toowoomba. He came across the one he'd taken of Lola that day with jacaranda flowers in her hair and smiled.

Things had been a little weird to start with between them but they seemed to have settled down into an easy kind of co-existence. It wasn't the flirty banter of their relationship a few months ago, or sex on the couch, which he probably wouldn't say no to, but it was something he could walk away from when his time in Sydney was up.

Because the more he got to know Lola, the more he knew, she was city right down to her bootstraps. And it didn't matter how *wicked* his thoughts got alone in his room each night, Lola wasn't going country for anyone.

Just then a call came over the radio and Jenny threw the last of her sandwich down her neck. 'Buckle up,' she said as they climbed into the vehicle and she flicked on the siren.

Hamish turned his phone off, shutting down thoughts of Lola as adrenaline flushed into his system and he concentrated on that as they screamed through the Sydney streets.

They arrived at the home of a fifty-six-year-old man called Robert twelve minutes later. He'd had a probable MI—myocardial infarction or heart attack. He had no pulse and wasn't breathing.

It was Hamish and Jenny's second of the day. The heat wave they were experiencing was no doubt contributing to that.

Two advanced care paramedics were already on scene. They'd arrived six minutes previously and were administering CPR, having taken over from the patient's wife and a neighbour who was a nurse.

The fact that Robert had had lifesaving measures carried out immediately on collapsing could probably mean the difference between him dying today and living.

Jenny quickly intubated the patient and stayed at the head, delivering puffs of oxygen into Robert's lungs via the breathing tube, while one of the advanced care paramedics, another woman, continued to do compressions. The other was busy inserting a couple of intravenous lines and Hamish was managing the emergency drugs and the defibrillator, which had already been connected when they'd arrived.

'Recommends another shock,' he said, as he flipped the lids on another mini-jet of adrenaline and wiped his brow with his forearm. It was stiflingly hot in the little, inner-suburban shoebox house.

Jenny gave a few quick hyper-inflating puffs of oxygen before she joined the others, who had shuffled out of contact with the body. 'All clear,' Hamish called, double checking everyone was away before he pushed the button and delivered the recommended shock.

The patient's body jerked slightly—not quite like the dramatic arch seen on TV shows—and all eyes watched the heart trace on the monitor.

A hot flood of relief washed over Hamish as the previous frenetic, squiggly line suddenly flipped into an organised pattern. 'Sinus tachy,' he announced, although he didn't need to. Everyone there knew how to read an ECG trace.

Jenny and the other female paramedic high-fived before she said, 'Okay, let's get him locked and loaded.'

They'd revived the patient, brought Robert back from the brink, but heart-attack patients were notoriously unstable in the hours immediately after the heart muscle dying, which meant Robert needed a tertiary care facility pronto. Somewhere with a cath lab, a cardiac surgeon and an intensive care unit.

'We'll take him to Kirribilli General,' Jenny said.

They unloaded the patient in the emergency department twenty minutes later. Hamish listened to Jenny's rapid-fire handover to the team. Lola was right, she was an excellent paramedic.

'I wonder where the third one's going to be,' Hamish said as they headed back to the ambulance.

Because these things tended to come in threes.

'Somewhere with air-con, I hope,' Jenny quipped.

Hamish laughed. It was nice working with someone who was not only good at their job but also knew how to make light of a situation.

It was the kind of job that needed it.

A call came over the radio as soon as they were seated. Another suspected MI. 'No rest for the wicked,' Jenny said, flicking the sirens on.

And Hamish's thoughts went straight to Lola.

* * *

Hamish sighed as he entered the apartment later that evening. It was good to be home. It was still warm outside but their apartment was getting a nice breeze from the direction of the beach and Lola had all the doors and windows open to catch it.

The sheer curtain at the sliding door to the balcony was billowing with it and Lola was shimmying in the kitchen to some music she was obviously listening to via her ear buds. She had her back to him as she stood at the counter, a bottle of beer in one hand and a fork in the other, attacking a container of leftover Chinese takeaway.

She'd obviously had a shower. Her hair was wet and she was wearing her short gown that brushed her legs at mid-thigh. He didn't know for sure what she wore underneath it but he had spent a lot of time speculating over it.

Tank top and lacy thong were his current picks.

She looked cool and relaxed and was a sight for sore eyes after a long day. Something he wouldn't mind coming home to every day, in fact...

He shoved his shoulder against the doorframe. 'You're chipper today.'

She startled and whipped around. 'Bloody hell, Hamish. You scared the living daylights out of me.'

She brought the hand holding her beer to her chest and Hamish's temperature kicked up a notch as the action pulled the gown taut across her cleavage and the tight buds of two erect nipples.

He dragged his gaze upwards. 'Is your patient improving?'

Lola had told him about the woman waiting for a heart transplant. Not any particulars of her identity, just her situation, and he could tell by how fondly she talked about the family and how often she seemed to be assigned to the case that this particular patient had slipped under Lola's barriers.

A hazard of the job. He'd been there himself.

'Yeah.' She grinned as she pulled her ear buds out and her face lit up. His breath hitched. 'She's really turned a corner. She's coming along in leaps and bounds now. Still needs a heart, of course, but...'

Hamish nodded. The imminent threat to her life had passed but she needed a transplant to survive going forward. He hoped she got one and that the family got something extra-special to celebrate as the festive season approached. Even if it meant some other family would have the worst Christmas of their life.

He remembered when his sister-in-law, Merridy, had got her kidney. In her case, his brother Lachlan had fortunately been a tissue match for her and had been able to donate one of his. What a joy, a relief, it had been, knowing they hadn't had to wait for somebody to die to give Merridy that gift. But also how sobering it had been for everyone, knowing that others weren't so lucky.

'You're drinking beer?' He'd only ever seen her drinking wine.

Why was there something hot about a chick drinking beer?

'That's because it's *Die Hard* marathon night.'

Hamish laughed. 'And that requires beer?'

She rolled her eyes. 'You think John MacClane drinks Sauvignon Blanc?'

'I wouldn't think so.' They both smiled and Hamish ground his feet into the floor as the urge to walk over and kiss her almost overwhelmed him. 'I thought we were out of beer? I meant to get some on my way home.'

'I picked some up from the liquor warehouse on my way home.'

Hamish grimaced. That place gave him the willies. A football stadium of booze was mind-boggling. 'Rather you than me.'

'It's okay, *Country.*' A smile hovered on her mouth. 'I know you don't get shops that big where you come from. I've got your back.'

Hamish laughed. Her teasing set a warm glow in the centre of his chest. 'Toowoomba isn't exactly a two-horse town. It's a fairly decent size.'

'You're going to be moving to a two-horse town, though, right? Once your course is done?'

'Hopefully. Those jobs don't come up very often. People don't tend to leave them once they're in.' Hamish laughed at her visible shudder. 'Newsflash, *City*, some people like living in small towns.'

'If you say so.'

'Plus, it's a professional challenge. Out there, it'll be just me on shift, no back-up. The next ambulance service could be a couple of hundred kilometres away.'

'Sounds terrifying.'

'Nah. There'll be a doctor and Flying Doctor back-up but the autonomy…the skills I'll acquire can only make me a better paramedic.'

'I think that would drive me nuts. I like working with a team. I thrive on being a small part in a well-oiled machine. I like the people I work with. I enjoy their company. I wouldn't want to work in isolation.'

Hamish shrugged. 'I don't want to do it for ever necessarily. But I'd like to do it for a while.' Clearly, though, she didn't. And it bothered him more than it should have.

'Well…' She looked at him like he was a little crazy.

'Each to their own, I guess.' She took a slug of her beer. 'Are you joining me tonight?'

'*Die Hard* marathon?' He grinned, shaking off the urban-rural divide between them. 'Absolutely! I'll just have a shower.'

She nodded. 'I'll pop the corn.'

Lola watched him go. Good Lord! The man took more showers than a teenage boy who'd just discovered the Victoria's Secret catalogue. Which led her down a whole other path she did not want to go…

She got busy in the kitchen instead, putting the popcorn bag in the microwave and grabbing two frosty long-necked bottles out of the fridge. When her mind started to wander to his shower, she distracted herself by rereading the latest postcard from May stuck on the fridge. She was in Mongolia, the usual *Wish you were here* in her lovely loopy handwriting making Lola smile.

By the time the popcorn had popped and been decanted into a bowl, Lola had cracked the lids off the beers, and the first movie was queued, Hamish was out of the shower. He reappeared in a T-shirt and loose basketball shorts that fell to just above his knee but clung a little due to the humidity.

It was what he usually wore after his shower—just a little more indecent tonight.

But that wasn't a particularly helpful thought right now as he stood there, temptation incarnate, his hair damp and curling against his neck. She had to remind herself that this *thing* she felt could go nowhere.

That they lived very different lives. Wanted very different things.

Still, the lights were out and the glow from the tele-

vision caught the ginger highlights of his stubbly jawline and he smelled like coconut and the deodorant he
used that reminded her of fresh Alpine air, heavy with
the scent of pine.

How could a man smell like the beach and the Alps
all at once?

'Beer?' Lola thrust a long-necked bottle at him.

'You read my mind.'

He took it from her and they clinked. He took a pull
of his as he sat beside her, the popcorn bowl between
them. It was a large bowl but it still put him closer than
was good for her sanity. Of course, if he thought about
what they'd done on this couch half as much as she did,
no amount of space was adequate.

'Okay, roll it,' he said.

Lola laughed and pressed 'play', taking a long cool
swallow of her beer as the credits did their thing. She
could do this. She could sit here on this couch with
Hamish, where they'd done the wild thing a few months
ago, and watch one of her favourite movies as if they'd
never laid hands on each other.

A sudden thought occurred to her and she turned to
face him slightly. 'You *are* a *Die Hard* fan, right?'

He smiled and her heart skipped a beat as he raised
his bottle to her. 'Yippie-ki-yay.' He tapped it against
hers again and settled back against the couch, grabbing
a handful of popcorn.

Lola was so damn happy she actually sighed.

After two of the most entertaining hours of her life, Lola
was sad to see the end of the movie. Normally she and
Grace just sat and watched it, gobbling it up like they
gobbled the popcorn. But Hamish was a much more ac-

tive consumer. He kept up a running commentary of interesting asides about the films or the actors and mimicked his favourite lines, even adlibbing better ones.

They'd also had a serious discussion about it being a rom-com. He'd been horrified in an endearingly masculine way when Lola had dared to suggest it.

'Well…thank you very much for your insights into the movie,' he said, as Lola hit 'stop' on the DVD remote. 'They're wrong, of course…' his lips quirked '…but it's given me a whole different perspective on it.'

Lola laughed and threw a kernel of popcorn at him. It was a spontaneous thing that fitted the mood of the moment but one she regretted immediately as the glitter of laughter in his eyes changed to a competitive gleam.

'Oh, it's going to be like that, is it?' He dug into their second bowl of popcorn and grabbed a handful of kernels.

'Hamish.'

If he heard the warning note in her voice he chose to ignore it as he slowly lifted his hand above her head.

'Don't you *dare*.'

He just smiled and opened it. Popcorn fell around her like snow. When they settled he plucked one out of her hair and ate it, his eyes goading her to do something about it.

'Right.' She grinned at him, plunging both hands into the frothing bowl and coming out with two fistfuls. 'You asked for it.'

He laughed, which only encouraged her further. He was prepared to swerve and duck, obviously, but not prepared for her to grab his T-shirt and dump the popcorn down his front.

'Well, now,' Hamish muttered, 'this is war.'

He reached for the front of her gown with one hand

and the popcorn with the other. Lola half laughed, half squealed, flinging herself back, trying to twist away, but Hamish was bigger and stronger and more determined, laughing as he followed her down, sending the popcorn bowl flying as he anchored her squirming body to the couch and stuffed a handful of kernels down the front of her gown.

Lola joined him in laughter as the popcorn scratched against her skin. She tried to remove it but he just shook his head and said, 'Nuh-uh,' as he grabbed her hands.

They were both panting and laughing hard from their playful struggle so it took a moment to register that he had her well and truly pinned, his hips over hers, one big thigh shoved between her legs, his hands entwined in hers above their heads.

He seemed to realise at the same time, the glitter in his eyes different now—not light or teasing.

Darker. Hotter.

Their gazes locked and Lola's heart punched against her rib cage, nothing but the sounds of their breathing between them now. Panting had turned into something rougher, more needy as she stared at him looming over her. An ache roared to life between her legs, right where his knee was shoved, and she couldn't fight the urge to squirm against the pressure to relieve the ache.

His eyes widened at the action and he pressed his knee against her harder. She gasped at the heat and friction building between her legs and he pushed again.

'Lola,' he muttered, his breathing as rough as sandpaper, his gaze boring into hers. Then, as if something had snapped, he swooped down and kissed her.

Lola flared like a lit match beneath the onslaught, moaning his name. Her hands, suddenly free from his, slid into the back of his hair, holding him there. His hands found her hips, gripping them tight as he ground his knee against her over and over.

Lights popped and flared behind Lola's eyes, her whole world melting down as his mouth and his body worked hers. She was hot, too hot, and her heart was beating too fast. There were too many clothes. She wanted them gone. Wanted them off. Wanted him naked and inside her, pounding away, calling her name.

She reached down between them for his shorts, needing them gone while she could still think, while his kisses hadn't quite stolen her capacity to participate. Her hand connected with his erection and she made a triumphant noise at the back of her throat as she grabbed it and fondled him through his shorts. He groaned, breaking off the kiss, dropping his forehead to her neck, his lips warm against the frantic beat of her pulse at the base of her throat.

He was big and hard and solid in her hand. She squeezed him and he swore into her neck, his voice like gravel, his breath a hot caress.

This. She wanted this. Him. Inside her. Right where his knee was pressed tight and hard.

Lola moved her hand to his waistband, sliding her fingers beneath it, her pulse so loud in her ears it was like Niagara Falls inside her head. But before she hit her objective, his big hand clamped around her wrist.

'Wait.'

He panted into her neck for a few more moments, his body a dead weight on top of hers. Lola also panted, blinking into the dark room, grappling with the sudden cessation of endorphins, confused yet still craving at the same time.

He eased himself up a little, his hand still shackling her wrist. 'Are you sure about this, Lola?'

His gaze bored into hers once again and she could see he was struggling with this as much as she was. His arousal was as obvious in his eyes as it had been in her hand. But there was conflict there as well.

'Because if we keep going like this we'll end up having sex on this couch again, and I'm telling you now I don't think I can go back to being just roomies again if we do.'

The implication of his words slowly sank in, the sexual buzz fizzling as Lola's brain started to kick in. It was like a cold bucket of water.

But it was the cold bucket of water she needed.

'Right.' She nodded and pulled her hand out of his, her breathing erratic. What the hell had she been thinking? 'Of course. Sorry... I...' She trailed off because she didn't have any kind of adequate explanation for what the hell had just happened.

'Don't worry about it. It's fine.' He rolled off her, his butt sliding to the floor, his back against the couch.

'No...it's not,' she said breathily, her hands shaking a little. He was right, they'd overstepped their boundary. And they probably needed to re-establish it. 'I think we need to talk about it.'

'Okay.'

He didn't turn and perversely Lola wanted him to turn and look at her. And, *Lordy*, she wanted to touch him.

She didn't.

'It wouldn't work out between you and me. No matter how good the sex is. We have different jobs and different lives and different *goals*.'

He nodded. 'I know.'

'I'm sorry that we got carried away but I think we both need to agree that if this living arrangement is to work out, we just can't go there.'

He nodded again before rising to his feet. He was looking down at her but his eyes were too hooded in the semi-darkness to really see what he was feeling. He shoved a hand through his hair. 'You're right.'

Lola reached for his hand but he pulled back slightly and it felt like a slap to the face. 'I'm sorry,' she whispered once more.

'Me too,' he whispered back then stepped away, feet crunching over popcorn as he headed to his room.

CHAPTER EIGHT

November morphed into December. The weather got hotter, the days longer. The Christmas tree had gone up in the apartment. Hamish had been in Sydney for five weeks and was working his first run of night shifts. He didn't mind working nights usually, he was a good sleeper and night shift in Sydney was a hell of a lot busier than back home. Which was great—there was nothing more tiring than trying to fill in twelve empty hours.

But Lola was also working nights, which meant they were home together during the day. *Sleeping.* A much bigger psychological temptation than being at home together and sleeping during the night.

Because the night was for sleeping. And being in bed during the day felt decadent. Like flying first class or a good bottle of cognac. Or daytime sex.

Totally and utterly *decadent.*

They weren't having daytime sex, of course. They weren't having *any* sex, thanks to their conversation after things had got out of hand on movie night. She was right, their lives were going in different directions and he respected that.

But it didn't help him sleep any better.

Having Lola just across the hallway from him was far

too distracting. Sure as hell *not* conducive to sleep. Not conducive to night shifts. Not conducive to being a safe practitioner when he was so damn tired when he was on shift he couldn't think straight.

Consequently, Hamish wasn't looking forward to heading home in a few hours to repeat the whole not-sleeping process again. But it was his third night. Maybe if he was tired enough he could sleep despite the temptation of Lola in the next room.

Hamish's thoughts were interrupted by a squawk from his radio. 'Damn,' Jenny grumbled. It was almost two in the morning, they'd been going since they'd clocked on at eight and they'd only just left the hospital from their last emergency room drop-off. 'Are we ever going to get a chance for a cup of coffee tonight?'

But her grumbles quickly ceased when the serious-ness of the call became evident. Some kind of explosion had happened in a night club in Kings Cross. It was a Saturday night in one of the city's oldest club districts. 'We have a mass casualty incident. Repeat mass casualty. Multiple fatalities, multiple victims. Code one please.'

Code one. Lights and sirens.

Neither Hamish nor Jenny needed to be told that. As intensive care paramedics, all their jobs were lights and sirens, but the urgency in the voice on the other end of the radio painted a pretty grim picture.

Jenny flicked on the siren. 'Hold onto your hat.'

Hamish had never seen anything like what greeted them when they arrived on scene twelve minutes later. A ca-cophony of sirens from a cavalcade of arriving emer-gency services vehicles—police, fire and ambulance, including several intensive care cars—*whooped* into the warm night air. The area had been cordoned off and over two dozen firemen were battling the blaze that currently forked out of the windows on the upper storey.

Others were running in and out of the lower floor, evacuating victims, masks in place to protect them from the smoke that billowed from the blown-out windows. It hung in the air, clogging Hamish's nose and stinging his eyes.

He and Jenny, their fully loaded packs in hand, reported to the scene controller. 'Some kind of incendiary device, although we won't know for sure until afterwards. Blast killed several people instantly and started a fire on the first floor, panic caused a stampede and the upper balcony collapsed under the weight of people trying to get out. The night club was packed to the gills, so we're talking at least a couple of hundred people.'

Hamish glanced around the scene as evacuated victims huddled in groups across the road from the night club. Some stood and some sat as they stared dazedly at the building, their faces bloodied, their clothes ripped. A lot of them were crying, some quietly in a kind of despair, others loudly in shock and rage and disbelief, railing against the police who had been tasked to question them and stop them from running back into the building to find their mates.

An incendiary device?

Someone had done this deliberately?

'Go to the triage station. There are several red tags there and more coming out all the time. The collapse has trapped quite a few people and the rescue squad are digging them out.'

'Red tag' referred to the colour system employed in mass casualty events to prioritise treatment. Everyone in the triage section would be tagged with a colour. Green for the walking wounded, yellow for stable but requiring observation, white for minor injury not requiring medical assistance.

And black. For the deceased.

Red identified patients who couldn't survive without immediate attention but still had survivable injuries.

Hamish followed Jenny down the street, adrenaline pumping through his system at the job ahead. He slowed as he passed an area that was obviously being used as a temporary morgue, a tarp being erected to shield the scene from the television cameras already vying for the most grisly footage. He didn't need to see them to know the dozen or so bodies lying under the sheets would be wearing black tags.

He glanced away, concentrating on what was ahead of them, not behind. On the people he could help, not the ones he couldn't. If he went there now, if he started thinking about such a senseless waste of life, about the horror of it, he'd get too angry to be of any use. He needed to channel his adrenaline, harness it for the hours ahead, not burn it all up in his rage.

A dozen paramedics, their reflective stripes glowing in the flare of emergency sirens, were working their way through the victims when they pulled up at triage. Jenny introduced both of them to the senior paramedic in charge. She calmly and efficiently pointed them to a section where two other intensive care paramedics were currently working among half a dozen casualties. 'Over there, please.'

Jenny shook her head in dismay as they made their way over. 'Who would do this?'

Hamish didn't have an answer, he was still grappling with it himself.

They got to work, steadily treating the red cards—establishing airways, treating haemorrhages and burns, getting access for fluids and drugs. In two hours Hamish had intubated four patients who hadn't looked much older than twenty and dispatched them for transport to one of the many hospitals around the city that had already activated their mass casualty protocols.

He'd hadn't been able to save two people and they'd died despite his attempts to treat their life-threatening injuries.

One, a girl wearing an 'Eighteen today' sash across her purple dress, was going to haunt his dreams, he just knew it. The dress was the colour of Lola's jacarandas, with the exception of the bright crimson blood spray across the front.

'Help me.' That's what she'd said to him, her eyes large and frightened, just before blood had welled up her throat and she'd coughed and spluttered and the light had drained from her eyes as she'd lost consciousness.

Hamish had worked frantically on her to staunch the bleeding, to stabilise her enough to get her to hospital, but he hadn't been able to save her.

He hadn't even known her name.

In all probability the chunk of whatever the hell had hit her chest had probably ruptured something major. What she'd needed had been a cardiothoracic surgeon and an operating theatre. What she'd got had been him.

And he hadn't been enough.

'This is the last of them,' a female voice said.

Hamish looked up from the chest tube he was taping into place, surprised to realise that dawn had broken.

He hadn't noticed. Just as he hadn't noticed the stench of smoke in the air any more or the constant background wail of sirens as they came and went from the scene.

He'd shut everything out as he'd lurched from one person to the next, concentrating only on the one in front of him.

Two rescue squad officers, a male and the female who'd spoken, placed a stretcher bearing a long, lanky male on the ground. He was sporting an oxygen mask and there was a hard collar around his neck. A small portable monitor blipped away next to his head.

Hamish nodded at a crew who were waiting to whisk his current patient away. 'Thanks,' he said as they snapped up the rails of the gurney and pushed the patient briskly towards the waiting ambulance.

He turned his attention to the new patient. 'He's breathing,' the female officer continued as if she hadn't stopped. 'His pulse is fifty-eight but he's unconscious, sats are good.'

Hamish didn't like the pulse being that low—it should be rattling along, working overtime to compensate for the trauma his body had sustained.

'He was right at the bottom of the collapsed balcony debris.'

The guy looked remarkably untouched, considering, but Hamish had been doing this long enough to know that sometimes it was the way of things. That internal injuries weren't visible from the outside.

He pulled off his gloves and grabbed a new pair from the box in his bag and snapped them on. The bag was somewhat depleted now. He crouched then knelt against the rough bitumen yet again. His knees protested the move but Hamish ignored the pain. Gravel rash was a minor inconvenience compared to burns, blast injuries and the other trauma he'd seen in the last few hours.

'Do you know his name?' So many of the victims hadn't had an ID on them but Hamish always liked to know who he was treating.

'Wesley, according to the driver's licence in the wallet we found in his pocket.'

Hamish nodded. 'Thanks.' The rescue squad officers turned to go. 'How many fatalities?' His voice was quiet but enough to stop the woman in her tracks. He'd been trying not to notice the line of bodies beneath the sheets growing but every time he lifted his head they were in his line of sight.

'Twenty-six.'

He shut his eyes briefly, the image of a purple dress fluttering through his mind like the sails of a kite. It was going to be a really terrible Christmas for a lot of families across the city.

'Wesley.' Hamish turned to his patient, his voice deep and authoritative as he delivered a brisk sternal rub.

Nothing.

'Wesley,' he said again, deeper and a little louder as he shone his penlight into the patient's eyes. Both were fixed and dilated. Neither responded to light.

Oh, no. Crap.

Jenny crouched beside him. 'Bad?'

Hamish nodded. 'Non-responsive. Pupils fixed, dilated. GCS of three.'

'Okay, then.' Jenny grabbed her bag. 'Let's intubate, get some lines in and get him to hospital. This guy has a date with a neurosurgeon's drill.'

Hamish didn't think Jenny really believed performing a burr hole was going to result in a positive outcome.

They had no idea how long Wesley had been in this condition. If he'd had surgery performed immediately post-injury, it *might* have helped, but it was probably way too late by now.

More likely the sustained pressure in his head from a bleed, which had probably occurred when his skull had crashed into the ground, had caused diffuse injury. If he came though this, the likelihood of a severe neurological deficit was strong.

But one thing he knew for sure was that sometimes people surprised you and it wasn't their job to make ethical decisions. It was their job to save who could be saved and Wesley had made it thus far. And, hell, Hamish wanted to believe that a guy who was still breathing, despite the trauma he'd received, could pull through this.

God knew, they needed a Christmas miracle after everything tonight.

Lola wasn't surprised to see Hamish pushing through the swing doors of her intensive care unit. Normally paramedics dropped patients in the emergency department and Emergency brought them to ICU if warranted. But when a patient was already intubated it saved time and handling for paramedics to bring the patient directly to ICU. They'd had two admissions like this already tonight from the night club bombing.

She was pleased it was him accompanying the patient this time, though. She'd figured he'd be there on scene somewhere and she hadn't realised how tense she'd been about it until she'd spotted him and the grimness of his mouth had kicked up into a familiar smile.

It wasn't that she thought Hamish might be in some kind of danger, it was more professional empathy. Lola could only guess at the kind of carnage he must have witnessed from what had already come in here and from the news reports they were hearing. Dozens of crushed, broken and burned bodies. Bright young things just out having fun. And so close to Christmas.

Things like that could do a number on your head.

'Bed twelve,' she said.

As one of the shifts runners, it had been Lola's job to get the bed space ready for their new admission. They'd been alerted to this arrival about fifteen minutes ago so she'd had time to customise the set-up for a patient with a head injury. And now it was action stations as two more nurses—the one assigned to look after Wesley and the nurse in charge—and two doctors—the ICU and the neuro registrar—descended on bed twelve.

They worked as a team, listening to Hamish's methodical handover as they got Wesley on the bed, hooked him up to the ventilator, plugged him into the monitors, started up some fluids and commenced some sedation.

The ICU registrar was inserting an arterial line as Hamish's handover drew to a close. By the time he'd answered all the questions that had been thrown at him, the arterial line was in, they had a red blood-pressure trace on the screen with an alarmingly wide pulse pressure and the registrar had thrust a full arterial blood gas syringe at Lola and she filled some lab tubes with blood from another syringe.

'Go and get some coffee,' she threw over her shoulder to Hamish and Jenny as she headed for the blood gas machine out back. Jenny knew where the staffroom was and they looked like they could do with some bolstering.

Lola was inserting the blood-filled syringe into the machine when Hamish appeared and said, 'Hey.'

He reeked of smoke and looked like hell. 'Hey.' She smiled at him for a beat or two, her heart squeezing, before she returned her attention to entering Wesley's details into the computer.

He didn't say anything, just watched her, and she waited for the machine to beep at her to remove the syringe before she said anything. 'Are you okay?' she asked.

It would take a couple of minutes for the machine to print out the results so she had the time to check up on him.

'Yep.' His smile warmed his eyes and was immensely reassuring. 'Just tired.'

She nodded. 'How was it out there?'

He didn't say anything for a moment then shook his head. 'Awful.'

Lola didn't have any reply to that. No easy words to soothe the terrible memories no doubt still fresh in his mind. So she did the only thing she knew how to do, what nurses always did—she touched him. She reached across and squeezed his arm.

'Go.' She squeezed his arm again. 'Get coffee. I think there's still some choc-chip biscuits someone brought in earlier too. You look like you need a sugar hit.'

He gave a half-laugh that sounded so weary she wanted to tuck him into bed herself. 'You look tired too.'

That was an understatement. It was almost six and Lola hadn't even had a break yet. Not even to go to the bathroom. She wasn't tired mentally, but physically she was exhausted. Her feet throbbed, her lower back twinged, her stomach growled and she had a dull ache behind her eyes.

Being a runner usually meant a busy shift but some shifts were crazily busy. Like tonight with their third critical admission as well as several existing patients who'd decided tonight was the night to destabilise.

Emma was one of them.

Her blood pressure had shot up at the start of the shift and it'd taken them several worrying hours to get it down to a much safer reading. She was fine again now but it was just further evidence of the instability of her failing heart. A transplant couldn't happen soon enough.

Lola shrugged off her weariness. It was just the way it went sometimes. 'It's almost knock-off time.' That was the one consolation. In an hour and a half her shift would be over—so would his—and they could both get some well-earned sleep.

The blood-gas machine spewed out a strip of paper, which Lola tore off and studied. 'How is it?' Hamish asked.

'Not great.' She handed it to him. 'His carbon dioxide level's too high.' Which would increase his intracranial pressure—not the thing Wesley's brain needed.

'I've got to get this back to the reg.' He nodded and handed the slip over, stepping away from the doorway so she could pass. He fell in beside her as she walked briskly to the bed space. 'I'll probably be late home,' she said. 'This place is a mess and we're not going to get a chance to play catch-up until the morning staff come on.'

There was a roomful of discarded equipment out back that needed attention and things were in desperate need of a restock.

'I don't think I'm going to be home early either. Jenny mentioned something about the boss probably wanting to do a bit of an informal debrief with her before we leave so…'

Lola nodded. 'Good idea.' She pulled up beside the

registrar and handed over the blood-gas printout. 'Now
go get coffee.'

He smiled. 'Yes ma'am.'

CHAPTER NINE

LOLA HAD NOT long succumbed to sleep on the couch when the door opened and her eyelids pinged open. Between the hurricane-like roar of the fan overhead and the fact that she'd dropped like a stone into the deepest depths of unconsciousness, she was amazed she'd heard a thing.

She must have really been attuned to the key in the lock!

Squinting at the time on the television display—it was almost ten—she swung her legs to the floor. 'Hamish?'

'Sorry,' he said from somewhere behind her. 'I didn't mean to wake you. I thought you'd be in bed. What are you doing out here?'

Lola's thoughts floated in a thick soup of disorientation. What *was* she doing out here? 'I'm…waiting for you to come home.'

'Sorry, I didn't realise. Debrief went on for ever.'

He appeared in front of her, lowering himself down on the end of the coffee table and setting his backpack on the floor. There were a few feet separating them but, as always, she felt the tug of him.

'You didn't have to wait up.'

Lola shrugged. Did he think she'd just go to bed after the things he'd seen last night without checking in with him first? Just because she didn't think they should get intimately involved, it didn't mean they still couldn't care for each other, have empathy for each other.

'It's fine,' she dismissed, suddenly realising that he was in shorts and T-shirt instead of his uniform and that his russet hair was damp and curling at his nape. 'You had a shower at work?' He didn't usually.

'Yeah. Everything stank of smoke, even my hair.'

He ran his palms down his thighs, drawing her gaze to the gold-blond hairs on his legs and the state of his knees. They were criss-crossed with tiny livid cuts and areas that had been rubbed raw.

'Do they hurt?'

'A little.' He shrugged as if it was just a mild inconvenience. 'How's Wesley?'

Lola had been waiting for the question, knowing it would come. She wished she had better news to tell Hamish, even though she knew *he* knew full well the severity of Wesley's injuries. 'He'd not long come back from CT when I left.'

He nodded slowly. 'Bad?'

'Diffuse brain injury with severe cerebral swelling. They were prepping him for Theatre.'

'Right.' He nodded and rose from the table, heading to the kitchen. She heard the fridge door open and he called, 'You want a beer?'

'No.' Lola didn't think twice at Hamish consuming a beer at ten in the morning. Quite a few of her colleagues had a drink or two before going to sleep after night duty. They swore it was better than sleeping tablets, which many shift workers resorted to.

He reappeared in the kitchen doorway, leaning against

the jamb as he took a few deep swallows. The hem of his T-shirt lifted slightly, flashing a strip of tanned abs.

'They're saying on television that the bomb was set off by some guy who's a disgruntled ex-employee,' she said.

'Yeah, I heard. Death toll's risen to thirty-four too.' He wandered closer as if he was going to resume his seat on the table but changed course, heading for the balcony, stopping short to just stare out the door she'd opened earlier.

Lola didn't say anything, waiting for him to say more. If he wanted to. When he didn't, she filled the silence. 'You want to talk about it?'

He shook his head. 'Nope.' But within a few seconds he was turning around, his eyes seeking hers, searching hers. 'I've been trying to wrap my head around how that guy justified this to himself.' He took a swig of his beer. 'I mean, you got sacked, dude. I get it. That sucks.' He shrugged. 'Rant at your boss or your wife, go home and kick the wall. But *why* would anyone think it's okay to seek revenge like this? To kill so many innocent people?'

Lola shook her head. 'I…don't know.' She wished she did. She wished she had the answers he sought.

He was obviously still in the thick of the action inside his head. Probably second-guessing his every move, wishing he'd done something differently. That stuff took time to fully tease out. Took a lot of reflection before a person came to the conclusion that they'd done the best they could.

'I don't know why some people do terrible things, Hamish, but thank goodness for people like you.' She smiled at him because he looked so lonely all the way over there by himself. 'For those who charge in to help when everyone else is running away. There'd be a lot more fatalities from last night without people like you around.'

He nodded. 'Yeah.' Tipping his head back, he drained his beer, staring at the bottle in his hands for a moment or two before he glanced at her and said, 'Think I'll hit the sack now.'

'You should. You look dead on your feet.' He was swaying and his eyes were bloodshot. She'd bet her last cent they were as gritty as hers. There were tiny lines around his eyes that she'd never noticed before and his impossibly square jaw was as tight as a steel trap.

'Says the woman with a cushion mark on her face and scary hair.'

Lola gaped for a moment before his lips spread into a smile and a low chuckle slipped from his mouth. She pushed her hands through her fuzzy mane to tame the knotty, blonde ringlets but there was no nope for them. She probably looked like she'd been pulled through a hedge backwards, while he looked good enough to eat.

Even exhausted, the man wore sexy better than any man had a right to.

'Your sense of humour's pretty tired too, I see.'

'Yep.' He grinned. 'We're both kinda beat.'

'At least you only have one more night. I have three.' Lola didn't mind night shift but when the unit was busy for a sustained period of time like it had been, a run of night shifts could really take it out of her.

'Some days off would be good,' Hamish said, cutting into her thoughts.

Yeah. He could no doubt use some mental time-out after last night. But, more than anything, right now he needed to sleep.

They both did.

'Okay, well, I'm taking my scary hair to bed.' It didn't seem like he was going to make the first move towards the bedrooms so she did it for him. 'Night-night.'

She didn't look at him as she turned away in case she did something crazy like offer to rock him to sleep. She just kept walking until she pulled her door shut, placing temptation firmly on the other side.

Hamish woke at two in the afternoon for about the tenth time. His room was on the side of the apartment that copped full sunlight for most of the day, and the curtains at the big window wouldn't block out candlelight, let alone the December sun in Sydney. It hadn't ever bothered him before and he could usually sleep like the dead after night shift.

But he hadn't just been through a normal night shift.

He was coming off an adrenaline high that had left him wrung out and edgy, his brain grappling with the images of the kids he'd helped and all those bodies under sheets. When he did manage to drift off, his dreams were haunted by a woman in a purple dress.

Just like he'd known they would be.

And now he was awake again. Exhausted, but too chicken to close his eyes, plus it was too hot to fall asleep, anyway. There was sweat on his chest and in the small of his back. The fan going at full speed did nothing but push the stifling air around.

He *had* to sleep. He *needed* to sleep. He had to operate a vehicle in six hours *and* be thinking clearly. He wouldn't be any help to anyone if he went to work even more exhausted than he'd left it.

Hamish rolled on his side, forced himself to shut his eyes, to breathe in through his nose and out through his mouth. To do it again and again until he started to drift. And then a flutter of purple fabric splattered in blood billowed through his mind and his eyes flicked open.

Grabbing his pillows, he plonked them on top of his head, shoved his face into them and let out a giant *yawp!*

'Hamish?'

Startled, he ripped the pillows off his head to find Lola striding into his room, her short gown covering her from neck to knee but hugging everything in between. He was pretty sure she wasn't wearing much of anything underneath.

Great.

'Lola?'

'Are you okay?' She stood at the end of the bed, her forehead creased, her arms folded tight against her chest.

'Yes.' Hamish flopped onto his back and stared at the ceiling. It was that or ogle her. 'Just…can't sleep. Have you been skulking outside my door?'

'No.' He smiled at the affront in her voice. 'I was just passing to get a drink of water and I heard a noise. I thought you were…upset or something.'

He gave a harsh laugh, air huffing from his lungs. *Great.* Lola thought he was lying in bed, crying. It'd be emasculating if he wasn't currently sporting an erection the size of the Opera House.

He thanked God for his decision to keep his underwear on today and for the sheet that was bunched over his crotch.

'I'm frustrated,' he told the ceiling. *In more ways than one.* 'I need to sleep but my brain is ticking over and the fan is totally useless in this heat.' He raised his head again. 'We even have air-con in the country, Lola, what gives?'

'Grace and I moved into the apartment in the middle of winter. And there were fans...they're usually enough.'

'How do you sleep after nights on days like this?'

'Well, my room is quite a bit cooler than yours. Grace said I should take it because she didn't work nights on her job. But I have been known to get up and walk through a cold shower then flop on the bed wringing wet and let the fan air-dry me. That's almost as good as air-con.'

Hamish shut his eyes and suppressed a rising groan as his head fell back against the pillow. That image was not helping the situation in his underwear. Not one little bit.

'Are you dreaming about it?'

About her being wet and naked on her bed? He sure as hell would be now. But he knew that wasn't what she was talking about. He sighed. 'Yes.'

'You want to talk about it?'

'No.' What he wanted was to drag her down on the bed, rip that gown off her, roll her under him and sink inside her, and just forget about it all for a while. 'I don't want to talk about it. I don't even want to *think* about it. What I want right now is to just forget it so I can get to sleep. I *need* to sleep. I want it to *not* be forty degrees in this room so I can just *go to sleep.*'

She didn't say anything for a long time and a weird kind of tension built in his abdomen. Hamish lifted his head and immediately wished he hadn't. The way she was looking at him shot sparks right up his spine.

'What?' His voice was annoyingly raspy and he cleared it as her gaze roved over his body.

She nodded then, as if to herself, before saying, 'I can help you with that.'

Hamish swore he could feel his heart skip a beat. Where the hell was she going with this? Was she going to fix him a long cool drink or was she offering something else? 'What do you suggest?'

'My room is cooler and sex is not only the best sleeping pill around but I've generally found that if it's good enough it can also induce a temporary kind of amnesia. I can only surmise from the kind of sex we've already had together that the amnesia will be significant. What do you think?'

Hamish blinked. What didn't he think? There was no hope for his erection now.

He should decline. It was all kinds of screwed up and he knew how it'd mess with the boundaries they'd put in place. But he'd be lying if he said he didn't crave the solace—the oblivion—she was offering.

Didn't crave the white noise of pleasure, her breathy pants, the way she called his name as she came. Didn't crave the company of another human being, someone to hold onto in a world that seemed a little less shiny than it had yesterday.

Someone he wanted more than he'd ever wanted anyone. His heart rattled in his chest just thinking about being with Lola again.

'Please, Hamish.' She took a step forward, her features earnest. She'd obviously taken his silence as a pending *no* instead of a considered *hell, yes*. 'I know we said we shouldn't do this and we've both been trying to respect that. But…our jobs are… There's a lot of emotional pressure and sometimes we need an outlet. Let me do this for you. Let me be there for you the way you were there for me that night when I needed comfort and distraction. Unless you're too tired?'

Hamish gave a half laugh, half snort. 'Too tired for sex?'

She shrugged. 'I heard that's a thing.'

He grabbed the sheet bunched at his hips and threw it back to reveal how *not* tired he was. 'It's not a thing for me.'

Her eyes zeroed in on his underwear, following the ridge of his erection, and Hamish felt it as potently as if it had been her tongue. Her gaze drifted down a little then back up again, finally settling between his legs.

'So I see.' She dragged her attention back to his face and held out her hand. 'What are we waiting for?'

Hamish didn't have a clue. He vaulted upright, swung his legs out of the bed and rose to his feet, reaching for her hand. His pulse raced now as they headed across the hallway. The last time they'd done this it'd been the middle of the night. It'd been unexpected, spontaneous. There'd been haste, urgency. They'd groped blindly, they'd fumbled.

This was broad daylight, and premeditated.

She opened her door and led him inside where the heavy blinds at the window blocked out the light and the sparseness of the furniture and walls made it feel cave-like. And with the fan on high speed the temperature *was* several degrees lower. It wasn't cool exactly but the edge had been taken off the heat.

'Bloody hell,' he grumbled. 'I've been sweltering out there in the desert while you've been hibernating in a cave.'

She laughed and her hand slipped from his as she moved towards the bed. 'I thought you country boys could handle the heat.'

'What can I say? You've already made a pampered city slicker out of me.'

'*That* I find hard to believe.'

Hamish smiled as he watched her open a bedside

drawer and bend over it slightly as she fished around inside. The gown rose nicely up the backs of her thighs and he didn't even bother to pretend he wasn't checking out her ass.

She found what she wanted and turned to face him, brandishing a square foil packet in the air for a second before tossing it on the bed. Then, as he watched, she tugged on the tie at her waist holding her gown in place. It fell open, revealing a swathe of skin right down her middle. The two inner swells of her breasts, her stomach, some lacy underwear and upper thighs. His mouth turned as dry as the dust in the cattle yards back home.

She smiled. 'You want to come a little closer?'

Hamish did, he really did. He strode over, his heart in his mouth as he stopped close enough to slip a hand inside her gown if he wanted. And he wanted. But he wanted to kiss her more. He wanted to kiss her until they both couldn't breathe.

He placed his hands on her face, cradling her cheeks, his eyes searching hers, looking for pity and finding only the softness of empathy. And a glitter of lust. He brushed a thumb over her lips and she made a noise at the back of her throat as she parted her lips. The breeze from the fan blew a curl from her temple across her face and he hooked it back with his index finger.

'You're so beautiful,' he whispered as he slowly lowered his mouth to hers.

Their lips met and her soft moan was like a hit of adrenaline to his system, tripping through his veins, whooshing through his lungs, taking the kiss from a light touch to a long, drugging exploration that left them both breathless and needy.

When he pulled back her lips were full and wet from

his kisses and a deep reddish-pink. She looked like she'd been thoroughly kissed and damn if being the one to put *that* look on her face wasn't a huge turn-on. His hands slid to her shoulders, his thumbs hooking into the open lapels of her gown, which he slowly pushed back. The gown skimmed the tops of her shoulders before sliding down her arms, and falling off to pool at her feet.

Hamish sucked in a breath at the roundness of her breasts, at the light pink circle of her areolas and the way the nipples beaded despite the heat. His hands brushed from her neck to the slopes of her breasts, trailing down to the very tips before palming them, filling his hands with their fullness.

'Hamish.' Her voice was a breathy whisper and she swayed a little and shut her eyes as he kissed her again. Kissed her as he stroked and kneaded her breasts, kissed her until she was moaning and arching her back, her thighs pressed to his.

His hands slid lower, skimming her ribs and her hips, using his thumbs once again as a hook to remove her underwear, breaking off the kiss as he slid them down, crouching before her to pull them all the way down her legs. He looked up as she stepped out of them and her hands slid into his hair and he dropped a kiss on the top of each thigh, his nostrils filling with the heady scent of her arousal.

Hamish kissed his way back up, brushing his lips against her hip bone and her belly button and the underside of each breast and the centre of her chest and her neck then back to her mouth, groaning as she slid her arms around his neck and smooshed her naked body along the length of his, grinding her pelvis into him.

'Mmm…' he murmured against her mouth, his hands tightening on her ass. 'That feels good.'

'It'd feel better if you were naked too,' she said, her voice husky.

Hamish didn't need to be told twice and quickly pulled off his own underwear to stand in front of her naked, his erection standing thick and proud between them.

'Oh, yes,' she whispered, her hand reaching out to stroke him. 'Much better.'

Hamish shut his eyes as she petted him, her fingers trailing up and down his shaft, the muscles in his ass tensing uncontrollably, electricity buzzing low in his spine, his heart thumping like a gong in his chest.

Her fingers grew bolder, sliding around him, and he groaned again as he opened his eyes. 'Enough.' He grabbed her hand. 'I'm not sure how long I'm going to last and I want to be inside you.'

'God… Yes, please.'

Hamish lowered himself onto the bed and pulled her down on top of him, revelling in the easy way she straddled him, in the way his erection slid through the slickness between her legs, in the way she grabbed the condom and sheathed him, in the way her breasts swung and she moaned as he touched them, in the way her blonde curls blew around her head as she looked down at him.

His hands tightened on her hips. She was magnificent on top of him, so comfortable with her nudity and taking charge. She lifted her hips and took him in hand, notching his erection at her entrance, closing her eyes to enjoy the feel of it for a moment.

She took his breath away. 'You look like a goddess.'

She opened her eyes and smiled. 'You can call me Aphrodite.' And she lowered herself onto him.

Hamish groaned, watching her as he sank to the hilt inside her, watching pleasure spread over her face and satisfaction take over as she settled on him, her bottom lip caught between her teeth.

'Oh, yes,' she whispered, raising her arms above her head and sinking her hands into her hair, her breasts thrusting, her back arching.

She was gloriously unrestrained and she was his.

'*Now* you're Aphrodite.'

He moved then and she moved with him, her hands still in her hair, rocking her hips, undulating her stomach, riding him like a belly dancer, taking his thrusts, absorbing them, consumed in the rocking and the pounding, building her, building him—building them—to fever point, the frantic whistle of the fan a back note to the wild tango between them.

Hamish's climax gathered speed and light and momentum, little daggers of pleasure burrowing into his backside, the tension in his stomach and groin starting to unravel, and he could almost reach out and touch the rapture. He slid his fingers between her legs, wanting her there with him, *needing* her there.

She moaned as he found the hard knot of her clitoris and she gasped as he squeezed it, the sensation jolting like a shock through her body, her internal muscles clamping hard around him.

'*Hamish!*'

She sobbed his name as the rapture took her, and he cried out to her too, as it collected him, his fingers digging into her hips as his spine electrified and his seed surged from his body. He pulsed inside her and she pulsed around him, the pleasure sweeping them along, ravaging them, their movements jerky, their dance disorganised, neither of them caring as they rode the rapture right to the very end.

It lifted as dramatically as it had descended, Lola collapsing against him, her curls spilling over his chest as she gasped for breath. She was hot against him but he didn't care. He was burning up too and moisture slicked between their bodies, but all that mattered was that they were burning up together.

She rolled off him eventually and Hamish groaned as he slid from her body. He turned his head to watch her. She looked utterly sated, a satisfied tilt to her lips. There was a line of sweat on her upper lip as well as on her forehead and her chest and in the hollow at the base of her throat.

'So that first time wasn't a fluke, then?' she said, slurring her words a little, obviously sleepy.

Hamish chuckled. 'Nope.'

He assumed she knew how special that was. To be so *simpatico* with another person? To feel as if you *fitted* together. As if you were their *perfect fit*. He'd never felt it with another woman.

He shut his eyes, enjoying the thought and the coolness of the air from the fan drying his sweat and the stillness in his head, surrendering for a second or two to the tug of exhaustion, before rousing to dispose of the condom. Lola was already asleep, her body rosy from their contact, her blonde curls frothing around her head, a small smile still touching her mouth.

He crawled back in beside her—it never occurred to him to return to his own bed. Not now. This might only be a one-off but he was going to hold onto it for as long as he could.

He was going to lie down beside her and sleep—wonderful, wonderful sleep—and he was going to worry about the rest later.

CHAPTER TEN

ON HER LAST night shift, Lola was assigned to Emma who, although stable, still desperately needed a heart transplant. She'd been listed for almost six weeks now, which was truly pushing it, and there *would* come a point where Emma started to decompensate, despite medical technology's best efforts to keep her stable.

Then she'd be just another *died on the waiting list* statistic.

Which was tragic at any age but at twenty-three it was just too awful to contemplate.

Despite the underlying desperation of the situation, Emma was chugging along and Lola found her mind drifting back to Hamish. In her bed. They'd slept together three days in a row and she was counting on making that a fourth.

They hadn't talked about what had happened between them that morning after the bombing. Lola had just *understood* what he'd needed and hadn't been able to deny him. Not when he'd been *her* comfort, *her* solace, *her* soft place to land that first night they'd spent together all those months ago.

And she'd wanted to be that person for him.

They hadn't discussed sleeping together again either.

When she'd made the offer, it had been a one-time-only kind of thing.

The rest had just kind of happened.

They'd arrived home that next morning at the same time and it had seemed like the most natural thing in the world for her to join him in the shower, to soap him up, lay her hands on him, her mouth on him, until he had her up against the tiles, driving into her, withdrawing as he came because neither of them had thought about their lack of protection when things had started to get handsy.

And then he'd carried her through to her bed, both of them still wet, and they'd drifted off, their skin cooling under the roar of the fan, her heart happy. They'd woken twice during the day to join again, half-asleep but reaching for each other despite the fact she had to work that night.

Lola wasn't used to being gripped by such…attraction. Sure, she'd been with good-looking men, but she didn't need a *hubba-hubba* reaction to a guy to go to bed with him and sex had just been an itch to scratch. A fun but necessary biological function.

But these last few days had blown that theory out of the water. There was sex, there was *good* sex and there was *whoa Nelly!* sex. She'd had some of the first, quite a bit of the second but never any of the third. Until Hamish. He was the whole package—physically attractive and a magician between the sheets—and it had been totally consuming.

'Hey.'

Lola glanced up after finishing a suction of Emma's tracheostomy tube—a breathing tube had been inserted into her neck a few weeks ago—to find Grace approaching. She'd been here when Lola had arrived on shift but it didn't stop the spurt of guilt Lola felt every time she saw her friend, especially given the direction of her thoughts.

'Hey.'

Heat crept into Lola's cheeks despite telling herself she'd done nothing wrong. Hamish was an adult. He didn't have to check it was okay with his sister to sleep with Lola and Grace had already dismissed those concerns anyway. But, deep down, Lola knew that Grace would want to know.

It might not be one of the Ten Commandments but *Thou shall not sleep with your best friend's brother without at least giving her all the gory details* was ingrained in the female psyche.

Lola thanked God for the low lighting Emma's stable condition allowed at the bed space and smiled, determined to act normal, even if she did feel like she was wearing an 'I'm sleeping with your brother' sign around her neck.

'How are you?' Lola asked.

It wasn't a standard throw-away question. It was a genuine enquiry about what Grace was dealing with tonight. Just prior to Lola commencing, Wesley, who hadn't recovered or responded in the seventy-two hours since the bombing of the nightclub, had undergone his second set of neurological function tests and been declared brain-dead.

It was a tragic end to such a young life and had raised the death toll from the bombing to thirty-five. The one glimmer of hope from the situation was Wesley's parents, who had generously and selflessly consented for his organs to be donated.

And it was Grace's job to co-ordinate everything. Which was a massive undertaking. Everything from ensuring all the correct tests were done and protocols followed, to liaising with other teams and hospitals involved with the recipients, to choreographing the harvesting that was going to occur in a few hours, to being there for Wesley's family fell under Grace's purview in this instance.

'Are you okay?' Lola pressed.

She knew how difficult these cases were to deal with. How talking with bewildered and bereaved people looking for answers you couldn't give them was emotionally sapping. How being strong for them required superhuman levels of empathy and patience and gentleness and sometimes meant bearing the brunt of their grief and anger.

Just watching Wesley's distraught family as they came and went from his bedside had taken a little piece of Lola's heart. It was simply heartbreaking to watch and there wasn't one nurse on the unit tonight who wasn't affected by it.

Grace grimaced. 'I'm okay.'

A silent moment passed between them. An acknowledgment that the situation sucked, that Wesley's death was a tragedy about to spawn a lot of happy endings for people staring down the barrels of their own tragedies.

Organ transplantation was truly a double-edged sword.

Lola stripped her gloves off. 'Everything sorted now?'

Grace gave a half-laugh that told Lola she wasn't getting home to Marcus any time soon. 'Things are coming together,' she said, obviously downplaying how much still had to be put in place.

It didn't fool Lola an iota.

'But I do have some good news.' She tipped her head to the side to indicate Lola should meet her at the bottom of the bed.

Lola removed her protective eyewear and washed her

hands at the nearby basin before joining her friend at the computer station at the end of Emma's bed. 'I thought you might like to be the first to know,' Grace said, her voice low. 'Emma's a match for Wesley's heart.'

Lola stared at Grace incredulously for a moment. The possibility had been in the back of her mind but she'd dismissed it as being highly unlikely. Lola *had* seen it once before a few years back when the donor and a recipient had been on the unit together but it wasn't common.

'Really?'

Grace beamed. 'Really. They're ringing Emma's parents now.'

Lola's heart just about grew wings and lifted out of her chest. It was a moment of indescribable joy. *Emma was getting a new heart.* The backs of Lola's eyes pricked with moisture and her arms broke out in goose-bumps.

'That's...*wonderful* news.'

Grace nodded. 'Right? It's nice in this job when you get to give happy news.'

Lola gave her friend a hug because she was overjoyed but also because Grace probably needed it after all she'd been dealing with. Of course, it didn't take long for the logistics to dawn. To know that her night was suddenly going to get a lot busier, following all the pre-donation protocols and getting Emma ready for the operating theatre.

But the realisation that a usually anonymous process might not stay that way dawned the heaviest.

The truth of the matter was that families of ICU patients talked to each other. The unit had a very comfortable, well-equipped relatives' room, where people hung out. And talked. They talked about their loved ones—

about the ups and downs, about the good days and the bad days, about the improvements and the setbacks.

Often they became *very* close, particularly in long-term cases like Emma's.

But donation was supposed to be anonymous. In most cases, donor families never met recipients. Usually about six weeks after the patient had died and their organs had been transplanted, the donor family was written to and given some basic information about the recipients in very generic detail.

Like, the right kidney went to a fifty-eight-year-old male who had been on the waiting list for ten years. Or the left lobe of the liver went to an eighteen-month-old baby girl and the remaining lobes were transplanted into to a thirty-one-year-old father of three.

But never names. Identities were always kept confidential. The whole process was ruled by a protocol of ethics and anonymity was strictly adhered to. It was too potentially fraught otherwise for recipients if donor families knew their names and where they lived. Also fraught for donor families.

If a recipient died due to complications after transplant—which did happen—what extra burden of grief could that put on already fragile families?

Organ donation was the ultimate altruistic gift and the lynchpin of that was anonymity.

Except now there were two families in the relatives' room—one whose son was brain-dead and about to have his organs harvested and the other whose daughter was about to get a heart transplant.

It wasn't going to take great powers of deduction to figure out the link.

'Have Wesley's family been interacting much with Emma's family?' Lola asked.

'Apparently not. They're still in that numbed, shocked stage and have kept to themselves. And Emma's family are down the coast for the night at some family thing so hopefully Wesley will be gone from the unit by the time Emma's family arrives back.'

'Fingers crossed we'll get lucky and neither will figure it out.' The other time it had happened, they'd managed to maintain the anonymity of the process. It had been touch and go for a moment but it had all worked out in the end. 'Are they going to use the Reflections Suite?'

Reflections was a self-contained unit two floors up that families of deceased patients could use to spend time saying goodbye to their loved ones, in private, before they were taken to the morgue. It was roomy with comfy chairs and couches and a kitchenette with a fridge. They were able to take all the time they needed to grieve as a family and be together in their loss.

Grace nodded. 'Yes. I'll go up with Wesley to the suite after the operation is finished and sit with the family for a bit if they want.'

Lola nodded. Grace was going to have a long, emotionally challenging night. 'Isn't that what the on-call social worker is for?'

'He'll be available to them too. But it's me they've been dealing with through this process so...' Grace shrugged. 'I want them to have some continuity and be able to answer any lingering questions they might have.'

'Yeah.' Lola nodded.

Caring for ICU patients meant caring for their families as well. And continuity, especially in acute situations, made everything much easier for grieving families.

Grace's pager went off and she pulled it off her belt, reading the message quickly. 'That's the Adelaide co-ordinator. Gotta go.'

Lola smiled. 'Of course. Go. I'll see you later.'

Grace darted off and Lola glanced at Emma and smiled before getting back to work. It was going to be another long night.

Lola was mentally exhausted as she entered the apartment eight hours later but her body was buzzing. In just a few days it had become scarily accustomed to Hamish being there and this morning was no different. In fact, it was probably worse.

They'd relaxed the rules about their roomie-only relationship and her cravings were growing.

Not even the prospect of telling him about Wesley's death seemed to put a lid on the hum in her cells. Lola knew Hamish was holding out hope that Wesley might make some kind of meaningful recovery, even though the news had been dire since the beginning. Hamish had asked after him every morning and Lola had filled him in on what she knew.

She doubted Wesley's death would come as much of a surprise but it would no doubt take a piece of Hamish's heart as it had taken a piece of hers.

'Hey, you.'

Lordy, he was a sight for sore eyes, lounging against the kitchen benchtop, a carton of orange juice in his hand. Her breath hitched as she pulled up in the doorway. He'd obviously just had a shower as his hair was damp and all that covered him was a towel slung low on his hips. His chest and abs were smooth and bare, his stomach muscles arrowing down nicely to the knot in the towel.

'I was hoping you'd still be in bed.'

He gave a nonchalant shrug but ruined it with a wicked grin. 'I've been for a run.'

'Of course you have.'

Lola laughed, feeling like an absolute sloth in his presence as she walked straight into his arms. His hands moved to the small of her back as hers slid up and over his shoulders on their way to his neck, revelling in the warm flesh and the taut stretch of his skin over rounded joints and firm muscles.

She sighed, grateful that the temperature had eased yesterday afternoon and she could get this close and personal without being a ball of sweat in five seconds flat. She pressed her cheek against a bare pec, the steady thump of his heartbeat both reassuring and thrilling. When he tried to break the embrace she held on harder.

'Lola? Everything okay?'

She could hear the frown in his voice and she pulled away slightly, gazing up into his face. His face did funny things to her equilibrium. How had his face come to mean so much to her in such a short time?

'Lola?' His hands slid to her arms and gave a gentle squeeze. 'What?'

Even with his brow creased in concern, his blue eyes earnest, she wanted to lick his mouth. 'It's Wesley.'

He didn't say anything for a moment but she was aware the second he knew what she was about to say. 'Oh.'

Lola stroked her fingers along the russet stubble decorating his jaw line. 'He was declared brain dead just before I started last night.'

'Yeah.' Hamish nodded. 'Guess that was inevitable.'

'Doesn't make it suck any less.'

He gave a half-laugh. 'No.'

Lola cuddled into him again, her cheek to his pec, hoping her body against his would be some kind of comfort. His arms came around her as he rested his chin on the top of her head.

'He'd be a suitable donor, right? Did his family consent?'

'Yes.' Lola broke away to look at him.

'Yeah?' Hamish brightened. 'That's fantastic.'

Lola beamed at him. She couldn't agree more. 'And guess what?'

He smiled. 'What?'

Strictly speaking, what she was about to tell him was breaking patient confidentiality, but healthcare professionals often did discuss patients past and present, particularly in overlapping cases where there'd been multi-team involvement, so Lola didn't have a problem divulging. And she figured Hamish would appreciate this particular silver lining.

'Guess who got his heart?'

He frowned for a moment but it cleared as quickly as it had formed. 'Your patient on the list?'

Lola nodded. 'She's in Theatre now.'

'Oh, God.' His smile almost split his face in two. 'That's...wonderful news.'

'The best.'

He kissed her then. Hard. And Lola melted the way she always did as her cares fell away and her body was consumed by the presence of *him*. His pine and coconut aroma fogged her senses. His touch dazzled and electrified everything in its path, drugging and energising in equal measure.

His fingers hummed at her nape, his lips buzzed

against hers, the rough drag of his breath brushed like sandpaper over her skin. His heart thumped hard beneath her palm and the steel of his erection pressed into her belly.

She was so damn needy she wanted to simultaneously rub herself all over him *and* crawl inside him.

'Mmm…' He broke off and every nerve ending in Lola's body cried out at the loss. 'I missed you last night.'

Lola smiled. 'I have three days off now.'

He smiled back. 'Whatever shall we do?'

'Well…there is the Christmas shopping.'

'We *could* do that.'

Lola pretended to consider some more. 'We could take a drive along the northern beaches. Find a nice spot for a picnic?'

'Yep. We could definitely do that.' He ground his erection into her belly. 'I was thinking of something a little more indoorsy.'

The delighted little moan that hovered in Lola's throat threatened to become full blown as Hamish adjusted the angle of their hips and the bulge behind the towel pressed against her in *all the right places*.

'Oh, yeah?' She shut her eyes at the mindless pleasure he could evoke with just a flex of his hips. 'What did you have in mind exactly?'

'Something that doesn't require clothes for the next three days would be awesome.'

Somewhere in the morass of her brain Lola knew she should reject his invitation. Try and pull things back now their night duty stint was over. She was already dangerously attached to Hamish—three days of naked time with him would only make this insane craving she had for him worse.

Oh, but she *wanted* him.

Wanted to spend three days talking and sleeping and kissing and getting to know each other *really* well.

Lola tossed caution to the wind. Hell, it was Christmas, right? She grinned at him as she grabbed for the knot sitting low between his hips. 'I think clothes are overrated.' She pulled it and the towel fell to the floor, the thickness of his erection jammed between them.

Oh, yes, that was better.

She glanced at it before returning her attention to Hamish's face. 'I need a shower. I'm having very dirty thoughts.'

'But I like it when you're filthy.'

Lola grinned, kissing him quickly before shimmying out of reach, her fingers going to the buttons of her work blouse, undoing them one by one as she walked slowly backwards, opening the shirt when she was done so he could get an eyeful of her blue lacy bra.

'Come and get me,' she murmured, before turning tail and sprinting to the bathroom, a large naked man hot on her heels.

CHAPTER ELEVEN

EMMA WAS STILL ventilated when Lola went back onto the early shift after her days off and wild horses wouldn't have stopped Lola from requesting her to look after.

To say Emma was markedly improved was a giant understatement. She was breathing for herself and almost weaned off the ventilator. Her blood pressure was good, her heart rate was excellent, all her blood tests were normal and there were no signs of rejection. All her drains were out and her exposed surgical incision was looking pink and healthy.

She'd come a long way in such a short time.

Her eyes lit up when Lola said hello first thing and she reached for Lola's hand and gave it a squeeze.

'She remembers you,' Barry said.

Lola smiled. She had looked after Emma a lot these past weeks. Had held her hand, talked to her, reassured her. But Emma had been very ill for most of it and the drugs she'd had on board had often caused memories to be jumbled. Lola wouldn't have been at all surprised had Emma not remembered anything or anyone.

In fact, given the long, intensive haul she'd been through, it was probably not a bad thing.

'You look amazing, Emma,' Lola said.

Emma smiled and pointed to her tracheostomy, mouthing, 'Out.' The position of the tube in her throat rendered her unable to vocalise.

Lola laughed. 'Hopefully today, yes. After the rounds this morning, okay?'

She rolled her eyes and kicked her feet a little to display her impatience. 'I know.' Lola squeezed her arm. 'Not much longer now, I promise.'

'I told you, Emsy,' Barry said, kissing her hand. 'Soon.'

Lola smiled. Barry had come a long way too.

'You think she'll be on a ward for Christmas?' Barry asked.

Lola shrugged. Christmas was still a week away. 'That's the way to bet. *But—*'

'Did you hear that?' Barry said, interrupting Lola to beam at Emma. The way he looked at her caught in Lola's throat. 'You'll be out of here soon.'

'Maybe,' Lola stressed. She didn't want to rain on their parade but Lola had been doing this far too long not to be cautious about her predictions. 'Don't forget, it's one day at a time in here.

'We know, we know,' Barry said in a way that led Lola to believe they were already planning Emma's homecoming.

And Lola didn't have it in her to stop them. Inside Emma's chest beat Wesley's heart. His family's tragedy had become Emma's family's miracle and hell if Lola wasn't going to let them bask in that.

A few days before Christmas Hamish found himself sitting at the back of a packed cathedral in full uniform. He'd imagined a lot of different scenarios playing out during his urban stint in Sydney but attending a memorial service for the victims of a bombing had not been one of them.

Lola, one of the many hospital personnel in attendance, was by his side as the mayor talked about the tragic events that had unfolded that night and how the efforts of the emergency services had doubtless saved countless lives. He shifted uncomfortably in his seat, pulling the collar of his formal uniform shirt off his neck. It was stifling hot in the cavernous cathedral and praise such as this added to his discomfort.

He and everyone else who had attended that night and all the health care professionals who were caring for the injured—doctors and nurses like Lola and Grace—had just been doing their jobs.

Words like heroes and angels didn't sit well on his shoulders. He'd just done what he'd been paid to do.

A squeeze to his leg brought him out of his own head and he smiled at Lola, her hand a steadying presence spread over his thigh. He'd spent a lot of time in her arms avoiding thinking about the carnage of that night, but it was unavoidable today and he'd been discombobulated ever since meeting Wesley's parents earlier.

And somehow she knew it.

Jenny sat on his other side. She was rigid in her seat and tight-lipped, the buttons on her dress uniform as shiny as the tips of her black dress shoes. She shot him a small, strained smile as the minister at the front asked everyone to stand for the reading of the names.

They rose to their feet. Hamish knew how important these sorts of memorials were. That public grief, remembrance and acknowledgement brought communities together and paying respect helped people move on. He knew it would help him and Jenny move on from that night—eventually.

It still felt a little too raw right now, though, the girl in the purple dress still a little too fresh in his brain.

Abigail. That was her name. He'd seen it on TV.

Lola's hand slipped into his as the minister read the first name out and a candle was lit in their honour. He was so damn grateful to have her here. She'd become his distraction, his safe harbour, his soft place to land. She'd become vital—like oxygen and sunshine—and the thought of leaving her in a few weeks was like a knife to his heart.

Because he'd fallen in love with her.

The weird tension he'd been carrying in his shoulders for a while now eased at the realisation. If anything, it should have tightened because that was not part of *the plan*. Not that they'd talked about any plan. In fact, they'd studiously avoided it seeing that their last plan to keep their hands off each other—obviously hadn't gone that well.

He should be worried. He should be grim. He should be nervous. Hell, he should at least be trying to figure it all out, work out his next step. But he was thirty years old and in love for the first time and right now, on this darkly emotional day, it was like a blast of light through the stained-glass windows of the cathedral.

It was enough.

The service ended fifteen minutes later and Hamish was finally able to breathe again. Jenny peeled off to talk to somebody she knew as they walked out into the fresh air and sunshine. Grace, who'd been up at the front supporting Wesley's family, waved and Lola's hand slipped from his as they headed in her direction.

Hamish missed the intimacy immediately and resentment stirred briefly in his chest before he got over himself. He didn't need Grace on his case as he tried to navigate this next couple of weeks. He kissed his sister on the cheek and she and Lola introduced the group of nurses they'd joined.

They made polite small talk for a few minutes but it was the last thing Hamish wanted to do. He wanted to be at home with Lola. He wanted to strip her out of her uniform and bury himself inside her and tell her with his body what he couldn't tell her with his words. Not yet anyway. Not until he'd figured out just how to do that without losing her in the process.

If that was even possible.

'You okay?' she asked, her voice low as the conversation ebbed and flowed around them.

Hamish nodded and smiled reassuringly. These people were clearly her work colleagues and friends and he needed to pull his head out from his ass. They'd all been part of the bombing and its aftermath in some way. 'Yes.'

'We'll, it's after twelve.' A male nurse who'd been introduced as Jay rubbed his hands together. 'Who's up for drinks at Billi's?'

There was a general murmur of, 'Count me in,' including from Grace and Lola.

'You, Hamish?' Jay asked.

Not really, no. He didn't want to go and psychoanalyse to death every part of that night, which was exactly what he knew would happen. It was inevitable when you got a bunch of health professionals together—it's what they did.

He just wanted to be alone with the woman he loved.

But Lola had already indicated she was going to the

bar and he wanted to be wherever she was, even if it meant he couldn't touch her and he had to pretend everything was platonic between them. 'Um…sure.'

He glanced at Lola and smiled. But her eyes narrowed slightly and Hamish swore he could feel her probing his mind as she searched his face. 'Actually… I might take a rain-check.'

She turned back to Jay, the movement inching her closer to Hamish. He felt the slight brush of her arm against his, was conscious of their thighs almost touching.

'I still have some Christmas shopping to do and this is my only day off between now and Christmas.'

Hamish could have kissed her. Well…that was a given…but he *knew* she was blowing off her friends for his benefit and he seriously wanted to grab her and kiss the breath out of her. He sure as hell wanted to drag her beneath him and love her with all his strength.

All his heart.

'Oh. Right. Actually, that's a good idea,' he concurred, hoping he sounded casual and that his sister wasn't picking up on the mad echo of his heartbeat.

Grace glanced between him and Lola before cocking an eyebrow. '*You* want to go shopping instead of drinking beer?'

He shrugged. 'To be honest, I'm not sure I'm up to much company today.'

'Oh…absolutely. Of course.'

Hamish felt guilty as Grace's cynicism faded, to be replaced by an expression of concern. He didn't want her to worry about him but he'd say whatever he needed to say to be alone with Lola right now.

'Just don't let her drag you into a bookshop. You'll be stuck for two hours at the travel section.'

Everyone laughed, including Lola, before they said their goodbyes and quietly slipped away.

'Thank you,' he murmured as they headed for the car park. 'I really didn't want to make polite conversation today.'

'I know.'

Hamish sucked in a breath. It was simple but true. She did know. And he loved her for it.

Lola usually worked on Christmas Day. It was a good excuse not to go back to Doongabi and she got to spend it with people she really liked, doing what she loved. Instead of with people who wished she was different in a place that felt just as claustrophobic as an adult as it had when she'd been a kid.

And hospitals always went out of their way to make everything look festive and inviting throughout the season, and Kirribilli General was no different.

But this Christmas morning was different.

Good different.

Waking-up-in-the-arms-of-a-sexy-man different.

Hands touching, caressing, drifting. Lips seeking, tasting, devouring. Coming together in a tangle of limbs and heavy breathing, desire and December heat slick on their skin. Crying out to each other as they came, panting heavily as they coasted through a haze of bliss and floated back down to earth.

Hitting the shower to freshen up and cool off, only to heat up again as the methodical business of soaping turned to the drugging business of pleasure. Hamish kissing her, Lola kissing him back until she couldn't breathe, couldn't stand, slumping against the tiles for support, Hamish supporting her, urging her up, her legs around him, pushing hard inside her again and groaning into her neck as he came, whispering, 'Yes, yes, yes,' as she followed him over the edge.

And that was before they got to the best bit—opening the presents.

There were only a few beneath the tree. Grace and Marcus's presents were the biggest—she'd bought them his and hers matching bathrobes as a bit of a joke present but they were top-notch quality and had cost a small fortune. They were coming over for lunch today and Lola couldn't wait to see the looks on their faces.

Hamish had also bought Grace a present and it was there along with the one Lola had bought him. It was just a novelty thing.

Nothing special. A snowglobe. With the Harbour Bridge and the Opera House planted in the middle. It had made her smile and she figured it'd be a memento of his time here.

And maybe he'd smile too every time he looked at it, the way he'd smiled when he'd talked about the innkeeper's daughter in Mykonos.

The biggest surprise, though, was Hamish's present to her, which had appeared a few days ago. In Lola's experience, men didn't really *do* presents for people they *loved*, let alone those they just…slept with.

Or whatever they were doing.

What that was, Lola didn't know. But an offer of solace had definitely turned into something more. Something she didn't want to over-analyse. Hamish's last shift was on the second of January and he was leaving on the third and starting back at his Toowoomba station on the fourth. Which meant they had just over a week left together.

Why mess up a week of potential good horizontal action—which she'd miss like crazy when he left—to put a label on something they'd already agreed couldn't go anywhere.

'So.' Lola, who'd thrown on shorts and a red tank top with 'Dear Santa, I've been very, very bad' splashed in glittery letters across the front, was pouring them both a tall glass of orange juice in the kitchen. A Christmas CD was playing 'Frosty the Snowman' in the background. 'What say we go out to the balcony with these and open our presents?'

Hamish wrapped his arms around her from behind. He hadn't bothered with a shirt at all, just boxers, which left a lot of bare, warm skin sliding against hers. Strong thighs butted up against the backs of hers as he lowered his mouth to nuzzle her neck and Lola almost whimpered at the pleasure of it.

'I'll grab the presents,' he said.

Lola followed him out with the drinks. She sat opposite him—all the better to see him—and placed the drinks down with a tapping sound on the tabletop. The balcony was still in shade and with the Christmas music drifting out through the open doors it was a pleasant morning.

Hamish swigged half of his juice in three gulps before handing over his gift. 'Ladies first.'

Lola, who'd already had a good feel of the present the moment he'd left the apartment, fingered it again. It was only palm-sized but quite heavy. She was dying of curiosity but also unaccountably nervous.

'No. Guests first.' She pushed his over. She'd rather

break the ice with something gimmicky—have a laugh first. He started to protest but she shook her head. 'Please, Hamish, indulge me.'

He sighed dramatically but grinned and ripped the paper off. The boom of his laughter as the box was revealed had been worth it.

'Oh, my God.' He grinned as he pulled the plastic snowglobe out and shook it, holding it up between them. She watched him as his gaze followed the flakes fluttering down around the famous Sydney landmarks. 'This is awesome.'

'Yeah? You like it? I thought you'd appreciate something to take home from Sydney to remind you of the place. And the muster across the bridge.'

And her.

'Are you kidding? You know I'm nuts for all this tacky, tourist crap.' He grinned. 'It's perfect.'

Lola laughed. 'I think I win Christmas, then.'

'I think you do.' He shook it again as he held it up. 'I love it.'

His casual use of the L word caused a skip in her pulse as her gaze narrowed to the snow falling in the dome. When she widened her gaze he was staring through the globe straight at her.

'Now you.' He placed the snowglobe on the table and tipped his chin at the present he'd given her earlier.

'Right.' She smiled as she picked it up, her fingers fumbling with the paper a little, suddenly all thumbs.

Inside the paper was a plain, thick cardboard box that had been taped by someone who obviously had shares in a sticky-tape company. Lola glanced at Hamish. 'Seriously?'

He laughed as she sighed and started on the tape.

'It's fragile. I guess they wanted to protect it as much as possible.'

Fragile? What the hell could it be?

After a minute of unravelling layers of tape, Lola was finally able to open the lid. Inside was an object secured in bubble wrap and yet more tape. She pulled that out, working away at it, going carefully as she finally revealed the most exquisite glass ornament Lola had ever seen.

It was a jacaranda tree in full flower. The gnarled trunk and its forked branches were fashioned in plain glass. The flowers, a perfect shade of iridescent blue-purple, hung from the branches, frothing in a profusion of purple, each individual bloom a teardrop of colour.

Lola blinked as she placed it reverently on the table. It was utterly breath-taking. It was delicate and feminine and so very *personal*. She didn't keep trinkets because gypsies didn't do clutter, but she knew she'd take this to the ends of the earth with her.

'I…' She glanced at him. Nobody had ever given her such an exquisite gift. 'I don't know what to say… It's utterly…*lovely.*'

'Lovely' seemed like such a bland, old-fashioned word but it was actually perfect for the piece. It was pretty and charming and sweet.

It *was* lovely.

More than that, it was *thoughtful.* Only someone who *knew* her, truly knew her would know how much something like this would mean. And the fact Hamish knew her so deeply should have her running for the hills. But all she wanted right now was to run straight into his arms.

'You like?'

'I… It's perfect.' She dragged her eyes off its loveliness to glance at him as she deliberately echoed his words. 'I love it.'

'I guess that means *I* win Christmas.'

She laughed at the tease in his voice. 'Yeah. You totally do.' She sobered as her eyes followed the graceful reach of the branches before her gaze shifted to his. 'Oh, God.' She faux-groaned. 'And I got you a crappy snowglobe that cost ten bucks.'

'Hey.' He picked up his present and held it against his naked chest as if he was trying to cover its non-existent ears. 'Don't insult the snowglobe.'

Lola laughed. There was no comparison between the two presents but he seemed just as chuffed with his gift as she was with hers.

He placed the snowglobe on the table. 'You want to see how well I can win Christmas in the bedroom?'

Lola's nostrils flared at the blatant invitation. But… 'I think you've already done that this morning. A couple of times.'

'I was just getting warmed up. Third time's the charm.'

Lola shook her head regretfully. 'I have things to prepare for lunch and a pavlova to make. Your sister's going to be here in three hours. And I think it might be a good idea if we don't look like we've spent all morning bouncing on a mattress together when she gets here.'

'I'll act my ass off, I promise. Not that I'll need to. She only has eyes for Marcus at the moment.'

Yeah. Grace was totally immersed in her new relationship, that was true. But women in love also had uncanny radar about other couples too.

'Lola Fraser, if you don't get your ass into that kitchen in the next thirty seconds, I'm going to take you remaining seated as a subconscious invitation to toss you over my shoulder, throw you on your bed and go down on you until you're singing "Ding Dong Merrily on High".'

Lola's stomach looped the loop at both the threat and the promise. 'Hold that thought,' she said as she rose and fled to the kitchen to the wicked sound of his low sexy chuckle and the jingle of bells from the CD.

CHAPTER TWELVE

THE TWO GUYS had insisted they'd clean up after Christmas lunch so Lola led Grace out onto the balcony. It was warmer outside now after several hours of the sun heating things up but there was still a nice breeze blowing in from Manly.

'Oh, my.' Grace reached for Hamish's present to Lola as she sat, turning it over and over. The sunlight caught the flowers and threw sparks of purple light across the glass of the tabletop. 'This is exquisite.'

'Yes.' Lola sipped some champagne, still stunned by the gift. 'Hamish gave it to me for Christmas.'

Lola was too caught up in the beauty of the piece to realise at first how still Grace had grown. How the light had stopped dancing on the tabletop as her hands had stopped moving. It wasn't until she spoke that Lola became aware of the situation.

'*Hamish* gave this to you?'

Lola glanced at her friend, a slight frown between her eyes at the strangled quality of Grace's voice. 'Yes.'

Grace's gaze settled on the tree for a moment before she placed it back on the table. 'I see.'

Her gaze flicked up to Lola, who frowned some more at the sudden seriousness of Grace's expression. 'What?'

'There *is* something going on between you, isn't there?'

Lola had known that Grace had been suspicious about her and Hamish a couple of times but she didn't see how a Christmas present could spark this line of questioning. Especially when she and Hamish had been impressively *chummy* throughout lunch.

'That would be stupid.' Lola trod carefully. They'd managed to keep the particulars of their relationship quiet from Grace so far. 'He's going back to Toowoomba in a week.'

'I've been watching you two for the last few hours. You've been knocking yourselves out trying to prove you're both just pals, but it's not working.'

Damn. Lola blinked, her brain searching for a rapid-fire response. She could just make out the low rumble of male voices inside over the sudden wash of her pulse through her ears and hoped like hell they stayed there until she had this sorted.

'I think you may be projecting there, Grace. Just because you're all loved up, it doesn't mean everyone else is.'

Grace sat back in her chair with a big, smug smile that was worrying and irritating all at once. 'You think I'm so caught up in my own love life that I don't notice anything else? It's been obvious today you two are sleeping together.'

Double damn. Lola swallowed, her eyes darting over Grace's shoulder to check they weren't getting any imminent visitors. She didn't need Hamish out here, making things worse. 'Obvious?'

'Sure. It's in the way you look at each other when you think the other isn't watching, all starry-eyed. And even if I was so blinded by my own feelings I couldn't see the blatantly obvious, I'd know from this.' Grace reached forward and picked up the tree again.

'It's just a Christmas present.'

'Lola.' Grace was using her don't-mess-with-me nurse voice. All nurses had one. 'This isn't *just* a Christmas gift.'

Lola glanced at the piece, a tight band squeezing her chest. 'He's...really grateful for my...hospitality these past couple of months, that's all.'

'And normally some guy you've been renting a room to would get you something for the kitchen or, better still, a gift voucher to a home appliance shop. Roomie Guy gets you practical and impersonal. He doesn't get you something pretty and frivolous. Something that's fragile and delicate and beautiful. And *meaningful*. He doesn't get you a work of art that speaks to you so deeply, that represents a place he knows you love, a place that's part of your shared history.'

Lola squirmed in her chair. She'd been so touched by the beauty of the blown glass, by its perfection, she hadn't thought about it having a deeper meaning.

Or maybe she hadn't *wanted* to.

'This is a gift of love, Lola.' Grace placed the sculpture down again. 'My brother is in love with you.'

Lola breath hitched as her gaze flew to Grace's face. *No*. How utterly ridiculous. 'He's just...a really thoughtful guy.'

She shook her head slowly. 'Trust me, I know him. He's really not. He's my brother and I love him but he's more the gimmicky gift giver.'

Lola thought about the T-shirt he'd bought Grace and his penchant for tacky snowglobes. Was Grace right? Adrenaline coursed through her system at the thought of it. She knew Hamish *liked* her. A lot. And it was reciprocated. They got on really well, enjoyed each other's company and they were magic between the sheets.

But they'd only known each other for a couple of months. It was just…fun.

Starry-eyed, Grace had called them. But really good sex *could* put stars in your eyes. It had certainly put stars in hers. And Grace's, for that matter.

'He's…going home in a week.'

'Yes.' Grace nodded, her expression gentle but earnest. 'Broken-hearted probably.'

Lola's blood surged thick and sluggish through her veins as she stared at the miniature glass sculpture. This wasn't the way it was supposed to be. They may have blurred the boundaries but he knew her attitude towards relationships and about her gypsy lifestyle. She'd thought he'd understood.

He *had* understood it, damn it. So Grace had to be wrong.

Lola was going to confront him about it as soon as Grace and Marcus had left. He'd deny it and they'd laugh over his sister's silliness and it'd be okay.

Although maybe they should *stop* sleeping together…

'More champagne, good women?'

Marcus's jovial voice coming from behind ripped Lola out of her panic. Her gaze briefly locked with Grace's, who was still eyeing her meaningfully before she turned and smiled. 'Yes, please.'

Hamish was there too, smiling at her, and the stars in his eyes blazed at her so brightly it was like a physical punch to her gut. *Crap.* She turned quickly back to escape their pull, her gaze landing squarely on Grace and her imperiously cocked *I told you so* eyebrow.

It couldn't be true. She wouldn't *let* it be true.

* * *

Hamish was standing at the sink, washing up, a couple hours later when Lola returned from seeing off their guests. 'Did they leave or did they make a pit stop in my bedroom for a quickie?' He grinned at her over his shoulder. 'I swear those two couldn't stop looking at each other.'

A faint smile touched her lips but it didn't reach her eyes. She folded her arms as she leant into the doorframe. 'That's exactly what Grace said about us.'

Hamish's smile slowly faded. Lola looked serious. In fact, she'd been kinda serious this past couple of hours. *This couldn't be good.* 'Does she know we've been sleeping together?'

'Yeah.'

'You told her?'

'No.' Lola shook her head. 'She guessed.'

'Impossible.' Hamish smiled, trying to lighten the mood. 'I acted my ass off today.'

She didn't return his smile, just dropped her gaze to the floor somewhere near his feet. 'It was your Christmas present to me.'

Hamish frowned. 'The tree?'

'She said it was a gift of love.' She raised her gaze and pierced Hamish to the spot with it, her chin jutting out. 'She said you were in love with me.'

It was softly delivered but, between the accusation in her tone and the look in her eyes, the statement hit him like a sledgehammer to the chest.

What the hell? Was Grace trying to sabotage his chances with Lola?

'Is it true?'

Of course it was true. But he hadn't wanted to tell her

like this. Not that he'd given this moment much thought but he didn't want it to come when he was backed into a corner either.

Hamish dried his hands on the tea towel he had slung over his shoulder and turned round fully. 'Lola, I—'

'Is it true?' Her eyes flashed, her jaw tightened and her knuckles turned white as her fingers gripped her arms hard. 'I told her it was ridiculous.'

Hamish let out a shaky breath. She was giving him an out and he could see in her eyes that she wanted him to take it. He could pick up that lie and run with it and try and salvage something out of this mess. Paper things over, spend this next week with her as if tonight hadn't happened. Then take things slowly with her over the next year—settle into something long distance.

Woo her.

But loving her was bigger than that. Bigger than him and her. Bigger than any will for it not to be so. Too big to dishonour with denial.

Too *important*.

He rested his butt against the edge of the sink. 'It's not. Ridiculous. It's true. I've fallen in love with you.'

His lungs deflated, the air rushing out with the words. He'd held them in for too long and it felt good to finally have them out. He didn't realise they'd been a weight on his chest until they weren't there any more.

Lola, on the other hand, looked as if she'd picked up those words and was being crushed beneath them, her face running the gamut from shock to disbelief to downright anger.

'But…that's not what we were doing.'

'I know.'

'I told you, I don't do relationships. We want different things.'

'I know.'

'This is just...sex, Hamish.'

'No.' He shook his head emphatically. God knew where they'd go from here but Hamish wasn't going to pretend any more that this had only been physical. And he wasn't going to let her pretend it either. It had been deeper than that right from the start.

Right from the first time she'd turned to him. Their connection had been forged that night and he knew she'd felt it too.

'It's never been just a sex thing, Lola.'

Her arms folded tighter, her lips flattened into a grim line. 'It has for me.'

A sudden rush of frustration propelled Hamish off the sink and across the kitchen, leaving only a couple of steps between them.

'Please don't lie to yourself, Lola. This is me, Hamish. I might not have known you for very long but I think you've let me in more than you've ever let anyone else in. You've told me about where you're from and your family and how you never fitted in and your Great-Aunt May and you've taken me into your bed time after time after time, even though you're the one-and-done Queen. Hell...you took me to your favourite place in Sydney. A place you've *never taken anyone else.* So don't pretend that all we've been doing is having great sex because that's ridiculous and we both know it.'

Hamish was breathing hard by the time he'd got that off his chest but he wasn't done yet either. If he was unloading everything, he should go all the way. He took the last two steps between them and slid his hands onto her arms and said, 'And I think you have feelings for me too.'

Now he was done.

She gasped, her pinched mouth forming an outraged O as she wrenched out of his grasp, pushing past him to pace the kitchen floor. 'Now *you're* being ridiculous.'

Hamish blinked at her vehement reaction. If he wasn't so sure about their connection, her dismissiveness might have cut him to the quick. 'Would it be so terrible, Lola?' His gaze followed her relentlessly back and forth as he leaned his shoulder on the doorframe. 'To let me love you? To let yourself fall in love with me?'

She stopped abruptly, her hair flying around her head as she glared at him. If anything, she was even more furious, her chest rapidly rising and falling. 'And how do you think that would work?' she demanded, her eyes wild and fiery.

'I don't know... I hadn't really thought about it.'

She gave a small snort. 'Well, think about it,' she snapped. 'Are you going to commute between here and Toowoomba or wherever the hell you end up?'

Hamish rubbed his hand along his scruffy jawline. 'I don't know.'

'Or are you going to move here?'

The rejection of that notion tingled on his tongue in a second. Sydney was a great place to visit but it'd drive him mad to live here permanently. The thought made the country boy inside him shudder. Also, he'd be putting his dream for rural service on hold. Maybe indefinitely.

But he could do it, especially if it meant being with her. 'Yes.' He nodded. 'I would move here.'

She gaped at him. 'You'd just give up all your dreams?'

'For you, yes.' He could get new dreams. What he couldn't ever get again was someone like Lola.

She was the *one*.

'If you were serious about being in a committed relationship with me,' Hamish continued, his thoughts starting to crystallise. 'Not if you're just going to keep me for a few months and discard me when your next wild adventure calls you. I'm happy to live with you wherever you want, but I'm not going to be just some filler, Lola, somebody to occupy yourself with between jaunts. I'm not going to be your *Sydney* guy.'

'God, Hamish…' She shook her head and started to pace again. 'I don't want you to give up your dreams.'

'Okay so…' Hamish shrugged. 'Come and live mine with me.'

She halted again. 'Oh, I see, so *I'm* supposed to follow you to Outer Whoop-Whoop.'

'I don't know. Maybe… Why not?' Hamish *didn't* know, but surely it was worth giving them a shot?

'Because I'm *not* going back to some speck on the map in the middle of bloody nowhere. I've paid my small-town dues, Hamish.'

'I'm not talking about forever, Lola. I'm talking about a couple of years. That's all. And it's not like it was when you were growing up in Doongabi. There's better roads and cars and more regional airports than ever being serviced by national carriers. Just because we might live in a small town, doesn't mean you're going to be *stuck* there. I'm not going to keep you a prisoner.

'You want to go to the nearest city for a week of shopping, go for it. You want to fly to Sydney to see the ballet or Melbourne to watch the tennis or the Whitsundays to lie on a beach and get a tan—great.'

She shoved her hands on her hips. 'I'm *going* to Zimbabwe in April.'

Hamish sighed. She was so damn determined to stay on the path she'd forged for herself. She been concentrating so hard on it she didn't realise she could change direction or forge a whole new path and that was okay. 'Then I'll carry your bags.'

She huffed out a breath, clearly annoyed by his logic. 'And what about my *job*?'

He shrugged. 'Rural areas are desperate for nurses.'

'But there won't be an ICU in the middle of nowhere, will there? Why should I let my skills languish?'

'Just because there won't be an ICU, doesn't mean there won't be patients who require critical care from time to time. Who are going to depend on you and what you do with what you have to keep them alive until they can be transferred to a major hospital. Think of the challenge and the experience you could come away with. I'm looking on it as a means to becoming a better paramedic, to push me, to challenge me. It could be the same for you. When was the last time you were truly challenged at work?'

An intensive care nurse had highly specialised skills but there was a lot of support in a big city unit with not a lot of autonomy.

She folded her arms and regarded him for long moments, which was a nice change from pacing and glaring, and for a second Hamish thought he might have won her over. But finally she shook her head.

'It's not just about moving to a small town, Hamish.'

He cocked an eyebrow. 'What, then?'

'I don't want to tie myself to one person at all but if I did, it wouldn't be a small-town guy. He'd have to be a kindred spirit. He'd have to have a gypsy soul, not someone who's content to live a small life with a side of snowglobe tourism.'

Her barbs struck him dead centre. She hadn't hurled them at him but he felt the bite of them nonetheless and a spurt of anger pulsed into his system. He didn't like her insinuation that because he wasn't as well travelled as her, he was unadventurous and lacking ambition.

Being happy with his life and his lot hadn't ever been a negative in Hamish's book. He'd never considered being content a *bad* thing and the fact that she was judging him for it was extremely insulting.

He may not be worldly enough for her but he knew people didn't get to pick and choose who they had feelings for—that just happened. And ignoring it was a recipe for disaster.

Whether Lola wanted to or not, she *did* have feelings for him. Feelings he suspected scared the living daylights out of her. And not just because she had them but because he was the opposite of what she'd always told herself she wanted.

Hamish took a steadying breath, shaking off her insult. 'I think you do want someone to tie you down. That you don't want to be a gypsy all your life.'

She shook her head vehemently. 'That's the most absurd thing I've ever heard.'

Hamish probed her gaze, holding hers, refusing to let her look away. The more he talked, the more convinced he was. 'Is it? I've never pretended to be anything other than a small-town guy, Lola, and yet you went there anyway. If you didn't really want this, want me, then why have you kept coming back? What the hell has this been?'

She took a deep breath before levelling him with a serious gaze. 'A mistake.'

Hamish wouldn't have thought two little words could have had so much power. Had she yelled them at him, he could have put it down to the heat of the moment, but she was calm and deliberate, her gaze fixed on his as she shot them at him like bullets from a gun.

He couldn't speak for a beat or two. Hamish knew that whatever happened between them after today he would *never* categorise their interlude as a mistake. He would look back at it with fondness, not regret.

But right now her rejection stung.

He nodded slowly. 'Right. Okay, then.' He pushed off the doorframe. 'I think I'm going to go and stay at Grace's tonight.'

There were only so many insults a man could take in one night. Lola had called him small town and insular and now a mistake. He couldn't work out if he was angry with her or disappointed, but he couldn't stay. They would either get into it more or they'd end up in bed together because sex seemed to be the only way they dealt with emotional situations.

And he didn't have the stomach for either.

A little frown knitted her brows and she opened her mouth. For a second Hamish thought she might be going to retract everything but her mouth shut with an audible click and her chin lifted. 'That might be best.'

Hamish nodded. Her dismissal hurt but what else had he expected? 'Merry bloody Christmas, Lola.'

CHAPTER THIRTEEN

IT WAS NINE that night when Lola answered the phone. She knew who it was before she even picked up. Aunty May always rang her on Christmas morning and where she was, in the Pyrenees, it was six in the morning.

'Merry Christmas, sweetie.' Her aunt's voice crackled down the line, not as youthful as it had once been but still shot with an unflappability that was uniquely May.

Lola almost burst into tears at its familiarity. She didn't, but it was a close call as she cleared her throat and said, 'Merry Christmas, Aunty May. How's the skiing?'

May launched into her usual enthusiastic spiel she went into when she was somewhere new and Lola was grateful for the distraction. She let her aunt talk, content to throw in the odd approving noise or question, not really keeping track of the conversation, her brain far too preoccupied.

Ever since Hamish had walked out so calmly a few hours ago, Lola had been able to think of little else. It had been an incredibly crappy end to such a great day. From the second Grace had mentioned the L word it had started to go downhill and had slid rapidly south.

Damn Grace.

And damn Hamish for ruining it even further by backing up his sister's outrageous claim. They'd had another week. They could be in bed right now, enjoying their last days together. Enjoying this day in the same way it had started.

But he had to go and tell her he loved her. Tell her he knew she had feelings for him too! The fact that he was right—there was something between them, although it couldn't possibly be *love*—had only compounded the situation.

'It's been a few years since I've done a black run but I'm very much looking forward to it.'

Lola tuned back in. 'It's just like riding a bike.' Aunt May had been skiing for the better part of fifty years—she could out-ski Lola any day.

May burst out with one of her big, hooting laughs. 'Been a while since I rode one of those too. Never mind… I've made some friends with a couple of hottie old widowers here so I won't be alone.'

And she launched into an entertaining description of the two gents in question in that irreverent way of hers that always kept Lola in stitches. Except for tonight. Because all Lola could think about was Hamish and how abominable she'd been to him.

Yes, he'd admitted he loved her and that had been a shock, but he hadn't deserved being told he was living a small life and that he was a mistake. As someone who'd made her fair share of mistakes she could confidently say none of them had felt as good as Hamish.

She'd even opened her mouth to apologise, to take it back, but then she'd realised it had been the perfect shield to fight the sword of his L word and she'd left it. But she hadn't liked herself very much.

And she liked herself even less now.

'Okay, sweetie. Are you going to tell me what's on your mind?'

Lola blinked. Aunty May was ten thousand kilometres away and they were speaking down a phone line but she still knew something was up. 'What? Nothing.' She forced herself to laugh. 'I'm fine. Just a little tired, that's all.'

'Lola Gwendolyn Fraser. This is me. When will you learn you can't fool your old Aunty May?'

Lola gripped the phone. It was some kind of irony that a woman who had been largely absent from her life knew her so well. They had that kindred spirit connection.

'Does it have anything to do with that guy who's been staying with you? What's his name again?'

'Hamish.' Even saying his name made Lola feel simultaneously giddy and depressed.

'That's right. Grace's brother.'

'Yes.'

'And you're in love with him?'

'No!' Tears blurred Lola's vision. 'I've only known him for two months.'

There was silence for a moment. 'You showed him your jacarandas, right?'

Lola was beginning to wish she'd never told May or Grace that particular bit of information. 'Yes, but I'm like you. A gypsy. We travel. We don't fall in love.'

'Poppycock!'

Lola blinked at the rapid-fire dismissal.

'It took me two minutes to fall in love with Donny.'

Donny? Who the hell was Donny? And since when had her spinster aunt been in love with anyone? 'Donny?'

'The one great love of my life.'

What the—? 'I...didn't know there'd been anyone.'

It was a weird concept to wrap her head around—her spinster aunt in love with a man. Lola had no doubt she'd been highly sought after but May had always been staunchly single.

'Well…it was a long time ago now.'

The wistfulness in her great-aunt's voice squeezed fingers around Lola's already bruised heart. 'What happened?'

May said nothing for a beat or two as if she was trying to figure out where to start. 'I was seventeen, working at the haberdashery in Doongabi, and this dashing young police officer moved to town. He was thirty. But when you know, you *know*.' She gave a soft chuckle. 'I fell hopelessly in love.'

'I see.' That was quite an age gap even for fifty-something years ago. 'And that caused a stir in the family? Or…' She hesitated. 'Didn't he reciprocate?'

Lola thought it the least likely option. May had always been a tall, handsome woman. Carried herself well, wore clothes well. But in the photos Lola had seen of her as a teenager she'd been striking, with an impish flicker in her eyes.

'Oh, he reciprocated. It was wonderful.' She sighed and there was another pause. 'But he was married. He had a wife and two girls who were joining him a little later. And I knew it and I embarked on a liaison with him anyway.'

Married? 'Oh.' Lola hadn't expected that.

'Yes. Oh… So I left. The day before his family were due in town. I was afraid if I stayed I wouldn't give him up, I wouldn't end it. That I'd risk my family's reputation and his marriage and break up his home because I was young and selfish and loved him too much.'

A lump lodged in Lola's throat. May was rattling it off as if it was something that had happened to somebody else but she couldn't hide the thickness in her voice—not from Lola.

'I'm so sorry. I didn't know.'

'It's fine.' May cleared her voice. 'As I said, it was in a whole other lifetime.'

'Is he still—?'

'No.' Her aunt cut her off. 'He died ten years ago. But you know…' She gave a half laugh, half sigh that echoed with young love. 'I would give up everything I've ever done, every place I've ever been, to have spent my life with him.'

Lola sat forward in the chair. *'What?'*

'Oh, yes. I've been with other men, Lola. Even loved a few of them. But not like Donny. He was always the one.'

'But…you've had such a wonderful life.'

'Yes, I have. I've been very lucky.'

'Right.' Lola nodded, feeling suddenly like she was the elder in the conversation having to point out the obvious. 'You've been to so many places. Seen so many things. Your life has been so full.'

'No, sweetie, it hasn't. I've been living a half-life. There's always been something missing. So promise me not to make the same mistake I did, choosing adventure over love. If this man loves you and if you love him, as I suspect you just might, be open to it. Humans are meant to love and be loved. We mate for life. And a gypsy caravan is big enough for two.'

Lola was too stunned to speak. Her whole world had just shifted on its axis. Not only had her great-aunt had a torrid affair with an older, married man but she'd have traded her gypsy life for a second chance with him.

'Lola? Promise me.'

Her aunt's voice was fierce and strong and Lola was spooked by the sudden urgency of it, goose-bumps breaking out on her arms. 'I promise.'

Lola was pleased to be back at work the next morning. Between what had happened with Hamish and the conversation with her great-aunt, her head was spinning. May—spinster of seventy-five years—had loved a married man she'd gladly have given everything up for. And Hamish *loved* her.

Loved.

On such short acquaintance. And having being warned that she didn't *do* love.

The whole world had gone mad.

At least work was sane. She knew what she was doing there. What was expected of her. And people didn't ask more than they knew she could give. She could care there, she could give a piece of herself, but she didn't have to give them *everything*. They didn't demand her heart and soul.

Only her mind and body. And *that* she could do.

'Lola, can you take Emma today, please? She's due to be transferred to the ward around eleven so can you make sure all her discharge stuff is completed by morning tea?'

'Yep. Sure can.' Lola leapt up from her chair in the staffroom, eager to throw her body and mind into a full, busy shift. And she was excited to be the nurse looking after Emma on her last day on the unit.

Everything since the transplant had gone swimmingly well and Lola was thrilled about Emma's transfer. Two months was a long time to be on the ICU and all the nurses had grown fond of Emma and her lovely supportive family.

For so long it had been touch and go and to see her
leaving the unit with a new heart and a new chance at
life was why Lola did what she did.

'Hey,' Lola said as she approached Emma's bed to take
handover from the night nurse. The background noise
of beeping monitors and trilling alarms and tubes being
suctioned formed a comforting white noise that blocked
out the yammering in her brain.

'Hey, Lola.'

Emma's voice was still husky but she beamed at Lola.
She'd lost weight, was as weak as a kitten and looked like
she'd been in a boxing ring with her smattering of scars,
nicks and old bruises, but the sparkle in her eyes told
Lola everything she needed to know. Emma's spirit was
strong, she was a fighter. And she was going to be okay.

'I'll just get handover and then we'll get you all ready
for your discharge to the ward.'

'Now, those are some beautiful words,' Emma
quipped. The small white plaster covering her almost
healed tracheostomy incision crinkled with her neck
movement.

Lola took handover. It was short and quick compared
to the previous weeks that had required twenty minutes
to chronicle all the drugs and infusions and changes as
well as the ups and downs of the shift.

'How did you sleep?' Lola asked a few minutes later
as she performed her usual checks of all the emergency
equipment around the bed.

Emma may be leaving in a few short hours but certain
procedures were ingrained for Lola. It was important to
know everything she might need in an emergency was

here, exactly where it was located and that it was in full working order.

Patient safety always came first.

'Wonderfully.'

Lola laughed. 'Somebody should have warned me I was going to need sunglasses today to block out the brightness of your smile.'

'I am pretty excited about leaving this dump,' Emma said with a smile.

Lola sighed and clutched her chest dramatically. 'People never want to stay.'

Emma grinned. 'I'll come back and visit.'

Lola grinned too as she put a stethoscope in her ears. 'Make sure you do.' She placed the bell on Emma's chest and listed to her breathing. A patient assessment was performed at the start of every shift.

'You want to know what I got for Christmas?' Emma asked as Lola removed the earpieces. 'Besides a new heart?'

Lola cocked an eyebrow—Emma was vibrating with excitement. 'Of course.' Hopefully it'd help take her mind off what Hamish had got her. The little glass jacaranda tree had caused a shedload of problems.

Emma held up her left hand and wiggled her fingers. The oxygen saturation trace on the monitor went a little haywire because the probe was on that hand but that wasn't what caught Lola's attention. A big, fat diamond ring sparkled in the sunshine slanting in through the open vertical blinds covering the windows.

'Barry asked me to marry him and I said yes.'

Lola blinked as the refraction shone in her eyes. Damn it, was the whole world conspiring against her at the moment?

'Crikey.' Lola kept her voice light and teasing as she

took Emma's hand and inspected it closely, her heart beating a little harder at the expression of pure joy on her patient's face. 'Did he rob that bank he works for?' Barry was a teller at a bank in the city.

Emma laughed. 'I'm afraid to ask.'

Lola smiled as she released Emma's hand. 'Well, I'm thrilled for you. If anyone deserves a bit of happiness it's you.'

Emma held her hand out to admire the ring, wriggling her fingers slightly to get a real sparkle going. 'To think I was never going to do this. Marriage and all that stuff.'

Lola had turned to grab a pair of gloves from the windowsill behind so she could remove the arterial line from Emma's wrist, but she stopped and turned back. 'Oh?'

Maybe this was why she felt such an affinity for Emma? She too didn't want to tie herself down.

'Yeah.' Emma dropped her hand to her stomach. 'Baz and I have only been going out for ten months and he's asked me twice to marry him now but I always felt like I was a bad bet for a guy. Why would I inflict a woman with a dodgy ticker on someone I supposedly loved without an easy out for him? Better for him to just be able to walk away, for us both to be able to when things got tough.'

'I see.'

'Barry's kinda hard to shake, though.' Emma grinned. 'He was determined to stick around. To show me that he here for the long haul as well as the short haul if that's the way it panned out.'

Lola nodded. 'He's been very dedicated, Emma. He was here every day.'

'Yeah, I know. But even with my new heart…well…' Emma grimaced. 'The potential for complications is real, right? Rejection, infection, complications from medication…and how long will it last till I need another one? But when he asked me yesterday morning to marry him, all that just fell away and love was all that mattered.'

A lump the size of Emma's bed lodged in Lola's throat. Isn't that what May had essentially said last night too? If Lola didn't know better, she'd say the universe was trying to tell her something.

Just as well she didn't go in for all that spiritual crap.

'Sure, my life's potentially shorter than that of other women my age and it might not all be smooth sailing, but none of us are guaranteed a long life, are we? I mean, I don't know how old my donor was but he or she didn't get a say in their life coming abruptly to an end, right?'

Lola nodded. It was still a miracle to her that they'd managed to pull off having a donor and a recipient on the same unit without either being aware of the other.

'Life's short, I know that better than anyone, so why shouldn't I get to live my life fully? Like other people? To love like other people. To share my life, no matter how long it is, with someone else? And I think I owe that to my donor. To live my life *fully*. Why should I restrict myself to a half-life?'

A half-life. Just as May had said last night.

'Of course you do,' Lola said, a little spooked that Emma appeared to be channelling her great-aunt. 'You deserve all the good things, Emma, and I think it's exactly what your donor would have wanted.'

Emma smiled and grabbed her hand. 'So do you, Lola.' For a second Lola's heart stopped—maybe her patient actually *was* channelling Aunty May—but then Emma glanced around the unit at the general hubbub. 'All the nurses do. You're freaking angels.'

Lola gave her usual self-deprecating smile. 'Okay, well, there's no time to shine my halo at the moment.' She squeezed Emma's hand before withdrawing it, all business now. 'I've gotta spring you out of here.'

Emma nodded and sighed and went back to looking at her engagement ring.

CHAPTER FOURTEEN

THERE WAS A knock on Lola's door later that afternoon. She'd just shoved the ice cream in the freezer and ripped into a chocolate bar. She might as well have one of those too if she was about to consume a one-litre tub of ice cream, right?

The knock came again and she put the bar down with an impatient little noise at the back of her throat. 'Coming.'

Her pulse accelerated as she walked towards the door—what if it was Hamish? She had no idea what his plans were for his last week. Was he coming back? His stuff was still all here, or was he going to move in with Grace for his remaining time?

She felt sure if it was him he'd probably just use his key but maybe, after their words yesterday, he didn't want to intrude uninvited. Her heart did a funny little giddy-up at the thought. It'd only been twenty-four hours but she missed his face.

It wasn't Hamish.

It was the police. Two of them—a man and a woman, both in neat blue uniforms and wearing kindly expressions.

Lola frowned. 'Can I help you?'

The woman introduced them. 'Are you Miss Fraser?'

'Yes, that's right...' Although she felt rather stupid being called 'miss' at the age of thirty. 'Lola.'

'You are the next of kin for a May Fraser?' she clarified.

The hair on Lola's nape prickled. 'Yes. She's my aunt. My great-aunt.' Lola had been down as May's emergency contact for the last ten years. 'Is something wrong?'

Had her aunt fallen on that black run and broken something? Her leg? Or a hip? She was going to be really cranky with herself if she had. But then something worse occurred to her. The police didn't usually come around just to tell someone their loved one had been injured in a foreign land.

But...what if it was more serious than that? What if there'd been an avalanche? A surge of adrenaline flew into Lola's system.

'Could we come in?'

The question was alarming. 'Please just tell me here.' Because if they could tell her here, *whatever it was*, on the doorstep, then it couldn't be too bad, right?

Lola didn't notice the barely perceptible exchange of glances that passed between the two police officers. 'I think it would be better if we came in, Lola,' the male officer said gently, his smile kind.

Oh, God. Dread burrowed into her veins and the lining of her gut and the base of her skull but Lola fell back automatically to admit them. Once they were sitting, the male officer took up the baton and delivered the news she'd been expecting.

'I'm sorry to have to inform you, Lola, but your Aunt May passed away earlier today.'

Every cell and muscle in Lola's body snap froze.

Aunty May was…*dead*? The pounding of her heartbeat rose in her ears as tears sprang to her eyes, scalding and instant.

May was dead.

'Did she…have a skiing accident?' Lola wasn't sure if it was the right thing to ask but her mind was a blank and it seemed logical given what she knew about May's whereabouts and her intended activity.

'No.' The woman took over now as if they were some kind of grief tag team and for a second Lola thought how horrible it must be to deliver this kind of news as part of your *job*.

Lola had sat through many end-of-life conversations in hospitals, holding the hands of distressed and grieving people. But this? Out of the blue like this? Everything chugging along then *bam*! Strangers on your doorstep.

'She was found in her bed,' the woman continued. 'She didn't turn up to meet some people she was going to go skiing with and they raised the alarm. Hostel staff entered her room to find her still in her bed. At first they thought she was sleeping but they couldn't rouse her. She'd died some time during the night in her sleep.'

Lola shook her head. Died in her sleep. *No.* Whenever she'd imagined her aunt's death it'd been her doing something adventurous when she was ninety-seven.

Going out with a bang, not a whimper.

'But… I was just talking to her yesterday.' Which was a stupid thing to say given her medical background—she knew how quickly and unexpectedly death could come knocking. 'She was fine. Are you sure?'

May's words from the phone call came back to her now and Lola shivered. They'd spooked her a little yesterday but even more so now. May's insistence that Lola promise her to give love a chance felt like some kind of portent today.

Was that only twenty-four hours ago?

Had her great-aunt *known* she was not long for this world?

Goose-bumps feathered Lola's arms at the thought.

'Yes. I'm afraid so.' The man again with his gentle voice. 'It's been confirmed by all the appropriate officials.'

'Could it have been…some kind of foul play?'

It seemed like a bizarre thing to ask but no more bizarre than her bulletproof aunt dying in her sleep.

The police officers took her question in their stride. 'The local authorities say that your aunt was lying peacefully in her bed wearing her sleep mask.'

Lola almost laughed at that piece of information. May used to collect the sleep masks from airlines and swore by them as an antidote to jet-lag. She'd never travelled without one.

'There'll be an autopsy, of course, but they're expecting to find natural causes.'

Lola nodded, the medical side of her brain already making guesses. It had probably been a massive stroke or a heart attack. It wouldn't have been a bad way to go, a quick death, taking her in the night. But the thought May had died alone was like a knife to Lola's chest.

It would have been the way her aunt would have wanted it—dying as she'd lived—but Lola wished she'd been able to hug her one last time and she thanked the universe for that phone call yesterday. She was grateful for the time they'd spent chatting, for having spoken to her beloved aunt one last time.

Even if May's words hadn't sat easily on Lola's shoulders.

The officers talked more about procedures and passed over some pamphlets regarding relatives who died overseas. 'Is there someone we can call for you, Lola? Someone who can be with you now?'

Hamish.

His was the first name that popped into Lola's head and a tidal wave of emotion swamped her chest. Her fingers curled in her lap as she thought about the solid comfort of his arms around her, about him holding her, keeping her together while her insides leaked out.

But she couldn't. Not after their argument. Grace came to mind next but as she had lied to her best friend about sleeping with her brother *and* ignored six phone calls from her in the last twenty-four hours, she didn't feel able to suggest that either.

Of course, Grace wouldn't care about any of that in the face of this news. But Lola wasn't exactly thinking straight at the moment.

'Um, no.' She shook her head. 'I'm good. I'm fine.' Her mouth stretched into a smile that felt like it had been drawn on her face in crayon.

'We don't like leaving people alone after this kind of news,' the male officer said. 'Especially at Christmas.'

Between the events of yesterday and working today, Lola had forgotten it was Christmas. 'It's okay. Really. I'm a nurse, I work at the Kirribilli in ICU. I'll be fine.'

That information seemed to relax them both.

'I'll ring my mum,' Lola assured them. 'May is *her* aunt. And we'll go from there.' She smiled more genuinely this time, realising that her last attempt had probably frightened the hell out of them. 'I'll be fine, I promise.'

They left with her assurances but the last thing Lola felt like right now was talking to her mother. She *would* ring her—in a while. Right now she felt too numb to use her fingers, to use words. She needed time to wrap her head around the fact she was never going to see her favourite person in the whole world ever again.

Lola sat on the couch and fell sideways, pulling her legs up to her chest. Tears pricked at her eyes. May was gone. No more Christmas Day phone calls. No more postcards. No more random drop-ins. No more *National Geographic*-like pictures or entertaining foreign swear words or endlessly fascinating anecdotes from her travels.

May hadn't just been some distant, eccentric great-aunt. She'd been Lola's family. She'd been the one who had understood her when no one else had. She'd been Lola's sounding board, her shoulder to cry on when life in Doongabi had seemed like it would never come to an end, and had championed her desire to travel and see the world.

Lola realised suddenly she was already thinking of May in the past tense and pain, like a lightning bolt, stabbed her through the heart with its jagged heat, stealing her breath. The first tear rolled down her cheek. Then the next and the next until there was a puddle.

And the puddle became a flood.

Hamish stood indecisively outside Lola's door much the same as he had almost two months ago now. Nervous and unsure of himself. He'd been furious when he'd walked out yesterday and while he'd calmed down significantly, he was still a little on the tense side. He couldn't remember ever knowing a woman he wanted to shake as badly as he wanted to drag her clothes off and kiss her into submission.

He got it, she was used to keeping her relationships

in a box, one where she made all the rules and had all the control.

But to not be open to something more? Something different? Something deeper?

Something *better*?

It was ironic that Lola had left Doongabi partly because everyone she'd known had been stuck in their ways and yet she was proving to be just as immovable.

He knocked, wary of his reception. Not knowing if she was even home. He knew she'd worked an early shift today, which meant she'd normally be home by now, but maybe she'd made other plans.

And what was he going to say if she *was* home? What was his plan? Hamish knew what he wanted. He wanted to come back here for his last remaining days. Back into Lola's house and her bed and her *life* and make plans with her. Plans about how their future might work out. It wouldn't be easy to come up with something they were both happy with but he knew they could do it if they put their minds to it.

If they both committed.

But if Lola didn't want any part of a future with him? Could he live here for the next week and pretend he was okay with her decision? Pretend he wasn't dying a little each day?

Whatever…they needed to have a conversation which was why he'd come now and not earlier when he'd known she'd be at work. They'd both had twenty-four hours to mull over what had gone down yesterday and he could sit and brood and look obsessively at the picture he'd taken of her that day with jacaranda flowers in her hair, or he could confront her.

He'd chosen confrontation. It was time to lay their cards on the table.

Hamish knocked again. When she still didn't answer he sighed and fished in his pocket for his keys. He'd have preferred to enter by invitation but if she wasn't home it wasn't going to happen. And, if nothing else, he needed his clothes for work tomorrow.

He inserted the key into the lock. He'd just grab his bag and go. Ring her later and see if they could make a time to talk. He entered the apartment and pulled the door shut behind him, the ghosts of a hundred memories trailing him as he traversed the short entrance alcove that opened into the living room.

'Hamish?'

Her head and torso suddenly popped up from the couch and scared the living daylights out of him. Hamish clutched his chest to still his skyrocketing pulse. 'Damn it, Lola.'

'Sorry.'

'I knocked but...'

It was then he noticed her red-rimmed eyes and her blotchy face in stark relief to the pallor of her skin. She looked...awful. Lost and scared and small. Like someone had knocked the stuffing out of her. Not the strong, feisty Lola he was used to.

Was this grief...over him? Over them?

And why was the thought as gratifying as it was horrifying? What the hell was wrong with him?

'Lola?' Hamish took a step towards her but stopped, unsure of how welcoming she'd be to his offer of solace. 'Are you okay?'

Her short hysterical-sounding laugh did not allay his

concerns. She shook her head, her curls barely shifting it was so slight. 'Aunty May died.'

Her words dropped like stones into the fraught space between them. 'What?' *Her aunt was dead?*

He was at her side in three strides, their animosity forgotten as he sank down beside her, his hand sliding around her shoulder and pulling her to him. She didn't argue or jerk away, just whimpered like a wounded animal and melted into his side.

He eased them back against the couch and her arm came around his stomach, her head falling to his shoulder. Hamish dropped his chin to her springy curls, shutting his eyes as he caught a whiff of his coconut shampoo in her hair.

'You want to talk about it?'

She shook her head. 'Not yet.'

So he just held her. Held her while her tears flowed, silently at first then louder, choking on her sobs, her shoulders shaking with the effort to restrain herself and failing. Eventually her sobs settled to hiccupping sighs and she was able to talk, to tell him what had happened.

'I'm so sorry,' Hamish murmured, still cradling her against him, his lips in her hair. He knew how much Lola's great-aunt meant to her.

Lola nodded. 'I thought she'd be around for ever, you know?'

'Yeah.' He dropped another kiss on her head. 'I know.'

She seemed to collect herself then, pushing away from him slightly as she scrubbed at her face with her hands. 'Sorry for crying all over you.'

'Don't.' Hamish cupped her cheek, wiping at some moisture she'd missed. 'I want to be here for you, Lola. You *have* to know that.'

He wanted to be here for her for ever. If she'd let him.

Emotion lurked in her big green eyes, waiting for another surge of grief. They slayed him, so big and bright with unshed tears.

So…damn sad.

'Hamish.' Her hand slid on top of his as their gazes locked. She absently rubbed her cheek into his palm and tiny charges of electricity travelled down his arm to his heart. From there it was a direct line to his groin.

Which made him feel like seven different kinds of deviant.

Traitorous body! *This wasn't about that.* This was about something deeper and more profound.

Comfort. Not sex.

Yet the two seemed to have a habit of intertwining where they were concerned. Even now he could feel the threads reaching out between them, twisting together, drawing them nearer.

Her breathing roughened and Hamish responded in kind. A strange kind of tension settled over them, as if the world was holding its breath. Her eyes went from moisture bright to a rich, wanton glitter.

'Lola.'

It was a warning as much for himself as for her. They couldn't keep doing this, letting desire do their talking. She was grieving. And he wanted to give her more than a quick roll on the couch. They *mustn't* let their hormones take over.

'I missed you last night,' she said, her voice barely louder than a whisper.

Apart from *I love you* she couldn't have chosen better words to say to him, especially when they were full of ache and want and need. Her voice was husky and it crawled right inside his pants and stroked.

'*Lola.*'

He was only a man. And he loved her.

She shifted then, moved closer, pressing all her curves back into him again as her mouth closed the gap between them. Their lips met and he was lost.

Gone. Swept away.

In her taste and her smell and the small little sounds of her satisfaction that filled his head and rushed through his veins like a shot of caffeine.

Hamish's other hand curved around her face, sank into her hair as he kissed her back, his nose filling with the smell of her, his tongue tingling with the taste of her. She moaned and he half turned and their bodies aligned and he totally lost his mind.

He'd missed her too.

It was a crazy thing to admit. It had only been twenty-four hours but he hadn't been able to stop thinking about her, to stop wanting her, to stop wishing he'd just shut the hell up and not pushed for more.

It wasn't fair that one woman had so much power but that was love, right? You laid yourself bare to one person. Laid yourself bare to their favour as well as their rejection.

'God... Hamish...'

Her voice was thick with need as she slid her leg over the top of his and straddled him. She kissed along his neck and pulled at his shirt and he was drowning. Happily. Being sucked down into the depths of Lola's passion, dying in her arms, every part of him aching to give her what she wanted. What she needed.

And to hell with what he wanted, what he needed.

But somewhere, something was fighting back. A single brain cell screaming at him to *stop, stop, stop.* To have some respect. For himself. And for Lola.

Groaning, Hamish wrenched his mouth away from her kiss, from her pull. 'Wait.' He shut his eyes and panted into her neck as her hands fell to his fly, her fingers not waiting one little bit. And he wanted her hand on him so damn bad.

'Stop.'

He shifted, grasping for sanity, for clarity as he tipped her off his lap. Ignoring the almost animalistic moan from Lola, he pushed to his feet and strode to the opposite side of the room. Shoving his hand high up on the wall for support, Hamish battled to control the crazy rattle of his heart and the crazier rush of his libido.

'I can't.'

She made a noise that sounded like another sob and Hamish whipped around. He couldn't do this if she started crying again.

She wasn't. But she *was* annoyed.

'I'm sorry.' It seemed like the least he could say given the frustration bubbling in her gaze and how hard her chest rose and fell.

She rubbed a hand over her face as she exhaled in a noisy rush. 'Hell, Hamish. I just…needed some comfort.'

'Yeah.' An ironic laugh rose in his throat but he choked it back. 'That's what we do, you and I, when we're feeling emotional. We have sex. That's the problem.'

'Why is it a problem?'

Her casual dismissal was like the slow drip of poison in his veins, eating away at him. 'Because we don't talk, Lola. We just take our clothes off and let our bodies do the talking. And I need more than that now. We need to start using our mouths to communicate, not our bodies.'

She blinked at him like she couldn't believe what was coming out of his mouth. But he meant every word.

'I love you. I want to *be* with you. I want to be in your life—*part of your life*—not just the person you turn to when you need some distraction between the sheets.'

Hamish broke off, his heartbeat flying in his chest. Was he making any sense? It all seemed totally jumbled inside his head.

'You want me to help you with the funeral arrangements and repatriation of May and being there when you talk to your family and rocking you as you cry yourself to sleep tonight? I can do that. I *want* to do that. I want you to lean on me, Lola. I want it all.'

She looked at him helplessly and Hamish felt lower than a snake's belly. Denying her didn't give him any satisfaction. But it would be too easy to slip into their old routine. Find himself in the kind of relationship he *didn't* want, and he couldn't bear the thought. His insides shrivelled at the prospect.

He wanted to be all in. And if that wasn't on the table then he needed to be all out.

'I…can't deal with this now, Hamish.' She rose from the couch and paced to the open balcony door. The last rays of afternoon sunlight slanted inside, gilding her shape. 'Can you please just go?'

Hamish nodded. He'd dumped a lot on her today, on top of the news about May. Which was an awful thing to do but, damn it, she drove him crazy. He wanted to be her *person*, not just a warm body with the right anatomical parts.

He sighed. 'I'll just grab my stuff and go. I'll be at Grace's until my plane leaves on the third.'

She nodded, her back erect. 'Okay.'

Hamish waited but she didn't turn around no matter how hard he willed it. 'I'll ring you tomorrow to check on you.'

She nodded again but didn't say anything, a stiff, forlorn figure in the fading gold of the afternoon light. It was like a knife to his heart to walk away. But a wise man knew when to choose his battles and live to fight another day and he was going to fight for Lola.

Even if it meant playing the long game.

CHAPTER FIFTEEN

THE APARTMENT WAS silent as Lola let herself in at almost ten thirty on New Year's Eve. Her shift had finished at nine but with the road closures around Kirribilli because of the New Year celebrations, she'd had to take public transport to work. Which had been fine on the way to the hospital but on the return journey the buses had been loaded with families trying to get home after the early fireworks. Add to that the detours in place and the trip had been much longer than usual.

Throwing her bag and a bundle of mail on the coffee table, Lola used the remote to flick on the television. Every channel was showing New Year revelry in Sydney, from shots of the foreshores to the concert on the steps of the Opera House. She settled on one channel and headed for the kitchen.

Grabbing the fridge door, Lola paused as her gaze fell on May's postcard. Her heart squeezed as she pulled it off and read it again, smiling at May's inimitable style. It still punched her in the gut to think she was never going to get another postcard from her aunt to brighten her day and make her smile every time she saw it.

The last few days had been a flurry of activity, making the arrangements to repatriate her aunt's body and coping with all the associated paperwork and legal requirements. Which had been a good thing. Something to keep Lola's mind off Hamish and how much she missed having him around.

May's body was expected back in Sydney in four days and Lola was travelling with her to Doongabi. May hadn't made any specific funeral requests, just that she be cremated and that Lola scatter her ashes somewhere wild and exotic.

Lola didn't think May would mind going home after all this time, especially knowing that her aunt had left out of propriety, not animosity. It wouldn't be her final resting place, Lola would make sure of that, but funerals weren't for the dead. They were for the living. And the town and the Fraser family wanted to be able to grieve her passing, even if it had been over fifty years since May had left.

Including Lola's mother, who had been surprisingly helpful with all the arrangements and genuinely upset at May's passing. Lola had always thought her mother had disliked her aunt for her gypsy ways and for seducing Lola to join the dark side, but her mother's grief had been raw and humbling and had made Lola look at her mother in a different light.

She put the postcard back on the fridge with a sigh, knowing without a shadow of a doubt that May's last written communication would stay right where it was for ever. Opening the door, Lola grabbed the half-empty bottle of wine and poured herself a glass. She was going to sit on the balcony in the dark and watch the revellers whooping it up at the park across the road.

She was going to think about everything that had happened this past year. About May and her mother and going back to Doongabi. About the explosion at the night club and Wesley and Emma.

And Hamish.

From their first meeting on the bridge to him walking out of here the other day, rebuffing her need for comfort. She was going to *wallow* in all of it. Probably even cry over it a little.

But when the clock struck twelve, that was it. A new year. A clean slate. Looking forward. Not back. And there was a lot to look forward to. Seeing family again. A job that she loved. Her trip to Zimbabwe. And maybe it was time to take a sabbatical and do some more extensive travelling. Her aunt was gone, someone had to pick up her mantle.

Someone had to take May's place.

Work would probably let her take a year off without pay. And even if they refused, she could quit. It wasn't like she couldn't get another job again on her return to Australia. She was highly skilled. She could go anywhere with a hospital and pick up a job.

From Sydney to some two-bit town way out past the black stump. Which brought her squarely back to Hamish.

And just how lonely she felt suddenly, her life stretching out in front of her, a series of intersecting roads and her walking down the middle. All by herself.

Lola had never felt lonely before. Serial travellers made friends wherever they went but were also happy with their own company. When had she stopped being happy with her own company?

Maybe it was to do with her aunt's death? Knowing she was out there somewhere in Lola's corner had counteracted any isolation Lola might have felt without May in her life. But deep down she knew it was Hamish—she'd only started feeling lonely since he'd come on the scene.

Damn the man.

To distract herself, Lola contemplated going out. Throwing on her red dress and getting herself dolled up and hitting Billi's. She could probably still make it before the countdown. Flirt with some men, do some midnight kissing.

But the thought was depressing as all giddy-up. The truth was, she didn't want to be with just anyone tonight, kiss just anyone. She wanted Hamish.

Lola scowled and stood up. *It would pass.*

It was just a break up-thing, the loss of the familiar. Which was why she didn't do relationships. No relationships, no break-ups. No feeling like death warmed up on New Year's Eve or any other night for that matter.

They were too different, she reminded herself. They wanted different things. It would never work.

She went and poured herself another glass of wine, picking up the mail off the coffee table as she passed. But she didn't open it straight away, distracting herself instead with her phone and friends' social media posts.

All round the world, it seemed, people were in varying stages of preparation for the New Year. Lots of overseas friends stared back at her from photos full of happy, smiling people, all having a great time together. She tried to smile too, to feel their joy, but she felt nothing except the heavy weight sitting on her chest.

It was grief, Lola understood that, but knowing that didn't make it any easier.

She should have volunteered to work the night shift tonight instead of the late shift she'd filled in for as at least it would have kept her mind on other things. Like how she and Hamish had requested this night off so they could sit on the foreshore together and watch the fireworks, show the country boy some real city magic.

The thought made her smile, which made her annoyed, and Lola grabbed for the mail. Maybe a few bills might help keep her mind off things until the fireworks went off and her slate was magically cleaned. She hadn't checked the box since before Christmas so she had quite a stack to deal with.

Most of it was bumf from advertisers. There were three bills, though—it was the season for credit cards after all—and a letter from the local elected representative wishing his constituents all the best for the festive season.

And there was a postcard. From May.

Lola's heart almost stopped for a moment before it sped up, racing crazily as tears scalded the backs of her eyes. It was of a snow-covered mountain, the peak swirled with clouds. The caption on the front read, 'Beauty should be shared.'

On the flipside, May had written, 'One of nature's mighty erections.' Then she'd drawn a little smiley face with a tongue hanging out. Lola burst out laughing and then she started to cry, the words blurring. Her aunt had signed off with, 'Merry Christmas, Love, May.'

'Oh, May,' Lola whispered, turning the card over again to look at the picture, her heart heavy in her chest and breaking in two. 'I'm going to miss you.'

The mountain stared back at her, and so did the words. *'Beauty should be shared.'* May's strange insistence from their Christmas Day phone call that Lola choose love over adventure, replayed in her head. *'A gypsy caravan is big enough for two.'*

Lola's heart skipped a beat as the words from the post-card took on a deeper meaning. *Beauty should be shared.* Was her aunt reaching out from beyond the grave? The feeling that May had somehow known she wasn't long for this world returned.

Suddenly Emma's words joined the procession in Lola's head.

'Why shouldn't I get to live my life fully? Like other people? To love like other people. To share my life, no matter how long it is, with someone else. Why should I restrict myself to a half-life?'

Lola shut her eyes as the words slugged hot and hard like New Year's Eve fireworks into her chest. Oh, God. That was what she was doing. She was restricting herself to a half-life. Choosing adventure over love.

Yes, love.

Because she *did* love Hamish Gibson. No matter how much she'd tried to deny it. How much it scared her. And it did scare her because they were so different and she knew squat about being a couple. Squat about being grounded after being a gypsy most of her adult life.

But he'd crept up on her, slid under all her defences, and her heart was full of him. Bursting with him. And now she couldn't imagine her life without him.

She didn't know what shape her life would take next, all she knew was that two wise women had given her advice this festive season and she'd be a fool to discard the lessons they'd imparted.

She chose love. She chose a full life.

If she hadn't already blown it.

Lola stood. Not stopping to think about what she was doing next, she was already on her phone, ordering a cab, which would probably cost her a fortune in a surcharge on New Year's Eve but she'd had two glasses of wine and she didn't care. She grabbed the postcard off the table and strode into the living room, snatching her keys out of her handbag before heading for the door.

She *had* to see Hamish. She had to tell him she loved him and beg him to forgive her and hope like hell she *hadn't* blown it. Because now Lola realised she was living a half-life and she wanted her full life, *with Hamish*, to start immediately.

Lola arrived at Grace's apartment with fifteen minutes to spare before midnight. She knew Marcus and Grace had gone to some fancy party in the city so they wouldn't be here. She also knew Hamish wasn't working.

Because they were supposed to be together tonight.

She just hoped like hell he was at the apartment and not out somewhere whooping it up, because he wasn't answering her calls or her texts. If he wasn't here she didn't know what she was going to do, but if it meant she had to sleep outside this door all night, torturing herself with images of who he might be whooping it up with, she would.

Lifting her hand to knock, the door opened before she got a chance to make contact and Lola pitched forward. Right into Hamish's chest. His hands came out to steady her.

'Lola?'

'Hamish.' He smelled *so* good—coconut and pine— that for a second she just stood in the circle of his arms and breathed him in.

Too quickly, he eased her away and Lola noticed he had his keys in his hands. 'You're on your way out?'

'Yes.' His grin was really big, and that impossibly

square jaw of his was looking absolutely wonderful covered in ginger scruff. 'I was coming to you.'

He kissed her then, pushing her against the open doorway, and Lola *melted*, moaning deep in the back of her throat, her hands going up around his neck to shift nearer, to bring him closer. Her head filled with the scent of him and the sound of his breathing and the taste of beer on his breath.

'Oh, I missed you,' he muttered, and his words filled her head too, making her feel dizzy.

Intoxicating her.

She was drunk. Drunk on the feel and the taste and the smell of him. On his heat and his hardness. But… they had to talk first.

There were things he needed to hear, things she needed to say. And if they kept this up there'd be no talking. There'd be nudity in the hallway and sex on the doorstep. God knew, she wanted him badly but she had to prove to him she *could* talk with her mouth, not just her body.

Lola pulled away, placing a hand on his chest as Hamish came back in for more. Their breathing was heavy between them as his gaze searched hers. 'We need to talk.'

'Lola, I don't care.' He dropped his lips to her neck and nuzzled. 'I don't bloody care.' His words were muffled and hot on her neck and Lola's eyes felt as if they'd rolled all the way back in her head as he teased her there, his tongue and his whiskers a potent combination.

'I've held out for as long as I can and I just don't care any more. You win. Whatever kind of relationship you want, I'm in. We don't have to talk ever. I just need you too bloody much.'

His words were like a rush to her brain. And places significantly south. But they didn't give her any great satisfaction. She'd treated him like a sex object. Like a life support for a penis and that had been wrong.

'Hamish.' Lola broke away again.

He pulled back, his pupils dilated with lust, his breathing raspy. 'Come to bed with me. Let me show you how much I missed you.'

And he kissed her again, long and drugging, and she clung to him, blood pounding through her breasts and belly and surging between her thighs as the dizziness took her again. The man could definitely kiss. He sure as hell made it hard to stop.

But. This was important. It was their future.

Lola pushed hard against his chest this time and Hamish groaned as he pulled away again. 'You accused me of not wanting to talk.' She was panting but determined to see this through. 'And you were right. So I'm going to do this properly. We're going to *talk.* And then you can take me to bed and do whatever you want with me.'

He searched her gaze for a moment before breaking into a smile. 'Whatever I want?'

Lola's heart swelled with love. 'Anything.' She'd give this man anything.

He grinned. 'You're on.' Then he stepped back, grabbed her hand and urged her inside. 'Let's go to the balcony. I won't be tempted to take off your clothes out there. *Probably.*'

Lola laughed. She didn't care where they talked, only that they did, and she followed him out to the balcony with its view of the Manly foreshore in the distance. She could hear the distant noise from New Year's Eve revellers floating to her on the balmy night air.

Hamish stood at the railing, his arms folded across his chest as if he couldn't be trusted not to touch her, and Lola smiled. She settled against the railing too, leaving a few feet between them.

'Speak.'

She didn't speak. Instead, she reached into the pocket of her work trousers—because she hadn't stopped to change—and handed over May's postcard. He took it impatiently, staring at the picture. 'What's this?'

'It's a postcard from May.'

'Well, yeah, I figured that. I mean why are—?'

'I got it today. It's postmarked the twenty-first.'

He glanced at her swiftly. 'Oh, Lola.' He took a step in her direction and stopped. 'Are you okay?'

Lola nodded. 'I am, actually.'

'It's kinda freaky, yeah?'

'Yeah.' Lola smiled. 'A little.'

'Listen, I've been thinking. I could come with you... to Doongabi...keep you company.'

Hamish no doubt knew about all the funeral arrangements. She'd only responded in a perfunctory manner to his texts and hadn't answered any of his calls, but Grace was up to speed with all the details.

Lola's heart filled up a little more at Hamish's offer. 'You have to be back at work in Toowoomba.'

'I'm sure I can figure it out with my boss.'

'Well...yes, thank you. I'd like that.' She took a step towards him. There was only about a foot between them now. 'I'd like to introduce my family to the man I love.'

She could hear Hamish's breath catch and caught the

blanching of his knuckles as he gripped the railing. 'The man you love?'

'Yes.' Lola nodded and her heart banged in her chest. This was it. The moment of truth. 'I love you, Hamish. I'm so sorry it took me this long to see it. That I was so blind to it, too wedded to this idea of being a gypsy, too frightened to deviate from the path I'd set myself all those years ago, to see what my heart already knew.'

'You *love* me.'

He was very still suddenly and Lola rushed to reassure him. 'Yes. *God, yes.*' Her hands were trembling and she folded her arms to quell the action. 'It took a postcard and some words from Aunty May and my heart transplant patient to realise that I've only been living a half-life and a gypsy caravan is big enough for two and I want to share mine with you.'

'You do?'

'Yes.' Stupid tears threatened and Lola blinked them back. She was done with crying. 'And I treated you like a...sex object—'

His laugh cut her off. 'Well, that bit wasn't so bad.'

Lola laughed too. 'That bit was pretty damn good. But it was wrong of me. You were *always* more than that. You were the guy who made me laugh. The guy who held me when I was sad. The guy who watched *Die Hard* with me. The guy who bought me the most beautifully perfect gift I've ever been given. I've been falling in love with you all this time and lying to myself about it because I've been single for so long I don't know how to be part of a couple.'

'Lola.' Hamish took that one last remaining step and brought his body flush with hers, his hands sliding possessively onto her hips. He smiled. 'You should stop talk-ing now and kiss me.'

Lola shook her head, pressing a hand between them as worry that she might screw things up grew like a bogeyman inside her head. 'I mean it, Hamish, I don't know how to do this. And we're so different, we want different things. I still don't know how we're going to work it all out.'

He smiled gently. 'Do you love me, Lola?'

She nodded. 'Yes. *God, yes.*'

'Do you want to be with me? In the forever kind of way.'

'Yes,' she whispered. 'I want forever with you.'

'Good answers, *City.*' He smiled and Lola relaxed and fell in love a little more. 'All that matters is that we love each other. We can work the rest out. Sure, it'll take com-promise and we'll probably argue a little and go back and forth a hundred times over the same old things but as long as we're committed to staying together, we can overcome anything. We'll be all right, Lola, I promise.'

Suddenly, Lola knew he was right. She could feel it in her bones. Because nothing was more important in her life than Hamish. And she knew he felt the same way about her.

They were going to be better than all right. They were going to be freaking amazing.

'Now.' Hamish removed her hand from his chest and urged her closer. 'Are you going to kiss me or what?'

Lola smiled, lifting on her tippytoes to kiss the man she loved, twining her arms around his neck and sighing against his mouth as their lips joined and everything in her life clicked into place.

In the distance the countdown started and they were still kissing as the crowd yelled, 'Happy New Year!'

The first firework shot into the sky with a muted *thunk* and exploded seconds later in an umbrella of red sparks. Lola and Hamish broke apart, laughing. She stared in wonder at the fireworks and at Hamish.

'I think I just saw stars.' Lola laughed up at him as the night sky erupted into a kaleidoscope of noise and colour.

He grinned. 'Me too. Now, let's go make the earth move.' And he tugged on her hand and led her to his bedroom.

EPILOGUE

A COOLING HARBOUR breeze blew cross the park on the warm November morning. Flurries of electric purple jacaranda flowers swirled and drifted to the ground, carpeting the road and the footpath and the edge of the park where the ceremony was being held in a stunning lilac carpet.

'Do you take this woman...?'

Lola's hands tightened in Hamish's as she smiled up at her soon-to-be husband and her heart did its usual *ker-thump.* It had been his idea to have the marriage service here, in this place she loved so much. And, if it was possible, her heart expanded a little more.

Having Grace and Marcus joining them to make it a double wedding was the icing on the cake. They'd already said their vows and were waiting eagerly for Lola and Hamish to get through theirs so they could all be declared husbands and wives.

Grace was looking radiant in her figure-hugging cream lace creation, her gorgeous red hair piled into a classy up-do. Marcus was darkly handsome in his suit and still only had eyes for Grace.

Lola had chosen a more gypsy-style dress of embroidered cotton that flowed rather than clung. It had shoestring straps and fluttered against her body in the breeze, the garland of jacaranda flowers in her loose, curly hair the perfect finishing touch.

'I sure as hell do.'

The wedding guests—a mix of friends and both families who'd travelled to Sydney for the occasion—laughed at Hamish's emphatic answer and Lola's heart just about burst with happiness. He was breathtakingly sexy in his fancy suit with his purple shirt. His clean-shaven jaw was as rock solid as always, his reddish-brown hair flopped down over his forehead as endearingly as always and his bottomless blue gaze was full of promises to come.

It had been a whirlwind year—falling in love, getting engaged and planning a wedding in such a short space of time but, as Aunty May had said, when you knew, you *knew*.

Hamish hadn't gone back to Toowoomba, he'd stayed on in Sydney to complete his course, finishing it while Lola had been in Zimbabwe then joining her there for the last week, taking Aunt May's ashes with him. Together they'd scattered them from a canoe across the mighty Zambezi River, a place as wild and free as May herself.

Tomorrow they were leaving for two weeks in London before heading to western Queensland. Hamish was taking up a two-year rural post and Lola had a job at the local hospital. *And* she was looking forward to it.

It had taken her very little time with Hamish to learn that home was wherever her heart was and her heart would always be with him. They'd even talked about having children when they returned to Sydney.

Children!

Lola had always assumed she'd remain childless, like May. Now she couldn't wait to be running around after a little blonde girl and little boy with cinnamon hair. She'd been a lot of places and seen a lot of things but what she craved most now was home and hearth and family.

It was official, she was a hundred percent, head-over-heels gone on Hamish Gibson.

'And do you take this man…?'

The celebrant was smiling at her. Grace was smiling at her. Her mother was smiling at her. And Hamish… Hamish was smiling at her.

'Yes,' Lola said, her eyes misting over. 'For ever and ever.'

More laughter but Hamish squeezed her hands tighter and, as the jacaranda flowers twirled around their heads in the breeze, she knew she'd never spoken truer words.

He was hers. And she was his.

For ever.

* * * * *

MILLS & BOON

Coming next month

THEIR NEWBORN BABY GIFT
Alison Roberts

'Give Grace a cuddle from me...'

Evie's voice seemed to echo in the back of Ryan's head every time he was near the baby. Like now, as he held his stethoscope against that tiny chest to listen to her heart.

He had never 'cuddled' one of his patients.

He never would.

How unprofessional would that be?

It wasn't that he didn't care about them. He couldn't care more about their clinical outcomes. He found enormous satisfaction—joy, even, in a successful outcome and he had been completely gutted more than once when he'd lost a patient despite his best efforts.

But those emotions were about the case, not the person.

And, somehow, that careless remark of Evie's had planted the idea that maybe there was something wrong with him. What if he hadn't been in control for so many years and deliberately choosing to keep his distance from people to avoid the kind of pain that emotions automatically created? What if he wasn't even capable of feeling strongly about someone else?

Would that make him some kind of heartless monster?

The complete opposite of someone like Evie?

The abnormal heart sounds he could hear were getting louder again and Ryan suspected that the blood flow to the baby's lower body wasn't as good as it had been straight after the procedure to widen the narrowed part of the aorta. Grace started crying as he pressed the skin on her big toe to leave a pale spot, looking for evidence of how quickly the blood returned to make it pink again.

Ryan made notes on Grace's chart as her cries got louder and then hung it back on the end of her crib. He looked around to see if someone was also hearing the sound of a baby that needed attention. Feeding, maybe. Or a nappy change.

Or just a cuddle…

Continue reading
THEIR NEWBORN BABY GIFT
Alison Roberts

Available next month
www.millsandboon.co.uk

COMING SOON!

We really hope you enjoyed reading this book. If you're looking for more romance, be sure to head to the shops when new books are available on

Thursday
1st November

To see which titles are coming soon, please visit
millsandboon.co.uk

LET'S TALK
Romance

For exclusive extracts, competitions
and special offers, find us online:

f facebook.com/millsandboon

⊙ @millsandboonuk

𝕏 @millsandboon

Or get in touch on 0844 844 1351*

For all the latest titles coming soon, visit
millsandboon.co.uk/nextmonth

*Calls cost 7p per minute plus your phone company's price per minute access charge